TO CATCH A SPY

Also by Chris Scott

BARTLEBY

Chris
Scott

TO CATCH A SPY

A RICHARD SEAVER BOOK
THE VIKING PRESS   NEW YORK

for Heather Sherratt

First published in 1978 by The Viking Press
625 Madison Avenue, New York, N.Y. 10022

Published simultaneously in Canada by
Penguin Books Canada Limited

LIBRARY OF CONGRESS CATALOGING IN PUBLICATION DATA
Scott, Chris, 1945–
    To catch a spy.
    "A Richard Seaver book."
    I. Title.
PZ4.S424To 1978 [PR6069.C584]   823'.9'14   77-21953
ISBN 0-670-71663-4

Printed in the United States of America

Set in V.I.P. Times Roman

Knowledge of the future cannot be acquired from the gods or demons, nor can it be obtained by comparisons, measurements, or calculations. Knowledge of the enemy is acquired only by human agencies. The kinds of spies that are used are five in number: there are the native spies and the spies within, the spies that return from the other side, the spies of life, and the spies of death. If all five kinds of spies are employed, then nobody will ever learn their secret ways. That is what we call a divine secret. It is the most priceless possession of the lord and master, who must control his spies' work in person. The spies that return are those that render the best knowledge of the enemy, so show particular nobleness unto them.

—SUN-TSE, *Treatise on the Art of War,* circa 480 B.C.

When everyone is dead the Great Game is finished. Not before.

—RUDYARD KIPLING, *Kim*

Author's
Note

At the end of May 1951 (almost two months after the close of the Rosenberg trial in the United States), British society in general and the intelligence community in particular were shocked by the defection of two middle-rank diplomats. They were Guy Burgess, former first secretary to the British Embassy in Washington, and Donald Maclean, head of chancery there from 1941 to 1948. Both men had been members of the Communist Party since their undergraduate days at Cambridge in the 1930s; both were university contemporaries of Kim Philby's. It was Maclean who, as Britain's secretary to the Combined Policy Committee (responsible for coordinating postwar nuclear research in the United States and the United Kingdom), would give the Russians the complete plans for the Blyvooruitzicht low-grade uranium-ore extraction plant in South Africa; it was Burgess, a houseguest of the Philbys' in Washington, whom Kim Philby would warn of the impending investigation into Donald Maclean. Philby's role as the "third man" in the Burgess and Maclean affair has been ably documented by the *Sunday Times* team of Bruce Page, David Leitch, and Philip Knightley. Truly remarkable is the fact that ten years later Philby was still on the books of the British Secret Intelligence Service and continued to be employed as a field agent until his own defection in January 1963. The identity of his recruiter has never been publicly established. We do not know who ran him—who protected him for so long and why. We do not yet know who succeeded him. But recruiter, controller, and successor there must have been. Such, in essence, is the background of this novel.

Part One JOHNSON

He had often noticed that six months'
oblivion amounts to newspaper death,
and that resurrection is rare.
Nothing is easier, if a man wants it, than
rest, profound as the grave.
—*The Education of Henry Adams*

1

Unencumbered
Sleepers

In that carefully manicured section of Moscow's Novo-Devichy Cemetery reserved for aliens who have rendered the state some service, there lies a modest gravel plot, frosted, at this time of year, with uncertain snow, like the icing on a Christmas cake. The grave is surmounted by a smooth, grey granitic headstone that bears the simple legend, albeit inscribed in gold with red borders:

George Michael Stevens
(1918–1974)

It is a month since the funeral; fifty-seven years to the day since the Red Guards stormed the Winter Palace in another city, another era. Now the streets of Moscow and the Lenin Hills are clad in red bunting. There will be a military parade, a celebration of a kind; speeches in Red Square, drinking and toasting, lots of that, and possibly, if the atmosphere is not altogether too sodden with vodka-induced tears, some remembrance of things past. And there will also be the customary batch of annual pardons—for the long dead, the Old Guard; for those who condemned them and were in turn condemned, for those who knew no such resting place as George Michael Stevens—posthumous rehabilitation.

Johnson's companion sighed, a cloud of condensed breath floating above his head like ectoplasm. The Russian moved stiffly, dropping the wreath with a lateral flick of his hand. The wreath could have been a bundle of papers, the grave an out tray. File and forget.

The reporter stamped his feet, slapping his hands to the sides of his body. It was cold, colder than London, and quieter. Johnson studied the inscription. It wasn't much, really, a life in parentheses. Then what else had he expected—some corner of a foreign field that is forever England? He smiled. Cemeteries were the same the whole world over, yet this one was different. No angels.

For the last three weeks he had been pursuing a dead man. He had met Stevens' two wives, one in New York and the other in London. The first had been a waste of time and money, neither of which was Johnson's; the second had been drunk and had wept hysterically. He'd met Stevens' old secretary, who was willing to gossip, and her new master, who was not. He'd met Charles, the chinless *Wunderkind* of Stevens' first marriage, and had been told, in most un-Etonian terms, what to do with his press card. He had asked too many questions and had received too many answers. Worse, he had lied to himself, meticulously assembling a composite picture until he knew that it was no more than a jigsaw puzzle with all the key pieces missing. Clichés, but Stevens' life—and his death—had been one long series of them: colonial administrator's son, public-school boy, Cambridge Classics First, gentleman operative with SIS in Occupied France, spy, traitor, and pariah, dead of a broken liver in Moscow at the age of fifty-six.

The Russian's hand flicked again, a bureaucratic gesture: case closed.

Vladimir Andreyevich Dimitrov studied the English reporter. "You were not a friend?" he asked, hesitating before he pronounced the word "friend." His speech was unaccented.

Johnson said that he was not a friend.

He was thinking of Burgess and Maclean and their boss, Kim Philby. Johnson was six years old when the Burgess-Maclean story broke, and he could remember his father coming home in a foul temper, something to do with Communist spies and public-school boys. In those days his father was a technician with the Ministry of Defence, and that night, for the first time ever, the son was actually made to watch television. It was a lesson, and Johnson had not forgotten what he had seen: mug shots of Guy Burgess looking like a blotchier version of Dylan Thomas, and Maclean looking like Sir Donald Diplomat; then the polite, embarrassed remarks of a Foreign Office spokesman—well, yes, you could say they were traitors, though the term "defectors" was preferable.

Johnson was in his last year at grammar school when Kim Philby, the "third man" in the affair, had disappeared. The reporter wondered if Dimitrov knew the man; Stevens certainly had. It was Stevens who had warned Philby, just as Philby had warned Burgess and Maclean.

A detached observer and a good reporter of the Middle Eastern scene was Kim, a man for all seasons and parties. Johnson remembered the story of a photograph that Philby liked to show his friends, a photo of Mount Ararat taken on one of his walking tours— only the characteristic double-hump shape of the mountain was the wrong way round because Kim had been on the Soviet side of the frontier instead of the Turkish. Some of his friends thought it had been made with a reversed negative, and they all agreed that Kim liked walking. One day in 1963 he left his flat in Beirut and walked all the way to Moscow. It was time for another polite, embarrassed spokesman to make polite, embarrassed remarks; the same voice, the same suit and tie, except this spokesman had been wearing a different head.

Stevens had replaced Philby's successor, H. C. "Carlo" Peat, as acting head of Section IX, the division of MI6 responsible for anti-Communist and anti-Soviet intelligence. There had been a good deal of speculation as to what that made George Michael Stevens, but nobody was talking, nobody with the answers, at least. And now his memoirs had turned up, the autobiography of a dead superspy. KGB disinformation, Carlo Peat had called the manuscript four days ago when Johnson had been summoned down to Cambridge for sherry and enlightenment. Carlo had lectured him donnishly on the miracle worker Apollonius of Tyana and his biographer, Philostratus —"of the salon of Julia Domna." Manuscripts ancient and modern, Johnson thought. So much for enlightenment.

Dimitrov lit a cigar, a Romeo y Juliet. "Cuban," he said, a little man, blandly smiling.

Johnson stared at the graves, which reminded him of teeth. Everything was excessively neat and dental. Antiseptic.

" 'Unencumbered sleepers,' " the Russian said. "It's from Wilfred Owen's poem 'Strange Meeting.' "

"I know," Johnson said.

"You studied—journalism?"

"German, actually. Ghost-writer, that's what Carlo called you." Johnson volunteered this information, and Dimitrov let him continue. "It's funny, you know. I've been getting a lot of literary references in the last few days. I wouldn't have believed it, somehow. Not from people in your profession."

"And yours, Mr. Johnson? Forgive me for saying so, but your background is not that of the ordinary journalist."

Johnson did not know what to make of this remark. "That's life," he said.

"You were in America for a while?"

"You mean that's not life?"

The Russian laughed politely. "I meant recently. You were in America recently?"

"Yes."

"And before that, some years ago, with your newspaper?" Dimitrov did not wait for an answer but turned towards the waiting car, his feet crunching on the gravel driveway.

"Would you like a cigar, Mr. Johnson? I forgot, just now, to offer you one. My mind was elsewhere."

"Mine too," said Johnson, and accepted gratefully. They paused while Dimitrov lit Johnson's cigar, snapping the lighter from his coat pocket and returning it with practised ease. The battle towers of the Novo-Devichy Convent stared down on them, and nearby a modern high rise loomed through the early-morning mist, its windows catching the light of the pale sun.

"Is something wrong, Mr. Johnson?"

"No. Why, should there be?"

"You didn't know George Stevens, did you?"

"Vicariously," Johnson said.

"So." Dimitrov's hand rested on the door of the Volga saloon. "Then you know nothing, my friend," he observed correctly. "Nothing at all."

2

Monday's
Moon
Children

Outside Googie's Bar the Moon children gave him a leaflet urging love to all mankind. A girl who looked like a Raggedy Ann doll said, "Father Sun Myung Moon wants you to know that the twentieth century is the landing site of Christ." She had the eyes of a dead fish.

Father Moon was a South Korean with KCIA connections, also an ex-friend of ex-President Nixon's. A Byzantine combination —or was it? A sign of the times, anyway. A gross pubertoid called Maharaj Ji was hailed as the Messiah in a Rolls-Royce, the Maharishi Makesh Yogi was peddling mantras and TM to the masses, His Divine Grace A. C. Bhaktivedanta Swami Prabhupada espoused curried vegetables and the sound of oblivion, while inside the bar Oral Roberts advertised *agape* as the final solution to your very own spiritual problems.

Johnson looked at his watch. It was two-thirty p.m., Monday, 14 October 1974. For all the monkeys in Vrndavana, he could not have known that it was the beginning of a terrible time in his life.

Greenwich Village had changed since the psychedelic sixties. The junk stores selling off decades of English historical detritus had vanished. Johnson wondered if they'd used up the past and had run out of things to sell. And the flower children, who had declared war on war, they were gone too—gone to salvation every one. Instead of hair and acid, it was no hairs and cosmic consciousness; instead of tatty Union Jacks, faded Queen Victorias, and antique commodes, it was prayer wheels, vegetables, and Indian food stores.

"You're waiting for her and she's late," the barman said. He wore a knitted woollen hat like those worn on oceangoing tugs, and was inclined to conversation because the bar was empty. Here was a new face, a new victim. "I can tell. You keep looking at your watch. You're English, aren't you?"

Johnson said that he was.

There was sawdust on the floor and a skull with a Davy Crockett hat behind the bar. Googie's was small and cozily gloomy, a hangout for students from NYU. It said something about Louisa Alcott Stevens, née Perkins, that she had chosen the place. Maybe she was just lazy. She lived around the corner, on the fringes of Washington Square.

Johnson asked for a scotch. He was feeling nostalgic and slightly nauseated. Jet lag, he supposed. The scotch didn't help.

"Mrs. Stevens?" He saw her framed in the doorway, the light playing over her hair.

The barman busied himself with a glass and watched Johnson stand up.

"It's been a long time since anyone called me that."

"Of course. How foolish of me."

An all-American grin flashed behind the bar. "Yes, ma'am," the barman said, and asked what she was drinking.

"Just a beer—a bock beer."

She was well preserved, handsome in a sexless sort of way, with delicate, aquiline features and green eyes. She was not an American type, not of her generation somehow. Her hair was its natural colour, mousey and greying. Maybe that was it.

He had expected she would look older and made the mistake of saying so.

"You must be Charlie's age" was all that she said.

"I know. We met last Monday." That had been the day after Stevens' funeral, and the memory of their encounter still rankled.

Still, Charlie was better than Charles.

"You don't waste much time, do you, Mr. Johnson? George has been dead only a week."

"But gone for ten months." He waited for a reaction. There was none. "I did a story on him when he went over the wall. Through, actually. With the connivance of our people and theirs. Did you know that? It wasn't the way it was supposed to be."

She shook her head. "Do tell me. I'm all ears."

"He went through Brandenburg Control as a West German garage proprietor." Johnson attempted a smile. "After all, he had been a mechanic in his day. He was visiting an aunt in the zone. That was the story. It was Christmastime, and the Vopos are quite understanding about missions of charity. So is the BND."

Louisa sipped her beer and gave him a little-girl look. "The BND?"

"The West German Intelligence Service." Johnson swallowed his drink. Signals were getting crossed. He was edgy and didn't like the sound of his own voice.

"Christmastime? You said it was Christmastime. I thought it was February."

"Officially, yes. Maybe they were pretending he wasn't missed." Johnson remembered the press release: "Whitehall, 11 February 1974, 2:12 p.m. George Michael Stevens, a civil servant attached to the Foreign Office, disappeared three days ago in the city of Berlin." And that was all. There had been no press conference this time, no polite, embarrassed spokesman. Bloody lies, Johnson's editor had called the bulletin. Hasketh was annoyed because there was a D notice out and they could print only what they were told to print.

"You said something about a mission of charity, Mr. Johnson?"

"That's right. Especially when ten little nephews come the other way. Also mechanics, but not so experienced as your—as George."

"Ah." She savoured this information. "An exchange."

"Yes. You can see why the Russians were in a hurry. There wasn't much time left, was there?"

Ten months. Enough time for a debriefing. But then it was Hasketh's opinion, delivered, as were all his important pronouncements, on a Monday, last Monday, that the Russians had killed George Michael Stevens.

"Why should they do that, Terry?" Johnson had asked.

"Kill one of their own?"

"But was he, dear boy? Was he one of their own?"

Talk, it was just talk. Yet Hasketh had sent him to see little Lord Fauntleroy, and now he was here in New York talking to the darling Charlie's dam. Something was bound to turn up, according to the Micawberish Hasketh.

Johnson was suddenly worried. "You mean nobody's been to see you—nobody's told you all this?"

"No, Mr. Johnson. Why should they?"

"Well, there's George."

"There was George," she corrected him. "A long time ago. I suppose you'll want to know why we were divorced?"

Johnson said that he did not wish to appear impertinent.

"God!" She laughed then, and he found himself liking her—for a while.

"You were saying—about George?"

"I was?" She looked surprised. "We met in '35 or '36, before he went up to his college. That's the English way of saying it, isn't it?"

Johnson nodded.

"It was in Vienna. I remember—the Italians had just marched into Addis Ababa, so it must have been '36. . . ." She had seen him again that summer, in London; and then three years later in New York. They were married in '42, she said. She had figured that he would settle down after the war. He hadn't. "Not that he was selfish or anything. In fact he was quite impulsive, really he was. But he became, I don't know, introverted somehow. We were married eight years, and I felt like I never really knew him."

A sincere little speech, Johnson thought. "And now you know why," he said.

"Not exactly, Mr. Johnson. You never understand things until it's too late." Her hand went up to her hair. "Do you have another name?"

"Bill."

"Mine's Louisa."

"I know."

"What a lot of things you know, Mr. . . . Bill."

"Only when it's too late. You never remarried?"

Her father had been dying, and she had felt obliged to take care of him in his final illness. It had lasted for ten years.

Amos Bronson Alcott Perkins had been a big man on the New York Stock Exchange. Johnson asked why he hadn't been able to afford a home help of his own. Of course he had, but that wasn't the point. They had been very close, after her divorce, in England and in death. Old Amos had gone home to sleep with his ancestors.

"It sounds kind of incestuous." She laughed.

"Was it?"

"Now, that's prying."

"George remarried, though."

She gave him a quizzical look.

"I haven't met her yet," he added.

"But she's on the agenda?"

"When I get back. Thursday or Friday."

"The best of luck, Mr. Johnson."

"Yes. I think I might need that. Do you know her?"

"I do, but I'd rather—"

"Not get into that. When did you last see him—George?"

"My father's funeral. Fourteen years ago, Mr. Johnson. He didn't say anything, you know, like, 'Boo, guess who's a Russian spook.'"

"Do you think he was?"

"I don't *know.* . . ."

"One more thing." Johnson couldn't bring himself to call her Louisa, so he called her nothing. "Do you think the Russians killed him?"

"No. He drank himself to death."

Johnson was silent.

"How do you get by in this business?" she asked him. "I like asking people how they get by. It's an art."

"Getting by?"

"Asking questions. You'd make quite a good interrogator, really you would. George was. During the war when he was in France, the Germans pulled him in for questioning. There was nothing they could do to him."

"They could have tried shooting him."

"That's what I mean. I imagine you get by very well, Mr. Johnson. You remind me of him—of George. He was never quite there somehow, if you know what I mean."

"Yes," he said. "But I am—here. You're sure no one came to see you?"

"Quite sure. They must have forgotten all about me." She raised her glass. "You could come to supper, you know."

"I have a prior engagement," he lied.

"You're quite a Puritan, aren't you?"

"No," he said. "They're outside."

"Ah, well. Give my best wishes to Charlie. And Ponsonby."

"Ponsonby?"

"Number two."

The Moonies pursued him outside Googie's Bar. "The twentieth century is the landing site of Christ!"

Johnson told them to piss off. There was no sign of the Raggedy Ann girl.

He went to see the Belfast man who keeps the English pub at the Avenue of the Americas and Bleecker Street. It was when he ordered a pint of Worthington E at an outrageous price that the Louisa Alcott connection clicked: *Little Men* and *Little Women*. Her father, like his namesake, had given his all to charity. Cancer research. He had forgotten to ask Louisa whether she was writing her memoirs.

The Belfast man said he felt safer in New York, and Johnson believed him.

He found time for number two on Friday. Not until Mrs. Marjory Stevens, née weeping Ponsonby, threw him out of her Hampstead Gardens *pied-à-terre* for asking impertinent questions did he realize that both wives were in substantial agreement. Only the phraseology differed.

"He killed himself!" cried the tearful Ponsonby. "The lousy Commie lush!"

"How very British of you," he said.

"Please, I'm upset. Can't you see that I'm upset? It's too much. Everything's too much!"

Johnson was left with a watery impression of scrawled red hair, dissolving mascara, and a lingering odour, like that of hyacinths, which he associated with death. It was odd, but no one seemed to miss George Michael Stevens. The bereft Marjory mourned for herself. She could have been pretty, but she was a spoiled brat, trained from the cradle up in the art of tears. Then, Mrs. Stevens number two had an excuse. It takes a lush to know a lush. Besides, she couldn't help it. She was about half the age of Mrs. Stevens number one.

Another war-surplus baby, Johnson thought bitterly.

3

Forever England

Hasketh was twenty years older than Johnson, middle-aged, and it seemed to Johnson that Hasketh had always been middle-aged, that he had issued from the womb complaining of dyspepsia, piles, sleepless nights, and impending retirement. "You can't be too careful," he was fond of saying. "Not in this business." And he would speak eloquently of unexpected horrors: incapacitating strokes that transform a man into so much useless protein or sudden madness replacing the old, comfortable personality with a new, alien self.

"Have a nice weekend, did you?" Hasketh had just finished reading Johnson on Ponsonby. It was unprintable.

"It was all right, Terry."

"So you see this Ponsonby and you still don't know what Stevens was doing in Vienna."

"Why would he have told her that, Terry?"

"Because he met number one there, that's why. Because Ponsonby would have asked and you didn't. What do you know about women? What do you know about anything? Come to think of it, what do I know about you?"

Johnson thought about this.

"Has anyone ever told you that you look like a badger?" he said. "It's that slick of hair down the middle of your head that does it. You'd better watch out, you had. You're an endangered species."

"Not me, boy. You. Philby was there, you know." Johnson gathered he meant Vienna. "His first wife was Viennese. What was she called? Litzi something-or-other. A real pretzel she was. A Jewish lady, also a party member. Kim was her number two. Check out the dates, will you? See if George ran into them at the Karl Marx Hof. You *know*, the local Conservative Club."

"It burnt down, Terry."

"Litzi Friedman," Hasketh said. "You know what your trouble is, don't you? You don't listen to people." Hasketh banged the space bar of his typewriter, upset his coffee, and swore. "Mr. Bill bloody Johnson, what bloody use are you? Same with this Louisa, you didn't listen to her. You found something out, and you didn't even know what it was. Nobody called on her, you see, nobody with regrets and commiserations."

"I told you," Johnson said. "They've been divorced for twenty-four years. I mean, she's not exactly his next of kin anymore."

"That's not the point, dear boy. Nobody contacted her when George went over the wire. What if you were the Russians, mm? What if you knew that nobody dropped in, not even a vacuum-cleaner salesman with so much as a calling card?"

"I'd think they couldn't afford the fare, Terry. That's all."

"Or that she knew? Just a theory. My idea."

"You can't have it both ways," Johnson said. "You can't have him joining up at the Karl Marx Hof, then going to Moscow to spread the gospel and restore the Romanovs."

"And why not? Maybe that's what he wanted to do."

"Don't be daft, Terry."

"The absurd is the first truth. That's Camus, a Frenchman. You won't get far in this game if you can't hold two contradictory ideas in your head. Who's next on your list?"

"The major general," Johnson said.

"Gilbert-and-Sullivan time again." Hasketh gave an acidulous grin. "My ulcer," he said, then, "Be good to him, won't you? I knew him during the war. He's not so stupid as he tries to make out.

And something'll turn up. You mark my words.''

"That's your job," said Johnson, and left.

"Yes—" Hasketh watched him go. Then he turned to the copy, altering the words "hysterical" to "grief-stricken" and "gin-swilling" to "chain-smoking."

Johnson ducked into the narrow Queen Anne building on Broadway, near the St. James's Park underground. He was confronted by a wheezing retainer who wore a costume that advertised him as an employee of the Government Communications Bureau.

"Which floor will it be, sir?"

"Four," Johnson told him.

The retainer gave him a conspiratorial look. "Then four it is," he said.

Johnson smiled at the TV camera in the roof of the lift cage. On the fourth floor he halted at a mahogany door bearing a plaque that read DIRECTOR OF COMMUNICATIONS. PLEASE KNOCK. Johnson knocked, and Dorothy Winters' voice allowed that he could enter.

She was Stevens' old secretary, and Johnson had managed, after a great deal of trouble, to see her back in February. A quiet man was Mr. Stevens, reserved, you know, but kind and very thoughtful. Good at remembering little things, birthdays, anniversaries, and suchlike. Easy on his staff, too. He would often let them go early and stay behind after hours. No, of course she had never dreamed that he was a Russian spy. That would have been disloyal of her, positively disloyal.

Dorothy Winters remembered Johnson but tried hard to look as though she did not.

"You are rather early," she said.

"I wasn't asked for identification," he said. "Not like the last time."

"We know who you are," she said, and he enjoyed the "we."

He sat down. "Pity about Stevens," he said.

She was silent.

"It'll be lunchtime when I'm through with his nibs," he said. "How about a drink?"

Dorothy shuffled papers. Johnson, who was clever at some things, noticed that her knuckles were white and bloodless.

A buzzer sounded on her desk. "Lunch, then?" he said, and was surprised when she agreed.

Major General Donald Macpherson (RSG, ret.) was an imperial Scot who had been landed with the task of investigating the chaos that the good Lord and George Michael Stevens had jointly wrought. Macpherson had "come over" from MI5's liaison office in the Ministry of Defence, where it had been decreed that he would function most happily among the shades of the dead and defected. The minister, who believed in new blood, had insisted on using someone from outside MI6 and had chosen Macpherson because of his experience in counterintelligence. As far as hoi polloi were concerned, that experience amounted to an incautious statement he had once made to the press: "MI6 are the spies. We in MI5 have the job of catching the spies." Everyone had applauded his foresight.

Macpherson had his points. As well as being a member of White's and the Turf, he was a KCB and a KCMG, twice a knight—Sir Donald, the title Maclean had aspired to. He was also a grand officer of the Legion of Honour; a member of the Legion of Merit (United States), a grand officer of the Order of Orange Nassau (Holland), a grand officer of the Order of Leopold Crown of Belgium, a commander of St. Olaf (Norway), a member of the Order of Polonia Restituta (Poland), and a member of the Order of the Black Star (Ghana—rescinded). Not bad for a man who was basically a policeman, Johnson thought. If Macpherson was not yet a hero of the Soviet Union, it was because he still had to run true to form.

He was a skilled navigator in that trivalent zone where the security forces of the realm occasionally met and passed like ships in the dark. Sometimes there were collisions: too many ships. There was the Special Branch of Scotland Yard, which came within the home secretary's bailiwick and also functioned as the detective arm of MI5. Originally formed to infiltrate the Irish nationalists of 1916, it had returned to its ancestral duties with something less than a historic sense of mission. There were Macpherson's own people, "the Plods in Five," as SIS called them, who lived in the penumbra between the Home Office and the Ministry of Defence and whose job it was to catch foreign spies operating in the United Kingdom.

Then there was Foreign Office security, supposedly to police MI6, the secret intelligence service itself—"the Friends," as SIS liked to be known. But the Plods in Five had a better name for the Friends in Six. They called them "the Enemies."

So Macpherson had come over from Whitehall, and now he was running SIS as a presbyterian elder would a Boy Scouts' camp. A bizarre set of events had led to his elevation. Before Stevens defected in December of 1973, the controller of SIS, perhaps reading an oracle of straws, had vanished. Whereas Stevens had surfaced all too quickly in Moscow, the controller was not to be found anywhere on the face of the earth. After a year the son had sniffed him out in the attic of his country house. "Percival," as the Friends called him, was badly decomposed, but no one seemed too interested in positive identification. After all, if it wasn't Percival, who was it? There was a suicide note (in the deceased's handwriting), a gun (his own), and a bullet in the corpse's head. The gun and bullet matched, a ballistic detail that had persuaded the coroner's jury to return a verdict of death by misadventure.

Johnson had raised the subject with Macpherson back in February. "Let us not talk of the dead," the major general had said then, and that was strange because the body hadn't turned up yet. This had triggered a dispute over the meaning of the word "missing." Macpherson, using the service definition, had said it meant assumed dead until found otherwise; the reporter had asked why not assumed otherwise until found dead. Back in February, Johnson had wondered which formula applied to Stevens, who was then listed as missing. Now, he supposed, he had his answer.

"There've been a lot of changes around here," Macpherson said aggressively. He was the kind of man who seemed permanently angry.

"I can imagine," Johnson said.

Sir Donald sported a regimental tie and a clipped moustache. His cheeks were scribbled with little red veins and his eyes were inflamed with presenile keratitis. He was also known to suffer from gout. Macpherson hated the press, for they were not gentlemen but gutter trash. Even the *Times* people were not exactly gentlemen, and this reporter was not from the *Times*.

"What can I do for you today?" he asked.

"Just a few questions," said Johnson. "Who were those men you exchanged Stevens for?''

"I cannot tell you that." Macpherson put his hands together under his chin. "He was a defector."

"You make him sound like he was defective."

"Aye, well, so he was. In the moral sense."

Johnson felt like adding "d'ye ken." He said nothing.

"Anyway," Macpherson said, "you did not ask me that question before."

"Oh, but I did, Sir Donald." Johnson was on his best behaviour. "You denied that they existed."

"Then how do you know about them?"

"Secrets of the confessional. About Stevens . . .''

"That man!"

"Aye." The temptation was too much.

"A blackguard!"

"Do you think the Russians killed him?"

"Who?"

"That man."

"Now, listen . . .''

"I'm listening, Sir Donald, but you don't have to say anything. He drank himself to death. That's what everybody tells me. Wife number one says so and wife number two says so. Even dear old Dorothy as good as said so, and when three women agree, what the hell is anyone supposed to think? Then there's the Russians, and you agree with them. So it must be true, right? That's the official story. But what's the unofficial version? What went wrong, Macpherson?''

Johnson felt better now. Their hatred was quite mutual. He could live with it.

"I have absolutely nothing more to add, Mr. Johnson."

"All right. Did you see the body, Sir Donald? That's the point I'm trying to make. Did any of your people get a sniff at the meat?"

"You've made your point, Mr. Johnson, and you've made it very well." Macpherson tugged at the roots of his moustache, exposing tiny yellow teeth. "As a matter of fact, we did get a look at him. They laid him out on display, dressed him up, you know, just like Lenin." Macpherson gave a foxy laugh. Evidently the comparison amused him.

"Postmortem?"

"What?"

"Did you actually examine the body?"

The veins in Macpherson's face darkened. A nervous tic developed at a corner of his mouth, and his Adam's apple moved up and down. "Before I ask you to leave," he said, "I think there is one thing you should know. We did not examine the body because we had no rights in the matter. None whatsoever. You see, George Stevens had been a Soviet citizen since 1950."

Macpherson recovered his poise, magnanimous in victory. "Will that be all, Mr. Johnson?"

"Thank you very much," said Johnson, who was equally gracious in defeat. "It seems that his wife was not the only thing he divorced in 1950."

He took Dorothy Winters to lunch at the Press Club. None of the Broadway people would be seen dead or otherwise in there, and it amused him to think that the story would get around sooner or later. Sooner than he thought, he realized as they sat down. A colleague from a rival newspaper came by and lurched thoughtfully at their table. "Aha," he said, "the spy catcher." And then, eying Dorothy, he gave a sleazy wink and drifted on his way.

"Do you know him?" she asked.

"No. Do you?"

They had martinis, which Johnson detested. This time he made an exception. He had no idea why. The gin reminded him of Ponsonby: tears, junipers, lavender water, hyacinths. When it came to ordering the food, Dorothy asked for quiche Lorraine, an error. Johnson, who was not in a good mood, did not feel like enlightening her. Nobody in his right mind would eat a Press Club quiche. He chose something called steak Reykjavík, a gastronomical innovation. It turned out to be a euphemism for charred roast beef, which, in its previous incarnation, had been a long time frozen. Probably since the last ice age. They ate in silence.

A sour taste invaded Johnson's mouth. He stared at the wreckage of Dorothy's quiche, a fulvous mess of dribbled eggs, crumbled bacon, and stale pastry, and he felt a momentary access of panic, a passing nausea for the morning that was gone and the week before, for the life behind him and the life in front, for time stretching away into infinity.

When Dorothy asked what he was thinking about, he said, "A man called Hasketh. My editor."

Dorothy gazed at the quiche, then at Johnson. "You're not eating," she said.

"No."

The world had taken a tilt on its axis. The martinis, of course. He needed another drink, a brandy. "Mr. Johnson," he heard her say, "I think there's something you should know."

"As long as it's not too late," he said.

"I'm afraid it is," she said. And over brandy and coffee she told him.

At the beginning of July, she said, there had been a flurry of telex traffic from the Moscow embassy. One of the messages had been sent *en clair*, and Johnson asked if this was unusual.

"Not for the ordinary traffic," she said. "Most of that goes through the diplomatic bag anyway. The ambassador doesn't like our people, and satellite time *is* expensive, you know. But this was different. Our man was in a hurry. Not that it mattered, his being denied use of the coding machine, I mean. The Russians must have known what was in the message."

The gist of the telex, which she'd glimpsed on Sir Donald's desk, was that the agent was afraid the Russians were going to use some kind of truth serum on George Michael Stevens. The *implication* was that they were holding him as a double agent so that a deal could be made.

"Canned goods," Johnson said.

"I'm afraid I don't quite follow."

"Dead bait."

"He was still alive, Mr. Johnson."

"All right, then. Live bait."

"Yes. But the thing was, you see, we couldn't very well exchange George as a British agent, having already done so as a Russian."

"That makes sense," Johnson said, "that makes a lot of sense. Do you get double time for that kind of thinking, or is it just the spies? Look, somebody was putting the mockers on him. It's obvious, isn't it? Their big chief in Moscow thinks George's blood is a bit too blue for his liking, so he tries this on, just to see how your big chief will react."

"It could have been that," she agreed. "George still had some operational usefulness left, and the Russians could have put him to work in Moscow."

"As they had in London?"

"As they *thought* they had, Mr. Johnson. They had to make sure that he was secure first."

"And you think he was? From your point of view, if not from Sir Donald's?"

"I worked for George, Mr. Johnson. From choice. I do not work for Sir Donald from choice."

"I can believe that," Johnson said. "I'm sorry, do go on. You didn't negotiate, I suppose?"

She hesitated. "We didn't, no. Your idea's an interesting one, by the way. That somebody in Moscow was fishing. But it also works the other way round. Suppose George were a Soviet agent, then it could have been our own people who were trying to put the mockers on him, as you say. But there's only one thing wrong with that, only one thing wrong with that in both cases. . . ."

"Which is?" Johnson asked.

"Why, it was so late in the day. The Russians would have tried in December to save themselves the trouble of debriefing George, and our people would have tried it before the debriefing could begin. Anyway, to answer your question, someone did negotiate, or tried to at least. Whoever it was must have had Cabinet authority. I don't think it was any of the Friends, you know. They just don't have that kind of influence anymore."

"You make them sound like a bunch of Quakers," Johnson said.

"Oh, no, Mr. Johnson. They're not pacifists."

"So it's 'Come home, George, all is forgiven.' Then the Russians top him—with honours. Doesn't that strike you as being in the least bit odd? I suppose it was his funeral, by the way? Or are you going to tell me that he's alive and well in the Lubyanka?"

Dorothy Winters smiled. "I don't think so," she said. "But, yes, it did strike me as odd. At the time."

Johnson asked what had changed her mind.

It was a small thing, she said. A change of routine. The day after the funeral, the embassy doctor was recalled. The transfer papers and accreditation for his replacement would normally have gone through the diplomatic bag. They hadn't.

"It's just another coincidence, Mr. Johnson. First the telex and the funeral, then the doctor comes home. We could have done it, you see, his own people. We could have killed him. I don't know, I just don't know anymore. . . ." Johnson hoped she was not going to cry. "I expect you're probably wondering why I'm telling you all this?"

"I think I know why," he said. "Could you get me a copy of that telex?"

"I'm afraid that's quite out of the question." She reverted to her behind-the-desk manner. "The Official Secrets Act, you know."

"The Covenant of Works. Oh, nothing," he responded to her glance. "And what would you expect me to do now? Complain to Brezhnev, or would he be the right man?"

She dipped into her handbag for a mirror. "Why, nothing," she said, looking at her face. "I expect you to do nothing, Mr. Johnson. Brezhnev wouldn't be much help, would he? I think you should forget about this. I've been rather silly, that's all. I've said too much as it is, really far too much."

"Not at all. I appreciate your help." Useless help, he thought. Dorothy's swan song for the dead Stevens. Unrequited love is the deadliest of poisons. Or had someone told her to talk? That was possible; anything was. What a can of worms.

"I'll see you to a taxi," he said.

"There's no need. I can manage, thanks. I'm sorry about the lunch. And, please, don't say a word of this to anyone."

"Mum's the word," he said, hating himself.

"I hope so." She finished her coffee. "Good-bye, Mr. Johnson."

He watched her leave, a lonely old woman making her way out into the golden afternoon of October London. And she was also lying; of that he was certain.

Johnson moved to the bar and ordered a double scotch. He thought of calling Hasketh but waited for Hasketh to call him. The phone rang almost immediately, and as if by some mysterious telepathy, the barman gave the receiver into Johnson's hand.

"Where are you?" Hasketh sounded as if he were on another planet.

"I dunno, Terry. I was hoping you could tell me."

"Listen . . ." Johnson caught something about a modern major general. "He's bloody annoyed with you. I want you back here."

"I have to see a man in Windsor."

"Eh?"

"About a famous old boy." Johnson looked at his watch. "Zulu sixteen-thirty hours, Terry." It was plausible, he thought. Then he realized that the line was dead.

A white lie, Johnson thought. The appointment was for tomorrow morning—at nine-thirty.

Johnson had called Philpotts-Barker, Stevens' ex-housemaster, before leaving for New York. He had said that he was doing a story on famous old boys, knowing that Philpotts-Barker would never agree to talk about Stevens.

"Indeed?" an ethereal voice had said. "Whom do you have in mind?"

"Well, there's Pinchas Newman. . . ." Philpotts-Barker couldn't refuse to talk about him because Newman was a Jew and P hyphen B was now the headmaster of a famous school that was not anti-Semitic.

"His experiments!" The voice was invisibly moved. "He was always experimenting!"

Johnson winced at his recollection of this statement. Newman's experiments consisted of statically detonating tethered goats with five-hundred-pound bombs—during the war. Since then he had progressed to more exciting things, and was now known, for various reasons, as Sir Pinky.

"You must drop in and see us sometime, Mr. I-didn't-catch-your-name."

Johnson had used the alias Hoare.

"Hoare! Well, yes, definitely do. Call my appointments secretary. Life isn't all cream cheese and strawberry teas. Not nowadays."

And HM had clicked off.

Johnson asked the barman to refresh his glass. And then, as a man so often will in the middle of the afternoon when he has had too much to drink but has not yet decided to get drunk, Johnson began a mental inventory of his real and imagined woes.

There was England, for one thing. He had been back a week, and he was hating it already. Tweedledum and Tweedledee in high places, and all those grubby little hatchet men in Smith Square, the Transport House racketeers. Not that the Tories were any better. Hang the horse thieves! Bring back the birch! It was all so bloody Dickensian, a comic-opera island, and he should have gotten out years ago, permanently.

He had joined the paper nine years ago after graduating with a degree in German (during the white-hot heat of Harold Wilson's technological revolution—the ship of state sailing merrily on, three sheets to the wind), and he had long since abandoned any attempts to make sense out of the world. Because his own life had been a series of disparate places and people (a spell in Bonn, another in Washington, university—light-years ago—at Keele), he assumed that others endured similarly disconnected lives. He had never felt the urge to marry, and the kind of domesticity enjoyed by a man like Hasketh frightened him. It was something to be visited, not lived. Even then, and he thought of his parents, it was bad enough. Their house, their little house in Croydon, suffocated him with its cosiness. And when his father died, as he looked like doing soon, there would be a lifetime's memorabilia to dispose of. He would have to persuade his mother to sell, of course. Another chore. And another drink. Yes, he could do with that.

"When are you going to settle down?" his mother had said that weekend, and he knew what she meant.

"I don't have the time," he replied.

His father was dying, and all she could think of was the propagation of the species. He felt amused, in a sour kind of way, and resentful. A man of deep and unspecific resentment, he knew and resented this as well.

A man should die once and cleanly. Jack Johnson was dying slowly. "Your father has had a serious coronary," the doctor had told him six months ago. "But with a little care . . ." Over the weekend he had noticed how his mother cosseted the man. If he so much as moved or expressed an interest in life, she would remind him of his condition. "Oh, Jack, mind your heart, Jack." Mind your heart, Jack. Pull away the ladder.

"You should come home more often, Bill. You know how your father likes to see you."

It had been an awful weekend.

Think German, Johnson told himself. He admired the Germans for their resilience. They were methodical and dispassionate, and Johnson respected that. It was good to be methodical. That way you could discover who was lying the most. There was no such

thing as the truth, only lies, empirically verifiable lies. Dorothy
Winters had been lying. If she was going to break security in a
little way, telling tales out of court, she would break it in a big
way. Which was why he'd asked for the telex. Verification.

Think German. How could he without the facts? The Germans
were all right. They couldn't help it, and that was the trouble.

He asked for another drink.

"Bad day?" the barman enquired.

"Mondays."

"Life is like a duck's arse," the other declared philosophically.
"Short and full of shit."

"I know," said Johnson. And then he set about the business of
becoming seriously drunk.

He didn't remember much of the drive to Windsor the next
morning. But he was on time, nine-thirty on the dot. Johnson was
always on time.

Philpotts-Barker was disappointed to find that the reporter was a
grammar-school boy. Not only that but red brick as well. Such
people were responsible for the loss of the colonies.

"Pinky," he said, surprising Johnson. "It was Pinky you
wanted to, ah, rap about?" Philpotts-Barker's slender hand adjusted
his rimless glasses. His mouth forced a smile, pleased with its
neologism.

Johnson said that he was more interested in the past.

"Good. Oh, very good." Philpotts-Barker beamed. Perhaps
the young man was not so dreadful after all. Though he did look
a little jaded. Not enough exercise. Too many potatoes.

"Famous men," Philpotts-Barker said enthusiastically. "Did you
know that Pinky proved, beyond all shadow of a doubt, that the
Luftwaffe had a kill rate of 0.8 persons per ton of bombs dropped?
During the war."

Johnson was prepared for this. "Between August 1940 and June
1941," he said, "fifty thousand tons and forty thousand corpses.
Whereas the RAF could kill only 0.2 Germans per ton of British
bombs. Improvements had to be made."

"I say!" Philpotts-Barker was impressed. "You have swotted
this up. Hard work, research." He gestured expansively. "I'm
all in favour of that."

"So am I," said Johnson. "My dad just happened to do Pinky's sums."

"Ah, yes." Philpotts-Barker twiddled his thumbs. "There's pure research and there's applied research. I suppose it all depends on your point of view. With Pinky, now, it was all so abstract. Hamburg, Dresden, fire storms—that sort of thing, you know. He'd worked it all out in his head."

"That sort of thing"—Johnson felt terrible—"do you approve of it?"

"Man proposes, God disposes—Thomas a Kempis. You can't blame Pinky for what he did. Look how they treated his own people. Auschwitz and all that."

"He worked on nuclear weapons, didn't he?"

Philpotts-Barker nodded. There was something decidedly unusual about this young man. And he was so sickly-looking.

"I read a story about this spy," Johnson continued. "What's-his-name? You know who I mean. One of Pinky's contemporaries."

"Stevens. But you're not here to talk about him."

"No. It was just something I'd read."

"He was a bounder. And, confidentially, he was more than that. *Un ivrogne*, just between ourselves."

"A what?"

"A drunk, to use the vulgate."

"No, really?"

"What's more"—Philpotts-Barker leant across his desk—"he was also a dreadful womanizer. A wastrel."

"Yes," Johnson sighed. "He did let the old school down a bit, didn't he?"

"But you're right about Pinky." HM folded his arms. "He was particularly interested in the effects of radiation on living tissue. Those Japanese fishermen, for example . . ."

Johnson drove back to London through the mists of a sickening hangover. The car radio informed him that George Michael Stevens had been linked with Kim Philby and that the prime minister had promised vigorous action.

"Disaster in central India," the BBC announcer intoned. "Two hundred pilgrims were killed early this morning when they were swept off the roof of the train on which they were travelling. It is believed that they were bound for a religious festival in Jabalpur and that the train passed under a low-lying bridge. . . ."

He knew that he had nothing concrete to write and that he should return to the office. But that would mean Hasketh. What, then? Work, work and hide.

In town he parked illegally outside the British Museum. The law would tow his car away. So what? Let them. It would be a good excuse for not seeing Hasketh.

He spent that afternoon in the Public Reading Room, checking out dates. Stevens had missed Kim Philby and Litzi Friedman in Vienna by more than a year. But that didn't matter. Stevens could have met Litzi anytime, anywhere. *If* they had met.

Johnson even followed the career of Stevens' father in *Who's Who* for the years 1913 to 1955, whereafter he was dropped. Too old to ride to the hounds or go on safari. Johnson went to *Webster's Biographical Dictionary*, an American source of which Philpotts-Barker would have disapproved. The father merited an entry; the son did not: "Stevens, Anthony St. Clair, 1884–1961. British colonial official in Africa, amateur anthropologist, explorer. Member of Parliament, 1918–1931. Author of *Nigerian Nemesis, Gold Coast Imbroglio*," etc. That was all. His books were terrible. Johnson knew because he had read them. And none of the sources so much as hinted at what all the people in the right places knew. The elder Stevens had been a crook—a con man.

"To use the vulgate," Johnson said aloud, and was roundly shushed by a tramp who was devouring the second volume of Leon Trotsky's *History of the Russian Revolution*.

4

"You
are old,
Father
William . . ."

Johnson made his way through the solitary dusk of Bloomsbury. Rush hour had faded, the commuters gone to suburban dreams. A profound hiatus reigned, neither-nor time in London town, as if the city, waiting for something but unsure of what, had taken time out to commune with itself in the long shadows of the decaying sun.

His car was missing when he left the museum. There would be a phone call in the morning and a fine to pay. Emergency regulations. And in the morning also—Hasketh: "What have you found out, mm? What have you got?" Nothing, Terry. Sod all. How could you reconstruct the mind of a man like Stevens? Was he a fool or an idealist? Maybe he'd needed the money. Or was it the love of fame, notoriety? What had he been, this man—a Soviet agent murdered by his Russian masters because they no longer believed in him or a British counterspy disposed of by his own people because someone was covering a bungled operation? Whichever way you looked at it, Johnson thought, the betrayer had been twice betrayed.

Johnson rented a bachelor flat in a building called Crescent

Towers, not far from the Baker Street underground. The building, like the apartment, was cube-shaped, and justified neither the substantive nor its adjective. It was built in 1910, and boasted an entrance lobby that reminded Johnson of a third-class lounge from the *Lusitania*. Or the *Titanic*. Something of the sort. He didn't feel like going home to that, not to the sinking ship, his typewriter, and a blank piece of paper. As blank as the grave wherein they laid friend George. And all the Harley Street quacks round the corner, with their Bentleys and Rolls-Royces that do not come on the National Health, and all the little rich chicks fluttering to see them, all the Marjory weeping Ponsonbys.

Maybe the embassy doctor would retire to Harley Street. They'd have given him the glad handshake, all right. The kiss of life to keep his mouth shut. Hasketh would say, "Didn't you get his name? Aren't you going to see him? Why was he recalled? *Why?*" There were all sorts of things that Hasketh would say. But it's no use, Terry, because Dorothy is a nonattributable source, because they'd slap a D notice on the story and we'd go to jail if we published it. Because our friends are worth more than the freedom of the press, because ours is the God-given freedom to defend a lie, because *we* are keeping *you* free.

He remembered that he hadn't eaten for a long time. There was a little Italian place nearby, and he needed something to drain the blood away from his head.

Johnson couldn't face pasta so he ordered veal scallopini with a carafe of Chianti. *Vino* plonko *classico*. The waiter looked at him as if he had just crawled out of a sewer, but that didn't bother Johnson. There was nobody to look at, nobody to look at him. The walls were adorned with technicolor views of the via Posillipo and the Bay of Naples. When the bill arrived, unasked for, with coffee, Johnson wondered if he should confess that he had been hired by a rival outfit just to sit there and look like death warmed over. Bad for trade. A deterrent to all the bright young things who would be coming in soon.

Brandy? No, you have to write a story. Well, something . . . He demanded more Chianti, an unpopular move. People were drifting in now. There was a girl with a Pre-Raphaelite face and a boyfriend who looked like a pale echo of George Gissing. They don't make 'em any paler. Lytton Strachey next. Funny, that tramp reading Trotsky.

Some revolutions are more permanent than others. Was it worth it, Leon, for an ice axe in the head? Snatches of conversation drifted across, and the *superiore* began to take its toll. *"He's really into that. Astrology . . . the stars and Mars. Scorpio . . ."* The girl stared at him and he stared back. Was she an American? The stars and bars of outrageous fortune. Maybe he should go over and ask her to take her clothes off. It would be interesting to see Gissing's reaction, the proud man's contumely and so forth. No. What was it the young man said? " 'You are old, Father William.' " No, I'm not. "And your hair has become very white." Not yet it hasn't. There's a pub just a block away, the Half Moon. "And yet you incessantly stand on your head." Untrue. "Do you think, at your age, it is right?" Quite all right. A pint of Guinness, or two or three. If I leave now, the Gissing girl will come round later. Bound to. It's in the stars.

The Gissing girl did come round later, but Johnson didn't get a chance to talk to her. He was propping up the bar in the Half Moon, wondering what Stevens' sun sign was, when the bomb exploded: a concussive blast and, far, far away, the tendrils of blood and flame. The Gissing girl was dead, and everyone had something to scream about, everyone except Johnson. I didn't have the time, he kept saying to himself, over and over again. No time.

He gave a statement to the police and got out before the media could arrive. Somehow or other he found a cab.

"You've had a spot of bother," the cab driver said.

"What's that?"

"Trouble, mate. I can tell. There's blood all over your face."

So there was. Used blood.

The early-morning edition of Hasketh read Johnson's copy in silence. It wasn't like Johnson; but it was all right, it would pass. And now he would have to give Mr. Bill Johnson a nice friendly chat.

"The police called up while you were away."

"The police, Terry?"

"Yes, Mr. Johnson. The constabulary, the fuzz. Asking if you was the sort that leave a bomb in his car. Did you have any Irish connections? Not Johnson, I said, not him. Then would I happen to know where you were? In Windsor, I said, that's what he told me. Then why was his car outside the British Museum? I said I don't know, I don't *think* he's got anything against the British Museum. Who is this, anyway? Special Branch, they said. You've really pissed somebody off, you have. So where the bloody hell have you been, exactly?"

"I was in that pub, Terry. Last night."

"Oh, God. I'm sorry." And then, embarrassed, Hasketh grumbled. "Spending all your time in exploding boozers. Haven't you got a home to go to? Well, go on, then. Go home."

5

Of Manuscripts, Ancient and Modern

October declined into November. Stories die as stories will, and Johnson was grateful that Hasketh made no further reference to exploding boozers. And then he received a phone call asking him down to Cambridge that Saturday, 2 November. It was the first major break, and Hasketh was moved to declare that something had indeed turned up.

H. C. "Carlo" Peat was Stevens' old tutor. He was also the man who had recruited him for the Friends—in 1940. Carlo was sixty-five years old, and his cranium had long since outgrown his hair, remnants of which circled his head like a white crown. Pince-nez spectacles hung from his ears, a grubby bow tie from the nethermost of his chins. His eyes were blue and merry, most unruthless. Though it was cold in his rooms, he was wearing a light cotton jacket, the kind that Flinders Petrie might have donned for one of his jaunts down the Nile Valley. But Carlo was a fat man and his jacket was crumpled and stained. He was a bachelor, very fond of cats, several of which inhabited his study, including an obese Persian called Blotter, asleep on his desk. When Carlo extricated himself to peregrinate about the room, plucking isolated words from the air, which he did often and to the intense annoyance of Blotter, a broad band of underwear was visible at the frontier of his shirt and trousers. He was not a man who cared for personal appearances.

"Glad you came." Carlo stood up to greet the reporter. "Knew you would, though. Sherry?"

Johnson nodded. He took stock of the room, which reminded him of the set for Roy Dotrice's dramatization of Aubrey's *Brief Lives*. Dim light filtered through an elm-entangled window, and a calendrical clock next to the door measured the passing of the months and seasons. A broken-down gas fire stuttered and flared in the hearth, the fireplace strewn with charred paper, a communal bowl of milk to one corner. An astrolabe stood to the right of the fire; to the left, a bust of Julius Caesar with a college scarf incongruously tied round his neck. Above the mantelpiece, a portrait of Sir John Dee, the Elizabethan magus and spy, stared down on Carlo's back, and an aged Underwood typewriter squatted at the centre of his desk, which was otherwise littered with papers that formed a convenient bed for the slumbering Blotter. The walls behind the desk were lined, higgledy-piggledy, with antique volumes. At one end of these, to Carlo's left, a hatstand reclined drunkenly in a small alcove. Underneath this was affixed the only other living being in the room apart from Carlo, the cats, and Johnson, a desiccated-looking individual with crinkly hair and a moustache.

The remaining walls were covered with photographs of undergraduate groups, all with Carlo centre, in varying stages of his existence. In one of these Johnson recognized a 1930s prototype of the desiccated-looking individual. Stevens was there as well, wistfully smiling, and Johnson, who'd acquired one of the few extant photos of George Michael Stevens (he was known to have hated the process), compared the two. The younger Stevens clenched a pipe in his mouth and was dressed for cricket; the older Stevens was flabbier, but the eyes were the same, also the line of the jaw. A patrician face, a cross between Trevor Howard and the poet Wystan Hugh Auden, on a late-night talk show.

Carlo poured a glass of Findlater's and motioned to the hatstand: "Sorry—Sweet." For a moment, until he saw Sweet's head nod, Johnson thought that Carlo meant the sherry. "Sweet used to be with D—propaganda, broadcasting, and documentation. It was Sweet who thought of laundering mail in high-altitude test chambers. The

Blitz, you know. Water damage. Osmosis. During the war."

There it was, that phrase again. It was a magic formula to these men, something that abolished the last thirty years. During the war. It meant shog off, sonny boy. You don't exist.

Sweet nodded again. He made it look like a terrible effort, and Johnson decided that D must have worn him down a little.

"Your passport's expired," Sweet said, "and you don't have a visa. But don't worry. Your papers will be in the mail tomorrow."

"Pity you read German instead of Russian," Carlo said, his eyes twinkling.

Johnson gathered they were trying to tell him something.

"What you think to Grimmelshausen?" Carlo asked. He didn't mean a concentration camp but a book, *The Adventuresome Simplicius Simplicissimus*—and Johnson was beginning to feel like its hero. Bewildered.

"Fine," he replied. "If you like the picaresque. It doesn't exactly fit everyone's idea of the German mentality, though."

"Ah, well. There's this and there's that." Carlo stood up for one of his periodic excursions. "Here's to 007," he said, raising his glass to Sir John Dee. "His signature, you know. To Walsingham—Master Secretary Francis." He had an odd way of speaking, soft yet staccato, like a machine. Now he halted mid-room and gazed at Johnson. "That Zeus might change me into a winged bird, as Euripides says. If you see what I mean."

"No, I don't. Not really."

"I wonder." Carlo perched on the edge of his desk. "Sorry, Blotter. It's all been taken care of, Mr. Johnson."

"It has?"

"Oh, yes." Carlo hauled up his pince-nez and began searching through his papers. "Don't like flying, myself. Neither does Sweet, do you? No, of course not. That's why you were in D." He glanced at Johnson over the top of his glasses. "They've agreed, you see."

"They?"

"The KGB."

"Now, wait a minute. . . ."

"My fault. Why is everything always the wrong way round, Mr. Johnson?" Carlo chose an avuncular tone. "Do you mind, by the way, if I call you Bill?" Then, abruptly, "You can leave on Monday."

Yes, there was this and there was that. Meaning the Aeroflot tickets and the Stevens Papers, Moscow round trip with George's memoirs thrown in for free.

"Terry Hasketh thought it was a good thing, Bill."

"Did he?"

"We are paying the expenses, you know."

"That figures, then."

"You were going to ask, were you not, whether George's memoirs are genuine."

"Something like that."

"Problematical," Carlo said. Stylistic analysis (his own) revealed that George had definitely written the manuscript, under KGB supervision, of course. Computers? Good Lord, no. They wouldn't use those, too American. Scholars such as Ephorus and Philostratus ("of the salon of Julia Domna") had managed quite nicely, thank you, without computers. As had authorities closer to our own time, the sixteenth-century French-Swiss bibliographer Isaac Casaubon, for example. Transmission? *Samizdat*, via the underground. A put-up job, no doubt. But the manuscript was genuine, in the sense that Philostratus' *Life of Apollonius* was genuine: full of mysteries and lies.

"*Dezinformatsiya*," Carlo said. "If you want to write a book of mysteries—and remember that Apollonius was considered to be in every sense more remarkable than Jesus of Nazareth—then it's best that you invent your sources. Philostratus' authority was a certain Damis of Nineveh, who never existed, in Nineveh or any other city. The next thing is to add *merely* dubious sources, the books of Moeragenes, say—no longer extant, but we do know from Origen that they did at one time exist; then you admit some *very* dubious sources, such as the account of one Maximus of Agae concerning some miracles wrought by Apollonius in that city; mix it all up with personal reminiscences, and in the end your reader can't tell fact from fiction. It's an old formula, and it's what we have here in George's case. Disinformation, and very cleverly done too."

"For example?" Johnson said.

"Those men we exchanged him for." Sweet's voice startled Johnson, who'd forgotten all about him. "He claims we told him to set them up. Says it was part of an operation to get him over there."

"And of course it wasn't?"

"What do you think?"

"How the hell should I know? I'm just a stooge around here. You could be setting me up too. That's what it looks like." Johnson was trying to think of a line of Lewis Carroll's. Something about a crocodile and his gently smiling jaws.

It was best to be cautious, Carlo agreed. He had just rescued his pipe from Blotter. Now he stood up, ambled over to the fire, and lit the pipe with a piece of paper from the hearth. Then he turned round to face the reporter. "What I am going to tell you is strictly on a need-to-know basis, neither more nor less. Listen to me, Bill, then you can make up your mind. . . .

"We're looking for three people. One is the man who recruited Kim Philby. Two is the man who controlled him in London. Three is Kim's successor. The recruiter's code name is Niemand, the controller's Nemo. It's possible, *remotely* possible, that Niemand is dead or has been retired. It amounts to the same thing anyway." Carlo made a lot of smoke with his pipe and returned to his desk. "We do know, however, that he found a replacement for Kim. We know this because we lost an entire network in East Germany, long after Kim went on his travels. Now, it's possible that the controller is the successor, which simplifies things for us, because it means that we're looking for only two people. To be quite candid, it's also possible that George was Philby's successor. But there's yet another possibility, which is that the successor, as distinct from the controller, was one of the agents involved in the exchange. There's a list of them in the manuscript, mostly Russians and Warsaw Pact people, a couple of Englishmen. But this one is different, a German we call Shelley. He's a naturalized citizen and had worked for us for a long time. Well, according to this theory, he had himself arrested in East Berlin so that he could contact the recruiter and warn him that we were close to the source of the trouble. I must say, now that we have Shelley back in the fold, that this theory is no longer very tenable. So that leaves us with George. Or it did until recently." Carlo looked very unhappy. "Then the manuscript turns up, oh, a couple of days before the funeral. Impertinence, but why? And for what reason? Those are the questions we have to answer, but it does mean sending someone to Moscow. Bill"—Carlo made his appeal—"we could use one of our own people, but he'd be spotted straight away. And you must admit your cover's pretty good.''

Sweet laughed, an action of which Johnson thought him incapable. "That's not the reason," he said. "It's because you're an outsider. *Tabula rasa*."

"Well, there's that, too." Carlo extinguished his pipe. "You will go, won't you?"

Johnson said that he would be out of a job if he didn't.

"You can look upon it as a free-lance assignment," Sweet said. "Sort of on Her Majesty's unofficial service."

Like hell, Johnson thought.

"Details," Carlo said. "You're writing a book about George, that's the idea. You'll be met by a man called Dimitrov, KGB first chief directorate, a colonel. Vladimir Andreyevich—Volodny to his friends. We call him Ghost-writer. Bill, we don't expect trouble, but this may come in useful." Carlo handed Johnson the torn half of a Findlater's Dry Fly label. "Our Moscow resident has the matching half. His name is Soper, Reginald Soper. You are to ask him if he likes sherry after cricket."

Johnson shrugged, convinced that he was a one-eyed man in the kingdom of the blind. "Isn't this rather—American?"

"Cricket?" Sweet was convulsed.

"You know what I mean. . . ."

"Questions?" Carlo said.

"Only one. Exactly *what* am I going for?"

"Why, Volodny is just as anxious as we are, don't you see? He wants to find out, too."

"Find out what?"

"Who George was working for, of course."

Fallen leaves lent the air a taint of corruption as Johnson left the college; a cloistered sun in a pastel sky, gingerbread crenellations and gingerbread men. Johnson breathed in deeply.

He found the list of agents in the manuscript after he returned to London:

AVATAR: Komarowski, Stefan; a military-intelligence officer formerly with the Free Polish Air Force, arrested Krakow, 6 August 1970.

BABY: Graebe, Julius; citizen of the DDR employed by Section

IV of the SSD (Staatssicherheitsdienst, the East German State Security Service, counterespionage section), arrested East Berlin, 5 September 1968.

CONCH: Schlierbach, Hans; citizen of the DDR, a captain in the VfK (Verwaltung für Koordinierung, Administration for Coordination, the intelligence branch of the East German armed forces), arrested East Berlin, 30 December 1969.

DUMBO: Deriabin, Anton; a Soviet citizen formerly with Kommissariat 5 (an auxiliary arm of the MGB operating in East Germany after the war), arrested Moscow, 10 September 1970.

EKKA: Stanton, John Philip; British subject in NID (Naval Intelligence Department), disappeared Tekirdağ, Turkey, 7 April 1971.

FEY FERN: Chvalkovski, Eduard; a Czech subject in the Ministry of Commerce, arrested Prague, 8 September 1973.

GRUMBLE: Parks, Keith Edward; British subject with the trade mission in Leningrad, arrested there, 23 October 1972.

HARITON: Tyulenev, Kirill Aleksandr, a colonel in the Soviet military space program, arrested Baikonur, 4 June 1972.

IMPORTER: Druzhinin, Gregori; a Soviet citizen formerly with the MGB (Ministerstvo Gosudarstvennoye Bezopasnosti, the Ministry of State Security and immediate forerunner of the KGB), arrested Moscow, 6 August 1973.

SHELLEY: Ritter, Manfred; a naturalized British citizen, formerly with MAD (Militärischer Abschirmdienst, the counterespionage arm of the West German armed forces), a radar technologist, also employed by SIS-IX, arrested East Berlin, 8 May 1973.

MAD was about it, Johnson was thinking when the phone interrupted his reading. It was Hasketh calling to wish him bon voyage. Johnson asked his boss how long he'd known Carlo.

"Since before you were thought of," Hasketh said, and rang off.

Johnson returned to the manuscript, and a line from Meister Eckhart came into his mind: "In silence man can most readily preserve his integrity."

Integrity was something he valued, as indeed does the one-eyed man his sight.

6

Herr
Keller

The air hostess announced the flight number, cruising speed, altitude, ETA, and Moscow weather in Russian. The translation followed in Radio Moscow style, fruitier than the BBC's. "There will be a light fog on arrival," the girl said. She resembled Joel Grey at his decadent best, scarlet lips and a white face framed in a Joe Gardenia hairdo. A type more Weimar than Soviet. Light fog was appropriate, Johnson thought.

The Tupolev's jet whine and angle of ascent reminded him that the aircraft had originally been designed as a bomber. The decor, however, was Petrograd Imperial. Like a flying Pullman, he thought as the runway dropped behind and the airframe shuddered, poised between the infinite abyss and the triumphant resolution of Newtonian physics.

"Steep," observed a thrombotic figure in the next seat.

Johnson's neighbour was a German businessman with Krupp International. Apart from the reporter and a diminutive Burmese who was engrossed in a 1912 Baedeker, he was the only other non-Russian on the flight. Later he remarked that he had been in Russia during the war. *Drei Jahre in Russland*. But all that was forgotten now. Johnson wondered by whom.

They were over the grey North Sea when the air hostess dispensed two boiled sweets to each passenger. Johnson deduced that one of them was for takeoff and the other was for landing, but there had been a foul-up in the five-year plan. The sweets tasted of barley sugar and childhood, and the Russians sucked glumly. Johnson imagined the pilot wearing a sailor suit like the tsarevitch Aleksei. Poor little bleeder.

A samovar appeared, then caviar for the delectation of a returning bevy of KGB diplomats.

"I bet they don't get this at the GUM," he said in a wan attempt at humour, "the fish eggs." He disliked caviar. Its texture reminded him of tapioca.

"Beluga," his neighbour said. "From the sturgeon *Acipenser huso*. With your permission." And he leant over, seizing Johnson's portion. "My name is Keller and I am from Essen."

Herr Keller from Essen asked where Johnson was staying. He was forced to admit that he didn't know.

The German assumed a look of polite enquiry. "But you are on business?"

"Sort of."

"Myself, I am in steel. Have you been to America?"

Johnson said that he had.

"America is a good country, but it is full of men with dirty jackets. It is your first visit to Russia, yes?"

Johnson nodded.

"Ah, then you are expecting to be met at the airport. And from there you go to your hotel."

"That's right."

"Do you expect to be in Moscow long?"

Johnson, who was beginning to find Herr Keller's phrasebook interrogation a little curious, said that he didn't know how long he would be.

"But your visa." Herr Keller frowned. "The duration of your stay must be clearly specified along with the points of entry and exit."

"Of course. I was forgetting. I'll be there for a week."

Johnson's new passport and Soviet visa had arrived the day before in a resealable OHMS war-economy envelope. Either D's resources were not infinite or someone had been planning on a longer war. Johnson had wondered how Sweet had been able to produce the documents so quickly. Now he was struck by the thought that they had probably been forged. He couldn't remember anything about duration of stay or points of entry and exit.

"Perhaps you have a special visa," said Herr Keller soothingly.

"Yes," Johnson agreed. "Open-ended."

"I have heard of such things," Herr Keller said, nodding sagely, "but I have never seen one." A wet smacking sound issued from his mouth as he helped himself to more caviar. "But why," he enquired sedulously, "should you need this open-ended visa if you are staying for a week only?"

"Because that is the minimum duration of stay," Johnson replied, "and the maximum will be specified at the time of expiry."

"Ah." Herr Keller was evidently satisfied with this answer. "I understand."

The tedium of the flight and Herr Keller's company gave way to a feeling of diffuse resentment. Carlo and his type were living anachronisms, aged cavaliers eking out their days of faded glory. Old men, they were drunk on the past. And that was another thing: Weren't they supposed to retire them now at fifty-five? Wasn't that one of the improvements made after the Philby affair? Sweet must be Hasketh's age, though by the look of him he wasn't much longer for this world. And Carlo was a relic from another day, when gentlemen had played the game according to gentlemanly rules. But Stevens, now, he had been something else. A romantic, he had repudiated the past. He was a man who had repudiated other things as well. The manuscript was shot through with references to his habitual drinking. Sober, he described himself as Dr. Jekyll and Mr. Hyde all of a piece together—drunk, Don Quixote without Sancho Panza, the Knight of the Sorrowful Countenance apart from his risible squire. "Liquid bones in a glass reliquary, booze is the balm of the soul," he wrote, "the lost soul." Booze had been his familiar, yet it had also been his guardian angel. For who would have believed that Stevens, a funny man really, and pathetic, had been a spy?

Two other familiars had haunted the man. One was Miles Cavendish, characterized by Stevens as "the only free spirit I have ever known," another contemporary, another famous old boy. "Our friendship had Augustan qualities," Stevens wrote. "Drunk, he could walk but not talk, whereas I stood, or rather lay, in the opposite case. Symbiotic comrades we were, one to ask for more, the other to fetch and carry." Cavendish's friends had called him Balthazar. "A sobriquet not from the name given to the biblical Daniel (though perhaps that, too) but from the wine bottle that holds thirteen incontinent quarts U.S." The owner of this nickname had achieved some notoriety in his life as a kind of Aleister Crowley figure, a would-be wizard, playboy *manqué*, and drunk, found dead on his bathroom floor—in Detroit, of all places. That was in 1970. Cause of death: heroin OD.

The second familiar was still very much alive: Vladimir Andreyevich Dimitrov, a graduate of the Lubyanka academy at number 2 Dzerzhinski Square. His career began inauspiciously enough under Lavrenti Pavlovich Beria, Stalin's chief of secret police. For a while he seemed destined to indecent obscurity, and then a grotesque incident had hastened his promotion.

After Stalin's stroke in March 1953 the faithful Lavrenti was summoned to the great leader's *dacha* outside Moscow, taking Dimitrov along for company. Molotov, Kaganovich, Malenkov, and other members of the Central Committee suggested that Beria should enter the sickroom to discover the true state of Koba's health. This he did, only to retreat appalled and terrified. For Beria found Stalin, paralyzed and speechless but fully conscious, eyes open, lying on the floor in a pool of his own filth. One by one the heirs apparent crept in to confirm Beria's report, and one by one they were subjected, as so often before, to the dictator's silent gaze. But now they would make no reports, advocate no measures, take no action. Least of all would they dream of summoning the doctors, the same doctors who were supposedly conspiring against Koba's life.

Shortly thereafter the first witness to this scene was shot. But his servant, who testified against him, survived; and under Ivan Serov, Beria's successor, he flourished. And when, in the course of nature, Serov's star began to decline, Vladimir Andreyevich Dimitrov observed another in the ascendant.

According to the manuscript, it was Dimitrov who had recruited Stevens for the KGB in 1941, the year after he joined the Friends: "Peat furnished me with an introduction to Dimitrov; I was to join the other firm, if they wanted me, which of course they did. After the war it was a well-known secret that I had been an officer in the Russian secret service, a cultivated schizophrenia rationalized in the name of the united, if temporary, front against the common enemy. I was hailed as *Tovarich* in all the best clubs. Volodny found this troublesome at first but soon understood that it was the English way. 'Nobody would ever think I'm a spy, you see,' I remember telling him, 'because they all know that's what I am.' "

Johnson glanced at his neighbour, who had fallen asleep. A cherubic smile creased the German's face, giving him the look of a man who was assured of life's simplicities, its points of entry and exit.

The seat-belt sign rang with a Pavlovian stimulus.

Herr Keller awoke. "I was dreaming," he observed. "Here is a short stop scheduled."

The aircraft banked. Twelve thousand feet above the divided city of Berlin, Johnson gained a moment's visionary insight into the world of paranoia, where all accident is the result of careful predetermination: *What if Keller were an agent of the KGB?*

He closed his eyes and tried to picture the faceless Dimitrov. Instead the radiant countenance of Philpotts-Barker floated before him. "The thing about Pinky, you know," he was declaiming enthusiastically, "was that he'd worked it all out in his head."

Indeed he had, Johnson thought, indeed he had.

7

"When the
Kremlin burns,
the devil
has left hell . . ."

Johnson disembarked at Sheremetyevo International with Herr Keller. The sky was murky, the horizon invisible. No one seemed in a hurry, no one except Herr Keller. The German gave a mock salute. "I wish you a pleasant stay," he said, and disappeared into the arrivals building.

The passengers separated into groups and stray individuals, and the corridor echoed to the muted sounds of Russian and the harsh clack of official stamps. Johnson hated arrivals. There was always this blue-green corridor, this ceremony in a vacuum with your existence checked off at the end. First Circle, he thought, welcome to the bureaucrats' paradise. Then he ran into trouble. He wasn't on the passenger list, and a crazy Aeroflotnik was trying to tell him that if he wasn't on the list, he couldn't have been on the flight.

"Now, look—" Johnson clutched his travel papers in one hand, a briefcase with Stevens' manuscript in the other. Somewhere he heard his name being called. He saw her amid a cluster of green-hatted border police and knew immediately that she was waiting for him. One of the guards moved a crash barrier aside and motioned brusquely in his direction. Her name was Anna Samsonov, she said, taking him by the arm, and she was very sorry but Vladimir Andreye-vich had been called out of town.

"Firearms?" she asked. "Ammunition?"

He shook his head, and she smiled. She had beautiful eyes, grey ringed with black, and classic Baltic features, high cheekbones and a fine, delicate nose. Her smile reassured Johnson. Perhaps it was the way she dealt with the officials, but she was utterly self-pos-sessed.

"I'm a good guide," she said. "That's why they gave me to you."

"Gave?"

"In a manner of speaking."

They walked down the main concourse. "Your luggage is being taken straight to the hotel," she said. "You'll be staying at the Rossiya, if that's all right. It's just off Red Square. I have a car and driver outside."

They passed a large poster showing a bottle mated with a crutch. It reminded Johnson of a design for an experiment in visual per-ception, and was overprinted with a legend in the Cyrillic alphabet. He could guess what it meant.

She anticipated his question. "It says that if you learn to drink, you'll end up on crutches."

"Do you believe that?"

"It depends."

"On what?"

"On what they mean by 'learn,' "

"Then I'm a student, too," he said, and they were outside.

"It is thirty-two kilometres to Moscow," she said as the car turned onto the Moscow-Leningrad highway, "and the road we are on now continues in the other direction to the Finnish frontier. In a few moments, to your right, you will see the monument honouring the defenders of Moscow. It is shaped like an antitank barrier, and—"

"Where's Dimitrov?" Johnson asked.

"I do not know where he is. He has to attend preparations for the festival."

"The festival?"

"The anniversary of the Revolution. You have much to learn."

"I said I was a student."

"There." She pointed out of the window. "The sculpture symbolizes the heroic aspirations of the workers' battalions who, with their Red Army comrades, administered the first repulse to the Fascist hordes.''

The Brobdingnagian tank trap loomed through the mist. "There was a German on the flight," Johnson said.

"It is important to have a sense of history," she rejoined. "Hitlers come and go, but the German people and the German state live on."

"Stalin said that, didn't he?"

"Stalin was an expression of the times, like Churchill or Roosevelt."

"Stalins come and go, too. Maybe he was thinking of himself."

She was silent.

"Where did you learn to speak English?"

"Places."

"It's quite fluent when you don't sound like a guidebook. What has Dimitrov to do with festivals? I didn't think they were in his line of work."

The next few miles passed without a commentary. "The Petrovsky Palace is coming up on your left," she said as they reached the suburbs. "It was built in 1775 and is now the Engineering College of the Soviet Air Force. Napoleon stayed here in 1812, after he was compelled to abandon the burning of the Kremlin."

"Wouldn't it catch fire?"

"No." She smiled. "There's an old saying: 'When the Kremlin burns, the devil has left hell.' ''

"Do you know why I'm here?" he asked.

"Not to set fire to the Kremlin," she said.

"Napoleon, was he just an expression of the times?"

She gave it some thought. "He was a revolutionary, a revolutionary who chose the wrong path."

Johnson sighed. "What did you say you did for a living?"

"Be patient. You'll find out. What shall I call you? William is so Germanic."

"Try Johnson."

"Johnson, you must learn that it is a personal question in the Soviet Union to ask someone what he does for a living."

"That's my job," he said. "I'm supposed to find out the truth."

"What is that?" she asked. "We are now travelling down Gorkovo, which means 'the street of Gorki.' That is the truth, Johnson. It is like Regent Street, yes?"

"No," he said.

They drove through a vast square flanked by a mustard-coloured building with a white colonnade. "Manege Square," she said. "Red Square is to your right. Please don't try to burn the Kremlin, Johnson. Such an action could have unforeseen consequences. We are turning into the Karl Marx Prospect now. Traffic is forbidden in Red Square."

They made a left turn, then a right, towards the river. The Hotel Rossiya was transplanted Park Avenue International, a stone-glass monolith set in ornamental gardens.

"Welcome to Moscow," Anna Samsonov said, and asked to see his papers.

"Why?"

"Oh, *nichevo*. There's another old saying: 'Kiss the devil and he'll grant your wish.' Only I'm not sure if you're the devil, Johnson. There." She returned his passport and kissed him lightly on the cheek. "You should change to our time," she said.

His watch showed twelve-thirty p.m., 4 November. Exactly three weeks had passed since he had been in Googie's Bar waiting for Louisa Alcott Perkins. Johnson advanced his watch by two hours and did not feel as though he had missed them.

"Passport, *pazhahlsta*." The clerk's hands were sweaty and trembling, and he kept looking nervously over his shoulder. He placed the passport, upside down, in a pigeonhole, then began searching for a set of keys. "*Tam, tam*," he muttered, and found them.

"We must see the *dezhurnaya* now," Anna said. "Like a concierge, only more so. Here there is one for every floor."

"*Da, gospodin*." The clerk flashed a silvery grin.

The *dezhurnaya* of the twelfth floor surveyed her territory from a table at the end of the corridor. She was instantly alert and voluble.

"She is telling you that she is here to look after your welfare," Anna translated. "The main door of the hotel closes at twelve every night, but she has a system of secret buzzers. It is an honour to have such a guest. She can open or shut any door on this floor. Never does she sleep or leave her position. She has been here longer than the hotel and nothing goes on without her knowledge. The food is very good, but not so good as the American corned beef she tasted during the war. Be careful, Johnson, she disapproves of the cocktail bar—no, it's the drinks, the mixture of drinks. Vodka is all right, but you should not mix it with cognac. She says you have a powerful aura and that she will be especially vigilant for your sake, may the souls of Marx and Lenin watch over you."

"Tell her I am pleased to have such a custodian, but I am tired and would like to rest."

"*Da, da.*" The old lady laughed and nodded her toothless head.

"Johnson, if you are not too tired, I would like to take you out tonight."

"Yes, I'd like that," he said, and meant it.

"That's settled, then." Anna wrote down a number: 44-15-81. "You can reach me here in case of an emergency. You have three hours," she said.

"Win a few, lose a few."

"Yes, Johnson."

Later, as he lay on his bed and stared at the ceiling, he thought of her. Intourist and Aeroflot people were overseen by a special department of the KGB. Johnson tried to remember which but couldn't. The room was Scandinavian clinical, not at all the Empire style he'd expected. And the mattress was unyielding.

She had made reservations at the Seventh Heaven, three-quarters of the way up the TV tower at Ostankino. Johnson watched the intermittent stars from a window seat. Snowflakes brushed against the glass and dark clouds rolled by, obscuring the city lights vaingloriously twinkling far beneath.

Anna Samsonov nibbled on jellied pike. Johnson started to ask about Dimitrov, and she told him to relax.

"Is he a friend of yours?" he tried again.

"Johnson, for a minimum of eight roubles you can have a maximum of two hours in heaven. Enjoy it while you can."

A froglike man and his overdressed wife listened in at the next table. Johnson returned their gaze.

"Russians enjoy watching people," she said. "They find you different. Strange."

"Is that how you find me?"

"No." She pursed her lips. "But I think the *dezhurnaya* was right. It's an aura you have. Like cheese."

"Remarkable," he said, his self-esteem offended.

"A strong cheese." Anna smiled. "*Bien fort.*"

The froglike man belched loudly and his wife laughed. Johnson imagined them squatting on a lily pad: croak laugh, the love song of frog and wife.

She asked him if anything was wrong.

"Nothing," he said. "I'm all right." And then he found himself talking, of the Gissing girl and the pub blast, of his job and a life whose meaning escaped him.

Johnson was still talking as they drove downtown to the Labyrinth Bar. For the capital city of a state that espoused socialist realism, Moscow boasted a number of unlikely-named spots. It was snowing heavily now, and tramcars trundled through the night, monocular and baleful. Anna's driver, a patient man shrouded in taciturnity, dropped them outside the Hotel Intourist on Gorkovo and said that he would wait. The Labyrinth was like a bunker. Bracketed wall lamps cast a suffused glow on raw concrete, and the noise from the jukebox was frenetic: "Revolution." It was like going back in time in more senses than one. Beatlemania was alive and well in Moscow. They had to fight for a table.

Anna ordered a bottle of Starka. It was older than the usual vodka, she said, and stronger. Johnson drank and took in the crowd. Lost syllables came to him, a medley of voices, the languages of Europe and Africa and Asia. Everything was a question of wavelength, that was all; humanity in the labyrinth, not nearly so cunning as Theseus, but alive, warm, confiding. Johnson raised his glass. "Fraternal something or other," he murmured.

"To the peoples of the world," she said.

"And the Minotaur." His gaze wandered from her eyes.

"Jee-zus!" The figure hailed him, glass in hand, whisky-voiced. The shock of recognition coiled in his stomach. It was Gosling, their Moscow correspondent. "Bill Johnson!" he cried, shouldering his way through the crowd and waving his free hand in greeting. "What news bringest thou to Moscow?"

Gosling was balder than Johnson remembered, and his face glistened with sweat. Lank strands of hair framed his fleshy features, leaving a denuded patch at the top of his head that he rubbed and polished, an irritating mannerism that gave him an air of perpetual astonishment. He was wearing an old corduroy jacket, threadbare at the elbows and cuffs, and his beer belly protruded from a fawn-coloured sweater that was stained with the alcoholic and gustatory accidents of his professional life. A green pair of pants completed his attire. Waspish of gut and baggy at the knees, they had once fitted a younger, slimmer man; now they radiated the patina of age. Gosling seemed permanently sozzled, and his appearance troubled Johnson, who always took care with such things.

"Anna, this is Howard Gosling—Anna Samsonov," he said.

Gosling sat down. " 'Scuze the rags." He screwed up his face, a jolly man. "I don't think we've met before. No, I don't *think* we have. My pleasure."

Though not ours, Johnson thought. He saw Anna stare at Gosling, who was making dutiful enquiries about their brand of poison.

"Well." Gosling eyed the Starka bottle and dug into his pockets, depositing an assorted pile of schillings, zlotys, and dollars on the table. "Me sinking fund," he mumbled apologetically, "liquid assets. *Visky!*" he hollered at the miniskirted waitress, and then he turned to Johnson. "Or is it a holiday?"

"Not exactly."

"Ah."

Anna stood up and excused herself. "So long as you know what you're doing"—Gosling made sure she was out of range before he leant across the table—"that's the main thing." His mouth fell open and he was seemingly on the verge of a confidence when the waitress appeared with his drink. "Fact is, I'm sloshed, piddled. I'm not like this every day, but I've just won a bet. With myself. Funny"—he blinked and nodded—" 'cos the other half of me has just lost a bet."

"Look, Howard," Johnson began, "maybe you should—"

"I know, I know. There's no need to mobilize the Salvation Army." Gosling slopped his drink. "Cheers. Terry sent you out dead-spy hunting. I got a cable yesterday. See, I'm not the only one who's split-minded around here. There's no need to think you're poaching, you know"—Gosling rubbed his temples—"no need at all. Fact is, I'm a bit bored with Moscow. Anyway, I can see you've got things to do. That girl, now . . ." Gosling saw Anna returning and rose to his feet, making an exaggerated show of formality. "I was just saying that Johnson is fortunate to have a, well, you know . . ."

"Yes, I know," she said.

Gosling sat down again. "Hey, there's a friend of mine. Hey, Komo!" he shouted. "Come and join the party!"

Komo announced that he was a student of mech eng—from Ghana. Johnson thought of Stevens, who had been born in Ghana. His first mistake, as he put it in the manuscript—being born. Right now Johnson didn't have a very high opinion of people from Ghana, not this one anyway.

"I am unfortunately out of pocket," said Komo.

Gosling waved at the cash nexus on the table.

"Most kind, most gracious."

"Not at all." Gosling grinned as Komo fled to the bar. "He's okay," he said. "Generous, too, when he has the wherewithal. His granddaddy was a witch doctor or some such thing. Ah, well, it takes all sorts. Where're you staying, by the way?"

"At the Rossiya." Johnson glanced at Anna.

"The Moscow Hilton." Gosling took a hefty drink. "Like it?"

"I just arrived this afternoon."

"Maybe I could show you the city? Introduce a few people."

Anna glared at him. "That is my job."

"The three of us, then?"

"I am sure that you have your work to do, as Johnson has his," Anna declared. "I trust that you haven't had any trouble with your cables recently?"

"Only from home," Gosling said. He finished his drink. "All right, I get the message. Time for bye-byes." He yawned theatrically. "Come and see me sometime, Bill. If I'm not here I'm at the Central Telegraph Office, and if I'm not there I'm at the Varshava. That's where I hang out, cheap but comfy. Good food, you know. Well, be seeing you, then. . . ." And he lumbered out of the bar, trailing pity in his wake.

"Why do you sigh, Johnson?" Anna asked. "The man is a fool. He will end up on crutches."

He wondered if this was a threat. Then he remembered the poster at the airport. "Sometimes I think we all will," he said.

"Excuse, please." Komo had returned from the bar. "Howard has gone?" He gazed abjectly at the table. "How absentminded of him to have forgotten his monies. What will he do for provender? Poor Howard." Komo flashed a brilliant smile. "I shall take it for safekeeping. He is my friend."

"Take it," Anna said. "I don't care if he's your enemy."

"No, no." Komo shook his head. "What can one do if one cannot trust one's friends? Nothing, nothing at all." He counted the money. "Without friends a man does not exist. There is quite a lot here. He will not mind if I deduct another drink for the favour. He is careless, Howard, to leave such a sum. . . ."

Anna cut him off with a "*Spahkoynoy nochiy.*"

"Good night." Komo bowed gravely.

"Johnson," she said, "I would like to sleep with you."

"What? I mean—where? When?"

"Tonight, at your hotel."

"But . . ."

"The *dezhurnaya*? I can take care of her. *Nichevo*, Johnson."

Illuminated in awful splendour, the *dezhurnaya* of the twelfth floor accepted Anna's ten-rouble note. "*Da, spasiba balshoye.*" Another voluble address ensued, Anna translating.

"She would like to know what you want for breakfast and at what hour."

"Tell her boiled eggs at nine o'clock."

"*Da, da, yaitso f'smyatky.*"

"Come, Johnson," said Anna primly. "Let us retire."

The corridor rang to a wicked laughter. "I don't understand," he said. "What's so funny?"

"You asked for eggs," she said at the door to his room. "*Yaitso*— in Russian the word also means 'testicles.'"

Her lovemaking was energetic and practised; his, tired and lacking enthusiasm. But she did not seem to mind. "You are a parasite," she told him, "a capitalist parasite."

"Which makes you the host," he said.

Johnson cursed the adamantine qualities of the bed. Anna served sex, he thought, as a waitress would food at the Seventh Heaven. It was a commodity, nothing more. And what was he, then, but a jaded servingman, a worshipful slave groaning in enforced ardour at the font of Aphrodite?

They made love for a second time, in the shower. It was distinctly novel but somewhat slippery.

The water was never really hot, and after ten minutes or so the shower coughed and spluttered. Johnson scarcely had time to react before the stream of water on his back approximated to the temperature of the night air outside. He howled in shock, cracking his shin as he leapt from the tub. Anna ran giggling into the bedroom. "You bastard!" he cried, wet and shivering and miserable. "You did that on purpose!"

"No, Johnson. It was an accident."

She was already dressed when he came back into the room. "Where are you going?" he asked.

"To work," she said.

"After midnight?"

"Yes, after midnight."

"Your hair's still wet."

"*Nichevo*, Johnson."

"Will I see you tomorrow?"

"Maybe."

"When?"

"Oh, you know, whenever. And, Johnson, please don't set fire to the Kremlin."

He watched her leave. Then he noticed his clothes in a heap at the side of the bed. Damn, he thought, and sneezed.

8

Fog

Brazen alarms rang in his sleep. The phone jangled him into consciousness. Groaning, he picked up the receiver.

"Good morning, Johnson." Her voice was level, unmodulated. "Your friend Gosling is waiting for you in the breakfast room."

"What time is it?"

"Time for your eggs. Johnson, I've an apology to make. Volodny cannot see you today."

"Anna, will you tell me what's going on?"

"Tomorrow morning at nine o'clock Comrade Dimitrov will come to the breakfast room of your hotel. He sends his regrets."

"Like hell. What's Gosling want? I mean, how do you know he's there? No, forget it. What are you doing today?"

"Work, work, always work . . ."

"And you're my host, Anna."

"Spend the day with Gosling. He offered to show you round."

"I can't imagine a better guide."

"I'm sorry, Johnson. You have a free day. Use it."

"Will I see you tomorrow?"

"Perhaps. Well, yes. All right. And, Johnson . . . ?"

"Yes?"

"Enjoy your eggs."

"Thanks, Anna."

Gosling was huddled in a solitary heap behind a copy of the
Moscow News, the local English-language tourist rag. He greeted
Johnson knowingly, without speech. There was one other person in
the room, a tweedy-looking character about Johnson's age.

"Thought there'd be more activity," Gosling said, "what with
the impending bash-up. Hey, you know what?"

"No—what?"

"Guy Fawkes Day today." Gosling nodded. "You see, they'll
start arriving this afternoon, all the provincial apparatchiks.
Come tomorrow, you won't be able to move in here. Then Thursday—huge, big drunk, everybody, and I mean everybody, absolutely
smashedsky. Anyway, I just thought I'd drop in for a spot of brek-
kers." He made inefficient attempts at folding the paper. "You seeing that girl, then?"

"Not today." Johnson was feeling slightly hung over and wondered how Gosling continued to function.

The waiter appeared, carrying eggs swaddled in a napkin.
"You're supposed to crack them in a saucer," Gosling said. "No
eggcups, see? Balls, that's what they call them. Balls," he added
merrily.

"I know." Johnson cracked an egg. The yolk was pale, the
white transparent. He prodded it with a spoon and it squirmed
in the saucer. It was almost raw.

Gosling watched. "She tell you that, then? You could have had
them fried—the eggs."

"Live and learn," Johnson said.

"Foggy last night," Gosling mused.

Johnson stared at him. "It was snowing."

"Well, it's foggy now." Gosling cleared his throat. "Bad for me
chest. Look, I know it's none of my business, but . . ."

"But what?"

"That girl. She's, well, she's Comrade Dimitrov's lady."

Johnson said nothing.

"Not that I'm prying, mind. What's the matter? You laying her or something? Just be careful, that's all. First day in town and you screw the comrade's lady!''

"In the shower," Johnson said, "if you must bloody well know."

"Oh, he won't mind," Gosling went on happily. "Free love, it's part of the system. They were probably trying to get a look at you, that's all, trying to measure you up for size. I bet he's having a good laugh at the pictures now. The next thing you know, they'll be asking you to join the firm."

"You could have told me this last night," Johnson complained.

"Don't say I didn't try. And another thing"—Gosling lowered his voice—"don't look now, but that guy behind me—he's following you."

"I haven't been anywhere yet," Johnson said.

"I wouldn't say that." Gosling leered. "Anyway, I know the type. Listen, this is what we'll do. And don't *worry*. You can trust old Howard. I've done this sort of thing before."

The air was acidic, heavy with a petrochemical smog that seared the lungs. Gosling stood on the hotel steps and pointed out a little church, its tower visible through the fog. "The Church of the Conception of Anna," he said. "They restored it, but no one goes there anymore. Anna was the Georgian Virgin—unlike some Annas we know."

Johnson ignored this remark. He was thinking of Beria, the prying, porcine eyes of Lavrenti Beria as he watched his master dying on the *dacha* floor. Both men were Georgians, and Beria had shown a predilection for virgins—one of his few human characteristics.

"Let's go," Gosling said. "Act naturally, like you're seeing the sights."

"You must be kidding," Johnson said, their own footsteps sounding in hollow pursuit.

"Used to be a bad district, this," Gosling muttered. "The Zaryadiye, it was called. Muggings, knifings, and so forth. The Bolsheviks cleared it up. Listen." He halted as a third set of footsteps, unsynchronized with theirs, stopped some distance away. Johnson imagined he heard a fourth set of footsteps—an echo, that was all. "Come on," Gosling said. "We'll lose him in Red Square."

Johnson said, "Howard, how come you know so much about

Dimitrov? I mean, you could be mistaken. She might not be his woman. Maybe you just saw them together and . . ."

"She is his *property*. Jesus, man, I've been following him around for the last couple of months. Lost him a couple of days ago, though. I've been trying to fix a meeting with him, see, been trying to find out what George Stevens really died of. They had him in the Kremlin Hospital, best place for an old soak like that. Only, the funny thing was he was being treated by a psychiatrist, a man called Druzula. Maybe his liver had slipped or something. But she's his lady, all right, so don't go worrying about it. She wouldn't be seen dead in a *nekulturny* joint like the Labyrinth unless he'd told her to take you there. Another thing, your room is probably bugged. And your phone definitely."

"She gave me a phone number," Johnson said.

"Yes, and I can tell you what it was: 44-15-81, Ministry of Foreign Affairs, Press Department. Right?"

"Yes. They must have known I was coming for a long time."

"They must have *seen* you coming. Who did you talk to in London?"

"Well, I saw Macpherson. Then a man in Cambridge last Saturday."

"Fat man, looks like an old baby?"

"That's right."

"Carlo. And a thin man who looks like a corpse?"

"Yes."

"David Sweet. He took over from Carlo."

"Really? I thought Stevens replaced Carlo."

"George was only the acting head, see? For a few months in 1968. Then this Sweet took over."

They were walking uphill now, and the fog had cleared somewhat. An endless queue coiled round Red Square, the faithful come to view an embalmed dialectician. "Lobnoye Mesto"—Gosling pointed to a round white stone platform—" 'Place of the Skull.' It's where Ivan the Terrible used to deal with the Loyal Opposition. Boiled 'em in oil, he did." The Kremlin chimes were striking ten o'clock; there was no sign of their pursuer.

The two journalists turned right at the Tomb of the Unknown Soldier into Alexander Gardens. "There he is," Gosling said, and

Johnson caught sight of a trench-coated figure hurrying after them. Trench Coat slowed as the militiaman on traffic duty outside the Central Exhibition Hall held up the traffic for a convoy of army trucks. Johnson recognized the mustard-coloured building he'd seen the day before. Now it was covered with scaffolding. Preparations were already under way for the parade to be held in two days' time, when Red Square would be filled with tanks, rockets, and the massed phalanxes of revolutionary goodwill.

They made another right turn into the Prospekt Marxa. There was a metro entrance across the street, and Trench Coat was waiting outside, a newspaper hiding his face. Somehow or other he'd gotten in front of them. "Clever bugger," Gosling said. "C'mon, let's run for it. . . ."

A car horn blared, the vehicle speeding between them. The man had vanished when they reached the subway, and Johnson, who was not feeling at all happy, studied a wall poster of a human caricature sprawling in the street. Bottle and gutter, a variation on a theme.

"What now?" he asked as Gosling made a great show of consulting the map.

"Looks like we're following him," Gosling replied, and tapped him lightly on the shoulder. "Come on."

Their descent, flanked by the porphyry columns of Stalinist baroque, was illumined in the radiance of quartz chandeliers. Trench Coat was waiting for them, less than a car's length away, on the platform. It was the same man who had been in the breakfast room of the Rossiya, no doubt of that, and he also looked desperately ill at ease.

Johnson was eying the other passengers (a desultory crowd of perhaps twenty or thirty people) when a sudden whoosh of air announced the impending arrival of a train. "It's the on-off routine," Gosling said, and bundled Johnson into the car, waltzing him off again just in time to see Trench Coat stepping back onto the platform. "Now!" he cried, and they reboarded the train. Johnson, surprised at Gosling's agility, stumbled. Before he could recover, Gosling's portly frame escaped through the closing doors and the train shuddered into motion, throwing him into a seat as Trench Coat, similarly unbalanced, sat down next to him.

"I say!" he gasped. "That *was* professional."

When Johnson arrived back at the hotel, he was roundly cursing Gosling, who had set him up for the meeting with Soper. For an infinite moment he was convinced that Trench Coat was an officer of the KGB about to make an arrest. Johnson had registered a vertiginous series of emotions—panic, fear, relief, renewed suspicion—and then, as logic strove to reassert itself, the profound conviction that someone had made a dreadful mistake, an incredible mistake. But not until later, much later, when he attempted to sift these impressions in the relative security of his hotel room, did he understand the fantastic charade that Gosling had mounted in order to arrange the meeting; and then, and only then, did he understand that Soper had not in fact been referring to Howard Gosling but to another.

"Just left him standing there, you did. My name's Soper, by the way." And Soper had extended his hand, which Johnson shook merely from force of habit.

"Nothing like a public place for a private meeting, is there? Listen, Mr. Johnson. We've got the cassette and we'll make the switch soon. It'll be very easy. . . ." The train slowed and Soper stood up, glancing ostentatiously at the newspaper that he left on the seat. "You'll be seeing our mutual friend tomorrow," he said, "so take care. You might be interested in the cricket scores, by the way," he added, smiling. And then he was gone like a bird on the wing.

Johnson didn't know anything about a cassette. He had no idea what Soper was talking about, and he had no intention of finding out. "Look," he'd wanted to say, "I'm not a spy, not some sort of courier." Still, he'd picked up the newspaper that the avian Soper had left behind, and by the time he arrived back at the Rossiya it seemed to Johnson that he had had no choice in the matter. None whatsoever.

There was a brown paper envelope inside the newspaper and inside the envelope a sheet of handwritten instructions with the matching half of the Findlater's Dry Fly label:

You will be under constant surveillance [Soper had written], so there is little point in using the drop-off system. Should you require a personal meeting, any report that you file at the Central Telegraph Office beginning with the words "Request immediate clarification of

contract'' will bring me to the Place of the Skull in Red Square one
hour later. Fallback time and place, two hours after filing, at the Karl
Marx statue on the Prospekt Marxa. If for any reason you are unable
to make either place in time, call 31-95-55, extension 7, and ask for
Mr. David Evans of the Consular Section. You will be told that Mr.
Evans is unavailable. ''I was expecting him at noon,'' you will say,
and the person at the other end will ask you for your present
whereabouts. The same procedure is to be used if I fail to appear at
either meeting place, where you are to wait *no more* than ten minutes.
I need hardly add that you should destroy this note once you have
committed its contents to memory.

Soper's handwriting, like his style, was crabbed and formal.
Johnson read and reread the note. Then he took it into the bathroom and flushed it down the toilet with both halves of the sherry
label. Good riddance, he thought. Or was there a KGB man lurking
down there in the sewers?

He spent the rest of the afternoon in a futile search for Howard
Gosling. The Labyrinth Bar was closed, didn't open again till six,
and looked like the Führerbunker after the optimists had cleared out.
Gosling wasn't at the Varshava either. Nor was he at the Central
Telegraph Office, and Johnson wondered if he should file the cable
requesting immediate clarification of contract. But that would be
playing their game (whatever it was) and would probably cause the
riot squad to storm Red Square.

Soper's note had an unnerving effect on Johnson. It was something he couldn't get out of his mind, and the more he tried, the
worse it became. He knew, of course, why Anna hadn't turned up
that morning. Both sides were softening him up for something. But
for what? Nothing was the way it was supposed to be. Strange
faces in a strange city, in shop windows and in crowds, began to
take on a disturbingly familiar aspect. It took him three hours before he isolated and identified one of them, a man whose long
grey overcoat and blank stare advertised him as a member of the
security police. Johnson had seen him before, standing on the platform in the metro just before the doors had closed and Howard
Gosling had slipped out of the train and into the crowd, Moscow
swallowing him up, receiving him as surely as one of her own drab
grey citizens into the void.

He tried phoning Anna after dinner that evening. A recorded message answered—in Russian. Johnson went to see the desk clerk and asked him to call a cab.

"Cap?" The other gave him a look reserved for children and idiots. "Which means it, 'cap'?"

"A taxi, don't you understand? A taxicab."

"*Tahksi!*" Illumination shone in the clerk's eyes. "*Doh?*"

"What?"

"Ah. Vehr to?"

"The Labyrinth." Johnson sighed.

Gosling was not in residence, but Komo was. The Ghanaian greeted Johnson effusively with a "*Mir i Druzbah!*" and sat down.

"Peace," Johnson said. Ivan Grey Coat, Ivan the Glum, was sitting two tables away, watching.

"Tonight I am buying," Komo announced, and asked if Johnson would join him in a *peeva.* "It is called that because it makes you go for a pee." He giggled.

When Komo, still laughing and smiling, returned from the bar, he asked if Johnson had seen Gosling. "By any chance?"

"Yes, this morning. But somehow I don't think he'll be in to-night—if that's what you want to know."

Komo winced as he tasted his beer. "It has been foggy," he said, regarding Johnson thoughtfully.

"Yes."

"Very foggy. So I am still out of pocket and cannot repay Howard his monies."

"I see. And you want me to help?"

"No! No! No! I am not sponging off my friends. Howard will have his monies back when my stipend comes, oh, yes! But, Mr. Johnson—Howard told me your name—there is this thing, this other thing. A clerical matter." Komo made it sound vaguely Anglican, Johnson thought. "They are refusing to renew my visa. I must go home if I do not graduate at the end of this term. That means a big disgrace for me, Mr. Johnson, a big disgrace. So what am I to do?" Komo took another sip at his beer and came to the point. "Mr. Johnson, I am not one for poking my nose into the business of other people, but Howard mentioned this girl in the Ministry of Foreign Affairs . . ."

"Anna?"

"Exactly! The very same! Now, she is connected with what they call OVIR, that is the Office of Visa Registrations, and so it occurred to me that you might—how do you say it?—put in the good word for me. . . ."

"I'll see what I can do," Johnson said.

"Most kind!" Komo drained his glass. "And now the quid pro quo, as it is called. At the same time as he spoke of this lady, Howard also mentioned the reason for your presence here. Mr. Johnson, be very careful, very, very careful." An awful sincerity crept into the Ghanaian's voice, and Johnson was amazed to see that his large and limpid eyes were glistening with tears. "Mr. Johnson, this spy, George Stevens. Howard told me that something so bad happened to this man that they could not even bury him when they had finished."

"Not according to my information," Johnson said. He glanced across the table at Ivan the Glum, who was still there. Lipreading, Johnson thought.

"That is what I have been told, Mr. Johnson. You do not have to believe me. Ask Howard. He is in the know."

Komo waited for his reward. Wearily Johnson asked him what he was drinking.

"*Visky!*" he cried, imitating his benefactor of the night before.

It was a passable imitation, Johnson thought, as passable as the world wherein he lived.

9

Our
Mutual
Friend

Dimitrov appeared punctually at nine o'clock the next morning. He came alone into the breakfast room and walked past the table where Soper was sitting, pecking at some grey morsel of food. When Johnson looked up, his compatriot had vanished. So had Ivan, his subway familiar. It was a game, Johnson thought. Musical spies.

Dimitrov seated himself, and the waiter appeared, with great celerity, at his side.

"*Kohfay*," he snapped. He was wearing an Astrakhan coat and a fur hat, which he removed and deposited on a napkin. "I seem to be interrupting your breakfast," he said. "My apologies. And my apologies, also, for yesterday."

"That's all right," Johnson said. "Anna explained."

"She did? That was good of her."

Johnson recognized Dimitrov's look, the same one that Anna had given Gosling the night before last. So they taught each other tricks, he thought; that was nice to know. It also confirmed what Gosling had said.

Dimitrov gave the impression of a man who had managed to live well in himself over the years. His English was fluent and precise; his face, unremarkable except for the eyes. They were glaucous and slightly protuberant, and Johnson wondered if the comrade suffered from a thyroid condition. Watching him, he thought it unlikely. The Russian might have been a senior civil servant at the height of his career, a description that would have fitted him exactly except for something Johnson could not pin down, a sense of distance, a remoteness that brought to mind Louisa's description of her husband. The comrade wasn't there somehow; he was not quite present enough.

"Mr. Johnson, I do not know how much your people have told you about what I want, but it is a great deal."

"Oh?"

"A great deal."

The waiter returned with coffee. Dimitrov acknowledged neither his presence nor his Heepish regard but removed one glove and then the other, placing them next to his hat—a simple act, anatomically performed. It was a bloodless operation, Johnson thought; everything about the comrade was singularly bloodless.

"Therefore you and I should not play games with each other, Mr. Johnson. For example, yesterday morning, in the company of Howard Gosling, you led one of our agents a song and dance through the Zaryadiye, eventually losing him at the Prospekt Marxa metro. . . ."

Johnson started to protest, but Dimitrov silenced him. "Listen to me, Mr. Johnson, and mark what I say. You boarded the train not with Gosling but with this man Soper, who was sitting here in this room even as I came in. He has left now. I wonder why, Mr. Johnson. No matter. It is known that he left the train at Dzerzhinski Square, which was not very wise of him perhaps. You remained on the train until Kirov Square, whereupon you turned round and came back. Mr. Johnson, if you were to tell me that you had never seen this man before in your life, then I might possibly believe you. But if you were to tell me that your association is innocent, then I would never believe you. For you see, Mr. Johnson, when the pair of you boarded that train, Soper was carrying a newspaper and you were not, but when you left the train, you were carrying a newspaper and Soper was not." Dimitrov studied the backs of his hands. "You will not see this man again, Mr. Johnson, not while you are in the Soviet Union."

"Is that right?"

"Yes, that is right. If you do, I will have you arrested."

"On what grounds?"

"Grounds, Mr. Johnson, do I need 'grounds'? Surely it is enough that your friends have provided me with those already."

"You've got me wrong, you have. I'm not working for those people."

"Oh, come, Mr. Johnson. Your documents are forged. They were put together by a man called David Sweet." Dimitrov watched the reporter. "So that's illegal entry, good for at least five years' hard labour, I would say. Then we have other charges. . . ."

Johnson wondered if Dimitrov was bluffing. Probably not, he decided. Now was the moment when he should say, "I don't scare so easy." Something like that. He said nothing.

"Believe me, Mr. Johnson, it would be the easiest thing in the world to arrange your disappearance. Legally."

"As you did with Stevens?" Johnson said. Evidently Dimitrov wasn't going to enumerate the "other charges."

"No, Mr. Johnson, not as with Stevens. That was not so easy." Dimitrov picked up his gloves. "Bear in mind what I have told you. And now, when you are ready, I would like to show you George's grave."

"Yes." Johnson remembered Komo's information. "I would be very interested in that."

The Russian eyed him with exaggerated solemnity. "Personally," he said, "I have no interest in graveyards."

En route to the cemetery, Dimitrov discoursed amiably on biographical method, enquiring whether Johnson thought twentieth-century technology, with its marvellous ability to encapsulate the spoken and visual moment, gave the modern biographer an advantage over his predecessors.

"All biography is official in the Soviet Union," he said. "After Beria's execution the *Soviet Encyclopaedia* greatly expanded its article on the Bering Strait. You cannot imagine what interesting geographical facts they found, just to fill the space left by my boss.

However, that is the way we are.''

Johnson was still thinking about those other charges. He was also distracted by a peculiar smell in the car. At first he thought it came from a wreath of roses that he was surprised to see on the backseat of the car. Dimitrov, observing his surprise, had moved the wreath aside.

"A token of my appreciation," he said.

A strange remark, Johnson thought, and the odour was even stranger. A rancid smell like that of cabbage water, it clung to the car's upholstery, permeating the entire vehicle. Perhaps his senses were acutely sharpened that morning, for he now made out another, distinct odour, which emanated from the person of Dimitrov himself. It had passed unnoticed in the hotel breakfast room, but in the closer confines of the car it grew more and more cloying as the journey progressed: the odour of musk or civet.

Johnson recognized it as Anna's perfume and was amused to think that Dimitrov had this weakness, that he would share not only his mistress but her perfume as well. Vaguely he wondered if there was just the one deodorant in general use, one perfume to mask the animal odour of both sexes, an olfactory correlative of their social equality. Surely this was not the case in a land famed for its distillation of vital essences! Was there, then, some primitive reason for the comrade's stench? Had he leapt from Anna's bed daubing himself in her perfume as a mark of possession and a warning to others, a warning that unequivocally stated, "Stay away from her; she is mine"? Or was there a stranger explanation yet?

Johnson opened the window on his side of the car, as if a breath of fresh air could dispel not only the perfume but his thoughts on those other charges as well.

Dimitrov regarded him with some amusement. "It is overpowering, isn't it?" he said, adding, "Anna threw it over me this morning."

The Novo-Devichy Cemetery is stocked with the famous dead. Gogol rests here, the Gogol whose hero Pavel Ivanovich Chichikov bought the title deeds on dead serfs that he might raise cash by mortgaging them; likewise Ilya Ehrenburg, propagandist of the Revolution, and Vladimir "Read it—envy me—I am a citizen" Mayakovski, futurist and suicide; among the many musicians, Scriabin, whose oeuvre was intended to bind heaven and earth as a prelude to the Second Coming, and Prokofiev, who died on the same day as Iosif Vissarionovich Stalin, to be honoured, unlike the dictator, with posthumous awards. Here also lie the remains of Nadezhda Sergeyevna Alliluyeva, Stalin's second wife, another suicide—from nine grams in the head. And still others are commemorated, if not exactly buried here, such as the generals executed in the aftermath of Stalin's death, a row of marble effigies attesting to the one thing they had in common, the year of their death.

Vladimir Andreyevich Dimitrov paused with his hand on the door of the Volga saloon. "No, no, my friend." He turned to the English reporter. "In order to know a man you must meet and talk with him, you must live something of life with him, you must see how he enjoys it and also how it makes him suffer. So do not tell me that you knew George Stevens vicariously."

An odd mood came over the Russian, who backed away from the car even as he seemed on the point of entering it. "Don't you understand?" he cried, his eyes catching the fire of the morning sun. "Don't you understand anything at all?"

Johnson was at a loss.

"Come, my friend." The Russian clapped him on the shoulder. "Follow me."

Dimitrov gave a parting look at the grave. He had walked a hundred yards down the driveway when he stopped and turned. "What do you see over there?" he asked abruptly.

"Why, the monastery, of course," Johnson said.

"Why, the monastery, of course," Dimitrov mimicked. "And over there?" His hand shot out, pointing.

"An apartment block. At least, that's what it looks like. . . ."

"Then you really do not understand!" Dimitrov punched a fist into his hand, his foot stamping on the driveway. "I cannot believe it! But from you, my friend, yes, from you! They didn't tell you, did they, they really must have forgotten. . . ." The Russian fought against his laughter. "Oh, how we have been waiting for you, my friend! How we have been waiting! He's alive, don't you see, George Stevens is *alive!*"

Vladimir Andreyevich surrendered to his humour. His laughter sounded resonantly in the Cemetery of the New Monastery of the Virgin, and at last Johnson understood the deceptions, the lies, the silences. They had kept Stevens because they were unsure; they had kept him while they waited for an approach. But Carlo must have known, and it suddenly occurred to Johnson that, right from the beginning, Carlo and his friends had done everything within their power to draw the Russians' attention to his existence, including the forgery of his documents and, most probably, ordering Soper to contrive a meeting that would be observed.

Then he remembered Herr Keller from Essen and Carlo's words: "We could use one of our own people, but he'd be spotted straight away."

Sweet Jesus, what a fool he'd been!

"Those other charges," he said. "What are they?"

"Attempted murder," Dimitrov said. "Conspiracy to commit espionage against the Soviet Union, conspiracy to assassinate a government official—these carry a mandatory death sentence. But don't worry, my friend, you're an accessory before the fact. You only get life."

Johnson understood everything, especially the fate of George Michael Stevens, to whom something so terrible had happened that he could not even be buried.

INTERMEZZO

From
the
Stevens
Papers

I was born in Kumasi, capital of the once independent kingdom of Ashanti, now a province of the present-day state of Ghana, on 1 June 1918—an only child. My father was with the Colonial Office there and by the time of my birth had already left for England, having enjoyed a gentleman's war observing the marches and countermarches in the Cameroons through a haze of gin and fizz. In the month of my birth the Germans launched their final offensive, and were to be held for a second time at the fateful line of the Marne. To visionary men eager for profits, it was evident that the war was all but done, and my father therefore returned to his reward: the joys of a rural constituency and a seat in that good grey Parliament of hard-faced men who had done well out of the war. In aftertime he would often lament, with a bluff English nostalgia, that he had not died uncommonly in the common cause. It was a role in which he invested much time, energy, and insincerity. For thirteen years he played the part, until fate, Wall Street, and his own cupidity compelled him to assume another guise.

In 1918 he was content to leave Africa and his wife to the business of bearing him a son. She was too "ill" to make the journey home or even down-country to Accra, but she need not have worried. African women are so much better suited to midwifery than their pale, insipid sisters. Such were my father's words of parting to my mother, who was attended by an Ashanti woman, Mampong, named after the settlement where she was "found"—by British soldiers in the war of 1900.

A man's first mistake is getting born, and it is hard to improve on that. Now, as I sit in my utilitarian apartment (the architect was sired by Jeremy Bentham upon Walter Gropius, with Kandinski thrown in for the fittings) and admire the view of the Novo-Devichy Convent, I recall, perhaps imperfectly, a line of Dickens: "His handwriting shakes more and more. I think he mixes a great deal of cognac with his ink." Not cognac for me but some vile imitation; not the Poteshny Palace of Peter the Great, where Bukharin eked out his days in splendid isolation, nor a solitary cell in the Lubyanka, yet a kind of limbo all the same.

Mampong, then. What an alliance we made, the black and the white, heathen and Christian, surrogate mother and adopted child, while my real mother languished in exile, dependent on the charity of the Colonial Office's outstation. My father did not send for her. Perhaps he had forgotten; he was quite capable of such a lapse. I spoke Ashanti before English. It was Mampong who told me of Nyame, the sky god who brings rain, and Asase Ya, his wife, and their descendants, the *abosoms*, gods of waters and trees. It was she who told George Michael, that child of England and heaven, of Ananse, the spider who prepared the clay of the first men for Nyame to infuse with life; she who told him of Tano, the thunder god and filler of rivers, and of the fraud he played on Nyame's elder son, Bia, so that he could inherit the fertile lands of the Gold Coast, leaving only the arid wastes of the Ivory Coast for his brother. "Nyame, he was old and blind then, or he would not have allowed it. But Tano, he was clever and young. And fast, George, he was so fast. . . ."

"How fast?"

"Faster than the snake."

"How clever?"

"Cleverer than any man."

I was four years old when my mother died, of ennui and its complications. I did not weep for her, only for Mampong, who disappeared at the same time. Perhaps she returned to her birth-place. I do not know.

I was taken in charge by a white woman who disapproved of my pagan ways and whom I was told to address as Nanny. Her name reminded me of the spider god, and there was something spiderish about her, as if she had been born with too many arms, for scrubbing and beating and cleansing and scouring. She had come up from the Coast, and there we returned to have my existence photographically determined. "Sit still, will you! Watch the birdie!" Thus Nanny, as the proboscis of the camera lens uncurled like the eye of God and a soiled yellow canary lolled at the end of its jack-in-the-box spring.

After an indeterminable length of time, of gulls and waves and flying fish, of docks and ships and trains, I arrived home to a rambling aedicule in Sussex, a mock-Elizabethan shrine of oxidizing silverware, insistent clocks, and pulmonary servants, all presided over by my father. "George, by God!" I recall his first words to me. "You look just like your mother!"

Anthony St. Clair was a stupid man but not unkind or cruel. He had been trained, as he put it ("and I mean trained, my boy, for it has to be in the blood, like a horse"), to share in the governance of an empire that coloured the map red. My first years in England consist of memories of that colour, a formative influence, no doubt. A proconsul, my father, mentally somewhat more sophisticated than our ancestral ape *Proconsul africanus*, to whom at times he seemed distantly related. He had left his wife and son in Africa because that was where he himself longed to be, and what was good for Anthony St. Clair was good for the rest of the world. A simple man, then, fond of the deceased laureate whom James Joyce dubbed Lawn Tennyson. My father also liked croquet, but most of the players were dead.

He had several companies and his interests often took him abroad. In 1930, partly as a result of the world financial crisis and partly because of long-established rumours, Anthony St. Clair was the subject of a Stock Exchange investigation. Most of his companies (Ashanti Bauxite, West African Gold, etc.) were imaginative fictions, even rarer than the precious metals they pretended to exploit. He had attracted investors and paid them dividends by investing the capital elsewhere, borrowing additional funds on the strength of his imaginary holdings. It could have been an intelligent operation, except for his pretended unawareness of its illegality. And so, protesting his innocence, he was quietly forced to resign his seat. No charges were pressed.

The story has a coda. After a few years' decent obscurity, Anthony St. Clair emerged from retirement as a champion of the extreme right and attempted to reenter Parliament on the Mosley ticket, an action that cost him a lost deposit. In 1939 he at last abandoned England for his beloved Africa, flourishing in his old age as an unlikely advocate of colonial independence. He died in 1961, at the age of seventy-six, a friend and confidant of Kwame Nkrumah, the Immortal Redeemer of all Africa, to whom the city of Accra owes its triumphal arch and an American-style highway that leads into the bush. Both men had a great deal in common, including the love of exalted schemes and a fond, maniacal regard for Adolf Hitler.

"It was you who warned Philby, wasn't it?"

"It was."

"How did you go about that?"

"Well, I was told to do it."

"By whom?"

"You know that. It was Carlo. He was the section chief in those days. It was just an errand. I had to see John Stanton, who was with naval intelligence in Tekirdağ. I flew to Nicosia and then to Izmir. On the way back I took a military transport to Beirut."

"What was the weather like in Beirut? Was it a fine day?"

"There was a light wind from the west, about five knots. It was sunny, for January, but then I was thinking of England. The temperature was in the mid-fifties Fahrenheit. So, yes, I suppose you could say it was a fine day."

Every interrogator has his style. Donald Macpherson's was to ask questions about the weather.

"Wasn't that unusual for you—to be thinking of England?"

"No, I often thought of England when I was abroad."

"Where did you meet Philby?"

"In the bar at the Hotel Normandy."

"What did he have to say for himself?"

"Not much. He said, 'When the cow stumbles, the butchers

start to run.' It's a Lebanese proverb."

"Did he know you were his successor?"

"Who says I am?"

"Please answer the question."

"I've no idea what Philby knew."

"Why do you think Carlo wanted him to run?"

"He didn't want a cancellation. Bad publicity."

"Very well. Let's go back again. Tell me how you got out of France. I want to hear that again."

And so interminably on. Every interrogation brings back memories of the preceding one. There can be an interval of weeks, months, or even years, but the memory remains—of the asides, diversions, and chronological switches designed to trap the unwary agent. It seems as though my entire life has been spent under interrogation, though in reality I have endured but three: a grilling from an *Ic/ Abwehroffizier*, a major, in Paris, January 1944; my "interviews" with Macpherson in HM prison Wormwood Scrubs, London; and the debriefing sessions with Vladimir Andreyevich Dimitrov in the little Lubyanka, Moscow, otherwise known as the Centre, the headquarters of the KGB.

It was Volodny who recruited me, with Carlo's knowledge, in July 1941, a month after the German invasion of Russia. I had been assigned to the government Code and Cypher School at Bletchley Park in Buckinghamshire, where Carlo saw to it that I was given the task of analyzing intercepts from Fremde Heere Ost, Branch 12 of the German General Staff. This was mostly routine logistical traffic sent over their enigma machines: casualty figures, operational strengths, requests for reinforcements and supplies— the bookkeeping of war. By the time of Stalingrad I was supplying the Russians with considerable amounts of information, and in this, as in so many other things, I was acting under Carlo's explicit direction. Not until long after the war did we discover that the Russians had been receiving the same information from the Lucerne publisher of Catholic tracts, Rudolf Rössler, Lucy, whose source was General Fritz Thiele, the second-in-command of OKW signals. Nevertheless, they accepted our information in good faith, if only because we supposed it to be secret.

In December 1943 Carlo told me that there was trouble among the brigands in the Special Operations Executive. There had been a retrograde development: This time the Germans were reading our codes, a "pianist" and suspected Abwehr agent, Jimmy Polk, having been mentioned as the source of the leak. I was given the SOE short course at Beaulieu in Hampshire, and six weeks later arrived in Paris masquerading as a Belgian Todt Organization worker in transit to the Atlantic Wall.

The day before my arrival, Jimmy Polk had been shot and killed at the keys of his set, the cell closed down, and its members arrested. The next day (not knowing any of this), I went to an apartment in the rue du Faubourg de Saint Honoré, where I found the Gestapo already in residence. I was arrested and taken to their headquarters in the rue des Saussaies.

Neither the Gestapo nor the SS seemed too interested in me. After two days, in which time I was allowed to reflect on my operational obsolescence, I was summoned before that *Ic* major, who said his name was Clemens. We spoke in French, his fluent, mine halting and heavily accented, as befitted a lowly Flemish servant of the master race. It was the only advantage I had, and at the end of an hour Clemens said, in English, "Your name is George Michael Stevens, and you were born in Kumasi on June the first, 1918."

Years later, after I had arrived in Moscow, Volodny would ask me for a description of Clemens. We had been through it all before, but this was an official debriefing for the record.

"I didn't see him standing up, so I couldn't tell you his height. I judged his weight at around seventy-seven kilos. He had a duelling scar on his right cheek, a *Korpsstudent*, I would say. He wore glasses and was in his middle thirties, hair brownish, slightly receding, hazel eyes. Very prominent cheekbones. Softly spoken."

"Weren't you surprised when he let you go?"

"Yes and no. I guessed that he was taking a risk and wanted to have me tagged. Later on, when I gave it more thought, I decided that he must have been one of your people. Carlo came to pretty much the same conclusion. He made some remark about the advantages of cooperating with our allies."

"Was he surprised?"

"Very."

"How did you actually get out?"

"Fallback procedure. I had to place an ad in the *Paris Soir*. Something about a lost kitten. The next day I was to look for one of two responses. 'Lucille thanks her friends' meant that I had to go to the Gare du Nord left-luggage office and ask about that kitten again; 'Charles arrives tomorrow' meant an address in Neuilly. It was the Gare du Nord. I was told that my cat was in Saint Pol and that they'd arranged transport. They flew in a Lysander. No trouble."

"Good. Let's go forwards in time, to May of 1968. What was the name of the agent in the SSD that you employed?"

"Julius Graebe."

"Code name and function?"

"He was code-named Baby and worked in Section Four. His job was to supply us with their counterespionage stuff. If any of our people were in danger, then he'd give us the tip-off. He'd been at it for years—since 1953, when the SSD was made a state secretariat under Wollweber."

"So he was an important agent?"

"Yes, they all were. They had to be."

"Who was running him?"

"That would be one of the SIS men—Grove, Philip Grove."

"Baby couldn't have guessed, could he, that you'd been giving us your own people there?"

"He didn't know that I was doing it, obviously. He told Grove that there was a deep-penetration agent in the Friends and Grove told Carlo. That's why I gave you Grove."

"But before that Carlo ordered you to give us Baby?"

"Yes, that's it."

"All right, George. So we picked up Grove, then the station chief, Carmichael. Now, I want to get this absolutely right. We're talking about two separate operations. One you undertook on your own initiative, and the other was Carlo's. I'm sorry to press the point, George, but did Carlo realize that it was you who gave us the network? Betraying foreigners who've already betrayed their own country is one thing. Rolling up one of your own networks, as you did, is quite another. Did Carlo suspect you at all—in any way?"

"No, it was his hobbyhorse. He was obsessed by the idea that Philby could have been loyal. He was always saying, 'What if Kim had been working for us? We'd have had him in Dzerzhinski Square by now!' "

"Then his operation was exclusively concerned with building up your bona fides?''

"Yes, with a view to a trade. That's why they had to be good agents."

"And also for Macpherson's sake?''

"Yes, it had to look convincing.''

"He wasn't told about the infiltration?''

"Not while it was under way.''

"One thing interests me. Why, at no time, did you reveal the code names of those agents, merely their positions and actual names?''

"Carlo's instructions. He had a thing about code names. They were scratched after each arrest, and I suppose he was worried by the possibility of someone being picked up and turned—or of someone else operating under the same code name.''

"Well, we can return to that later. I'll want a list of those code names. Did Macpherson ask you about the East German network?''

"No, he was interested only in the ten. Carlo's ten.''

"Didn't that surprise you?''

"Yes, but then I thought it wasn't part of his brief.''

"I wonder why not. Carlo had no plans for your recovery, did he? Or if he did, you weren't told about them?''

"Obviously not. That would have compromised me.''

"Perhaps. Let's see, I would like to find out how long this scheme was in Carlo's mind. Let's go back again, George. Further back. To 1941 and London . . .''

Thirty-three years have passed since Volodny asked me why I was prepared to risk the odious title of traitor. ''Why are you doing this? We have nothing to offer you. You don't need the money; you're not even a Communist.''

"Not even? No, I suppose not. Let's say it's from the spirit of peace and international goodwill.''

"Let's say anything. You may have other reasons, of course.''

"Such as?''

"A sense of theatre. I can believe in that. It's so much more revealing than real life.''

I understood him then. We had succeeded in making language meaningless and rejoiced in our communion, a fit exemplar for the age's idiot imitation.

But all that was such a long time ago.

Part Two DIMITROV

The Revolution is like Saturn—it eats
its own children.
— GEORG BÜCHNER, *Danton's Death*

10

Dzerzhinski Square

The square commemorates Lenin's head of the Cheka, the Polish aristocrat Feliks Edmundovich Dzerzhinski, whose thirty-six-foot-high statue presides over the traffic in monumental scrutiny. It is joined on the southeastern side by New Square and Serov Proyezd (named, Muscovites will tell you, after Ivan Serov, Khrushchev's chief of the KGB and the wartime boss of SMERSH) and on the southwestern and western sides by the 25th October Street and the Prospekt Marxa. Detsky Mir, the Children's World department store, is situated on the northern corner, its glass arcades affording a fine view of the Lubyanka Prison, located across the square on the rise of a hill at number 2 Dzerzhinski Street. Before the revolution this building, with its yellow façade, tidy white curtains, and brass fittings on the doors, housed the main offices of the Rossiya Insurance Company. The curtains and fittings are still there, though the windows are now covered with heavy mesh screens. A grey stone extension, completed by political prisoners and German POWs after World War II, today houses the Secretariat and Collegium of the Komitet Gosudarstvennoye Bezopasnosti, the main administrative organs of the Committee for State Security.

On the morning before the fifty-seventh anniversary of the
Revolution, Yuri Andropov, chairman of the KGB, sat in his third-
floor office—a well-appointed room, with a bar, embroidered sofas,
mahogany-panelled walls hung with tapestries, the floor deep under
Oriental rugs, a room with enormous windows and a seventeen-
foot-high ceiling, a room with a view and an adjoining private
shower and bedroom. The chairman sat behind an impressive desk
that housed a bank of six telephones. One, the Kremlevka, connected him with the Kremlin; another, the Vertushka, with the
Politburo; others with the Ministry of Defence and military
intelligence, his assistants, and the main KGB *rezidentura* throughout the world. A portrait of Dzerzhinski himself gazed down
over the chairman's shoulder and seemed to be absorbed in the
file with which Andropov was preoccupied. The chairman was
entirely familiar with its contents, though the words "present at
the death of Iosif Vissarionovich" never failed to create in him
feelings of guilt and fear. The chairman reassured himself in the belief
that he needed to rouse precisely such feelings, to let them course
through his veins and revel in the psychic energy thus released,
and to subjugate them, of course, as he always did, with the thought
that Chernukhin, his assistant and a Jew, had chosen as his *nom de
guerre* the very ordinary Russian name Dimitrov.

The chairman knew everything there was to know about Yuri
Simonovich, everything in the file at least. His father was an old
Bolshevik (revolutionary name, Malyuta), born 5 April 1880, Tiflis,
Georgia, which made him a compatriot of Stalin and Beria. A former
archivist at the Hermitage in Saint Petersburg, he had been an exile
in Zurich, where he had married his assistant, Yekatrina Mogilev-
chik. She had died in Maidenek concentration camp, Poland, 3
November (?) 1943. Her husband, Simon Avseyavich, had prede-
ceased her by a good five years—*ex*: Moscow, 22 March 1938—
a victim of the Great Purge.

Their son, Y. S. Chernukhin (or Vladimir Andreyevich, as he
called himself—something that irked the chairman, whose first name
was Yuri, patronymic Vladimirovich), was educated at Moscow
State University and the Red Army's M School. Instead of saying
Yevrey, his internal passport described him not as a Jew but as a
citizen of the USSR, the decree of the Central Executive Committee
of the Council of the People's Commissars, 27 December 1932,

having been waived in his case for extraordinary services rendered. Those services included obtaining the complete plans (research, development, and coordination) for the Witwatersrand gold-ore and low-grade-uranium processing plant, back in the days when he was running the English spy Maclean from Washington, D.C. The chairman had known him personally since November 1956, the month of the abortive counterrevolutionary coup in Hungary, where Andropov was the then Soviet ambassador. It was Chernukhin who, as one of Serov's men, had lured Imre Nagy out of the Yugoslav Embassy with written guarantees of safe-conduct. For this he had received the Order of the Red Banner—from Chairman Khrushchev himself. And another thing about Chernukhin: At the age of fifty-five he was five years younger than Andropov—old enough for seniority, young enough to be a threat.

Comrade Chairman Andropov secured the file in his desk shortly before its subject entered the room.

"Well?"

"Anna's report was negative. So was Keller's. It seems that the journalist is what he claims to be. Nevertheless, his papers are forged."

"Sit down." Andropov motioned to one of the sofas. He rose, crossed to the window, and looked out at the statue of Feliks Dzerzhinski. Then he sat down next to Vladimir Andreyevich, whom he dwarfed, a tall, scholarly man, hands clenched between his knees, speaking in a gravel-voiced whisper. "Has he seen Stevens yet?"

"Tonight. Soper will try to contact him again this afternoon to give him the cassette. He may have done so already. We're listening, of course. We've had an audio device on Johnson since he arrived. Now his luggage is bugged, all of his clothes, even his pajamas."

The chairman frowned. "Pajamas?"

"An Anglo-American sleeping suit."

"Ah, yes." The chairman savoured the word, sniffing. "Now I remember." He was disturbed by the most unaccountable smell.

"By the way," Dimitrov said, opening his briefcase, "you may like to read this. It's the English version of Stevens' manuscript. Johnson left it in his room while he was at the cemetery this morning."

"More disinformation, Comrade?"

"It's been edited."

The chairman was suddenly anxious. "What do you think?"

"You are no longer in any personal danger."

"And Stevens—will it work?"

"There may be problems. He's been through a great deal. I'm no longer sure if he knows what the truth is—if he ever did. But he's been thinking, and should be able to distinguish his own lies from other people's. I hope that I have his confidence. . . ." Dimitrov looked at his watch. It was almost twelve. "Both of them should be on that train by this time tomorrow."

"Let us hope so," the chairman said. "For all our sakes, let us hope so, Yuri Simonovich, Comrade Chernukhin."

Dimitrov showed no surprise at this. "Yes," he said simply, "our fathers gave us both the same name."

"The same Christian name, but your father was no Christian."

"That is true," said Vladimir Andreyevich. "He was a Marxist."

11

Nexus
and
Crunch

Any intelligence network resembles the structure of the human brain. Vladimir Andreyevich developed this comparison on the afternoon of 6 November. Brain cells age and die. The sudden death of too many will cause cerebral catastrophe; the mutation of others, impaired functioning. How like a cancer is a double agent, and how numerous the carcinogens: commitment to a cause, real or imagined; a personal grievance, misplaced loyalties, the desire to atone or avenge, some ethical imperative such as the hankering after justice—and money, always money. How many the ways of death and deceit, how infinite the means of corruption. Yet how childish the traitor often was, how theatrical his impulses. There was Oleg Penkovsky, who had asked for, and had obtained, a U.S. Army colonel's uniform from his Western masters. It amazed Dimitrov that a costume should be the price of treason. He thought of another agent, who had used the proceeds of his treachery to buy a pleasure cruiser for trips down the Danube, thus fulfilling a childhood ambition; and of yet another, who had sold his country down the river for Benny Goodman records. How dreamlike this was! Yet what was a dream but a species of mental *dezinformatsiya*?

Nonspecific input, the neurophysiologists called it. A fine phrase, the conjuration of dream scientists. Doctors! Yet their work had its uses. It could empty a man's head.

Whatever the nature of that jelly inside a man's head, it needed to dream. Jelly, it was the code name of one of George's agents, and he had lied about that name. Why? Mental engineering, some kind of conditioned response? Or was there a more human and humane reason, such as willpower, denied by the materialists as an abstraction deserving only their scorn? Sometimes a man has to be caught lying first in order to convince his inquisitors that he is telling the truth later. A reformed liar is convincing; like a reformed sinner, he begs to be believed.

Everything had its uses. There were people at the time of the Great Terror who thought their dreams were being monitored by the secret police. Similar experiences had been reported from Germany. Had the British been dreaming at the time of the Philby affair, the Russians at the time of Penkovsky? Were they not both dreaming in the case of George Michael Stevens? Then the awakening could not be long delayed. The image pleased Dimitrov, who thought again of George Michael Stevens. When an agent is cornered, he goes to ground. Lizardlike, he seeks the earth, dark places, the single cell of all beginnings. He does what no brain cell can do. He divides within himself against himself; he becomes catatonic. This, Dimitrov had seen; this was real.

Such were his thoughts on the afternoon of 6 November as he sat in a radio truck outside the Hotel Rossiya. The truck was camouflaged as a baker's delivery van. In Dimitrov's hand was a warrant for the arrest of Reginald Soper, the British resident in Moscow, who was charged with attempted espionage against the Soviet Union and also with the lesser crime of attempted murder, the intended victim in this case being Vladimir Andreyevich himself.

He thought of the last time that a comrade had called him by the name he was born with. "Yuri Simonovich, what kind of name is that?" Commissar Yezhov had exclaimed. "A bastardized name, that's what it is. What are you, Yuri Simonovich? A parasite! A flea! Does a flea pay tax on the blood it sucks with such a name? What are you? A Jew? A Russian? Both? Neither? What can Simon Avseyavich have been thinking of when he gave you this name?"

This was in the late summer of 1938, five months after his father's trial and execution. Nikolai Ivanovich Yezhov had called him in for a personal interview before lecturing the students at Moscow's M School, the espionage academy of the Red Army. "I wanted to see the father's son," he said, gloating.

The father's son drew himself to attention and begged permission to ask a question. It was granted.

"Why did you kill my father?"

"Why, Comrade, *why*? A roach among garbage does not ask why; a roach can be crushed. It has to hide from the light of day. Will you scuttle when I turn on the switch, Yuri son of Simon? You'll have to be quick, quicker than Malyuta. Or will you crawl as he did? But you are a successful species. You endure, you seek, you survive—providing you do not ask questions. Remember that, Yuri Simonovich. And remember the terror, the *Yezhovchina*, for they have named it after me."

Nikolai Ivanovich Yezhov, who stood five feet high in his boots, was the people's commissar for internal affairs, Beria's predecessor and the director of the Show Trials. A few weeks after this interview it was rumoured that the commissar, in crushing the leftist opposition, had advanced the rightist. He was arrested, beaten, released, rearrested, and beaten again. And then he was created people's commissar of waterworks, and died.

Simon Avseyavich had pleaded guilty at his trial, but he had not admitted any crimes. "The crimes to which I have confessed are abhorrent to me. The crimes to which I have confessed deserve extreme punishment."

If Yuri Simonovich, as he once was, had not fully comprehended the distinction between confession and actual guilt, Vladimir Andreyevich, as he now was, understood it only too well.

In the beginning he had been nothing, one cell among many. His sole function was to convey information. A mere conduit, he did not ask why. He was expendable, he could be wasted. Thousands, millions were. Glial cells of the brain, unite! You have nothing to lose but your mind! But perhaps Nikolai Ivanovich Yezhov, who had wept so profusely at his own interrogation that Iosif Vissarionovich had given him the job of regulating Russia's water supply, perhaps the former commissar was right. It amused Vladimir Andreyevich to think of Yuri Simonovich, or what was left of him, as a cockroach. He was no longer a Jew, of course. Others had paid the price for that, his mother included. "Your father was right," she told him before he left for London at the beginning of the war. "Only the Revolution matters. Nothing else. It will pass, everything will pass. You must go along with them, do what they say."

Vladimir Andreyevich understood many things, but most of all he understood his ability to dissociate himself from the world around him. It was something he had seen in other agents, a kind of extreme passivity, as if a theatre audience, watching the events on-stage and knowing them to be unreal, had itself ceased to exist in the real world. But Vladimir Andreyevich, a man well acquainted with fear, knew that this abeyance of reality was itself a sign of fear. It was the agent's defence, his protective screen lest he be called on to judge or condemn the play, lest the killing of the king, the play within the play, be taken, as Hamlet had taken it, as the augury of doom, fate in all its theatrical finality.

A man could be frightened into passivity. Dimitrov had seen this in Lavrenti Beria. Strangely enough for a man who in every other respect had been a monster, Beria was not anti-Semitic, and when Stalin had hatched the Doctors' Plot, his chief of police should have had every reason to feel threatened. But he had shrugged the matter off. The play was unreal, he knew that; and although the actors were real enough, he could not bring himself to believe in them. Beria had been a devious man, but he was also quite uncompli-cated when it came to action. He was incapable of distinguishing between shadow and act in others, which was why he ordinarily crushed all conspiracies at the merest whisper of a plot. Yet the script for the Doctors' Plot had been too crude even for this simple man, and most untypically he had failed to take action. When Iosif Vissarionovich, likewise running counter to form, died (it was unique, this death, unprecedented, revolutionary; it was impossible, nevertheless it had happened), Vladimir Andreyevich understood that life and art occasionally have something in common: dramatic irony. Lavrenti Pavlovich had confided in Dimitrov. "Now they will believe in this madness. Now they will think I killed him." And, like a man in a dream, he had laughed at this absurd concatenation of events.

Initially, then, Dimitrov had conducted his business as a cock-roach, neither caring nor daring to ask why. His life, he'd decided long ago, was meaningless. The world's duplicity bored him, though he had gone on watching the play, never believing in the action but always marking the actors closely, how they said their lines and whether they were happy or unhappy in their roles. He would not make Beria's mistake, for he knew that many a great actor had appeared in an undeserving part. Over the years, too, he had come out of his shell, had opened his wings and dared to test himself in flight—a new species, a winged cockroach. And now that he could afford to ask why, he found (but not to his surprise) that there was no answer.

His second London appointment was to have marked the high point in his career. For a time his expectations were fulfilled. Stevens' information was good; if anything, it was too good. Between September 1968 and September 1973 George had given him the ten agents for whom he was eventually exchanged. At no time did he make any secret of the fact that Carlo was ordering him to betray these agents, which explained why things had continued for so long. But there had been other betrayals, culminating in the arrest of the Friends' Berlin resident, Philip Grove, on 2 January 1970, and his station chief, William Patrick Carmichael, a couple of days later. These men were dead, their agents eliminated. Which, Dimitrov knew, was far too high a price to pay for an infiltration. Carlo couldn't have ordered or condoned that; or if he had, Harland Caisho Peat was something other than what he appeared to be.

And yet it had gone on for *five years*. Time and place of assignment: three p.m., the first Saturday of every month, the Fossil Vertebrate Gallery, the Museum of Natural History, South Kensington. They had a fallback procedure, of course (a postcard inserted in the rack of the foyer to the Great Hall); even so, the Friends, who had been watching their every move, had crossed that manoeuvre. Dimitrov himself was arrested and held briefly in surety for the negotiations. After all, the Centre regarded George as a top-flight agent, and ten for one (two, including Vladimir Andreyevich) did not seem too expensive.

There were times when Vladimir Andreyevich came perilously close to disbelieving Stevens. It wasn't that George was a liar or a bad actor but that he seemed unaware of the role he was playing. Could it be that the spy was inseparable from his spying, the actor from his acting? Vladimir Andreyevich couldn't report that to his superiors. There were other times, too, when he told himself that Stevens was a man more deceived than deceiving. He pitied him and sympathized with him; he knew what George was feeling, but he could not believe in him. His disbelief was not empirically proven (perhaps it could never be); yet the more thought he gave it, the more he realized that he had never really trusted George Michael Stevens.

There was nothing unusual in this. Vladimir Andreyevich Dimitrov, or Yuri Simonovich Chernukhin, as he had once been, was not a man to trust himself.

The debriefing began after the New Year's holiday and continued, with a week's intermission in July, until the middle of September. By the end of April, Dimitrov knew that the crunch was not far off. Stevens was drinking heavily now, slipping away down the neck of the bottle. Without alcohol he was surly and petulant; with it, introspective and maudlin. Dimitrov let him drink and free associate, rationing the doses like a clinician with some experimental animal. But the laboratory was Room 505 in the Lubyanka, the animal was human, and this clinician took occasional draughts of his own poison. And after twenty years his marriage was going to hell, which didn't exactly help.

In the evenings when he got home, he would pour himself a drink and shut himself away with the tapes of the day's session. He began to dream of tapes, the reels slowly turning, the playback echoing through his mind: *Let's go back to July of '41. What did Carlo say? What did he tell you to do? Did he know who I was? How? Who told him? Let's go forwards now. I'm interested in August of 1970. This agent, what was his name? His code name and function? His code name, why didn't you give us that before?*

At the beginning of May he suggested that George write his memoirs. Stevens was agreeable, surprisingly so.

"They'll be published, won't they?"

Vladimir Andreyevich concurred. "In the West. It will be interesting to see what they leave out."

Meanwhile, the debriefing continued. There were three areas of interest to Dimitrov, three strands of the same rope. The first had to do with Carlo's plans for the recovery of his agent (assuming that he thought George was loyal); the second with the code names; the third, and ultimately the most important, with Carlo's suspicions of Stevens.

George claimed that he knew of no plans for his recovery, asserting that this would compromise him in the event of narco-analysis or rigorous examination. Yet an agent in his situation ordinarily has an intuitive grasp of the end game. It does not matter whether his intuition serves him true or false, merely that he has seen *a* possibility of recovery. If Carlo had trusted Stevens, plans for recovery there must have been. That George, who had concealed no other aspects of the operation, was unprepared even to speculate about such plans struck Dimitrov as being very strange indeed. But as yet he had no theory to explain this.

By the end of May they had reached the subject of Manfred Ritter, the radar technologist and eighth agent whom George had betrayed. Alone of the ten, he had been an employee of SIS-IX and was therefore personally known to Stevens. Dimitrov was anxious to discover exactly why Carlo had ordered Stevens to betray Ritter, who was the odd man out. The answer, when it came, was unexpected.

"I can't remember."

"What?"

"I've forgotten."

"But that's impossible! How could you forget?"

"I've told you. It's just one of those things. I can't bloody well remember."

"Very well. Perhaps you can recall his code name?"

"Oh, yes. It was Jelly," Stevens answered without hesitation. "Shelley! Christ, Volodny. I'm sorry. That was crass of me. It was Shelley, the poet's name."

Stevens sagged in his chair. "It's nothing—a headache. I'm sorry, Volodny, I don't seem to be in very good form today. Give me another drink, will you?"

On 29 June a bizarre incident occurred, one that greatly shocked Vladimir Andreyevich but that with the benefit of hindsight did not seem so very surprising.

"I want to recapitulate," he told Stevens on that day. "You remember Anton Deriabin, I suppose?"

"Deriabin, Deriabin," George repeated. "Yes, a good horse was Dobbin. He was with the MGB Advisory Section, a liaison officer

with K5. He told us a lot about you. We turned him around on
the fifteenth of March 1965. I remember the date because my wife,
my second wife, was . . ." Stevens looked up blankly.

"Was what?"

" 'Seesaw, Margery Daw, Jack shall have a new master.' What
comes next, Volodny?"

Dimitrov watched him silently; the mouth, hands, and eyes—all
the trouble spots.

"*Marjory*! I'd forgotten her name. Isn't that funny? And I'll tell
you another thing. It wasn't Jack either. It was Jacky. '*Jacky* must
have but a penny a day, because he can work no faster.' "

"Take it easy, George."

"I'm all right. You must have known Deriabin, just as I knew
Ritter. Well, did you?"

"Yes. Why?"

"No reason. Well, that is, there is a reason. What did I tell you
his code name was?"

"Dumbbell," said Vladimir Andreyevich.

"It wasn't, you know." Stevens looked sheepish. "It was
Dumbo. Carlo's coinage. Like Walt Disney's elephant, he said."

"You're tired, George. You need a rest."

"No, I don't. The writing's doing me a world of good. Really.
It's just that when I'm talking to you things get a little fuzzy round
the edges. . . ." Stevens stood up, startling Dimitrov. "I need a
drink or something," he said. "Fresh air . . ." And then he fell
unconscious to the floor.

Two days later Dimitrov visited the Kremlin Hospital, where he
talked with a Dr. A. M. Druzula of the Moscow Neurophysical
Institute. The doctor was a thin man with pink hands. His voice
was reedy, his manner condescending, and he reminded Dimitrov of
a pedantic bassoon, shiny, tubular, and slightly stooped.

"We are testing the patient's attention selectivity time at the moment," he intoned. "Come with me, you may find this interesting. . . ." And Vladimir Andreyevich, a slave in the temple of
Hippocrates, had followed as Druzula led the way to a room on the
fourth floor.

Inside, George Stevens faced a computer console. Electrodes
bristled on his head, patching him into an electroencephalograph

that purred sleepily as it transferred an endless reel of graph paper from one drum to another. The EEG machine was itself linked to an oscilloscope, which displayed a pattern of variable green squiggles and emitted a monotonous, rhythmic hum.

"An SES-10 computer," Druzula explained, "and the purpose of this experiment is to measure the patient's reaction to encoding and selectivity functions. The scope you see in front of him, Comrade Dimitrov, is a Textronic 503 of American manufacture. Before the run begins, a warning signal will appear on the screen in the form of a cross. Exactly .5 seconds later the first letter will appear. After an interstimulus interval, fixed in this run at 150 milliseconds, another letter will appear. The subject then responds 'same,' if he perceives the letters as physically identical, by pressing the 'same' key on the console. If he perceives them as physically different, he will respond by pressing the 'different' key. His eyesight is normal for his age, and you can see that he is approximately sixteen inches from the scope. At this distance the letters will be recessed at three degrees of visual angle. Basically it is a simple test."

Dimitrov watched the cross appear; the oscilloscope beeped wildly, and he said, "What's that?"

"A contingent negative variation, Comrade. It means that the patient's visual cortex was excited by the signal."

The letter *E* appeared on the screen, followed by another *E*. George pressed the "same" key. Fadeout. The cross returned. Warning. The letter *M* appeared and then a *K*. Stimulus. George pressed the "different" key. Response. And so it went: warning, stimulus, response.

"He seems perfectly normal to me," Dimitrov said.

"I think so." Druzula drew him aside. "Maybe you'd like to come to my office for a talk," he said affably.

Dimitrov asked if the comrade doctor could account for Stevens' behaviour.

"His *verbal* behaviour"—Druzula stressed the adjective—"allows several explanations. This Jelly-Shelley and Dumbo-Dumbbell confusion is a prime example of what we call acoustical confusion. According to one theory of memory, words are acoustically encoded in the brain, which rehearses the sound of the word rather than its appearance. If, at recall, the memory storage has partially decayed for some reason, the residual information may be enough to produce a word remarkably like the one the subject is trying to remember."

"Yes," said Dimitrov. "But this man is a trained agent. Why should he forget?"

"A thousand and one reasons. I looked for some organic cause. There was none. A chemical agency, then? Alcohol, for example."

"That didn't seem to bother him before," Dimitrov remarked.

"No? Well, there may be other reasons, Comrade. You saw that computer in there. The machine has a memory, just as you and I do. Ask it a question and you will get an answer, the right answer if the program is correct. But the machine does not have total recall. What I am saying is that there are certain organizational constraints on storage, a law that applies as much to ourselves as it does to computers. For example, you are trying to remember something that happened several years ago, something you have temporarily forgotten. After a great deal of effort you eventually succeed, and when you try a second time, it is not nearly so difficult. However, in order for the query to reach its goal, the number of irrelevant queries must be minimized. If too many associations exist in storage, some questions cannot be answered, and in computer terms you will have what we call 'noise.' You will be confused. Comrade Colonel, it is possible that you asked this man too many questions."

"You're the one who's confused," said Dimitrov. "You forget that I've been trained to ask questions."

"Well, then, there is another possibility, which should have interesting possibilities for you." Druzula paused, a conjurer about to pull a rabbit from his hat. "This man collapsed when all he had to do was answer a direct question, ordinarily a situation he understands, with which he is familiar. In a certain sense the situation is rewarding to him. At least, if his performance is satisfactory, he will be rewarded. But he cannot respond as he is supposed to. He responds negatively to a positive stimulus! The dog does not salivate, Comrade; he whines, he cringes, he is afraid. You will gather, of course, that I refer to the work of Ivan Petrovich Pavlov—in particular, a form of behaviour that Ivan Petrovich called ultra-paradoxical.

"As to its cause, we can only speculate. Remember the machine, Comrade. If too many associations exist in storage, noise results. Let us suppose that the computer's memory includes the words 'Jelly' and 'Dumbbell' but that unknown to us on the outside, it has a whole galaxy of associations matching these words that it has been programmed never to reveal. So we question the computer, repeatedly, insistently, as I'm sure you did, Comrade Dimitrov. The responses seem quite normal at first, but then they become increasingly aberrant. The machine is trying to protect itself, you see. It is noisy, belligerent, and finally forgetful. It may even switch itself off, as indeed the subject did. To this, Ivan Petrovich has given the name transmarginal inhibition. In dogs, as well as in machines and men, it can seem like a very perverse form of behaviour."

"A man is not a machine," said Dimitrov.

"Neither is a dog. But he can be conditioned." Druzula's hand swept over his files. "They're full of such cases, human cases. Life has conditioned us all, Comrade Colonel."

"This inhibition, is there any way round it?"

"Through, you mean through it. Yes, to make a complex answer simple. It would involve some form of narcoanalysis or hypnosis, perhaps the two combined. . . ."

"Then you will undertake this work."

Druzula smiled. "I, Comrade?"

"You, Comrade," Dimitrov said, standing up, "*if* necessary. One other question: Can this kind of behaviour be faked?"

Druzula made a cautious noise. "Yes, if the subject knew what he was doing. But surely this belongs as much to your province as it does to mine."

"So it does. Is there anything else you would care to tell me?"

"I have told you everything I know, Comrade Colonel."

"You have told me nothing."

"Everything and nothing"—Druzula quavered—"that is all I know."

Stevens was discharged from the Kremlin Hospital on 6 July, a Saturday. Contingency plans were already being made for his funeral. George Stevens had just four months of official life left, but he could not have known that. Or could he? It was a question that came increasingly to occupy Vladimir Andreyevich, who loathed and feared all forms of intuition.

At Druzula's urging, he left George alone that weekend. He would have done so anyway, even without the comrade doctor's advice.

Friday he saw the chairman, told him about the code names,

mentioned Druzula's theories (dismissively), and waited for a re-action.

The chairman lit a cigarette, a Chesterfield. "This stuff about acoustical confusion," he said. "Do you believe that?"

"No."

"What, then?"

"I find it impossible to see how Carlo could not have suspected Stevens. Either he was trying to get rid of him with this supposed infiltration, because a defection was more convenient and he wanted to avoid the scandal of a trial—in which case all well and good. Or else he was setting him up for something."

"Such as?"

"I don't know yet." Dimitrov hesitated. "It may take some time to find out. If we could return him to hospital . . ."

"Later, Comrade. Later. Let's see how his health progresses first," Yuri Andropov said. And then he showed Dimitrov the telex.

STEVENS KREMLINIZED STOP FEAR SHOOT-UP STOP INSTRUC-TIONS QUERY SOPER STOP

"Shoot-up" meant narcoanalysis, a possibility that evidently ter-rified the Friends. But the most extraordinary thing about the telex was that Soper had sent it in the clear, at the same time as the embassy cryptographers had made an unscheduled change in their primary key settings; Technical Services were no longer reading any of the traffic from HM embassy, Moscow. Noise and silence—it didn't make a bit of sense to Vladimir Andreyevich, but it did to the chairman, who thought that the Friends were trying to discredit Stevens.

"Continue the debriefing," Yuri Andropov said. "Another thing, Comrade. This girl you're seeing, this Samsonov. She knows noth-ing of this, understand?"

When debriefing resumed on Monday, Dimitrov did not mention his conversations with Druzula or the chairman. Nor did he refer to Stevens' previous behaviour but was determined to be as business-like and as factual as possible.

"I must be honest with you," he told George that morning. "I think Carlo knew that you gave us your Berlin station chief."

Stevens seemed perfectly in control. "Oh, no, Volodny," he said.

"Carlo trusted me. It was Ritter he suspected. He was the deskman, you see. Ritter was the deskman for the DDR, and Carlo thought it was him."

"Why didn't you tell me this before, George?"

"I wasn't asked. Rule number one: Answer only the questions you've been asked. Rule number two: *Never* answer questions you haven't been asked."

"But you're among friends, George."

"Am I? There's been a goon on my door all weekend."

"A precaution."

"On my *door*, Volodny? I didn't like that. I didn't like the hospital either."

"How about a drink, George?"

"All right."

Dimitrov put an unopened bottle of Starka on his desk. "Who came after Ritter?" he said.

"Druzhinin." Stevens smiled faintly. "Gregori Druzhinin. His code name was Importer. He was a hangover from the MGB days and served as an adviser in Department Ten of your Directorate. French Africa."

"There's nothing wrong with your memory today," Dimitrov said. "You know what I think? It looks as though Carlo anticipated this line of questioning. Maybe he was trying to get you off the hook or something, but he must have said, 'Volodny's bound to ask about Grove, Carmichael, those people. So you string him along for a while.' Then you say Ritter, it was Ritter. A week ago you couldn't even remember his code name."

"It was Shelley. . . ."

"Shut up, damn you! We had Ritter here. I interviewed him personally, in this room. What possible reasons could Carlo have had for suspecting him? He was loyal. *Loyal*! And maybe you are, too, because if this were an infiltration, and nothing but, then Grove and Carmichael and God knows how many others were the ground bait— and they are dead, George."

"What happened to that drink, Volodny?" Stevens gave his slack smile. Dimitrov made him pour the drinks. His hand was quite steady. "You killed them, old boy. Cheers." Stevens sank half the tumbler. "Anyway, what you're saying is insane. I gave you those agents freely and in good faith. I wasn't to know that Carmichael would betray everyone. It must have been a lousy shop he was running.

Another thing, you're forgetting the work I did for your people during the war."

"At Carlo's bidding."

"Maybe, but it was worth a Soviet passport, just the same as yours, Volodny. There's something else, too. Peat's out of the game. He was running the infiltration because they thought it was such a many-splendoured thing, but Carlo was through when Carmichael got the chop. It was Sweet who conducted the investigation."

"All right, George. I can check that out."

"You do that, Volodny. You do just that."

And so it went. The debriefing—or interrogation, as it became—continued in much the same vein for another seven weeks while Technical Services concentrated on that most cerebral of tasks, the attempt to break a modern electronic cypher. There was no overt hostility between the two men, only mutual distrust. George Stevens was behaving exactly as Dimitrov himself would have done under the circumstances, but Stevens presumably knew why and Vladimir Andreyevich did not—a nice distinction.

At the end of August, while they were going through the list of code names in the manuscript, George Stevens suddenly said, "I've been thinking about Druzhinin. His code name was Insect, not Importer." And then, at the beginning of September, something occurred that would test even Dimitrov's formidable disbelief. HM embassy, Moscow, in an apparently calculated access of stupidity, transmitted a group of signals that had gone out earlier, before the primary key change. Since the old key was known, it was only a matter of hours before the new one became available. When it did, Vladimir Andreyevich was again summoned to Comrade Chairman Andropov's luxurious office, where he was shown yet another message, not from Soper this time but to him, care of the Division of Chancery:

> Foreign Office Security
> Charles Street, SW 1
> 8 September 1974

> Message begins. Please be advised that Cabinet today granted you full powers plenipotentiary to negotiate the release of G. M. Stevens, if and when you should judge this expedient. Message ends.

> (Signed) BENTINCK (FO adviser)

"Well, Comrade, I think it is time for Liberation now," the chairman said, and Vladimir Andreyevich agreed.

Liberation was the code name for Stevens' funeral.

George Stevens took the news of his impending "death" stoically, which surprised Vladimir Andreyevich. "I hope it will be a good funeral" was all he said.

"Yes, George. But you must return to hospital first."

"I'd have preferred a quick death, a heart attack or something. Why the hospital, Volodny?"

"George, you must understand that you are not a *well* man. So you might as well get used to the idea." Dimitrov poured two glasses of Starka. "Here's to the funeral, *Tovarich*," he declared, swallowing his drink, Russian style, in one gulp.

And it was a good funeral, he saw to that. There was a period of lying in state, of course, with lots of photos, which pleased Dimitrov, who was reminded of Dostoevski's father Zossima. Yet here was no unexpected metamorphosis, no stench of earthly decay. For the body that wore the features of George Michael Stevens was a creation of Spets-Otdel, the KGB's Special-Effects Section, and although Vladimir Andreyevich was pleased to call it the Golem, it had never inhaled the divine spirit and never would.

Dimitrov was inconsolable. He fortified his grief, as only a Russian can, with prodigious amounts of vodka. And after the funeral, when he returned to the Kremlin Hospital, no blame should be attached to him if he failed to notice that he was followed by a man called Howard Gosling. For Vladimir Andreyevich, slightly mellowed with the exercise of his grief, was also intoxicated by the thought of a miracle.

It would be worthy of comparison with the Palestinian archetype. Yet because both participants on this occasion were mortal, it would take a little longer, maybe a month instead of three days. And the new embassy doctor, a man called Owens, would help.

12

K Complex

George was readmitted to hospital on the eleventh of September. His "death," Dimitrov informed Druzula on that day, was fixed for the fifth of October, in the early hours of the morning. The funeral would take place the next day, a Sunday, in the late afternoon. There was not, as the comrade doctor remarked, much time left.

"You're forgetting," Dimitrov said, "that you'll have some time after the funeral. I would estimate three to four weeks. That gives you seven weeks altogether, plus or minus a few days, depending on how quickly the British react."

"What you are asking is very difficult," Druzula complained.

"Nevertheless, it will be done."

"Oh, yes. It will be done. Comrade Colonel, since we are going to be working together, why not use first names? I am called Aleksei." The comrade doctor extended his hand, which had a soft, spongy texture. "It is strange, is it not," Aleksei Druzula observed, "the way the mind works? This ceremony we have, which all civilized peoples have—the shaking of hands—it reminded me of the Chinese. What an excessively clean race they are, Vladimir Andreyevich! For example, the term *hsi nao*, literally translated, means 'wash brain.' ''

Vladimir Andreyevich was angered. "I've told you," he said. "I do not want this man tortured. All I want are those code names. And the truth."

"Forgive me, Comrade. I was thinking aloud. Brainwashing, as it is called, engineered confession, menticide, thought control—name your own euphemism—is no more than a form of operant conditioning. The innocent must be guilty, Vladimir Andreyevich, that is the law. To this end the subject is deprived of sleep and food, of the society of his fellowmen, perhaps even of his reason. He must ask himself, 'Why are they doing this to me? Can it be because I am guilty?' What could be more ultraparadoxical, Comrade, than the innocent man who needs to believe in his own guilt? Yet he does this in order to save himself, as he thinks, so perhaps his behaviour is reasonable after all."

"You are a moralist," said Dimitrov.

"Perhaps." Druzula regarded him placidly. "Do you have any idea, Vladimir Andreyevich, how difficult it is to make a *guilty* man confess? You bring me this man Stevens, who you think may be lying. But you cannot tell, even you cannot tell. You ask for the truth, and you think I will brainwash him? I am not going to torture this man, Comrade Colonel. I will not starve him or deprive him of his sleep. In fact, I shall see that he catches up on his sleep."

"Ah, I understand. You will use hypnosis?"

"In essence, yes. There are many ways of putting a man to sleep. You yourself must be familiar with one, a sudden blow to the carotid sinus wall." Aleksei Druzula paused and tugged at the sleeves of his lab coat, an irritating mannerism. "However, I shall use a therapy that combines the speed of drug-induced sleep with the suggestibility of hypnosis—a form of narcohypnoanalysis. The drug I have selected is chlorpromazine hydrochloride. It can be taken orally, and will be administered to the patient in his food. I'll need a week to prepare him."

"That long?"

"Yes, Comrade Colonel. That long."

"Very well. Have it you own way. And then?"

"Then I shall hypnotize him, at the same time implanting the suggestion that he remember neither the hypnosis nor the questions you will ask him."

"You're not using a truth serum, sodium thiopental, nothing like that?"

Aleksei Druzula winced. "So crude," he said. "You see, Comrade Colonel, the patient will not answer you, but his brain will. . . . Shall we say a week from today, then? This may be inconvenient, but I wonder if we could make it in the early hours of the eighteenth, say at two-thirty a.m.? I would like the time to correspond, as far as possible, with the natural rhythms of sleep."

"Agreed," said Vladimir Andreyevich, who did not want to be seen visiting the hospital too often. It was a pity, he thought, but his intense dislike of Aleksei Druzula was just another of those things that he would have to put out of his mind.

Vladimir Andreyevich spent the next week reading about narcohypnoanalysis. He discovered that it was possible to make the subject believe almost anything, though he did not see why it was necessary to go to such lengths. Willpower, he learnt, was merely notational, the metaphysical preserve of decadent men like Schopenhauer and Nietzsche. Vladimir Andreyevich, who had never read a book of philosophy in his life, was unsure of this, but he was prepared to discard outmoded concepts.

It was not a question of making the subject do something against his will (whatever that was supposed to be) so much as neutralizing his resistances and inhibitions. Our experiences do not happen to us, he read, rather, we *are* our experiences, every man a vacuum in the process of exhaustion. If this smacked of the bourgeois-existentialist heresy, it had its uses nevertheless. For in extreme cases of functional impairment, the cause of the psychoneurosis could be recreated under analysis. Hence a combat soldier in battle trauma who has seen a comrade decapitated in front of his eyes could be made to relive this experience. He became the thing he feared, became in a sense a man without a head. All of Vladimir Andreyevich's authorities (American, British, and Soviet) agreed that this was an efficient cure, especially when the headless man discovered that his case was not so horrible as he had formerly supposed. Vladimir Andreyevich could see that brainwashing, as he still persisted in calling it, had come a long way since his father's trial and execution.

The man of science, as always, will vanquish the man of force. Then what was the difference, really, Vladimir Andreyevich asked himself, between the insane man who must lose his head in order to regain his sanity and the innocent man who must affirm his guilt in order (perhaps) to regain his freedom? None of Vladimir Andreyevich's authorities answered this question; none of them asked it.

When Dimitrov returned to the hospital in the early hours of 18 September, he was taken to a room on the fourth floor, where Aleksei Druzula had conducted his first tests on Stevens. Things were much the same as before, except that George, who was again wired to the EEG machine, was lying down, asleep in bed. But as well as the technician, whose name was Sergei, an anaesthetist was also present, fussing over his gauges and cylinders.

"What's the matter," Dimitrov said, "did you have to knock him out?"

"A precaution," Druzula answered. "Justified, as you may see."

Dimitrov grunted. The presence of the other doctor annoyed him.

"And you, Vladimir Andreyevich, you look as though you have forgotten something."

"My tape recorder. I left it in the car."

"Sergei," Aleksei Druzula said, giving the oddest smile, "would you be so good as to fetch the comrade colonel's tape recorder?"

"Yes, would you? It's in the black Volga. The door's open." Dimitrov looked at his feet. "I parked outside the morgue."

Druzula moved to the EEG and used the technician's absence to explain the experiment. "The traces you see here," he said, pointing to the graph paper, "are recording the activity of four major configurations of the brain, the frontal, parietal, occipital, and temporal lobes. The fifth trace is recording a deep brain function, that of the reticular cortex, located in the area of the caudal brain stem. The signals that trigger sleep originate here and also our dreams themselves.

"As you can see," Druzula said, pointing to the moving pens, "the brain is never fully unconscious. At the moment, the frequency of all five traces is regular and evenly spaced, no more than two to four cycles per second. This is the delta wave of deep sleep. Do not think of these lines as actual waves, Comrade; they are really electrical potentials amplified by the machine and transmitted to these pens. When the charge is negative, they swing up—down when it is positive. This gives us a mechanical and enduring record of what is more accurately described as a fluid field state.

"If this were a true hypnotic trance, Comrade Colonel, the rhythm would be that of the conscious brain, the alpha wave, say from eight to thirteen cycles per second, if the patient were relaxed; or the beta wave, from twelve to twenty-six cycles, if I induced an anxiety state in him. But this is not a true hypnotic trance." Druzula looked at his watch. "The subject was hypnotized an hour ago and was then told that he would go to sleep. Therefore, I have lost true hypnotic rapport with him. However, he has been conditioned to respond to a verbal stimulus from me and has also been told that you will ask him some questions. In a way, he is waiting for us."

"Waiting for us?"

"Yes, Comrade Colonel. I think you will find his answers interesting."

Dimitrov glanced from the machine to the door. It was Sergei, returned with the tape recorder. Dimitrov watched him run the microphone over to the oscilloscope next to the EEG. Sergei threw a filter switch on the audio system, and a level tone filled the room, the pens scribbling into life as the frequency shifted to a higher range. Sergei killed the noise. "I have a reading of one hundred and fifty microvolts," he said. "There's a lot of spindling now."

"He is dreaming," Aleksei Druzula said. "Let us leave him be for a while."

Druzula moved to a table at the room's centre, picking up a sheet of graph paper, which he unfolded and pinned to a corkboard on the wall farthest from the bed. "If you would care to look at this, Vladimir Andreyevich," he said, finding a pencil to use as a pointer, "you will see that it is a graph that Sergei here has so artfully transcribed from last night's reading."

The technician smiled while the anaesthetist looked on with an air of professional boredom. He reminded Dimitrov of a triangle player at the symphony, waiting his moment.

"In fact, it is a recording of the electrical potential from the subject's reticular cortex. The traces are rather flat, but that's something for later," Druzula said, keeping the treat in store. "The first trace is a delta wave, and the slight perturbation noticeable here"—he indicated a shift in wavelength—"is what we call a collateral afferent. More precisely, it measures the path of an impulse from the brain's temporal lobe to the reticular cortex. This occurred when I mentioned the name of the minor English versifier—your code name Shelley. It means only that the subject heard me, and if you follow the graph, you will notice that the signal subsided quickly. Much the same thing happened a few moments later with the word 'Dumbo.' Here is the evoked potential, you see"—he pointed again—"but, as before, the delta wave returns almost immediately."

"What does it mean?" Dimitrov asked.

"Nothing," said Aleksei Druzula.

"Nothing?"

"But look at this." Druzula pointed to another frequency change. "The perturbation is much more dramatic here. This, you could say, is a signal with a history, insofar as neural events are concerned. It lasted for almost four seconds—after the word 'Jelly.' Notice the spindling, the spikes. They are positively Alpine. The word 'Dumbbell' had exactly the same effect. Now, this kind of psychogalvanic response is known as a K complex. It means that the subject has definite, long-term associations with these words, so definite indeed that they almost woke him up. Hence my colleague here. Those are the code names, Vladimir Andreyevich—Jelly and Dumbbell."

Dimitrov absorbed this in silence.

"Delta wave again," the technician said. "Do you want to record, Comrade Colonel?"

"Yes. Why not?"

"I suggest that you begin by repeating my experiment," Druzula said. "Remember, it is the evoked potential that is significant. Try not to ask direct questions. I am going to count from one to ten now. Allow a few seconds when I have finished, then you may start."

Druzula began counting. "There's an EP from the temporal

lobe," Sergei said. "Alpha wave, one hundred and forty micro-volts. All other traces still delta. All right, Comrade Colonel. He's ready."

It was the strangest interrogation he had ever conducted. Vladimir Andreyevich repeated the experiment of the night before, with identical results. For a moment in that dimly lit room, the instruments ghosted in green light, the EEG pens scratching as if at the bidding of some hidden scribe, it was easy to believe that the art had been wonderfully simplified, that there was no longer any need for the conscious trickery of language. Here the captive mind lay open to investigation, the soul of an agent revealed as if to God. What secrets could not be thus extracted without their possessor's awareness? Yes, it was a historic occasion, Vladimir Andreyevich thought, but only for a moment.

He tried the code name Importer and got nothing. Insect produced a psychogalvanic response, a K complex. Which made no sense at all to Vladimir Andreyevich, because it meant that George, who had been lying when he said Ritter's code name was Shelley and Deriabin's was Dumbo, had finally told the truth when he said that Druzhinin's was Insect. . . .

The audio tone dipped and rose.

"Alpha wave from the temporal lobe," Sergei reported. The tone squealed. "There's spindling on all traces now. A very high-amplitude signal!"

"Anaesthetic, please," Aleksei Druzula said. "I am sorry"— he turned to Dimitrov as his colleague lowered the mask on George— "but that is enough. Sergei, will you clean up in here? And you, Comrade Colonel, perhaps you would come to my office. I have coffee there, and there is something I must tell you."

Dimitrov recorded his conversation with Aleksei Druzula, who made no objection. The comrade doctor was enjoying himself. Convinced that he had shown an old hand the ropes, his smugness became intolerable. Vladimir Andreyevich thought that he would have to do something for Aleksei Druzula, like arranging his transfer to the Serbsky Institute of Psychiatry, where he could cure the sane schizophrenics.

Aleksei Druzula began with a simple statement. "The subject has been hypnotized before."

"How can you tell, Comrade Doctor?"

"The same way as you can tell when a man is lying."

Vladimir Andreyevich overlooked the taunt. "What has he been hypnotized for? When? By whom?"

"Why don't you ask him, Comrade Colonel?"

"I will."

"Somehow I don't think you'll get the answers."

"What do you mean by that?"

"Exactly what I said. The man has been conditioned not to respond to that kind of questioning."

"Then you must decondition him."

"A man is not a machine. You said it yourself, Vladimir Andreyevich. But I doubt whether you understand." Aleksei Druzula plucked a necklace from his lab-coat pocket and let it fall on his desk. The stones were bloodred, the links silver. "A family heirloom," he said. "I use it for hypnosis. With this subject there was scarcely any need. He is very susceptible, hypersusceptible in fact."

"Impossible!" Dimitrov exclaimed.

"So, of course, I was immediately suspicious." Druzula trailed the necklace across the back of his hand. "He has been 'got at,' Comrade Colonel. Isn't that how you people say it? Oh, yes, you needn't look so surprised. I have already ascertained that he can remember nothing of the original hypnosis. If we could find out more about it, where it was done, for example, or the name and methods of the practitioner, then we might just be able to help him. Those traces from the reticular formation, Vladimir Andreyevich— they are very flat, very dull. One sees that levelling in certain depressive states. Somehow his mind has been tampered with. . . ." Druzula let the necklace fall again. "We must be very careful, Comrade. He may attempt suicide rather than break. You see, I am convinced that he has been programmed, possibly even to kill. If I am right, then he is waiting for a signal. He is a sleeper assassin, Comrade Colonel, waiting for this trigger stimulus that will set him ticking like a time bomb."

"Spare me the comparisons," Dimitrov said. "What kind of signal do you mean?"

"Anything. It could be a word or a symbol or something like this necklace. It could be anything, Comrade. But a word of advice, if you will allow me. The code names, they contain the key—of that I am quite sure.''

"The key?"

"What is it, Vladimir Andreyevich? What's wrong?"

"Nothing, Comrade Doctor. So you have told me something at last. Let me tell you something. Dead men do not kill. There are eighteen days until his funeral. Let us see if we can make use of them."

The key, Dimitrov thought, and helped himself to coffee from Druzula's flask, enquiring if the comrade doctor, perhaps, had some sugar.

Moonlight dissected the rear of the building, carving it into angular slabs, ghostly blue. Vladimir Andreyevich waited in the shadow of the morgue and watched the light from the fourth-floor window. It was a clear night, calm and still. Somewhere a dog bayed at the moon, its cry waning on the frosted air. A meteor or maybe satellite debris tracked across the stars, a brief arc of incandescence fading into nothingness.

Compared with the austerely classical grandeur of its façade, the back of the hospital was a slum. Humble wooden structures, detached from the main wings, clustered round the courtyard, which now functioned as a parking lot. Dimitrov recalled that the building at number 8 Kalinin Prospekt had been the principal residence of the Sheremetyevo family in prerevolutionary times. Land barons, they had owned half of Moscow. The morgue was a converted coach house. Vladimir Andreyevich smiled, amused at this use of the past. He looked at his watch. It was almost four o'clock, and the light in the window was out.

Unbidden, the words of a Russian proverb came to his mind: "When it happens to you, you'll know it's true." It was absurd, but he was sure that something was waiting for him in the side street next to the parking lot. Vladimir Andreyevich wasn't psychic, and he didn't believe in hunches. Yet the conviction was so immediate and forceful that he was momentarily undecided between investigation and flight. He could get in the Volga, drive out of there fast, and be home soon. Vladimir Andreyevich told himself that he had no choice. He left the tape recorder in his car and started walking towards the street. A large Chaika saloon belonging to the British

Embassy pool was parked on the left; a small Pobeda, the type of car used by the KGB for shadowing, on the right. Dimitrov approached the Pobeda. It was then that he realized his mistake. This was not a friendly vehicle. Its license series was unknown to him.

The Chaika's motor fired first. It reversed slowly, on full beam, while the Pobeda came for him, also on full beam—scissors. Dimitrov, who was unarmed, ran at the smaller car, heaving himself into a corkscrew dive. He brushed the front left fender and rolled into the gutter. The Pobeda had stalled, blocking the street, but the Chaika was starting its run now. Dimitrov waited until he heard the crash of gears, the Pobeda backing out, then made a break for the oncoming car, which went into a spin. He caught a lucidly crazed glance of its driver struggling with the wheel, mouth open, hands letting go, arms akimbo to cover his head. Then he heard the glissando of brakes and the impact of the collision, and he was running, zigzagging wildly down the street, expecting at any second the crack of small-arms fire. When he reached the parking lot at the rear of the hospital, he knew that he was safe. They were not going to shoot him—not yet, at any rate.

Dimitrov crouched in the shadows. He heard a car door open, a muffled groan, and an earnest English voice enquire, repeatedly, "I say, are you all right?" More voices and groans; the sound of somebody being dragged from the Pobeda. Whispers and slithers; footsteps—running, limping, fleeing. They were gone.

He waited until he was absolutely certain of that. There was another proverb: "If it hasn't happened to you yet, look again."

Dimitrov found the embassy Chaika abandoned in the street, its front end crumpled into the side of the Pobeda. Both cars were probably reported stolen, or would be soon. They had switched off the headlights, and he liked that because it was thoughtful. The engines ticked as they cooled, oil from the Chaika dripping onto the road. He looked inside. There was no blood.

Only then did he reflect on the narrowness of his escape. The houses were old, the side street barely wide enough for two cars to pass. Vladimir Andreyevich recapitulated the attack, putting himself behind the wheel of the Chaika. He saw himself caught in the headlights, stumbling from the gutter; he saw the driver's horrified gaze, and he knew and recognized that face. It belonged to Soper, the British resident. Soper had been surprised to see this figure leap out in front of him, but his reactions were fast and he had spun the wheel to the right, turning away from his victim and losing control of the car. Vladimir Andreyevich studied the skid marks. There could be no doubt that Soper had swerved to avoid him, and he realized what a fool he had been, throwing himself around like some kind of circus act. This would-be assassination had been nothing more than an attempt to scare him, perhaps not even that, and because of his fright, his miserable, puerile fright, he had almost caused the thing he feared.

He heard the distant wail of a siren. It was time to be going. Later, he thought, there would be time enough to settle accounts with Reginald Soper.

Dimitrov lived in the Prospekt Kutuzovsky, not far from Brezhnev's building. Like many other middle-aged men, he affected a domesticity that bore no relation to reality. A few months ago he had acquired an Alsatian puppy. This was against the house rules, but he needed company and solace now that his children had fled the roost. He had a son, Pyotr, born at the end of the war; and a daughter, Tamara Yekatrina, born a year later. He tried not to think of them. They were different, and that was all he knew.

He was sentimental about the dog and believed that it understood him as did no human being. He was an uncomplicated man, so he thought, who had been forced to live a complicated life. Now, as he drove home, he told himself that his dog would greet him but his wife would not. She would accuse him of spending the night with Anna when he had been fighting for his life. Such were the fortunes of love and war.

He heard music at the door of his apartment. Last year he had bought some German stereo equipment. It was expensive, far beyond the reach of the ordinary Soviet citizen, and as he listened he recognized the adagio from Shostakovich's Eleventh Symphony, an old Russian folk tune scored for muted strings. Was it possible that Vera enjoyed this music? She was always playing it. Sometime, when the Stevens case was closed and the file stitched into its folder, they would have to go to the State Symphony. Dimitrov closed his eyes and saw the scene the music was supposed to evoke: the crowd milling on the steps of the Winter Palace, the guard drawn up. A sabre flashed, and the crowd broke, spilling over the steps, their icons falling into the dust. He opened the door to the sound of revolutionary kettledrums.

Vera was sitting on the couch opposite the record player. She looked tired and drawn, but she had waited up for him. Surely that meant something?

"I was delayed at the hospital," he said.

He listened to this, and it sounded like a lie, as much a lie as Shostakovich's rhetoric. Violins moaned, accompanying the masses who were carrying off their dead. Vladimir Andreyevich disliked demonstrations, musical or otherwise.

Vera softened the volume and turned round to face him.

"I'd like a drink," he said.

She took his hand, guiding him to the sofa. Her eyes reminded him of the children's, also of Anna's—Anna, who was young enough or old enough to be his daughter. All the children, all the little children.

"What is it?" she asked. "What happened?"

"A little trouble," he replied. "Someone tried to make me think I was going to be killed tonight."

"Are you hurt?"

He did not answer her question. "I want to stop thinking," he said. "If only I could stop thinking."

She smiled. "Maybe I could help."

The music had stopped. Vladimir Andreyevich watched the pickup arm track to the centre of the record. It clicked and executed a flawless German salute.

"Yes," he said.

13

Catalepsis

He spent most of the next two weeks at the hospital. Working without Druzula, he discovered that the name Chernukhin elicited a K complex from the brain of George Michael Stevens. That was interesting, though Dimitrov was unsure of its significance —for Stevens as well as for himself. George had finished his memoirs now and in his lucid moments was quite anxious that the manuscript should reach London. Or Cambridge, Vladimir Andreyevich thought. On the twentieth of September he sent the list of code names to Technical Services with the request that they run a computer scan for a cypher, warning them to look for a classical language. On the twenty-ninth, ten days before the funeral, they came up with both: a monoalphabetic substitution cypher from English to Latin, *Mortuus, vivo pro tempore* —Dead, I live for the time being.

His first thought was that the cypher was an ingenious piece of improvisation on George's part; his second was extreme curiosity over how George could have known what was in store for him beforehand. Vladimir Andreyevich knew that he had been second-guessed; he had no idea how or why. Time would answer the why; the how was perhaps just one of those things that unhappily belonged in the same category as intuition. He was getting nowhere with Stevens, who couldn't—or wouldn't—remember anything about hypnosis and who was also exhibiting acute symptoms of what Druzula called transmarginal psychosis. There was another difficulty, too. Dimitrov was far from convinced that the comrade doctor's theories about programming were correct.

Against this he had to weigh the activities of the British resident. Technical Services had now decrypted all the embassy signals between Soper's astonishing telex of 5 July and its equally astonishing reply of 8 September. In slightly over two months' traffic there had not been a single mention of George Michael Stevens. Two months was a long time; two months of silence, an eternity. Either Soper and his friends had been operating out in the cold, without the support of their government, or the chairman was right and the whole thing was an elaborate deception plan. But why the clumsiness with the signals? Were the Friends trying to make it *look* as though they wanted to discredit George? So there were pluses and minuses for the comrade doctor, who could also be right. Multiply the minuses, Vladimir Andreyevich thought, and you get a plus. If Druzula were correct, the Friends could be stalling until they devised a means of contacting George with the trigger stimulus. Vladimir Andreyevich knew that he would have to let this happen eventually, though before he could, he had to be sure of two things: the target and the time.

He knew that he might be very close to cracking a major British operation and that much depended on the Friends' reaction to George's manuscript. He was certain of one thing. There would be no assassination, programmed or not programmed. After the incident with Reginald Soper, Vladimir Andreyevich departed from his normal procedure and started to carry a gun, a Walther PPK 7.65 mm, like his record player, of German manufacture.

He made a final attempt to break George Stevens a week before the funeral. George's own room was on the third floor, immediately under the EEG room. "The patient is physically well," Aleksei Druzula said as they walked down the corridor, "and he is most anxious to see you."

"Good. I want to talk with him as well."

"Under hypnosis?"

"That's right. Only this time I want him to answer me verbally. Can you do that?"

"Yes, of course."

"I want the target, the time, and that trigger stimulus—if it exists."

"Does a lock know what its key is, Vladimir Andreyevich?"

"You can turn a key," Dimitrov said.

"And pick a lock," Druzula rejoined. "The brain, however . . ."

They had reached Stevens' room, and the guard outside saluted. Inside, George was sitting at a writing desk, playing snap with another guard. "Volodny!" He laid down the cards and welcomed Dimitrov expansively. "When are you going to get me out of this place? It gives me the creeps."

"The creeps, George?" Dimitrov waved the guard outside.

"Bad dreams. My guilty conscience." Stevens grinned. He seemed quite relaxed and even looked younger and somewhat thinner. Hospital food, no doubt. Or was it the drug? Dimitrov made a note to check that out. "What have you done with the manuscript, Volodny?"

"It's on its way. I used a Leningrad literary agent. They're so much more . . ." He faltered. Something very unusual was happening.

The necklace chinked in Druzula's hand. George had paid no attention to the doctor when he entered the room. Now he stood up and walked over to the bed.

"That's right," Druzula said, holding the necklace so that its stones flashed in the light. "You are tired, George, and you want to lie down. You are so tired that you can hardly keep your eyes open. . . ." The necklace chinked again. It was the sound as much as its appearance, the sound of silver and red. "You are sleepy, so sleepy," Druzula intoned. "Close your eyes now, George, close them. . . ."

Druzula counted from one to ten. "Pull up a chair," he whispered, and Dimitrov obeyed. "You know this man, don't you? Of course you do. I want you to open your eyes and say hello to the colonel. He's going to ask you some questions, George."

Stevens sat up and looked at Dimitrov through the eyes of a ventriloquist's doll. "Hello, Volodny," he said.

Vladimir Andreyevich searched his expression for a hint, a sign, anything to suggest that he was acting. There was none.

George folded his arms complacently. Watching him, Dimitrov experienced the unaccountable sensation that the human being in front of him was George Michael Stevens only in the nominal sense, as if the man retained his name and physical identity, but the rest of him, his character and personality, had been invisibly, insanely extracted.

Dimitrov tried the chairman's name: "Andropov, Yuri Andropov. What are you going to do to Andropov?"

"Andropov? Nothing . . ."

"George, how are they going to contact you?"

"Contact me?"

"With the trigger stimulus—how are they going to reach you?"

"I don't know what you're talking about, Volodny." Stevens closed his eyes. His breathing deepened.

Dimitrov watched his hands clenching, unclenching. "Who are you going to kill, George?"

"No one."

"Who is it, George?"

"No one."

"Chernukhin," Vladimir Andreyevich said. "Yuri Simono-vich."

"No one!"

Stevens shouted the response, his head moving from side to side. His neck muscles tautened and his hands tore at the sheets.

The necklace glittered and chinked in Druzula's hands. "Sleep now," the doctor murmured. But it was unnecessary. George Stevens was unconscious.

Vladimir Andreyevich walked to the window. He looked out on the courtyard and the morgue. Then he drew the curtains.

"His condition approximates to a cataleptic trance," Aleksei Druzula said in his office. "I assume that my English colleague anticipated our moves and built in a series of resistances to thwart them. Unless the hypnosis is done by the original therapist, the subject's behaviour soon becomes transmarginal." Druzula dropped the necklace on his desk. "His mind is breaking into pieces, fragments of memories. I must warn you, Comrade Colonel, we may cause irreparable damage if we persist."

Dimitrov looked at him blankly. If there was a hint of a smile on his face, the comrade doctor would have described it as subcutaneous.

"What are the stones?" Dimitrov said abruptly.

"The stones . . . ?"

"In the necklace."

"Garnets. It belonged to my grandmother, the countess Yelena Kletinskaya."

"Times change."

"Quite. May I make a suggestion, Vladimir Andreyevich?"

"Please do."

"Where was Stevens living before you brought him here?"

"In an apartment . . ."

"Then I suggest you return him there. Leave him alone for a while. Later you can go to him and ask him what has happened, without drugs or machines or hypnosis. A simple, humane, direct approach. We must break the trance, Vladimir Andreyevich. And in order to do this, he must be fully conscious. He must *know* what is happening to him."

"He'll have to be moved, anyway," Dimitrov said. "After the funeral."

"Yes, Vladimir Andreyevich. I agree. In this hospital, and every other I know of, it is most unusual to keep a patient in his room after he has terminated."

"And the risk?"

"None, Vladimir Andreyevich. If he is watched."

Dimitrov rose to leave, and Druzula accompanied him to the door. "One thing interests me," the doctor said. "Who is this Chernukhin you mentioned?"

"No one, Comrade. The man no longer exists."

"Strange, but my grandmother knew a man of that name. He was an archivist at the Hermitage, I believe. But that was in the old days," Aleksei Druzula said, bowing, "and as you say, times change." So did the comrade doctor, who gave a kind of laugh. "Chernukhin is dead, and Stevens is dead. Setting a corpse to kill a corpse, Comrade—why, it's quite *ridiculous*. . . ."

"Yes, isn't it? Aleksei"—Dimitrov used his first name like a threat—"do you mind if I make a suggestion now? Check the subject's weight. You'll find that he's not been eating. When a man doesn't eat, Comrade Doctor, he grows weak and faint. It is called hunger, though perhaps you have another name for it. So give him some food, will you? I don't want him to die of starvation. Another thing, discontinue the drug. You can tell him you've done that, but he probably won't believe you. I'm afraid you'll have to sample everything for him, Comrade. Yes, you'll have to become the court taster. . . ."

That evening Vladimir Andreyevich asked his wife if she had heard of Druzula's countess grandmother.

"Yelena Kletinskaya? Oh, yes. She was quite famous in Saint Petersburg. One of Grigori Efimovich's circle."

"The monk?"

"Yes. Rasputin."

George's apartment commanded a fine view of the convent. Boris Godunov was elected to the throne here, after the death of Tsar Fëdor Ivanovich in 1598, having first ensured his succession by murdering the tsarevitch a few years previously. Peter the Great, renowned for introducing European civilization into Russia, incarcerated his wife and sister within the convent walls, hanging three hundred of their troops from the battlements and nailing the right hand of the archrebel Prince Khovansky to the front door. It was, as Vladimir Andreyevich remarked to Stevens, a room with a window on history.

"You can see your own grave down there." He pointed to the cemetery. "What's it like to be dead, George?"

"A hungry feeling, Volodny. Funny thing."

Stevens had sent one of the goons out for some ground steak, salad greens, and a bottle of Mukuzani, a red Georgian wine.

"Can't you call those gorillas off?" he asked when the guard returned. "I'm sick of the sight of them."

"They're for your protection, George."

"Yours, don't you mean?" Stevens' voice came from the kitchen.

"I didn't know you could cook, George," Dimitrov said.

"I can't. I'm making steak tartare. Raw."

"Yes, hospital food is always overcooked."

George appeared in the doorway, a salad shaker in his hand. "This food was drugged," he said, and vanished into the kitchen again.

Vladimir Andreyevich followed. "Druzula told you, then?"

"He didn't have to. I knew." George exfoliated an onion. His eyes watered. "Open the wine, will you, Volodny?" Stevens threw salt, pepper, and nutmeg into the beef, shaping it into a greyish-pink cake, which he crowned with a sprig of parsley. "All right, Volodny," he said, "I'll talk. The name of the doctor was Owens."

"*Is*," said Vladimir Andreyevich.

"He's here, then?"

"On the morning flight."

"He's a hypnodontist, actually, in South Kensington—just off the Cromwell Road. That's the front, anyway. I had toothache, you see, and Carlo recommended this man. I couldn't very well refuse. Eat up, Volodny. You're not eating."

"No."

"But you're listening. All right. You're wrong, you know. They didn't get to me."

Dimitrov said nothing.

"I had a friend once. Miles Cavendish. He used to dabble in this sort of thing, hypnotism and so forth. The thing to do is to go along with the hypnotist. You can get below the pain threshold, and they can stick needles into you, even cut you open, but they can't control your mind. That's impossible."

"Is it?" Dimitrov sipped his wine. "Druzula thinks otherwise. When you were in the hospital, someone tried to make it look as though they wanted me dead. It was Soper. You know him, don't you? Soper's been empowered to negotiate your release. You know what that means, don't you, George? Carlo's set you up. You're through. Finished."

"That's what you're *supposed* to think, Volodny. . . ."

"Maybe." Dimitrov rotated his wineglass by the stem. Stevens avoided his gaze and concentrated on the glass. He lowered his fork to the table and held the steak knife absently in his hand.

"Go on, Volodny," he said.

"Carlo had you in a trap." Dimitrov's eyes flickered to the knife, which Stevens placed on the table, a little self-consciously. "Why else would you agree to see this man Owens? You must have been aware of the dangers, but you couldn't very well run because there might have been unpleasantness. You remember everything that happened, don't you, just as you remember everything that happened in the hospital? By the way, that was quite a show you put up in there. Soper panicked because he was supposed to. He sent a cable, George, telling your people that you were in hospital, and he sent it *en clair*. You see, Carlo wanted me to think that you were dangerous, some kind of homicidal robot, and of course I would de-activate you—permanently. That's why he had no plans for your recovery, George. Simple . . .''

But for one thing, Vladimir Andreyevich thought—the code to Carlo. There was no way he was going to tell Stevens he knew about that. Instead he monitored George's reactions: pallor, facial rictus, shock.

"The target was supposed to be Andropov," Stevens said. "I couldn't have told you that, could I?"

"No," Dimitrov agreed. But you just have, he thought. "Time and place?" he said.

"The seventh of November. Red Square. I don't know who the contact will be, but I can give you the trigger stimulus." George stood up. "Let's go through to the other room," he said. "I need a drink."

George found a bottle of Starka in the living room, and a pen and paper. He poured a couple of drinks. "This is the sequence," he said, and wrote down two lines:

> For Cambridge people rarely smile,
> Being urban, squat, and packed with guile.

"Rupert Brooke," he said. "Carlo's idea of a joke. For some reason he hated Brooke. The code name for the operation was Poetry. I'm sorry, Volodny. I couldn't tell you any of this, and I didn't think you'd find out. I thought they'd try to make the contact, and when there was no reaction from me, they'd just give up. What are you going to do?"

"Let them go ahead. I hope your friend Cavendish was right, George."

Vladimir Andreyevich walked over to the window. Only a man who knows what the truth is can lie, he thought. George wasn't lying, nor did he know the truth. It was an extempore account, but perhaps it was meant to sound like one. That word again, *tempore* . . .

He braced himself before turning round. "Trust me," he said.

"I'll fix it. I must be going now. There's a man running round town killing women with an ice pick."

"Ivan the Terrible?" Stevens was momentarily distracted. "What's that got to do with you? I thought they'd caught him."

"They had. But there's been another murder. The chairman thinks he must be a foreigner. At least we know it's not you." Vladimir Andreyevich lingered by the door. "And, George," he added, "you didn't eat half your steak."

Outside, he reminded the guard that he was to shoot uninvited guests. "But don't kill anyone," he added mordantly. "There's a crisis in the Commissariat of Graves."

On Monday, 14 October, the same day that Johnson was in New York, Vladimir Andreyevich flew to Leningrad to see a man called Kron. Every agent has his special talent. Kron's was Germany and things German. He looked like his name sounded, a bearlike man with bristling black hair and prognathous jaws. His nose had been broken in his earlier days, and his face was scarred and seamed. Ivan Kron was tough, tougher than Dimitrov but not quite so clever. He had been purged after Stalin's death, hence the broken nose. And he owed Dimitrov a great favour: his release from the Lubyanka and subsequent rehabilitation. Vladimir Andreyevich was collecting a debt.

They had been students together in that terrible time before the war, and their careers had followed separate but similar paths. Kron had stayed with the army and was now a colonel with the GRU— Glavnoye Razvedyvatelnoye Upravlenie, or Main Administration for Intelligence, the Red Army's secret service. In the New Year of 1953 he had told Dimitrov of the coming troubles in East Germany and also that Iosif Vissarionovich was going to die. Since then he had respected Kron almost, but not quite, to the point of trusting him. For when he asked how Kron knew about Stalin, the answer had been that no one was immortal.

He found him eating *botvinya*, boiled fish laced with kvass. "Brain food," Kron grumbled, and listened patiently to what Dimitrov had to say.

"That's clear." Kron's voice belied his appearance. It was gentle and melodious. "Stevens *says* he's supposed to kill Andropov, and you think it's meant to look as though he's supposed to kill you. But you can't prove it. You have some noises on tape and that's all. What do you want me to do about it?''

"I'm going to put on a special train for the seventh of November,'' Vladimir Andreyevich said, "Moscow–Vyborg–Helsinki. Personally, I don't care what happens to the train after it reaches the border, because that's where Stevens and Carlo will meet. I'll be there as well. I can arrange things in my sector, but I'll need help in yours. That means the cooperation of the Leningrad security and transportation authorities and also the Finns. I'll want Vyborg sealed off and the train covered at every station en route to Vainikkala. I'll need a set of *bumagi* for Stevens, identity card, internal passport, and a Soviet passport with an exit visa. Another set of papers will be required for his contact man. Since I don't know who this will be yet, you can leave the photography to me. I could go through the Centre, and I have a girl who works for OVIR. But I don't want people asking questions in Moscow. The really important thing is the security. It's got to look good, but Stevens has to be given every chance to make a break. . . .''

Both men were silent. After a while Kron lit a cigarette. He inhaled, pursed his lips, and chewed on the cigarette. His next question was formulated painfully and deliberately, as if he found some miraculous power in language, a power to be used with awful economy. "What happens at the frontier, *mokrie dela*?'' Wet affairs. Kron meant bloodshed.

"I don't know,'' Vladimir Andreyevich said. "That's the truth.''

"All right.'' Kron made his decision. "The documents are easy. The security's more difficult.''

"It could be done as an exercise,'' Dimitrov said. "They are held occasionally. Also, if your army people have a spare footman in London, he could go to Cambridge. I'd like to get a look at the contact man before he arrives.''

Kron eyed him askance. "Anything else?''

"Yes, a lot more,'' said Vladimir Andreyevich. "I want you to tell me everything you know about Clemens, Johannes Heinz Clemens.''

The flight back was as uneventful as the flight out. It was up to Carlo now—Harland Caisho Peat, professor of classics, antiquarian, bibliophile, and sometime acting head of SIS-IX. According to his file, he had once made a study of the Manichees, the Gnostic sect that preached the duality of cosmic purpose. His father had been an Anglican clergyman. Light-dark, good-evil; only heretics possess absolute vision, Dimitrov thought—heretics, madmen, and the sons of the clergy.

Blank out your mind, Comrade, he told himself. *Blank out your mind.* The image of driven snow came to him and the sound of snow falling through the trees of the forest. There was a cottage in the forest, a cage in the cottage, and in the cage a little boy who was refusing to eat. So much for transmarginal psychosis, Vladimir Andreyevich thought.

In Moscow he called Anna and asked if she would like to join Foreign Affairs for a while.

Her reaction was predictable. It amused and saddened him that her only qualms concerned the physical appearance of her victim. Anna Samsonov didn't think she could work on an ugly man. In that case, Vladimir Andreyevich told her, she should be more objective.

"Not everyone enjoys his work," he said, and included himself.

Kron called on the afternoon of 2 November, the Saturday that Johnson was in Cambridge learning about manuscripts. He had some difficulty locating Dimitrov but eventually found him at Anna's, where he was perfecting her technique: B&B—body and bug.

"The exercise is fixed for the seventh," Kron said.

"Good. And?"

"The contact man is William Johnson, a journalist. His file should be on your desk by now. He'll be flying out on Monday. Keller will be with him all the way. Then it's up to you."

Vladimir Andreyevich began to ask how Kron had known where to find him. Then he realized that the line was dead. He smiled and turned to Anna. "Get dressed," he said. "That was Kron. Your boyfriend is arriving on Monday. I want you to meet him at the airport. Remember, a friendly gesture, a slight pressure on the arm, and then . . ."

"More friendly gestures later?"

"Yes. I want him infested."

"Don't be personal, Comrade. I wonder what he looks like."

"Come with me to the office and you can see for yourself."

In the elevator she said to him, "Volodny, you are the most moral immoral man I've ever met."

"Why do you say that?"

"Because you know that what is going to happen will be bad and you haven't told anyone."

Dimitrov winced. "A man is going to rise from the dead," he said. "Is that so bad?"

The late-afternoon sun loitered above the rooftops of Moscow. The scene possessed a certain ethereal beauty, which, to Vladimir Andreyevich, was as accidental as it was unnerving; this transmutation of base metals into gold, the cheap trick of a blind magician.

Vladimir Andreyevich felt as though he had something further to explain. Before he reached the car, he said, "The sun is ninety-three million miles away. Is that good or bad? I remember reading a story in *Tass* about the director of the Radio Institute at Gorki. He convinced himself that he was hearing signals from some alien space probe. It was noise, that's all. Just noise. These reports keep occurring: Academician So-and-so discovers evidence of intelligent life in the universe. As if this world isn't enough!" Vladimir Andreyevich halted. Apologetically he said, "In one form or another, humanity has been around for millions of years, but I do not think we have learnt very much. Is that moral or immoral?"

"Vladimir Andreyevich, you are a romantic!"

"No," he replied. "The romantics are always disappointed. They believe in noise."

14

Thanatopsis

"Hello, Johnson."

"Anna! Where've you been?"

"Places. Can I see you this afternoon?"

"Where?"

"Oh, at your hotel."

"When, what time?"

"Later. I can't say exactly."

"I went to the cemetery this morning. I know about Stevens, Anna. I know he's alive. Why didn't you tell me?"

"I thought you knew. Didn't you?"

"No, of course I didn't. Where are you? Listen, someone stole the manuscript this morning. While I was out, someone took it from my room. I didn't notice at first, but it's gone, stolen. . . ."

"Johnson, I want you to stay there and wait for me. Understand?"

"Yes. Why?"

"Trust me, Johnson. I can help you. Wait for me, Cheese. And relax. Everything will be all right."

"What do you mean, everything will be all right? What are you talking about? Anna? *Anna!*"

There were three men in the back of the truck, which was code-named Kestrel One and served as a command vehicle: a technician from Technical Services, two marksmen to cover Dimitrov, and Vladimir Andreyevich himself, who winced at the word "Cheese." He had managed to requisition three additional cars, each with a two-man crew, to cover the north wing, main lobby, and side entrances of the hotel. Excluding the technician, whose name was Vasily, he could count on eight men—more than enough. Johnson had been given the code name Gull; Soper, Fish.

Both marksmen wore drab green fatigues without insignia or badges of rank. The younger of the two was nicknamed Hametovich, after Rudolf Nureyev's patronymic. His hair was long and lank, his face bony, and he was methodically cleaning a .45 automatic modelled after the American Colt.

The elder man watched him with good-natured amusement. "Look at him!" he scoffed. "You'd think it was his prick. Loaded with piss, nothing but piss!"

"Shut up, Viktor." Hametovich scowled. He pushed back his cap and mopped his brow. The atmosphere in the truck was stifling.

Viktor frowned and asked if the comrade colonel was armed.

"Yes, a Walther," Dimitrov said.

Viktor shifted his girth uncomfortably. He hunched forward, his shaven skull bowed under the bulkhead housing the radio antennae. "Funny smell," he said, "like a civet."

"I had a disagreement with that young lady you just heard," Dimitrov said. "She doused me with perfume this morning."

"You should have changed your clothes." Viktor frowned again. "Hametovich could shoot you blind with that stench."

"It's true." Hametovich regarded the .45.

"But he wouldn't, Comrade Colonel. He wouldn't do that. He's afraid of the noise it makes."

"It reminds me of you farting," Hametovich said. "So I close my eyes and shoot by the smell."

Both men laughed. They were joking to relieve their tension, Dimitrov thought. Cigarette smoke curdled in the air and reminded him of blood under water.

"We recorded that at two-fifteen," the technician said. "Gull has had a busy day. After he got back from the cemetery, he went to the Central Telegraph Office and cabled London. That was at eleven-forty-five. An hour later he went to the Place of the Skull. No Fish. At one-forty-five he went to the statue on the Prospekt Marxa. Still no Fish. Then we recorded this, at two-twenty-five, just before you joined us, Comrade Colonel."

The tape squawked incomprehensibly and began turning again. Dimitrov heard dialling. The phone rang three times, then a woman's voice answered.

"Her Majesty's embassy."

"Extension seven, please." It was Johnson's voice.

The phone gave three more rings. This time a male voice answered, a smooth baritone.

Dimitrov listened as Johnson asked to speak with a Mr. David Evans of the Consular Section.

"I'm afraid he's not available at the moment," the voice replied.

"I was expecting him at noon," Johnson said.

"Where are you calling from?"

"My hotel," Johnson said, and hung up.

Dimitrov asked if Vasily recognized the voice.

The technician shook his head. "I've dubbed the tape to see if we have a voiceprint, but I don't think so. Do you know the voice, Comrade Colonel? There was an accent. . . ."

"Yes, Welsh. That was their new doctor."

Vasily frowned. "A doctor wouldn't answer the phone."

"This one might."

"Have you met him, Comrade Colonel?"

"No," said Vladimir Andreyevich thoughtfully. "Not yet."

Viktor said, "How much longer do we have to wait?"

"A long time," Vladimir Andreyevich said. "Years." It was easy to believe that time had no meaning, he thought. "So be patient," he added. "Be patient."

At five o'clock the radio stuttered into life. It was Kestrel Two reporting that the Fish had just entered the pond.

Viktor crawled to the back of the truck and opened the doors. "It's raining," he said, but everyone knew. "And it's nearly dark." Viktor was like that. Thorough.

Two minutes later the tape began turning. The four men listened as a curiously un-Russian voice explained to the *dezhurnaya* of the twelfth floor that it would speak with a Mr. Johnson.

The truck filled with a wicked laughter. "*Da, da, gospodin! Yaitso! Yaitso!*"

"Soper!" Johnson's voice was strained and tense. "Where the hell have you been? I've been trying to—"

"Good to see you. We can't talk here. Your room's bugged. Outside with you!"

Footsteps, another cry of "*Yaitso!*," elevator noises, and the distant sound of the evening's traffic. A few moments passed before Kestrel Two observed that Fish and Gull were walking towards the centre of the hotel's ornamental gardens.

"What the fuck's going on, Soper?"

"Now, now. I don't have time for tantrums. Our mutual friend is taking you to see George tonight. I want you to give him this."

"What is it?"

"It's not a bomb. Just the cassette with its own machine. Think of an excuse, you know, the little boys' room or something. As long as you leave it where George can find it."

"Look, Soper. I'm not working for your people. I don't want anything to do with this. It's raining and I'm getting wet. So leave me alone, will you? Just leave me alone."

"Don't be trite, Mr. Johnson. Your papers are forged. You'll never get out of the country without our help. Here, take it. That's right, there's a good chap. I thought you'd see reason."

Vladimir Andreyevich took the microphone in the command truck. "Catch the Fish," he said. "Ring the Gull."

Cerberus, the three-headed dog that guards the entrance to the underworld, stood watch over the gardens, the centrepiece of a majestic fountain radiating a network of crazy pavements among the rocks and lime trees. The statue was chequered by light from the hotel windows, and icicles hung from its gaping jaws like frozen saliva. Vladimir Andreyevich blinked as a white-coated figure drifted among the trees to the left of the statue. The light was polarized in the drizzle. His night vision was not good.

"Reginald Soper," he said in English. "You are under arrest. If you surrender now, you will not be harmed." He placed the megaphone to one side and withdrew the Walther from his pocket, easing off the safety catch.

Johnson had been picked up at once.

Dimitrov took up the megaphone again. "Two minutes," he said.

He heard a rustling to his right. It was Viktor, waving and pointing away from the fountain. Again he saw the apparition among the lime trees. A dull thwack came from the centre of the gardens, the report of an automatic pistol with a silencer, once, twice, and was answered by four tiny flashes of light, four shots from the other side. Dimitrov looked for Soper and understood that he must have removed his trench coat and thrown it into the trees.

"All right, Comrades! I give up!" Dimitrov heard him shout. There was a clatter as he threw down his gun.

Soper appeared, apparently unhurt, at the side of the fountain. He stepped back, raising his hands uncertainly, and saw that he was encircled. What rotten luck, he thought. What damned rotten luck!

Vladimir Andreyevich stood up, flanked by Viktor and Hametovich. Someone inside the hotel, probably the men who were holding Johnson, thought to switch on the fountain lights. Under the shadow of the three-headed dog, Soper was silhouetted in grotesque blues and greens. His right hand dropped impulsively for a second gun just as Dimitrov squeezed the trigger. Shots ricochetted from the fountain and Soper saw the lights spin. What a way to go, he thought, like *son et lumière* or something.

When they reached him, his body was half in and half out of the basin, his blood forming tendrils in the water and pinking the thin ice. The impact of the bullets had thrown him backwards, his legs draped over the side, his head and chest sinking underwater, the jaws of hell reflected in his birdlike eyes as if he strove even now to penetrate the fragile and slowly reddening layer that sealed over him, strove to see through the ice and comprehend absolutely the fire.

15

Anabiosis

The desk clerk was beside himself, wringing his hands and flashing silvery grins of despair. For surely everything was an illusion and would soon disappear. A wet corpse lay in the centre of the lobby. Blanketed for respectability's sake, at the clerk's insistence, it merely succeeded in drawing attention to itself. What right had it to lie there, to come in through the doors like a normal guest and then to flop down as no ordinary guest would, even when drunk, and to remain as if it had no intention of ever being removed? And the noise, the hubbub! The civilian police were everywhere and other people in green uniforms with guns and muddy boots. Mr. Johnson, the English journalist for whom he had called a "cap," sat dejectedly to one corner, evidently in a state of arrest. Another journalist (or was he a drunk?—a foreigner certainly) had crashed into the lobby and taken a flash photograph before his camera was broken and he was taken away by the custodians of law and order. The desk clerk shivered. A beautiful plate-glass window was starred with bullets; a lady had fainted, and outside were many vehicles with bright lights and noisy radios. That this should happen to the most modern hotel in all Russia! He shivered again as they dragged away the body, which left a pinkish trace on the marble floor. Wash up, he thought, absenting himself from his post to search out a mop and pail. When he returned, the silence shocked him. Everyone had left. All gone—gone with their mud and blood and boots and guns.

Johnson rode in the back of the car between Viktor and Hametovich. The large one stared ahead, arms folded. Ratface kept his distance and held a gun on Johnson, who considered disarming him but decided that it was too academic.

"Where are you taking me?" he asked Dimitrov, who was in the front passenger seat.

Dimitrov spoke in Russian and Ratface holstered his gun.

"What was that, Mr. Johnson? Did you say something?"

"I asked where you were taking me."

"You do not recognize the route?" There was mock surprise in Dimitrov's voice. "We are driving to the New Monastery of the Virgin. Be thankful that you are alive for the trip."

"Haven't you got any feelings?" Johnson was indignant. "A man was killed just now."

Dimitrov didn't like this. "The presence of death makes a hypocrite of you," he said.

"What are you going to do?"

"Before you arrived in this country," the Russian said, turning round, making a circle of his thumb and forefinger, "I read your file. It was a very thin file. I wondered why at first. Now I understand that there is nothing to know. But this thin file of yours will already be the fatter by several pages." Dimitrov flattened his hand. "Perhaps it has grown enough."

Johnson felt a sharp pain in his ribs. Viktor's elbow.

"Both men understand English, Mr. Johnson."

Viktor spoke. "If you are bad, you will be dead from us."

"Understand, Mr. Johnson?"

"I've got my rights. I'm a British subject."

"So was Soper. He existed, but you don't. You weren't even on the plane."

"*Nichevo*," Viktor said. "We look out for you yourself."

"Volodny tells me that you come to memorialize me. You can see that I don't look like a man in the grave." George Stevens smiled. It was a charming smile, reserved for hostesses and gentlemen of the press.

"No, you don't." Johnson turned to Dimitrov. "I'm going to put my hand in my pocket for some cigarettes. Also my wallet. I'm not armed."

Dimitrov laughed.

Johnson remembered the cassette in his coat pocket and was suddenly conscious that Stevens was staring at him. The journalist found the old Trevor Howardish photograph and laboriously compared the man with his image. "You've lost weight," he said.

"So Volodny keeps telling me."

Viktor had positioned himself by the door, and Hametovich moved across to the kitchen entrance. The English reporter would have to get by him if he wanted to leave the room. That was the expression they used. Where did they think it was to be left? The English were so very egocentric, Hametovich thought.

"Soper's dead," Dimitrov said, breaking the silence.

"What?"

"Shot. He was going for another gun, that's what I thought. There wasn't one."

It was a farcical scene, Johnson thought. Five men in that little room, all of them standing up, Stevens with one eyebrow raised and his hands clenched, Dimitrov, head and shoulders shorter, looking like a man who had just called about the plumbing.

The journalist murmured something about the bathroom, and the man near the kitchen door tensed perceptibly.

"Please give me that cassette," Dimitrov said, "and the recorder."

Johnson handed them over carefully, very carefully. The machine was smaller than the commercial type, no bigger than a pocket dictionary, and was made of a nondescript white plastic that shone dully in the palm of Dimitrov's hand. The Russian extracted the cassette and held it up to the light. It was about the size of a book of matches.

"Do you know what's on this, George? I do not think it is Rupert Brooke."

Dimitrov slipped the cassette back into the recorder. Johnson wondered if he was going to play it, but the Russian's hand closed over the machine. He was holding it very tightly, Johnson noted, and giving Stevens his best pop-eyed look. This morning it was Wilfred Owen; now it was Rupert Brooke—a poetic bunch of bastards.

Johnson felt the bile rising in his throat. "Really," he insisted, "can I go to the bathroom now?"

Dimitrov nodded, and Johnson sidled past Hametovich. It was to his credit, he thought, that he didn't throw up. He thought of Soper's dead eyes when they dragged him into the hotel lobby and of the living-dead gaze of the Moon children in New York. That was only three weeks ago. Then he thought of the Gissing girl, two weeks ago. The last few weeks seemed hideously overpopulated with zombies and corpses.

Johnson tried urinating, but —misery!—his bladder was oddly constricted. He leant over the washbowl and splashed his head and the back of his neck in water, cold water. Refreshed, he caught sight of the mirror, his favourite enemy. It was then he realized that Anna had framed him, or rather bugged him, as neatly as his face was framed now. He began a frantic search of his clothing but found nothing. Soper had picked out a tiny square wafer that had been pinned to the underside of his lapel, and Johnson knew there had to be at least one more. Later, when he returned to his hotel, he would find the damned thing if he had to search all night—*if* he returned to his hotel.

He heard angry voices from the living room. Stevens was denying something. "Untrue," he was saying. What was untrue? Johnson didn't want to find out. The idea came to him that whatever he heard would be transmitted by the bug, if anyone was still listening. "*That's damn well not true, Volodny!*" No, of course not. Nothing was true.

Johnson coughed. He dried his hands and neck, and edged towards the door, listening.

"You wouldn't have believed me if I'd told you the truth."

"George, when are you going to stop acting?"

"I don't know what you're talking about."

"No?"

"I *told* you . . ."

"Your friends will be waiting for you, George."

It was like a lovers' quarrel, Johnson thought. He flushed the toilet and the noise it made seemed like a threnody for a civilization, running water broadcast across the galaxy at the speed of light.

"The fly in the ointment," Dimitrov said, greeting his return. It was a long time since he'd heard the expression. "You asked me what I was going to do. We were just discussing the point."

"So I heard," Johnson said.

"That is your function." The Russian nodded agreeably. He was still holding the tape recorder in his hand. Now he dropped it into his briefcase and wagged a finger at the reporter. "I will make a deal with you, Mr. Johnson."

"A deal?"

"Under the back of your jacket collar you will find what you have just been looking for."

Johnson twisted round miserably. He found the electronic device and gave it to Dimitrov.

"You return my property, and I will return yours. The manuscript you missed this morning—you will have it back, Mr. Johnson. You should never, never have read it."

Stevens was staring out of the window. "Get it over with, Volodny," he said.

"In a minute," the Russian said. "I want to respect the wishes of the dead and also of the living. I find the two peculiarly difficult to combine. Your property will be returned tomorrow morning, Mr. Johnson."

"Someone just walked over my grave," Stevens said.

"I will have them construct a fence in the spring." Dimitrov dipped into his briefcase. "I have a set of papers for you, George, and for you as well, Mr. Johnson. You will also notice train tickets. One way, I'm afraid, but first class. You will be met at the frontier by duly accredited agents of your government, if it is still in existence. I know that you would sooner fly, Mr. Johnson, but I do have your safety to think of. As for you, George, it has been my experience that there is nothing like a long train journey for clarifying the mind. You will stay here tonight under armed guard. The hospitality of the Lubyanka will be yours for the night, Mr. Johnson. It should be a rewarding experience for you—something to write about. Both of you will be on that train at noon tomorrow."

Vladimir Andreyevich looked from one man to the other. "And now, George," he said, "how about a drink? A Starka, for old times' sake?"

The comrade chairman stared at the dull little man before him. His gaze switched to the wall-length portrait of Feliks Dzerzhinski and back to the cassette recorder on his desk. "A delta brain wave," he said. "Remarkable."

"Yes, Comrade Chairman. If you depress the play key, you will hear it."

Yuri Andropov obeyed, and his office filled to the amplified rhythm of George Stevens' sleeping brain. "Truly remarkable," he added.

"Yes."

Yuri Vladimirovich removed his glasses, polished them, and stared at Dimitrov expectantly.

"I'd read of such cases," Vladimir Andreyevich said. "People who claim they're immune to hypnosis often make very good subjects."

"But not good agents," the chairman said.

"They may have other talents."

"For example?"

"Total recall, a photographic memory. When Stevens couldn't remember the code names, I knew that something was wrong. It was the same with the hypnosis. At first I thought that Stevens really couldn't remember any of the sessions with Owens. But when he went there first, he wasn't hypnotized. He must have remembered that."

"Perhaps they used a drug or something," the chairman said.

"It was the 'or something' that interested me," Vladimir Andreyevich said. "When I saw him in the hospital, I began to think that he was acting. Not the signals that the EEG machine picked up, he couldn't have faked those—but the hypnosis, yes. I'm still not sure how far he was able to resist Druzula's charms or whether it was in fact some resistance that Owens had built in. George knew that something had happened to him, but he couldn't remember what. He was afraid that I would find out, and—this is the crucial point—he was even more afraid of finding out himself. But, providing he was kept in isolation, no harm could come of it."

"Total amnesia? Artificially induced psychosis that can be triggered by a brain wave?" The chairman looked at the cassette deck dubiously. "Vladimir Andreyevich, Soviet medicine, anyone's medicine, is years away from that kind of conditioning. It would have to be done surgically, with implants—electrodes in the brain." Yuri Vladimirovich had kept up on his reading.

"That's just it," Dimitrov said, "the amnesia wasn't total. That's why he told me the story about his friend Cavendish. He could remember going to see Owens but nothing thereafter. When he gave me the supposed trigger stimulus, he was trying to convince me that the treatment had failed. I knew what he was thinking of, by the way. It wasn't Rupert Brooke.''

"Cambridge," the chairman said.

"It's not important," Dimitrov said. "Put yourself in his position. What if you couldn't remember what had happened? You'd use the first thing that came into your head. Well, it just happened to be those lines from 'The Old Vicarage, Grantchester.'''

"And yet he knew I was the intended victim," the chairman said.

"Certainly." Vladimir Andreyevich, who didn't want to detract from the chairman's prestige, lied safely and dutifully. "But tomorrow you will be in Red Square and he will be on the frontier."

The chairman glanced at a folder on his desk. "Tomorrow's arrangements are rather complex," he said. "Why?"

"Stevens has to have a chance," Vladimir Andreyevich said. "I want to see which way he breaks."

"You think he will?"

"One way or the other, yes. Especially when he finds out that Carlo was Philby's controller."

"Which he was not," the chairman said.

Vladimir Andreyevich was silent. The controller's identity was unknown to him. He had no need to know, and it was not even something he wanted to find out.

"He'll want proof," the chairman said.

"We're working on that."

"You and Kron?"

"Yes. He told me that Clemens recruited Philby in Vienna. During the war he was ordered to open negotiations with the West. Covertly, of course. Also during the war Carlo sent George Stevens right to Clemens, or so it seems. If I were George, I'd want to know why."

"You're going to suggest that it was Philby's idea?"

"Something like that. I want George to make the connections for himself first. Then we'll see."

"Remarkable," said the chairman again, "most remarkable. Comrade Dimitrov, you have turned everything round!"

Vladimir Andreyevich acknowledged the truth of this statement with a yawn. "Comrade Chairman," he said, "it has been a long day, and tomorrow will be even longer. . . ."

"Of course, of course. You are going home now?"

"No, I still have one or two things to do." Vladimir Andreyevich looked at his watch. It was nearly midnight.

The comrade chairman accompanied him to the door, shaking him by the hand. "Your action has been quite pivotal, Comrade Colonel. Or should I say Comrade General?"

Vladimir Andreyevich disengaged his hand. "It isn't finished yet," he said. "You see, I do not know whether George Stevens is the devil or the devil's apprentice."

"And which is the lesser of two evils, Comrade?" Yuri Vladimirovich enquired.

"Judge for yourself, Comrade Chairman." Dimitrov stood in the doorway and yawned again. "It's an old Georgian folktale," he said. "A boy is apprenticed to the devil, and when he has learnt all that he can from his master, he wants to go out into the world and try his tricks there. But it is not so easy to leave the devil's service, Comrade Chairman. The devil catches the boy and locks him up in a dark barn, so the apprentice changes into a mouse and escapes through a crack from which he has seen a ray of sunlight enter his prison. The devil pursues him as a cat, and when the mouse changes into a fish, the cat changes into a net to land the fish. But the fish changes into a pheasant, the net into a falcon to kill the pheasant, the pheasant into an apple in the tsar's lap, and the falcon into a knife in the tsar's hand, ready to peel and slice the apple. Once again the apprentice changes, this time to a heap of millet in the tsar's courtyard. A hen and her chicks, the devil's brood, peck at the millet, but they are not quick enough to prevent the last grain from changing into a needle. The devil is clever and threads himself like the poor fellow he is through the eye of the needle—but the needle bursts into flames and burns the thread to ashes. Then the devil's apprentice reverts to his original shape and goes home free. . . .

"Good night, Comrade Chairman."

Yuri Vladimirovich watched him walk down the corridor, the strangest little man, who, for some unaccountable reason, smelled of civet.

He returned to his desk and was lured irresistibly to the window, where he drew open the curtains, the tidy white curtains of the Lubyanka, and lost himself in contemplation of the thirty-six-foot-high statue of Feliks Dzerzhinski, to whom he was such a worthy successor.

INTERMEZZO

From
the Stevens
Papers

In the summer of 1939, before he left England forever, Anthony St. Clair decided that I should also go on my travels and secured a place for me in the New York brokerage house of Perkins, Fischer, and O'Shea, who were impressed by the modern uses of ancient Greek. This was how I came to know old Amos Perkins and his daughter Louisa, who was to become my wife and intimate stranger in 1942. I had met her first in the summer of 1936, when she was "finishing" Europe before Adolf Hitler completed the job. She seemed to me then, at the captious age of eighteen, to represent an enlightened and a different breed of woman, more exotic than the chiffonaded blooms of my youth, who approached sex as they would afternoon tea, diaphanously. "It ain't lettuce, that's for sure," Louisa had declared at our first encounter. Nor was it love, but I could find no fault in her and looked forward to seeing her again.

Old Amos, as he was called in imitation of his father, a relic from the pioneering days of the Robber Barons, could not have been more than fifty, yet his opinions, manners, and dress were those of a bygone age. He was an isolationist, a believer in manifest destiny and unlicensed liberty, who swore that U. S. Grant had been a great president and Calvin Coolidge "God's veritable gift to these United States." Franklin Roosevelt he spoke of as would any Salem preacher the devil. Louisa's father, then, like mine, was a capitalist; unlike mine, he was successful, an American capitalist, moreover, in whom the accident of birth compounded the vice of nature. He was an honest bigot, dividing his prejudices equally and democratically between the Jews and the Catholics, though business, in the somnambulistic persons of Fischer and O'Shea, bade him forbear a little. The same instinct moved him to support the German-American Bund, despite his cordial detestation of the Nazi government, which he thought *arriviste*. Adolf Hitler he excepted, regarding him as a kind of male Jeanne d'Arc from the other side of the Rhine, a simple peasant soul given to visions. Under his tutelage, so Amos argued, Germany would keep the peace; the peace was good for business, and what was good for business was good for the USA—arguable assumptions all.

In August 1939, a couple of months after my twenty-first birthday, I had my first encounter with Manfred Ritter, the agent subsequently known to me throughout most of his operational career as Shelley. We met at a Bund function, a social evening in the Perkinses' Long Island residence, and Manfred was introduced to me as a machinist employed by the Douglas Radio Company of Manhattan. He was about my age, medium build, stocky, blond, and rather exacting in his conversation. When he understood that I was my father's son, recently arrived from Cambridge, he began to question me on the English political scene, about which he was remarkably well informed. I remember saying that my father's dedication to the Mosleyite cause was more sentimental than realistic, a defensive opinion that Manfred used to score a debating point. "Empires," he said, "are founded on sentiment." A curious remark for a man who claimed to be a machinist by profession.

"And violence," I replied, thinking it was a clever rejoinder.

He recognized the line. " 'Sentiment and violence, the envoys of divide and rule.' Surely Peat must have been your tutor?"

He must have seen something in my expression, for he claimed to have read Carlo's book on Manichaeism, *Mani: Father of Grandeurs and Prince of Darkness*, which had just then come out and had excited some comment in the American press: THIRD-CEN-

TURY WIZARDS NAZIS OF THEIR DAY, ENGLISH PROF. SAYS. But it wasn't the headlines that interested me.

"The heresy of malcontents," Ritter said, "though it was established as the state religion of the Uighur Turks."

"Yes," I said. "Their khan was given a Chinese title and princess, a case of violence and sentiment in alliance."

We drank to the thought.

During the few days that remained to me in America (a week and a half; we lived, or thought we did, at a frenetic pace, while the same headlines abandoned third-century wizards for twentieth-century war clouds), I did a lot of drinking with Manfred, who in a moment of vinous confidentiality confessed that he was an Abwehr agent looking for recruits. England had nothing to offer me; I was not even born there; Germany would win—would I join?

The test had been arranged by Carlo, who was already making his approach. It was my first experience of double agentry, for which I discovered I had a hitherto-unsuspected talent. I did not enquire too deeply into its source but, with the apocalypse just around the corner, played factitious bait to a German carp. Heady days! Manfred even gave me an Abwehr code number, A3517. It was something I would remember when that *Ic/Abwehroffizier*, whose name was Clemens, turned me loose in the rue des Saussaies in January 1944.

Socrates, when a stranger observed that his face revealed every kind of vileness and lust, replied simply, "You know me, sir!" I could not have known how Carlo worked, though I soon found out when I returned to England. Nor could I possibly have known that thirty-four years later, acting at Carlo's request and on my own behalf, I would turn Shelley over to the Russians.

Some obtuse logic made me book a passage on the *Athenia*, her last complete crossing before she was torpedoed on 3 September. Louisa (a friendly alien) followed in October to renew our personal war, which led to marriage three years later (the Unification of George and Louisa) and divorce in 1950 (the Dissolution of George and Louisa). Something must have happened in between.

I joined the service in January 1940, Carlo playing the role of best man at this wedding as he would at the later one. But he was also active in the guise of Pandarus, and, as with any pimp, blackmail was one of his stocks in trade. For Manfred Ritter (technically an enemy alien) had also followed me across the Atlantic. I had been royally set up.

Carlo, at the age of thirty-one, still had his hair, was not fat, knew everything about the seamy side of classical life, more than everything about split-minded religions, and was an authority on Chinese well architecture of the late Han period. I thought that he meant to develop the Abwehr connection, but Carlo had other ideas. It just wouldn't *do*, would it, to let everyone *know* that I'd joined the other firm first. I protested that I'd merely been playing Ritter along. Carlo puckishly remarked that I might have trouble proving this. His appeal to me was based on reason, he said. Whether I liked it or not, I had joined the Friends, exacting employers who demanded implicit obedience. In return, they guaranteed my security, material well-being, and life. The last commodity was insured for a tidy sum, default resulting in cancellation—of the insured party.

"Meanwhile we have a war to fight. But don't worry, you'll be going to the country."

And so to the country I went, far from the crowds and corpse heaps of Europe.

By 1951 the consensus in SIS was that the war had been a mistake: the wrong fight at the wrong time against the wrong enemy. In war as in love, hindsight multiplies the illusion of choice. One faction in the secret service believed we should have taken on Uncle Joe, another that Uncle Sam was the real threat. Carlo made a typical observation on this sad state of affairs. He said it reminded him of Xenophon's asking the oracle to which gods he should offer sacrifice before setting out on the Persian expedition. The oracle replied, "The appropriate gods."

The Korean War gave both factions enough to debate, and it soon became obvious that there were those who had long ago decided the colour of their votive offerings. On Friday, 25 May, occurred the mad, bad, and outrageously funny flight of Burgess and Maclean, via the midnight ferry from Southampton to St.-Malo and thence overland to Moscow. Maclean was under surveillance at the time (his interrogation had been scheduled for the following Monday), but his bowler-hatted surveyors, who thought it bad form to work over the weekend, had last seen him boarding the 5:19 from Charing Cross to

Sevenoaks. Don-Don, it seemed, was returning to the domestic hearth, so the Plods did likewise, retiring to hang up their hats over a pint of bitter in the local. Guy Burgess, meanwhile, was anxiously awaiting his brother-in-arms at Sevenoaks station. The two drove to supper with Maclean's wife, then off to the coast for the ferry. There was a touching little scene at Southampton, where they were in such a hurry to board the ship that they left their car door open. A docker drew attention to this from the quayside, and Burgess answered with a cry that has since become legendary among the Friends: "Back on Monday!"

Someone had tipped them off; there was a traitor among the Friends. I do not know if Carlo was the first to suspect Kim, but he made no secret of his suspicions to me. When I asked why he thought it was Kim, his reply was succinct: "Because he has permission to deal with the Russians." Then he added obliquely, "You must know by now that there comes a time when the actions of a loyal agent, however you look at them, are indistinguishable from those of a traitor. There's nothing I can do."

The age of the common man and his grand vizier, the TV reporter, was dawning. Macmillan himself, blustering, would soon detect the winds of change and (after Suez!) put the ship of state about, tacking before the storm. Poor Britannia, what a sorry image she cut in those years, beset on every quarter by mewling histrios who had learnt their art from the mother Parliament. Liberation, freedom, *uhuru*—these were the slogans that rang out on the distant African shore of my birth, where the white gave way to the black, one regime to another. We watched, bemused, horrified, or merely indifferent, as the best of men went down to the worst, our own politicos gibbering of progress and reform. "You've never had it so good." Macmillan's *dixit* made the masses enthusiastic while little men with provincial minds aired their views on culture and the cloak of dullness fell over all. But treason and conspiracy were abroad, and the greatest of scandals lurked in the wings of the political stage, a sordid tale of Venus and Mars cast in the persons of a society tart and the British minister of war.

Kim Philby left for the cedars of the Lebanon in September 1956, with a cover job as a correspondent for *The Observer* and *The Economist*. He was still on the books, still had permission, and for the next few years drank his way round the bars of the Middle East. It was now that things started to get operatic, in the *guerre des bouffons* sense. On Christmas Day, 1960, an agent with the self-styled code name Heckenschütze walked into the American Zone of West Berlin. He was Lieutenant Colonel Michal Goleniewski of Polish Army Intelligence, and over the last couple of years he had given more than two hundred low-grade KGB field operatives to the CIA. Goleniewski (or Sharpshooter, as he called himself after the woodsman who made a pact with the devil in Johann August Apel's Gothic tale *Der Freischütz*) had enough information to sink a Soviet spy of some nine years' standing who was then working out of the Friends' Olympia Station offices. This was George Blake, later to escape from Wormwood Scrubs and a forty-two-year prison sentence in October 1966. Goleniewski also had more bad news for the Friends: Harold Adrian Russell Philby was a Soviet deep-penetration agent of some thirty years' standing. Worse, his controller (KGB operational code name Nemo) had a hot line through to the recruiter (KGB operational code name Niemand), who was a senior officer in a Warsaw Pact service. Proof? Sharpshooter's credentials would have been enough but for one curious fact. For as well as himself, Michal Goleniewski also claimed to be the tsarevitch Alexis Nikolaevich Romanov, heir to the throne of all the Russias. So, while the CIA took their callipers to his skull and measured his nose and the space between his ears, the Friends muddled through, assured in their belief that all the world was a club ordained by their Heavenly Friend (who would one day call them to the Heavenly Club) as a bastion against the legions of the unwashed and unworldly, and no one listened to Lieutenant Colonel Michal Goleniewski, no one except Carlo Peat and the CIA.

Carlo sent me to Beirut in January 1963. It was his opening move. The dreamtime of an operation was over and he was preparing the infiltration itself. It would take another five years before he secured the final clearance, and I, too, became a man with permission. Vladimir Andreyevich made his approach early in 1968, humbly, like one who brings the apostolic succession. I knew what had to be done, unlike the gentlemen league of players. Our East German network was there for the taking, anonymous, drab, mercenary men. If I was going to be hanged, it might as well be for a sheep as for a lamb.

"Double agents mean double the trouble," Carlo was wont to say in his saner moments, like one of Hecate's sistren mixing the brew. I look on him without rancour, a man deceived by his own alchemy. Everything was prepared — how could it have gone wrong? But that is the story of another marriage and another defeat:

> Seesaw, Margery Daw,
> Jacky shall have a new master;
> Jacky must have but a penny a day,
> Because he can work no faster.

Part Three PEAT

Some truths there are so near and
obvious to the mind that a man need
only open his eyes to see them.
—GEORGE BERKELEY, bishop of Cloyne,
Principles of Human Knowledge

16

Cryptographia

Shadows slanted down the attic roof of Carlo's study, casting the walls and floors into zones of darkness. It was a foul night outside. Rain attacked the casement window, and the branches of the old elm trailed against the frangipane surface of the leaded glass. Tranquility ruled inside. The cat Blotter lapped its milk, the gas fire whispered in cryptic tongues, and the calendrical clock chimed the half hour: six-thirty p.m., 7 November. The cat answered with a strange cry, like that of a muted telephone ring. "C'm here, Blotter. C'm here. . . ." Carlo tracked the animal as it pounced, advancing and retreating with domesticated savagery, on a crumpled ball of paper, the telex that only yesterday had brought news of Soper's death. "Where'd you find that, Blotter?" But the cat tired of its game and sprang to the window ledge, where it tapped a paw at the watery outlines of the tree. "Nice puss, nice kitty," Carlo murmured, standing up slowly and painfully to retrieve the telex.

The memento mori still clenched in his fist, he lingered under the portrait of Sir John Dee and stared at his books. Leather-bound hoplites they seemed, rank on serried rank closing for the last stand, strong-thewed guardians of the pass. "*Quis separabit?*" he enquired of the portrait. It did not answer, and Carlo flapped his hands and shrugged. "Old Fork Chops," he muttered, turning to the photographs. His own gaze stared back at him from the past, donnish, mild, good-natured. There was George, pipe in mouth, dressed for cricket according to the custom of the country. That must have been in '37. There, too, was Miles Cavendish—dead now; and David Sweet, still alive but thinner than ever; and, yes, Soper. Another generation; '63 that must have been.

Carlo remembered the telex and was suddenly conscious of the cat's unblinking stare. What thoughts did it have, what dark red thoughts lay buried in its tiny skull? "*Prr!*" he mimicked, throwing the telex into the wastepaper basket. A killing machine, he thought, but grown old and fat like myself. The clock, it would need winding. "*Fiat lux!*" Carlo declared, and switched on the light by the door. Some of Blotter's fur had caught on the astrolabe and moved, frond-like, in the air currents. A dusting was in order, a cleansing of the old stable. For some moments, his hand poised, he seemed on the verge of picking up a feather duster that lay on the marble mantelpiece, but the hand itself distracted him. The skin was old and mottled, and, like a palimpsest, was scribbled over with veins. Carlo nipped the flesh between the tendons. A bruise-coloured welt formed and was a long time subsiding.

Carlo seated himself at his desk and began searching for the key to the clock. A copy of Erman's *Ägypten und ägyptisches Leben in Altertum* (Tübingen, 1885) lay unopened on the desk next to the Underwood typewriter. Next to this stood a battered portmanteau with a box of .45 cartridges and a Webley service revolver. What foolishness, he thought.

He found the key and recrossed the room. Clocks and devil's work are mechanical, he thought. Why had Soper exceeded his instructions? Seize the day, but put no trust in tomorrow. That was well said, but there was no use in bringing owls to Athens. The clock spring tightened against the turning key. There was a numbness in Carlo's fingers and he let the key drop to the floor. He peered at great Caesar's sightless head.

"Well?"

Great Caesar spoke. "I love treason but hate the traitor."

Carlo liked code names, for their aptness or otherwise. Hariton, used to designate Kirill Aleksandr Tyulenev, the colonel who had supplied information on the Soviet military space program, had pleased him enormously. In Gurdjieff's cosmic myth, *All and Everything: Beelzebub's Tales to His Grandson*, Hariton was an archangel who had devised a new type of spaceship for interplanetary travel. Hariton broke the rule that a code name should not refer to its subject, however obliquely. So did Avatar, the code name for Stefan Komarowski, the military-intelligence officer who had been with the Free Polish Air Force during the war—it sounded too much like "aviator." But Carlo had let them go because he liked them.

He had been surprised by the manuscript, which had arrived thirty-four days ago, two days before George's funeral. There was no question of its authenticity, and Carlo was pleased to note that, for the most part, George had lied by telling the truth. That, too, was a surprise: George Stevens was not a particularly intelligent man, unlike Carlo, who was. But when he came to the list of agents, he realized that Hariton had been the contact not of Importer but of Insect and that George had made some other changes as well.

Despite his unkempt appearance, Carlo was a methodical man. He made the first list:

MS Code Name	Date of Arrest (or Disappearance)	Real Code Name
AVATAR	6.8.70	AVATAR
BABY	5.9.68	BABY
CONCH	30.12.69	CONCH
DUMBO	10.9.70	DUMBBELL
EKKA	7.4.71	ERMINE
FEY FERN	8.9.73	FERN
GRUMBLE	23.10.73	GRIFFIN
HARITON	4.6.72	HARITON
IMPORTER	6.8.73	INSECT
SHELLEY	8.5.73	JELLY

Even if the Russians had known the real code names, George's list was close enough to allow any number of reasons for the discrepancies: stress, confusion, a faulty memory, difficulties in translation and transliteration. But they hadn't known the real code names, and since the dates were undoubtedly correct, there was no reason per se why the manuscript list should have attracted their attention. Except, of course, that George did not have a faulty memory. Everyone knew that. It was one of the few things about him that people did know.

Carlo made another list, or rather two. It was very simple. In the first series he found the corresponding letters for the days and months. Hence in column A the sixth letter was F, the eighth, H; in column B the fifth letter was K, the ninth, M, and so on. All he did was find the appropriate letters for the dates of the arrests, moving across and down the columns:

First Series

	A	B	C	D	E		Day and	Month
1.	A	V	A	T	A R		6	8
2.	B	A	B	Y			5	9
3.	C	O	N̲	C	H		30 (3)	12 (3)
4.	D	U	M	B	O̲		10	9
5.	E	K̲	K	A			7	4
6.	F̲	E	Y	F	E R N			
7.	G	R	U	M	B̲ L E			
8.	H̲	A	R	I	T O N			
9.	I	M̲	P	O	R T E R			
10.	S	H	E	L̲	L E Y			

A6-8 = FH; B5-9 = KM; C3-3 = NN; D10-9 = LO; E7-4 = BO

The first series would have been enough for a computer to find the key, if the cypher were consistent, which it was, up to a point. In the second series Carlo repeated the procedure for columns A to D. Because the code name Shelley broke the alphabetical sequence that had existed in the original list, he reverted here to column A, day 8 (the day of Shelley's arrest), giving the eighth letter, H. Then he moved into column B for letter 5 (the month of the arrest), which gave him K.

Second Series

	A	B	C	D	E			Day and Month	
1.	A	V	A	T	A	R			
2.	B	A	B	Y					
3.	C	O	N	C	H				
4.	D	U	M	B	O				
5.	E	K	K	A					
6.	F	E	Y	F	E	R	N	8	9
7.	G	R	U	M	B	L	E	23 (5)	10
8.	H	A	R	I	T	O	N	4	6
9.	I	M	P	O	R	T	E	R 6	8
10.	S	H	E	L	L	E	Y	8	5

A8-9 = *HI*; B5-10 = *KH*; C4-6 = *MY*; D6-8 = *FI*; A8-B5 = *HK*

The last couplet was supremely illogical, but that was George. Carlo then ran the two series together to form the cyphertext: *FH KM NN LO BO HI KH MY FI HK*. He knew from its appearance that he was dealing with a monoalphabetic substitution cypher. According to the principle of the most frequently recurring letter, cyphertext *H*, which occurred four times, would probably represent plaintext E, if the language were English; and cyphertext *K*, which occurred three times, plaintext T, the second most frequently recurring letter in English. But the language, as Carlo knew, was not English.

A relatively simple, if tedious, process of decrypting would have given him the solution, but Carlo was able to save himself much time and trouble by adding up the years and decades for a figure of 711. Moving the decimal two points west gave him 7.11 and the key to the cypher. All that remained was to transpose each cyphertext letter forwards by seven places in the plaintext alphabet (George had used the English, not the Latin, alphabet), counting an extra place for the cyphertext *Y*, where the transposition ran over the end of the plaintext alphabet—presumably George's idea of a trip for electronic scanning machines:

> *FH KM NN LO BO HI KH MY FI   HK*
> MO RT UU SV IV OP RO TE MP OR (E)

Mortuus, vivo pro tempore
Dead, I live for the time being

But that was just the beginning of Carlo's problems. A month ago the simplicity of the cypher had appealed to him. No more. It had really been too *clever* of George (it was one of his favourite words), far too clever, and Carlo knew that the cypher must have been read. Which meant that Poetry had been turned, and someone was going to try to kill him.

The clock was striking seven when David Sweet entered the study. He wore a sheepskin coat and a fur hat, neither of which sat well on his lanky frame, and, for all the wool, looked as though he had just been shorn and dipped. Tears of rain glistened on his cheeks. His complexion was its customary grey. "Everything's ready," he said.

"Oh, yes." Carlo interpreted Sweet's statement as a question. "Mrs. Wodehouse has agreed to look after the cats."

"Mrs. Wodehouse?" Sweet feared some bookishness.

"The cleaning lady."

The car was waiting to take them to the airport, Sweet said. He watched Carlo pick up the heavy service revolver and spin the cartridge cylinder. Carlo dropped the gun and ammunition into his portmanteau, sealing the clasps with an abstracted air.

"I hate flying," Sweet said.

"It can't be helped," Carlo said, reaching for his raincoat.

In silence the two men walked the corridor and in silence crossed the quadrangle. O conspiracy, Carlo thought, Russian nights are longer.

Not until later, when they were among the clouds and their course set for the Skagerrak, did he speak. "I've been thinking," he said, "and do you know what I've come up with, David? A limit to God's omnipotence. He can't alter the past, God can't."

And Sweet, a cautious man, regarding him through half-closed eyes, said, "As far as you know."

17

Past
and
Present
Friends

On the Sunday that George Michael Stevens was being buried in Moscow, Philip Bentinck sat in his room in the Foreign Office and listened to Carlo Peat. Bentinck enjoyed the Foreign Office, a solid building of marbled vistas, sweeping staircases, long corridors, and Venetian porticos. It pleased him that Sir Gilbert Scott's first essay in Gothic had been rejected, at Palmerston's insistence, in favour of the eventual Italianate design. This suited the Machiavellian temperaments of both lords (a hereditary viscount out of Ireland, a Labour life peer out of London's East End), though gone were the days when a British foreign secretary or his servants could hope to influence matters of design.

Bentinck was the FO adviser, whose lot it was to mediate between the Foreign Office and the Friends, subjecting some of their more quixotic schemes to the light of pure reason. He was a lugubrious, ugly man, with sleek hair and smooth, olivine skin. He did not enjoy sacrificing his Sundays, especially to men like Peat, who made him conscious of certain class distinctions that the party of his choice sought to eradicate. But Peat was an old man and surely not a threat. Or was he? Bentinck wondered. He was always telling himself that he had one disqualification for this job. He was too intelligent, though he had learnt to say little and delay everything. Sometimes he was forced to act; for example, at the beginning of last month when David Sweet had come to see him with an amazing story of brainwashing, an assassination plot, and a hypnodontist called Owens. This time the Friends or the Enemies had really overstepped the mark. Someone had even anticipated his action (he had no idea who—no one had), firing off a telex to Moscow authorizing the resident to negotiate Stevens' release. Forgery.

"You must have had clearance, ministerial authority?"

"Your predecessor," Carlo said. "He gave us that."

"Basil Callwell. A personal friend, was he not?"

Carlo observed a moment's silence. "Yes," he said.

"I suppose there's nothing on file?"

"Very little. You could say it was an ad hoc arrangement—initially."

"Set a traitor to catch a traitor. An old ploy."

Carlo did not reply.

"But 'initially' you didn't think it was Stevens?"

"I beg your pardon?"

"Last year, and for several years previously, you didn't think the traitor was Stevens? In fact, you thought it was Ritter."

"Well, it was plausible."

"Quite so. You realize how this is going to look?"

"Awkward."

"Ah, yes," the adviser purred. "And now Stevens is dead. Is there any doubt of that?"

Carlo looked at his watch. "They've just finished burying him," he said.

"Correction," Bentinck said. "They've just finished burying something."

"Do you suggest an exhumation?"

"In good time." Bentinck gave a quick smile. He tried another approach. "You'd no idea that Stevens could have been working for the Russians?"

"I didn't know then and I don't know for sure now," said Carlo, who knew that he would have to tell Bentinck about the cypher. "We were losing agents before we started. Nothing serious.

It could have been normal wastage; it could have been Kim's legacy. Carmichael was a major blow. He had all the cells, everything. Ritter was our deskman, and Sweet sent him to look into things. When he was arrested, Sweet flew to Berlin himself. Well, he found nothing and Percival committed suicide. I was much too busy with Poetry to be drawing the kind of inferences that you seem to be now."

"Poetry?"

"The code name for the Stevens infiltration. You won't find it on file. Callwell suggested that I retire to Cambridge and run things from there, so, strictly speaking, the East German network was none of my business. We had ministerial authority, as I said. I can't tell you what representations Callwell made to the minister because I don't know. Cabinet Records may have some information. The only people who knew about the operation itself were David Sweet, Basil Callwell, and Percival. George and myself, of course. Oh, there was one other person, Balthazar—Miles Cavendish. He was in at the beginning, but he didn't know very much. It was talk, that's all, just talk from the old days."

"Macpherson?"

"I don't know what he knows."

"And if you did you wouldn't tell me?"

"I meant he had no part in our discussions," Carlo said.

"Tell me about it," Bentinck said.

And tell him Carlo did.

A fumid evening, Carlo was thinking. He stared at Cavendish, who had just finished speaking, concluding his address with the word "malarkey." Balthazar was more than a little drunk, not that you would notice, not these days. He was sitting cross-legged on the floor, a tumbler of sherry in his hand. Findlater's. Sweet watched him, perched on Carlo's desk like an underweight Buddha with a moustache. Stevens lounged in the corner and tried to look bored.

They were in Carlo's old office in the Broadway building, discussing Kim Philby, who was operating in the Middle East as a field agent. That was like setting Abraham to spy on Jehovah, Carlo suggested. The wise thing would be to let the Russians know that Kim was blown, then allow them to find his successor. Better yet, find the successor for them.

"What do you think?" He turned to David Sweet.

"It won't work, Carlo."

"George?"

"I don't know. It might. . . ."

Cavendish laughed. "Our man in the Lubyanka? Oh, come on. You can't be serious. Turn on the radio, someone, for Christ's sake. Let's hear the news."

Stevens examined the dial on the old multi-wave-band Philips. The radio was housed in a wooden cabinet that made it look vaguely sepulchral, like an urn for someone's ashes, and was tuned to Radio Moscow. "Whose news?" he said.

"Ours," Cavendish said.

Carlo's office filled to the eleventh chime of Big Ben. It was 7 November 1955, an auspicious day.

"First, the continuing debate on the Burgess and Maclean affair . . ." The newscaster coughed and excused himself. "In Parliament today the foreign secretary, the Right Honourable Harold Macmillan, confirmed that Mr. Harold Philby was known to have had Communist associates during and after his university days at Trinity College, Cambridge. In view of the circumstances, he was asked to resign from his post at the Foreign Office in July of 1951. The foreign secretary also said that, while in government service, Mr. Philby had discharged his duties ably and conscientiously, and that there was no reason to conclude he had betrayed the interests of this country or to identify him with the so-called third man in the affair, if indeed there was one. However, Mr. Macmillan did say that Guy Burgess had been accommodated with Philby at the latter's house in Washington from August 1950 to April 1951, shortly before his flight to Moscow with Donald Maclean. The foreign secretary informed the House that searching and protracted investigations had been conducted into the possibility of a 'tip-off' and that they were still under way at this moment.

"Meanwhile, a government spokesman today confirmed the report of the White Paper issued last September, which—" Stevens silenced the radio, and the three men looked at Carlo.

"Our leaders vault credence," he said.

Without conviction, Cavendish said, "Suppose it's true?"

"Then I'll suppose anything," Carlo said. "How did we get Hess, remember?"

"Horoscopy." Cavendish stood up and poured himself another drink. He had reached that stage of drunkenness when the past seemed better than the present. "I fiddled that Hungarian's charts. Saturn in the tenth house. Bad lookout for Adolf." Cavendish balanced his drink on the palm of his left hand and made scrying passes with his right. "The Führer's aspect is *frighteningly* malefic. Six planets and a full moon conjoin in Taurus on the tenth of May. A mission of peace is indicated, a journey among the stars . . ."

"Hess was crazy," Sweet said.

"Maybe." Cavendish caught his drink. "But he's still alive."

"He did so *want* to believe," Carlo said.

Sweet was off the desk, prowling. In those days his moustache was too large for his face, and he brushed at it with the back of his finger. "You can do that sort of thing only once," he said. "It turned Adolf against wizards, remember? They were all locked up. Aktion Hess. Hitler's pet seer died in Buchenwald."

"This is different," Stevens said. "If you could convince the Russians that they had a replacement for Kim, well, it might work. David's right, though. It would be a one-time operation. No outs."

"And the ins?" Sweet said.

"You just heard the foreign secretary." Carlo beamed.

Sweet stared at him. "You're getting cynical in your old age," he said.

"Cynicism's just another name for experience," Carlo said.

"Bloody hell," Sweet muttered.

"I know Carlo," Cavendish said waggishly. "We all know Carlo. He wants to run the other firm. His middle name's Beria. . . ."

"Shut up, Miles," Stevens said. "That's not the reason. He wants to find Philby's controller, that's why."

"Now that's superclever, that is. Think they'd use the same man to run his successor? Not a kitten's chance in a bucket. I agree with our friend here." Cavendish indicated Sweet with a wave of his glass, which was empty again. He ambled over to the desk like a large child and placed the glass next to the bottle, where it remained, unfilled. Drinking sherry made him feel sick; agreeing with Sweet, even sicker.

"It's not kosher, you know," he said. "One thing you can bet on, the controller would go to Kim's recruiter. He'd say, 'Who is this man?' All right, let's say it's George. The recruiter would want his history, bed and breakfast companions, everything. Well, you weren't in the party at the right time, were you? But supposing you sold them a line about a change of heart. You'd never convince the FO adviser, and even if you did, there's still Kim. He knows everyone in this pond, who swims, who flounders, and who floats— all the fast fish and all the loose fish, who's bent, who's pliable, and who's straight. Then there's the question of bona fides. What would you sell them, Mickey Mouse microfilms? They'd want blood, the same as Kim gave them with that Albanian thing. *And* you'd have the Plods in Five after you. Jesus, they'd bury the lot of us."

"You're forgetting I worked for the Russians during the war," Stevens said. "Philby knows that."

"Everyone knows it, but you'll never be twice the traitor you once were." Cavendish looked enormously pleased with himself. He turned to Carlo, who had been watching owlishly. " 'I wonder if a man is less a traitor when he is twice a traitor,' " he said. "G. K. Chesterton, *The Wisdom of Father Brown*. Anyway"—he turned round again—"supposing, *just* supposing that I accept what you say. . . . Would the Russians? The black sheep returns to the fold? More like the sacrificial lamb."

"Maybe," Carlo said. "Your point about the adviser, Miles. Callwell's a friend of mine. I think I could bring him round. It's a question of the sky gods. Thunder, if you follow me."

"Meteorologically speaking, no," Cavendish said.

"Ah, well, it's like this. In Vico we read that thunder precedes the age of chaos. A learned man, Callwell, very fond of Vico . . ." Carlo lit his pipe. Poor Balthazar couldn't be so addled, not if he could pronounce the word "meteorologically" like that. "After the storm, theocracy," Carlo lectured his audience, "dictatorship divine. We live in a theocratic age, gentlemen. The gods are secular, of course—money, half-baked notions of progress, the GNP, and what have you. Democracy—I was forgetting that— an exportable item. What we need is an atheist in priest's clothing. Secretary Walsingham used them to carry letters. The sun's set on the empire, just as it did on Rome. Augustine was a Manichaean until he saw the light, and he was living in a similar age. Well, we need someone who will see the light of dialectical materialism. That covers your point about motives, Balthazar. It's never too late."

"The risks . . ." Sweet began. He didn't finish what he was saying.

"None," Carlo said. "Minimal. *We* find Kim's successor and promote him in Kim's stead. When it's expedient, we could even use him as the tip-off man. That would be a start, wouldn't it? As for the Plods in Five, they would cooperate by catching our friend, don't you see? Then we make a deal with the other side. It's all very hypothetical, of course, but it could be done. There is a difficulty, however."

"Only one?" Sweet asked.

"Two, actually." Carlo looked at his pipe, which sizzled. "Time and the man," he said.

Philip Bentinck stared at Carlo, who reminded him of a shabby schoolteacher, which in a way he was. He knew that Peat had told him some of the truth but by no means all of it. The adviser was determined not to mention Sweet's visit, not in so many words at least. Brainwashing. He wouldn't put it past Carlo—he wouldn't put anything past Carlo, murder included.

"My predecessor is dead," he mused. "Cavendish as well."

"Accidents of nature," Carlo said.

"Like Stevens, eh?" The adviser allowed himself a chortle. "This infiltration, what was the reason for it?"

"There was the thing in itself, you know," Carlo said.

"I don't." Bentinck made a cat's cradle of his hands. "But another person did."

"Really?"

"Owens." The adviser uncradled his hands.

"Ah," Carlo said. Someone had been talking.

"I know all about infiltrations," the adviser went on. "The Americans got hundreds of agents from Goleniewski, and so did we from Penkovsky till they took him away from us. So did the Russians from Philby. A thing like that, it takes half a lifetime. They would never have been satisfied with just those ten agents, never. Carmichael, Grove, the rest of our people—how many were there?"

"About fifty," Carlo said, "counting nonnationals. We retaliated, of course."

"Listen to me, Peat. We expelled their people, they killed ours.

There's the difference. The rest of our people, did you order Stevens to betray them as well? Come on, now, did you?''

Somebody had really been talking, Carlo thought. "No," he said, "but George could have done it with our best interests in mind. There comes a time when—"

"To hell with that," Bentinck said. His left arm felt as though someone were pumping air into the veins. Blood pressure. He didn't shout, didn't even raise his voice. "I know you have a confession from Stevens. Intelligent self-interest, naturally. I mean, you have to protect the flanks, don't you? You have to guard against unfavourable inferences. . . ." The adviser was reason incarnate. "But I think you should tell me what you *did* to Stevens, you and Owens. I'd be interested to hear your side of the story. Where is he, by the way, the doctor? What have you done with him?''

Philip Bentinck waited for an answer. It seemed to him then that something was hanging in the balance, something unspoken and perhaps unspeakable, as if a trapdoor had just been sprung. He could not have guessed at the prescience of this image. For Carlo was thinking of November 1918, his father, a sermon, and a rope.

"Dr. Owens is alive and well," he said, and Bentinck was disconcerted to see him smile. "So is George Stevens," Carlo added, "alive, anyway. I really think that Dr. Owens has the cure, don't you?''

18

"Dulce
et decorum
est . . ."

That year the weather was hard even for November.
A drizzle had settled in over the Norfolk coast and would later turn
to snow. Carlo would always remember this day, a day as cold and
flinty as the very fabric of his father's church, the spire of which
seemed the only vertical thing in a landscape dominated by the
horizon and sky. He would remember the righteous clustering
churchwards and the rickety gate in the churchyard wall clicking
open and shut, counting souls; the musty odour of sanctity and the
congregation humbled to coughs of quintessential piety; his father's
expression as he uttered the word "Lord," the Reverend Peat's
mouth a round black O, his eyes sealed in the deceptively
reposeful attitude of prayer, bunched sleeves crossed over the
front of his surplice like a man who was bound but not gagged,
an ordained lunatic with his arms pinioned in the folds of an
ecclesiastical straitjacket.

"Brethren," the Reverend Peat said, his voice awash over bowed
heads, "let us pray. . . ."

A sparrow twittered in the rafters, and Carlo heard a muffled
giggle from the choir as the bird dipped through the mote-flecked

light, its shadow and track followed by the choristers, whose
heads moved as one to watch it alight on the great brass eagle
that served as a lectern, their eyes turning again towards the
Reverend Peat.

"O Lord . . ."

Carlo buried his head in his jacket sleeve, chewing on the fine
worsted material of the cloth. *Worsted*, the word struck him as odd,
yet that was what it was called. He knelt close to his mother in the
foremost pew, hating the enforced ritual for his father's sake, his
father, who did not believe, could not believe in the Lord of Hosts,
whose name he was even now pronouncing, and he knew then,
though without knowing why, that this moment would remain forever
fixed and present, to be neither forgotten nor remembered but to
remain as a token of eternity. His eyes filled with tears when
he looked up. The sparrow, taking fright at his father's voice,
hopped from eagle's crest to eagle's wing and, unconstrained by
wings of burnished brass, fluttered aloft, a free and natural spirit
of the air.

Sundays had always been thus: the righteous clustering churchwards, the gate clicking open and shut, the boredom of psalms
and sermons endured until, after the service, the Reverend Peat,
nodding and smiling, shaking hands in the church porch, would
keep his wife and son close to his side, as if they were so much
human statuary and life an interminable Sunday imbued with
ceremony and sanctified gossip. Even the seasons came to possess an
all-hallowed usage, autumn and Harvest Festival declining to Advent
and peremptory goodwill to all mankind, thence, through the
lengthening of days and the chastening of the flesh, to summer's
brief, illusory freedom, every year of Carlo's young life bearing
its crop of fetes and bazaars. But their charitable intent had
grown warlike of late, alms for the poor yielding to guns for the
front. Other changes, too, were at work in the village of Carlo's
birth. The congregation of his father's church, shrinking in numbers,
increased in age, while the population of the little cemetery
swelled out of all proportion to the merely natural order of things.
But were not these fallen, these dead, transient souls? Were they
not tenants in their native clay (some of them), resting awhile
until triumphant hosannas would sound? So in the name of Christ

the Reverend Peat strove to assure the ageing, grieving remnants of his flock.

Even so did it come to pass that Harland Caisho Peat, at the age of nine, counted among his possessions four volumes of the *Boys' Own Paper*, wherein he learnt the names of Flanders' fields: Passchendaele, whose fruit was death; Messines; Polygon Wood; the Menin Road; Poelcapelle, and Ypres, which was called Wipers. Therein, too, were emblazoned the insignia of all the regiments of the imperial armies, with photographs of men and the machines of war: the lunarscape of the Sonnebeke Marshes caught in sepia halftones or the branchless trees of Remus Wood and the prisoner, smiling, content with his fate. Even so, as season ran into season and communiqué into communiqué, the massed infantry advanced on salient, pocket and flank, a generation trudging into the breach, for a hundred yards, a quarter of a mile, a half, and then—no farther. Even so there came a time to put away childish things.

"O Lord," the Reverend Peat intoned above the echo of a sparrow's song, "we give thee thanks for peace and rejoice."

And that was all.

Battle flags draped the church walls. The Great War, the war to end war, was over.

Carlo was no longer thinking of his father when he left Lord Bentinck at the Foreign Office. He had a journey to make and a bargain to seal, and much depended on the outcome of both. Owens had gone to ground next door to a Sikh temple on Terrace Road in Plaistow, a mouldering Victorian district not quite within earshot of Bow Bells. Carlo took a taxi from the FO to the Marble Arch underground, a Central Line tube from there to Stratford, and another taxi to Terrace Road. The journey, which was without incident, depressed him, as did most of London town these days.

Back in May 1973 Carlo had put it around that he needed to know how much a man like Stevens would reveal under narcoanalysis. Owens had obliged by using one of the mydriatics, the twilight-sleep inducer scopolamine, in an intravenous solution, and Carlo remembered that the good doctor had thought this unwise.

"They can tell, you know."

"Tell?"

"If this has been done before."

"Ah, but they would be expecting it. By the way, there's something else I may want you to do."

"What's that?"

"Nothing much. We'll see. . . ."

Reality is a mental act, or someone else's perception of the same. When the train surfaced in the East End, Carlo scarcely noticed the transition into daylight. *Dum-dum-dum-dum*; the motor idled in a station: East Ham. Bentinck's father had owned a bakery here. Carlo watched his fellow passengers, none of whom had boarded at Marble Arch. That was the *good* thing about travelling on Sundays, no crowds. The bad thing was that you were easily distracted.

Carlo studied the dried crust of Saturday-night vomit on the red and green pile of London Transport upholstery. Someone, perhaps the same inebriate celebrant, had scribbled "Sally sucks corns" in a black felt-tipped pen on an ad for Dr. Scholl's sandals. The train rumbled over a skeletal bridge, and Carlo stared down on the muddy waters of Barking Creek. He saw a Woolworth's store at the corner of two streets, a vista of row houses stretching into the grey distance. The cars and buses were toylike, the people matchstick figures in a dun-coloured canvas. "Bovril builds you up," proclaimed a painted sign on a factory wall. The paint had faded into the brickwork. On top of it was emblazoned a white cross in a white circle with SS lightning flashes and the legend "Niggers go home."

At the Terrace Road house Carlo enquired politely of an orange-beehive-haired lady for a Mr. Marlowe.

"You alone?" she asked.

"Yes."

"Come on up, then." She flashed her National Health dentures. "I think he's in. Don't go out much, does he?" The landlady turned, one hand on her back. "Well, actually, I *know* he's in. It's just that I thought you might have been one of them nig-nogs. Not that I'm prejudiced, mind. They're not a bad lot—apart from the feuding and that—not as bad as some. It's the curry what gets me, the *smell*."

Carlo sniffed.

"The cat's dinner," she said. "Fish, that's what I give him."

"I quite understand. That's what I give mine."

"Coo! You like cats, then?"

Carlo said that he did.

"I'd never have thought it. . . ."

Owens appeared on the landing. He was unshaven and wore carpet slippers that looked as if the cat had been at them.

"There's a gentleman here to see you," the landlady said as if it were a grievance. "He asked for you by *name*. . . ."

"That's all right, Mrs. Foulger." Owens nodded. His face was puffy and he had bags under his eyes, a debauched look that made Carlo wonder if he had been drinking. Tea, probably. The Welshman was teetotal.

"It's not a bad place," he said, closing the door to his room. "Once you get used to the smell."

"Fish or curry?"

"Both," said Owens dourly.

He moved to the window and drew aside the curtain. "She says the cat's her only friend," he murmured, "since her husband died. I've had all that from her, you know. Died of cancer, he did. Cancer of the bowels. The doctor said, 'Mrs. Foulger, we'll just have to unbung him.' That's what she told me. But they couldn't—unbung him, I mean. So he died." Owens' gaze flickered over the bay-fronted houses on the other side of the street and lingered on an old Riley that had been parked outside for weeks and was slowly decomposing as if it were biodegradable. "Did you see that car?" Owens spoke again, his head bowed. "They must have abandoned it. Just rotting, it is . . ."

It was half past three, a jaded and desultory time, and the street was empty. Owens was glad it was a Sunday because it meant that the children wouldn't be coming home from school at four. They had vanished, probably to the park nearby. Owens detested them. Weekdays at four, he seldom moved from this spot, expecting at any moment to see a stranger approach one of the kids and, looking up at the window, begin asking questions. He'd rehearsed the scene so often that he had it down to its finest details: the children gathering round with a knowing innocence, a seriousness that befitted this adult game of hide and seek; the angle of their interlocutor's head as he stole another glance at the house, his deferential, cajoling manner, even the words he spoke: "I think a friend of mine lives here, sonny. Do you know him? A bald-headed fellow, a Welshman."

Owens knew this for what it was, a neurotic piece of trickery, as if the encounter he dreaded could be forestalled by an imaginative act of the will. Now, as he turned from the window, his face sallow in the fading afternoon light, he sensed that the ritual of avoidance had worked and that he would not have to gaze out on Terrace Road for very much longer. It was nothing to rejoice about. For there came another realization, too, the thought that Carlo's presence, so ordinary and English, brought with it something of the unknown, something menacing and ineffable, like a child's fear of God. Owens, who failed to locate the source of this irrational fear, sought to exorcise it through a series of rationalizations. The news of George Stevens' death had shocked him, for as a physician he had known that there was nothing wrong with the man. He felt somehow guilty, implicated. His nerves were frayed. He had been out of touch for too long. It was the waiting. Ten months of Terrace Road and Mrs. Foulger—that was enough to drive anyone berserk. There was really nothing to fear.

"I've just come from the Foreign Office," Carlo said. "His lordship was asking about you."

"What is it?" Owens stiffened. "What's happened?"

"You haven't been to see him, have you?"

"I've never even met the man. Wouldn't know what he looks like. What's wrong?"

"Nothing," Carlo said. "The adviser thinks you should go to Moscow. Ah, Poetry—the final phase: 'The grave's a fine and private place,/But none, I think, do there embrace.'"

Owens sat down on the bed. "Stevens," he said, "he's alive, isn't he?"

Carlo nodded. He did not sit down but watched Owens closely. "When do you want me to go?" the doctor asked.

"Tomorrow," Carlo said. "I'll arrange a car—and diplomatic coverage, of course. The Moscow resident will be in touch after you arrive. Reggie Soper. I think you'll get along. You'll be safer there, in Moscow."

"Funny, that."

"Yes."

Something glittered in Carlo's hand. It was a cassette recorder, smaller than the commercial kind, and he placed it carefully on the bedside table.

"Give this to Soper," he said.

It was eight o'clock by the time he arrived back in Cambridge and settled into his rooms. *"Quid nunc?"* He turned to great Caesar's sightless head, which maintained its bland equipoise. "Sharpshooter," Carlo muttered, and a Siamese cat miaowed. "What are you trying to tell me, mm? If only you could *talk* . . ."

He reached for the phone and hesitated before making the call. A black Mark X Jaguar had been parked outside the college on his return, and he had mentally photographed the license plate. The Plods, they probably had a tap on his phone. They'd be using Bentleys next, like Macpherson himself. Bentinck must have called him about Stevens. It was nice to know how their minds worked, Carlo thought. He dialled and waited for Hasketh to answer. Newspapermen had their uses. "Peat here," he said. "About this Stevens thing. I know there's a D notice out, but . . ." It was Platonic in its way. Disembodied speech.

Hasketh wanted to know if the line was secure.

"I've paid my bills," Carlo said. "Listen, I received a literary property a couple of days ago. Would you like to see it?"

"What are you talking about?"

"It's by a friend of mine, Terry."

"Who?"

"He's recovering from a nasty illness. Serious, but not so bad as you would think from the headlines. He's abroad at the moment. His doctor's a friend of mine, too."

"Why are you telling me this?"

"Pro bono publico. Do you want to see it?"

"I'll think about it," Hasketh said, and hung up.

Carlo listened to the neural buzz of the receiver. He replaced it and thought of snakes and ladders. Uncle Alex had given him a set, his first game, and he could see it now, vivid in bold Edwardian reds and greens. Uncle Alex was his mother's brother, a naval colleague of Mansfield Cumming's, the founder of the service—C.

He inspected the veins on the back of his hands. Joseph Saragoza, the Sicilian Cabbalist, had conjectured that such phenomena were susceptible to hidden meanings. The name of God, maybe, was concealed in the superficial scrawl of the digital veins. Carlo had once thought of refuting this with the argument that an infinite God would not reveal Himself through finite attributes.

World, time, and Spinoza had intervened. Also Uncle Alex. That a game of snakes and ladders should serve as Carlo's introduction to the crepuscular world of secret agents was surely the act of some jesting deity, most unlike the dignified, gaitered God of his father. Carlo was fastidious; he was urbane. With a certain vanity, perhaps, he looked upon himself as a lazy man, sometimes, he thought, the laziest on earth. When work threatened, as it did now, he day-dreamed. This contemplative state he honoured with a formula, seductive and imprecise, like all of its kind: Minimum fuss equals maximum security.

There were times when this formula had been sorely tried. During the war, as director of Black Propaganda, an officially nonexistent department, Carlo had used the occasional corpse. They were employed for a variety of unwholesome purposes: one of the Reich Defence commissioners, inspecting a fireproof bombshelter, would be confronted with grisly proof of its inadequacy; a prominent official of the Vichy regime, on retiring for the night, would find a dead German corporal in his bed—just as the authorities arrived at his door. These tactical forays were supple-mented by larger, strategic exercises. In order to alert the Abwehr to the *Schwerpunkt* of the Allied invasion, the Friends had polluted the Mediterranean with a dead flying officer. One more wouldn't make much difference, but this flying officer was carrying a letter from General Sir Archibald Nye, vice-chief of the Imperial General Staff, hinting that Sardinia was the jumping-off point for the second front.

Experiment: War Department ink (*Atramentum belicosum*) was applied through a WD pen (*Stylus b.*) to WD paper (*Papyrus b.*), which was then sprinkled with a phial of seawater (*Aquamarina mare internum*). Result: secret plans unreadable to the enemy. Recommendation: Strongly advise that a dead flying officer on such a mission would be carrying his letters in a *waterproof* pouch.

Memories . . . The dead flying officer's boots wouldn't fit because his feet were too cold and stiff.

"I can't bend them," Cavendish said. "They'd break if I did."

"What a shame. He'd look odd without boots."

"Perhaps the force of the impact?"

"From a submarine?"

"But they don't know that. We *hope* they don't."

"Try to warm his feet on the fire."

"That's not very hygienic. He's going back into the freezer, you know."

"Yes, but it might work."

The whole project had worked, despite the civilian powers who had insisted that the next of kin sign release papers on the deceased's behalf, a bureaucratic nicety that had the effect of making corpses hard to come by at a time of plentiful supply. Hence it became the lot of young Hasketh (press-ganged from Fleet Street) to soften the heart of the most obdurate mourner, securing the loved one's mortal remains with appeals to higher sentiments. If it was sweet and fitting to die for one's country, how much more sweet and fitting to be of service *post mortem*. Carlo, who should have known, even went so far as to compare such undying patriotism with Christ's supreme oblation, which had nourished all mankind, Judas Iscariot excepted.

After the inevitable triumph of democratic nescience, Hasketh had retired to civilian life, to be called on from time to time in the public interest. His newspaper had denied that Philby was a Soviet agent, as it had that Greville Wynne was a British one. Contrariwise, the guilt of George Blake, Gordon Lonsdale, and George Michael Stevens had been openly proclaimed. It distressed Carlo that he had been forced to use the good offices of his old friend yet again, and he thought of the ever-widening ripples caused by a pebble cast into a pond. Carlo wanted a much greater splash. What was the word? *Tsunami*, a tidal wave. He made another phone call, to a lady—Dorothy Winters—and this time he heard the tap go on. Click-click. Yes, there was something he wanted to discuss but not over the phone. Lunch would be an excellent idea, the next time he was in town. Alternatively, he would call on her after work. No, he couldn't say when. Soon. How was the major general? Irritable. Ah, well, that was to be expected.

Carlo rang off, and his eye caught the list of code names in George's manuscript, native spies and the spies within, the spies who had returned. The intelligence services of the world depended on such agents, who, if they excelled in anything, excelled only in negative capability. Allegiance was meaningless to them; they gave little and expected everything in return. They were used now, finished because George had betrayed them, as he had other spies, spies who would not return. He had also used them as a cypher, and cyphers they were. What did that make him? Alive, he was dead, and dead, alive—neither a spy of life nor a spy of death, a marginal case. But then he had been washed up for years, since 1944.

Time was when the human element had counted for something. Not anymore; there was no honour left in the world. All the old friends were dead. Carlo would have preferred a more ascetic life. In his next incarnation he would avoid the service. Its old-boy chumminess bored him, the flag-waving also. Its backbiting was contagious; its quest for information amounted to motiveless greed. Yet his own life, he was forced to admit, had been equally without motive. He had become an intelligence officer by chance and a classicist by default, for his first and enduring love was for the languages and people of China. At Winchester, his public school, he had made do with the German orientalists, Franke, Grube, and Wilhelm, sinology not then being a subject of wide regard in the United Kingdom. By dint of a special, if minor, interest, he was a recognized authority on the well architecture of the later Han Dynasty. The more visible aspects of the culture he thought unworthy of a great civilization. Nor, with one or two exceptions, was he especially fond of Chinese thought. Confucius he considered (as had Plato his Cynic opponent, Antisthenes) an old man who had learnt late. As for Lao-tzu, he was a mystagogue to be classed with some barbarous Celt of the dark ages.

One of the exceptions was Li Ssu, the book-burning minister of Emperor Shih Huang-ti, who had proscribed all history and literature in the year 213 B.C. But Li, who had substituted his own secret script for writing and who had sought to recreate the world anew, had paid dearly for his presumption. He had fallen victim to a court conspiracy and was sawn in half by the longitudinal method—a fault, no doubt, in one so worldly wise.

Yet others had succeeded where Li had failed, among them General Lo Jui-ching, Mao's ex-chief of police, who had perfected the foremost instrument of revolutionary terror—mass indoctrination *with fanfare*. Ivor Owens had studied the techniques of Lo Jui-ching at first hand while a POW with the Welsh Guards in Korea. *Hsi nao*, or "wash brain," had been too rough and ready to have anything like a lasting effect, though few people had known this at the time, and even fewer had known about Owens' confession—something to do with biological warfare. But Carlo had known; it was his business to know things like that.

It was a pity that Li Ssu had not read his Sun-tse, Carlo thought; or if he had, the minister had ignored the philosopher's advice and burnt his books. Sun-tse had been a contemporary of Confucius, and his *Treatise on the Art of War* was Carlo's manual of tradecraft. A congenial blend of Machiavellian duplicity and Bismarckian *Realpolitik*, it had been written at a time of great upheaval, during the fifth century B.C., when the Eastern Chous had peddled kingdoms for armies. In an age of moral philosophers Sun-tse had applied the golden rule to espionage; two and a half millennia later his *Treatise* would be required reading in the military academies of the Warsaw Pact countries. The mandate of heaven depended on the divine secret, the divine secret on the five kinds of spies, the five kinds of spies on their lord and master, the lord and master on his knowledge of the future. The lord and master must rule his spies, but he must also rule the enemy's spy catchers, even if it meant using a sixth kind of spy: the spy of life who becomes the spy of death and does not return. No blame. George Stevens was such a spy.

When the physician is paid, the patient must be sick—so went an old Chinese saying—and the physician in this case had added a few refinements of his own to the techniques of Lo Jui-ching. But they were not so subtle as Carlo's or so dependent on that conjurer's trick, the sleight of hand.

The mind is a theatre, according to the Renaissance mnemotechnicians, with the seven pillars of wisdom as the proscenium arch. From the wings a magician steps onstage. "Ladies and gentlemen, the Amazing Dr. Waldemar!" Thus vaudeville in the summer of 1933, the old Variety, all balustrades and brass, chintz and moulded half reliefs, of Thalia and Melpomene, Janus masks of mirth and anguish, and Memory, the mother of the Muses. Mummery, Carlo thought. He remembered how the Amazing Dr. Waldemar had hypnotized a hapless gull from the audience, convincing him that his head had been surgically removed. The victim, who looked like a bank clerk, had careened about the stage screaming, "Give me back my head! Oh, *please* give me back my head!" Laughter from the gods and a profound silence (before the applause) when the audience realized that the victim could remember nothing of his experience but stood like one in a dream who must ask himself, Who am I? What am I doing here? Who are *they*?

It was a convincing demonstration of suggestion's power to Carlo, for whom everything was a mental act, even decapitation or sawing in half by the longitudinal method. The victim must have been a stooge of Waldemar's. Carlo made discreet enquiries and discovered that this was not so. Further enquiries unearthed the fact that Waldemar (the latest sensation in town), alias the Phenomenological Phreno, clairvoyant, ran a going concern as a society dip. He would pick the minds of the idle rich while an accomplice picked their pockets. A move was in order, an approach. Carlo contacted Waldemar-Phreno, whose real name by now he knew was Miles Cavendish. There was a niche for such talents, criminal and histrionic. The Depression, of course, had reduced many men of standing to desperate expedients. Road sweeping, strikebreaking, petty theft. Carlo and Miles understood each other perfectly; theirs was a gentlemen's agreement. Which was how George Stevens' file came to bear the entry that its subject was hypersusceptible to hypnosis. Party games.

Among the living, only four people had access to that file. They were David Sweet, Donald Macpherson, Manfred Ritter, and Carlo himself. It was a pity that poor Balthazar had cancelled himself, Carlo thought, slipping up on his pharmacology like that. Ah, well, let the dead bury the dead. But you had to be very careful with drugs, especially the mood modifiers. With the antidepressants — isocarboxazid, chlorprothixene, and imprimamine — a man could be made to remember too much. And sometimes he could be forced to forget. After all, if an entire society could be remade, why not an individual? The topic became a fetish with Carlo, so that people thought him a little daft on the techniques of scientific mind changing and the phenomenon of posthypnotic amnesia. "Leave that to the boffins," they would say. "In any case, you can't make a man do something against his will, can you? Not something that's morally *reprehensible* . . . ?" According to Dr. Owens, the question was badly put. It should have been, Can the hypnotic subject be made to do something that is socially dangerous? And the answer to this, as Carlo never tired of reminding people, was yes. Interdepartmental memos. The lord and master must be prepared for everything and must prepare his servants on the need-to-know basis.

The world was a cosmic egg, the snake its bearer. Carlo thought of alchemy and angelic visitations, of spectres, mirrors, and cyphers, of Sir John Dee and his improbable, impossible work of metaphysical cryptography, a first edition of which Carlo was pleased to call his own: *The Monad Hieroglyphically, Mathematically, Cabbalistically, and Analogically Explained.* He thought of Ophiuchus the Serpent Bearer, that malign constellation; of the Gnostic serpent, Ophiomorphus, endlessly consuming itself; of Trithemius, abbot of Sponheim, and his *Stenographia*: "a boke for which many a learned man has long sought and dayly doth seeke, whose use is greater than the fame thereof." He thought of his father and that Sunday in November 1918 and remembered running down to the village, past the chemist's shop with its blue and red apothecary's jars, past the butcher's with its Day of Rest enamelled platters tilted vacantly forwards, one of them stained with old blood, a sprig of dead parsley in the corner, through the marketplace with its striped awnings, to the country hospital with its lace-capped matrons of mercy. He remembered his father's last words, spoken above the echo of a sparrow's song, and his mother's frenzied *why? why? why?* which admitted of no answer. For the Reverend Peat's sermon had been a rope, and that most eloquent.

A casualty in God's undeclared war on the human race, he had left no note other than a line from Horace: *"Dulce et decorum est pro patria mori."*

Carlo picked up a pencil and sketched a sword cleaving a serpent in two, the emblem of the KGB. Then he wrote down the words "Ghost writer" and crossed them out. Owens would be en route to Moscow in a few hours, and Vladimir Andreyevich Dimitrov (or Yuri Simonovich Chernukhin, as he had been) would be expecting him.

"'The thing that hath been, it is that which shall be; and that which is done is that which shall be done: and there is no new thing under the sun.'" So thought Solomon, the wisest of the wise; and so wrote Harland Caisho Peat, adding, "Ecclesiastes 1:9." It was, he thought, better than Horace's silly ode.

19

Hsi Nao—
Washed Brain—
Welsh Style
with Fanfare

Tuesday, 15 October, the day after Dimitrov saw Kron in Leningrad, Carlo met with Donald Macpherson in Saint James's Park. He had no idea why the major general had chosen the park, except that it was close to his office. Perhaps he liked playing at spies. If it was because he wanted the meeting to go unobserved, he was in for a disappointment. Carlo was being followed by Igor Kulski, a GRU footman with the Soviet Embassy; and Igor was being followed by a man called Peter Smith, one of Macpherson's myrmidons. Carlo sat on a bench while Igor poisoned pigeons and Mr. Smith read a green-jacketed novel. The morning was like a French Impressionist's idea of autumn, only colder—the kind of day that Londoners call mild. Carlo studied the ever-moving chiaroscuro of clouds reflected in the pond. The ripples appeared of their own accord and, at ten-thirty precisely, a pair of Oxford brogues, colour of brown, twills, hem of herringbone coat (collar turned up). Carlo looked up as a jaunty Macpherson sat down, advertising his presence behind a copy of the *Times*. He was playing at spies.

"I've often wondered what some people do when the cricket

season is over," Macpherson said, rolling his *r*'s.

"He may have a directional microphone," Carlo said.

"I've got something better than that," Macpherson said. "Seen one of these before, Peat?"

It was a cassette deck, smaller than the commercial kind. Macpherson pressed a button: "Amazing Grace." "Stirring," he said, "the skirl of the pipes. How do they manage to capture that? The fidelity . . ."

Observing Macpherson's profile, Carlo reflected that clever men often conceal their intelligence behind a veneer of stupidity. In some cases it is superficial, a protective and easily damaged coating against a world that places little value on the higher functions of mind. Assuredly this was not so with the major general, whose soul was overlaid with many coats of varnish, a finely polished, close-grained soul, a soul of wood. He reminded Carlo of an angry walnut. Sir Donald's face was creased with pain, his ill humour exacerbated by an attack of the gout. For the major general spurned all medical advice, and in this Carlo sensed the redemptive glimmerings of a certain wit. No man could be so dense as Macpherson pretended to be, nor any so full of kindled wrath.

"Damned quacks!" he was declaiming. "How did you do it, Carlo, how did you go about it?"

"Simple, really," Carlo answered. "I made a phone call. 'A friend of mine has toothache,' I said. 'Oh, dear,' Owens said. 'Is the pain bad?' 'Terrible,' I said. 'Most unfortunate,' he said—"

"Not that, man!" Macpherson knew the technique. "I mean the confession. How did you get that? I couldn't crack him."

"Scopolamine," Carlo said. "We induced subcortical hypermnesia by chemically lowering the electrical resistances of the synapses in the brain." Chew on that, he thought, watching Macpherson's right eye blink.

"In plain English?"

"In plain English George told us that Philip Grove was Julius Graebe's nursemaid. I knew that, Sweet did—and Ritter. No one else."

"And then?"

"Why don't you ask David? He conducted the interrogation."

"I already have," Macpherson said. "I want to know what *you* did afterwards."

"I went home and had a bath."

"Before that."

"Make up your mind," Carlo said.

Macpherson nursed his wrath. "Bentinck's none too happy," he said. "On face value, he finds it hard to accept what you told him. He cannot understand why there's nothing on file. He cannot understand why you were running this and not Sweet. Above all, he cannot understand why you did not bring George to book. Listen to me, Carlo. . . ." Macpherson's gloved hands rustled the newspaper. He put it down and turned to face his protagonist, the strains of "Amazing Grace" skirling loud and clear. Igor had run out of poison and was cultivating the ducks; Mr. Smith turned a page.

"I know that George was out of circulation for the last three weeks in May of '73," Macpherson continued. "Asian flu, that's what *his* file says, and the report's signed by Owens. Now the Russians put Ritter in the bag on the eighth of that month, so it appears to me as if you had set up friend Manfred as a decoy for the East German imbroglio and were getting rid of him through George. At the same time, you knew, or were fairly sure, that Stevens himself was compromised, but you also knew that he was on the *qui vive* for trouble. Am I right so far?"

"Quite warm," Carlo agreed. Any warmer and Macpherson's gout troubles would be over, he thought.

"Good." Sir Donald said it the way they do in Glasgow. "And now I hear this tale about an assassination." He shattered the word syllabically. "The adviser also tells me this weird and wonderful story about messing up the embassy codes and the improper use of his name. . . ."

"Not guilty," Carlo said.

"He wants *me* to tell *him* all about it, the *first* I ever heard of it." Macpherson was rolling his *r*'s fiercely now. "Then there's Sweet, a good man and I don't deny it, but under your influence, Carlo. Under your influence . . ." Macpherson sucked in his cheeks. His nose was raw and bony. He gazed reflectively at Igor, picked up the newspaper again, and handed half of it to Carlo. "Sweet tells me there was some rough stuff with George," he said, and made a noise that sounded like "Aix." It could have been a cough or an expression of disgust. "What the hell am I supposed to think?'' he asked the editorial page. ''I want the truth,'' he said. ''I want to know what you did to Stevens, you and that damned quack Owens.''

Stevens could remember sitting in the dentist's chair, and Owens, who reminded him of Sweeney Todd, the barber pieman, then— nothing. When he opened his eyes, he was lying on an operating table under restraining hands. Coffer lights overhead. *Clack-clack-clack-clack*—machinery? No, a metronome set at MM 100. Maelzel's metronome. There was a shunt in his arm attached to an IV drip. Bubbles. Owens swam into view and stopped them. A barbiturate? Too slow. Whatever it was, it was fast acting and was wearing off. Stevens groaned.

''It's the East German network that interests us, you see,'' Carlo remarked conversationally. ''We know you gave those agents to Volodny. There's no point in being shy about it, George.''

''You admitted as much this morning,'' Sweet said.

''God,'' Stevens groaned again.

''Give him a drink of water,'' Carlo said. ''Does your wife know you're here, George?''

Stevens raised his head while Owens tipped the glass to his mouth. The water dribbled down his chin. He didn't know the day, the time, or the month. *This* morning, Sweet had said. That was important, but . . . At the head of the operating table there was a grey metallic box plugged into a wall socket.

''What?''

''Marjory—does she know you're here?''

''No . . . I don't know.''

''We'll think of something,'' Carlo said. ''I see you've noticed our new equipment.''

''What is it?''

''Ivor will explain. We're going ahead with the infiltration, George. But there's been a slight change of plan. I'm sure you can understand that.''

''Carlo, wait. Listen to me. . . .''

''Don't worry, you won't remember a thing.'' Carlo turned to Owens. ''Will he, Doctor?''

''This apparatus,'' Owens said, tapping the metal box next to the table, ''is used to simulate epileptiform convulsions.''

"ECT? You're not serious. Shock therapy? What for?"

Sweet monitored Stevens' reaction, which seemed genuine. For a moment he wondered if George had made a deal with Carlo and had been double-crossed.

Carlo was holding a gun on Stevens, the old, absurdly antiquated Webley service revolver. "What for, George? What *for*? Carmichael is dead. You killed him."

"Carlo!" Stevens cried. He had seen Owens advancing with a hypodermic. "Tell him to get away! Get him off me!"

The gun circled and Sweet thought Carlo was going to shoot. Instead he spoke again. "Of course you're not responsible for all the deaths," he said. "You gave them Grove at the beginning of January 1970, a New Year's present, and he led them to Carmichael. It was a slack time, wasn't it, George? Maybe you were just trying to raise the ante or something. Yes, let's be charitable. But they cracked Carmichael—they tortured him, George."

"He didn't have any eyes when I saw him," Sweet said.

"And of course you'd given them other people before as a come-on, little fish. Then Volodny flew in to find the defector-in-place. Your plans and mine, George, they must have fitted like hand and glove, that's what you must have thought. I'd wager you and Volodny had a good laugh about the infiltration. You might as well admit everything, George. It would save us a lot of trouble."

Stevens gazed abjectly at the hypodermic. "All right, Carlo. All right. Tell me you're not going to do this. . . ." His collapse seemed total.

"I'm afraid we must," Carlo said. "We're going to knock out a few circuits, that's all." He nodded to Owens, who moved closer to the table.

"There's nothing to be alarmed about, Mr. Stevens," he said. "This is a preparation of *Strychnos toxifera*—curare—you must have heard of it. The South American Indians use it to poison arrows. A motor paralytic."

Stevens looked on in terror. Sweet feared catastrophe.

"We don't want to give you real convulsions," Carlo said soothingly. "And we'll use a general anaesthetic, of course. Nitrous oxide."

"The dental anaesthetic," Owens said.

"Laughing gas," Carlo said, and cracked the gun barrel down on Stevens' head.

Donald Macpherson put down the *Times* and occupied himself staring energetically into space. Thirty yards away, Igor walked up and down, stamping his feet and frightening the ducks. Mr. Smith watched him, then remembered to turn a page. Macpherson tugged at the roots of his moustache. His right cheek twitched.

"Then he was a traitor," he said finally.

"Yes," Carlo said.

"How long have you known?"

"For a long time."

"Since the war?"

"Yes."

"I see why you called it Poetry," Macpherson said.

"Do you?"

"Very clever." Macpherson looked at the cassette deck, which played "Amazing Grace" for the nth time. "The things they put on tape. Sweet told me about the conditioning, you understand. He'd guessed what you were up to for those three weeks. A good man but lacking your nerve. He was worried in case it failed. But that's not really the point, is it?"

"Not really," Carlo agreed.

"How are you going to get the signal to Stevens?"

"I'm working on that," Carlo said.

"Hasketh?"

"Is there anything you don't know?"

Macpherson gave his foxy laugh. He was very close now, and his breath smelled of peppermints. "As a matter of fact, there is," he said. "Who forged Bentinck's signature?"

"I don't know," Carlo said.

"All right." Macpherson reclaimed the other half of the newspaper. He folded it, silenced the cassette deck, pocketed that, and stood up. "The hell with Sweet," he said, tapping Carlo on the knee with the *Times*. "Do it."

Carlo met Hasketh for lunch at the Maison Lyons in Marble Arch, the last of the old Lyons corner houses where the Friends had communed over wartime tea and damp sandwiches. The choice of locale had nothing to do with sentiment. Carlo was staking out the opposition, his own and theirs. Igor was getting to be rather a nuisance. So was Mr. Smith.

An aged Odysseus, he stopped his ears against the Muzak's sirenic wail and in a silence born of the horror of change watched Hasketh devour the choice of the day: meat pie, mash, and veg. That was the thing about Terry, he was always hungry. "I'm starving," he said. "Soggy," he added, though whether in praise or deprecation Carlo could not tell, "but warm."

"Ah."

"You not hungry?"

"Er, no. My head is full of the skirl of bagpipes. Verray inspiring."

"Oh, the Muzak." Hasketh followed Carlo's gaze and met with that of a dough-faced individual who was studying their table with undisguised intensity. The observer observed, Hasketh transferred his attention to a lustrous pink jelly that sat before him like some alien thing, conical, quivering, and possibly sentient, a medusa untouched by human hands.

"Tag?" he enquired.

"Yes."

"Something's turned up, then?"

"That's right. Why don't we adjourn to the pub across the way? The atmosphere is more convivial there."

"I wondered why you chose this place."

"To see if the opposition was serious," Carlo said.

In the pub he appeased his stomach with a brandy and port. Hasketh was buying. He ordered a half pint of bitter for himself. "There's a chap who might be in looking for us," he said to the barman mischievously. "If you could tell him we'll be over there— in the corner."

They sat down. "Horse piss," Terry said when he tasted his beer, "and they call this ale. Cheers, Carlo. You haven't changed."

"Nor you."

They both lied.

Hasketh frowned. "What are you going to do, Carlo?"

"Do? About what?"

"About Stevens."

Carlo sipped his drink. "I was waiting for that," he said.

"Me, too," Hasketh said. "For the favour, I mean. There's something you want, isn't there?"

"Yes, now that you mention it." Carlo smiled. "I was wondering if you might have a spare reporter. Someone already covering the case, perhaps?" Carlo smiled again. He had nothing on Hasketh, no leverage. "I could throw in the memoirs if you twisted my arm."

"After editing?"

"Well, of course. You know how it is."

"Not anymore, Carlo."

"Unedited, then?"

Hasketh shifted in his chair. Maybe it was the terrible beer, but there were not many customers in the bar. A frowzy blonde, with a leptorrhine nose and hair like steel wool, was engaged in earnest conversation with her companion, a sympathetic fat lady who wore granny glasses and a shapeless woollen sweater. Bits of disconnected talk drifted across. "You tell him what for." "That's no good." "If I were you—" "It's no good, I've tried. . . ."

A comfortable place, or it had been once. They had installed a jukebox. Hasketh watched the blonde feed it money. "You called it a case," he said as the bar filled to the galvanic chords of corpse music. Poised on the brittle edge of afternoon with a sour taste in his mouth, he felt as though he had something to explain. "It's not a bloody case to me," he said. "It's a story."

"Lots of human interest," Carlo suggested. "British agent buried alive in Moscow. I can just see the headlines."

"British? You said British?"

"Sorry, habit of mind. Well?"

"Well, what? Damn that noise." Hasketh glared at the blonde, who smiled, lynx-eyed. "All right, Carlo. There is someone. He's in New York, seeing Louisa. As a matter of fact, I wanted to send him to Moscow, but there's bound to be visa trouble. That's what I thought, and that's what I still think. I mean, they wouldn't take too kindly to some journalist sniffing around George's grave, would they?"

"No trouble," Carlo said. "Sweet can fix the visa."

"Chickenshit," Hasketh said. "That's what we called him."

"And what do you call the reporter?"

"Johnson."

"Politics?"

"None, so far as I know. His old man worked for the Ministry of Defence." Hasketh grimaced. "They canned him when he had a heart attack."

"What's he like?" Carlo asked.

"Number seventy-two," Hasketh heard the blonde say. "Past the Scrubs." Her friend with the granny glasses said, "That's where he'll end up." The music had stopped.

"There was a time when I used to think there were two kinds of people," Hasketh said.

"Yes?"

"Winners and losers. Johnson plays for the draw."

"Well, he's learnt something," Carlo said. "I'll have Sweet run a search on him—just in case. One other thing, Terry. He doesn't know about Stevens, your Mr. Johnson. As far as he's concerned, George is quite dead."

"Who said any different?" Hasketh finished his beer. He picked up a beer mat and tapped it gently on the table. "You've got some face," he said. "I haven't agreed yet."

"No, but you will."

"What if there's trouble?"

"Precisely because of that," Carlo acknowledged. "Trouble would make it worth your while."

"I was thinking, you know," Hasketh said. "We've been through all this before. Only things were the other way round then."

"The wrong way round," Carlo said. "Things have been the wrong way round for years."

"Money," the blonde said.

Hasketh stared at the pub entrance. The two girls were leaving. A grey city type, who had walked in after them, put down the book he was reading and stared glumly at his reflection in the mirror above the bar. The man from Lyons appeared framed in the doorway. He made his way to the bar, bought a scotch, said something to the barman, looked around him, then sat down obtrusively.

"Your friend," Hasketh said.

Carlo stood up. "I'll be in touch," he said. "And, Terry—thanks."

Hasketh saw him stop at the bar, where he bought another

half pint of the terrible beer and sent it over to Hasketh. Carlo turned, pointed to Hasketh, and made some jovial remark to the city type, who looked vaguely startled. And then he was gone.

When Hasketh left, five minutes later, Igor returned to the bar. "Mild weather we're having," he said to the barman, "for the time of year."

"Can't complain." The barman wasn't enthusiastic.

"Seen them before, have you?" Igor jerked his head at the empty table.

"What's it to you?"

"Police." Igor showed him a warrant card. "Special Branch."

"Never." The barman was shocked. "Gospel truth."

"That's what they all say." Igor scribbled down a phone number. "Give me a ring, will you, if you see them again."

The city type observed his exit. "I say! Nice day indeed," he remarked. Then, leaning across, he plucked the phone number from the barman's hand. "Thanks awfully," he said, and walked out, leaving the barman to wonder why everyone seemed to be following everyone else.

20

Tea
for
Two

Dorothy Winters wheeled out her Royal Worcester china smoothly and efficiently, an exhibit, like the rest of her house, with its Ackermann lithographs and Regency furniture, a house in which the silver did not tinkle, nor did it tarnish, as if the natural laws of the universe were held in suspended animation. In a way, they were. Her husband had been killed in an SOE drop, part of the mess that George Stevens had been sent in to clear up. The Friends had retained her services after the war.

She lived in a long, tall house in a row of long, tall houses off Brompton Road, and her neighbours, filmmakers and musicians, thought her unconventional.

"I came home early because of you," she said to Carlo, who hesitated tactfully.

"Ah, you didn't say why?" Not that it mattered, he thought.

"Did I tell Sir Donald, you mean? No, I didn't tell anyone. You look tired, Carlo."

"Yes, I am, a bit. Do you know where I spent the afternoon? In the Natural History Museum looking at dinosaurs. Most pleasant it was, Gladstonian, though there is so much walking to do."

"Gladstonian?" Dorothy smiled, a little wanly, at this reference to things past.

"The way everything is arranged. Systematic, logical. It's funny, the people you meet in museums," Carlo continued. "Peter Smith was there. You know Peter, don't you? Of course you do—Sir Donald's friend." He watched Dorothy, who coloured slightly.

"Tea, Carlo?"

"Yes, please. Ah, no sugar. Anyway, Peter said he was following Igor Kulski, who just happened to be following me. At least that's the way they started out, only they seem to have got things mixed up a bit. Do you know, I actually had to tell Peter where I was going. Our paths had crossed earlier, you see, and I didn't want him to think that I was trying to confuse him. And then we all bumped into each other with old Triceratops looking on. Horrid creature, that. Monstrous."

"That was where they used to meet, wasn't it? George and that Russian—like a tryst."

"A tryst." Carlo savoured the word. "What an odd way of putting it. I can see your point, though."

"You can?"

"Well, you could say that poor George was cuckolded," Carlo said in a wonderful access of poor taste, and then, seeing the effect of this remark, "What I meant was, it has too many horns—Triceratops."

"I know what you meant," she said.

"Defensive armament," Carlo said, recovering. "Anyway, it seems that Igor was passing himself off as a member of the Special Branch."

"You should have come down to the Circus," Dorothy said. "You didn't have to spend the afternoon in a museum."

"I suppose I was drawn to the place." Carlo stared into his tea, then looked up. "Can you think of a reason why?"

"You saw Macpherson this morning," she said. "You wanted to think things over, and you were pulling a switch. The museum was the best place, contained open ground. If Peter had really been following Igor, you wouldn't have run into them again. Then you wanted a favour from me, and you were thinking of the best way to go about it. Clever Dorothy," she said, and she was right.

"I'm looking for the owner of a Mark X Jaguar," he said, "license number JKA 218J."

"Not ours," she said. "Theirs."

"Oh." Carlo sipped his tea. It was scented. Cardamoms? "It was George I really wanted to talk about," he said.

"Harland, please . . ."

A cautionary note, Carlo thought. She mourned for a living man, exhibiting her grief like a trophy, something to go on the wall with the engravings and the Spode plates. Second best, of course, red ribbon, yet still more than she had ever expected from life. It would be a shame to disillusion her.

"Yes, I know," he said. "I wanted to apologize, that's all."

"Apologize? What for?"

"There's nothing you can do."

"No, I suppose not." He gave her a sympathetic look, which went with the tea. Another man would have felt remorse, but Carlo allowed himself a more corrosive sentiment, pity. *Mortuus, vivo pro tempore*; in the dog Latin of a poor priest or schoolboy, George had attained to a certain wisdom. It was as if he had glimpsed, in the course of operational necessity, the emptiness of his life, wrung dry like an old wineskin, and, parrying jest with jest, had thrown it away with hardly more than a shrug. His stoicism was commendable; it was also unthinking. And sad though it was, the same operational necessity prevented him from sharing the joke.

He became, at that moment, a man too preoccupied with irony to see the obvious. Dorothy Winters had read him plainly, without art or cunning—not, indeed, that he required too much study. He was taken aback when she smiled, handsomely, winsomely.

"What is it, Carlo? What do you want me to do?"

"Help me find George's killer," he said.

It was a plea he justified by converting a potential state into an actual one, as if an act of mind could abolish every distinction between life and death, as if life and death themselves were the slightest of verbal abstractions, rhetorical terms in a casebook of grammar.

"*Cheng*," she said. It was a Chinese word for serious play and also connoted "situation," "position," and "arrangement."

"Johannes Heinz Clemens," he said.

"Oh, Carlo, that was such a long time ago." She screwed up

her eyes, remembering. "He caught so many of our boys."

"And let George go."

"They were trying to open a line. Canaris' orders."

"Who handled that?"

"It was Harold Philby. You remember, Carlo."

Yes, Carlo remembered. Philby had quashed any attempts to deal with the German "opposition" because his Soviet masters were afraid of a separate peace.

"Himmler's people were after Clemens," she said. "He took a risk letting George go."

Carlo said, "Clemens was in the same position as Philby. He was working for the Russians, too."

"Yes, but he couldn't disobey an order, could he? Not if someone came down from Berlin and said, 'Who have you got in the cooler?' Clemens was in a *very* difficult position, what with the SD breathing down his neck. They put him in jail after the *Attentat*, you know. Would you like some more tea, Carlo?"

Carlo said that he would.

"I can read minds," she said. "Yours especially. You're wondering if Clemens made George an offer: 'I'll let you go if you work for us.' The Soviets, I mean."

"It's possible, isn't it? May I have that tea now?"

"Oh, Carlo, I'd quite forgotten. This is so *fascinating*." She poured the tea. "It's possible," Dorothy Winters continued, "but unlikely. One: Clemens had no guarantee that George wouldn't go back on his word. He might just report the whole thing to you and forget about it."

"He didn't," Carlo said.

She ignored this. "Two: in Clemens' position, why? If they were all that close, the SD, and they were, and if George fell into their hands, there's no telling how the *cheng* might have developed. Certainly not to Clemens' advantage. Are you hungry, Carlo? Have you eaten?"

"What?"

"I've got some salmon. Fresh. I mean freshly smoked. Oh, God, I don't know what I mean. . . ." He was amazed to see her rush out of the room. Carlo heard kitchen noises. When she returned with the salmon, her efficiency was restored.

Carlo was much more up-to-date. "I had lunch with Terry

Hasketh," he said. "But nothing like this."

Dorothy Winters smiled again. "That Mr. Johnson works for him," she said.

"Oh, really. You've met. What's he like?"

"Brash. Aggressive. He reminded me of . . ." She faded into the long past. "I'm sorry, Carlo. It doesn't matter. There was something else, wasn't there?"

"Back in July," he said, "someone switched the embassy codes, then used Bentinck's signature to try to make a deal with the Russians. Who was it? Do you know?"

"That was in September," she said. "I can tell you who it wasn't. It wasn't Macpherson. He was absolutely enraged. 'Mrs. Winters,' he said, 'we are dealing with a criminal mentality, a master criminal.'" She rolled her *r*'s. "You know what, Carlo? He thought it was you. But he couldn't understand how you'd done it. 'He disnae have the facilities.' " She laughed girlishly. "I feel so young sometimes," she said, "and sometimes so old."

Carlo nibbled on the salmon. It was tasteless. "Delicious," he said, and wondered where the fault lay. "I know the feeling," he sympathized. "Dorothy, this reporter. I think you'll be seeing him again. There are one or two things he should know, one or two things you should tell him. It's part of the *cheng*, Dorothy. . . ." The *agon*, he thought, the game. A ritual contest.

"What sort of things, Carlo?"

"The day after the funeral," he said, "someone recalled the embassy doctor. Now, *why*?"

Carlo listened to his own question, which sounded like a lie. How could a question be a lie? Many were. Does God exist? The devil? Is the human soul immortal? Speech was a lie, and all languages glossed with treasonable intent. Therefore be as silent as a mirror, and speak, if you must, as a mirror among mirrors, sinisterly.

He did not like what he was doing and salved his conscience, the agenbite of inwit, with the knowledge that what had to be done was best done well.

It was a mellow evening, and tranquil, when he walked home from the station. The Mark X Jaguar was parked in its usual spot, and had been joined by another car. They were watching each other now, watching and waiting. His rooms had been searched, of course. They had made a thorough job of turning everything upside down and putting it back together again so that things were slightly out of focus, little things, like the scarf round great Caesar's neck. Carlo wondered who had conducted the search and on whose orders, if orders there had been. But the point was academic, he decided, for he had long ago ceased to distinguish between the methods of one side and another.

It had been a routine search: nothing taken, nothing added. For the last consideration, at least, he was grateful. No bodies, living or otherwise. He made one phone call, to Macpherson. "About that signature," he said. "I've been thinking. Back in 1944, when George returned from Paris, I made a list of the people who knew where he was going. I know that has nothing to do with Bentinck, but I'm quite sure that whoever forged his signature is on that list."

Macpherson wanted to know if his own name was included. It was a reasonable request.

"It is," Carlo said. "Then, so is mine. So is David Sweet's."

"Anyone else?"

"Just dead people."

"Where is it, the list?"

"In the Clemens file," Carlo said.

21

Lappeenranta
Shuttle

The captain of the RAF transport told his passengers that the Met people had forecast a fine day for the Department of Kymi. "Our ETA for Lappeenranta is twenty-three hundred hours Zulu. It's less than half an hour's drive from there to the frontier," he said, lingering uncertainly in the cabin doorway. When this produced no result, the captain, aware that he had already said too much, asked if everything was "dinky-doo."

"Yes, thank you," Sweet said.

"Good, then. Well, back to the sharp end. Must wind up the elastic, what?" And the captain retreated, rolling his eyes.

"I prefer them with boots on, myself," Carlo said.

"He's all right," Sweet said.

"No, he's not. He's a fool."

"The Finns won't like this," Sweet complained.

"Then they'll just have to lump it," said Carlo succinctly.

"Still." Sweet unclasped his seat belt and lit a cigarette. "Did you see the PUS today?"

"I did not," Carlo said. "He telephoned—officially. He was all cut up about Soper."

A week before Soper's death, Carlo had been granted an audience with the permanent under secretary, to whom the Friends looked in moments of crisis. The PUS, whose name was Polfax, inhabited an office in a little-frequented corner of the now-defunct Ministry of Mines, Munitions, and Explosives. Successive modernization attempts drew attention to the building's antiquity, and the secretary's office, which had been cut in half for austerity's sake, had the look of a rococo coffin. Alabaster cherubs cavorted over the door, a velvet bellpull (as defunct as MM&E) hung next to the secretary's desk, and three of the walls were fringed with mock-Regency stucco at their juncture with the ceiling. The fourth wall, a thin pasteboard partition, which, if the coffin were laid on its side, might have been the lid, was lacking ornamentation.

Polfax, who did not exactly think of himself as a man buried alive, spent his days plotting the removal of this partition, which was the bane of his existence, for it made everything look so very eccentric. The fireplace, a bold essay in eclectic dysfunctionalism inlaid with the majolicaware tiles featuring various representatives of the vegetable kingdom, cabbages and cauliflowers ("in the French *manière*," Polfax would tell his associates), looked quite out of place on account of the room's division; and as for the ceiling, it was positively truncated. A charming chandelier, the gift of some tsar or other ("an amateur of naval architecture"), had once illuminated the office, suspended from a bas-relief moulding of radial cornucopias, now—alas—transected by the partition. The secretary's predecessor had waged war for the chandelier's preservation and, upon its untimely deracination, had retired to his club, there to revenge himself on the international philistine conspiracy. He had died unavenged, however, his letters to the *Times* unread and unpublished, returned on grounds of national security.

The PUS was gazing at the moulding, his mind brimming with vacancy, when Carlo entered.

"Come in, come in, do." He stood up, a grey-suited, abstracted man. "Is the door closed? I mean, will it—shut?"

Carlo opened and closed the door experimentally. A gang of navvies were delicately applying cream paint over green in the corridor, and the sickly odour of turpentine wafted into the office.

"Last year it was green on brown," Polfax continued. "Or was that the year before? Never mind. How time flies! Do sit down, Peat—by the partition there. Everything's so lopsided, I'm afraid. Enjoying Cambridge, are you?"

The PUS was nervous. "Recent developments" gave him cause to be.

"I've some news for you," Carlo said.

"News?" Polfax sat down. "Has something happened?"

"I've found someone to send out," Carlo said. "I'm seeing him this weekend. Saturday."

The secretary dithered with an inkstand. "Good man, is he?"

"Secure—a journalist."

The secretary frowned, a ridge of flesh cresting at the bridge of his nose.

"Unfortunately," Carlo added.

"I can't imagine what the minister will say." Polfax gathered his wits, drawing the inkstand towards him and directing a well-rehearsed *coup d'oeil* at Carlo. "A journalist? I mean, isn't that rather risky?"

"Not really. I was expecting that we'd have to use an outsider."

"Were you?" The PUS was unappeased. "Then do me a favour, will you, Peat? Spare me the details. I don't want to know about it, understand?"

"Yes, Under Secretary."

"*No*, Under Secretary. You haven't even been to see me. Because it's not happening, you see." Polfax elaborated. "None of this is happening. It is an historical nonevent, Peat. Because George Stevens is dead, officially dead. And a good thing, too, if you ask me."

"I quite understand," Carlo said. "You want deniability."

But Soper's death was not deniable, and the PUS had called— officially.

"What's gone wrong? The minister is beside himself. 'Wait till the Sundays get hold of this! Questions in the House! My constituents! A marginal seat!' I quote him, his very words. 'Murder in Moscow . . .' You see? He is an angry man, a very angry man. I didn't tell him about the journalist, Peat. You will have to tell him yourself. Yes, I'm afraid you will. . . ."

Carlo waited until he could hear Polfax's breathing. Then he said, "I'll want a transport. To Lappeenranta. Tomorrow night."

"What? Where?"

"Lappeenranta, Finland."

"Out of the question. The Finns—"

"The Russians are bringing Stevens to the frontier. I've already spoken to Wilkes. And Binghampton." Wilkes was the minister's personal assistant; Binghampton, one of the joint under secretaries, an aspirant for permanency.

"And Bentinck," Carlo said.

"Well, that throws a different light on the matter." Polfax capitulated. "I'll see what I can do."

"Was it an interesting call?" Sweet enquired. He sat in the window seat and thought of implosions. It was cold out there and dark. Sweet drew the blind and computed the chance of error, human, mechanical, and divine. It was then that Carlo made his left-handed remark about God not being able to alter the past.

"As far as you know," Sweet said, then, "It's the future that interests me, the immediate future."

"Ah, compossibilities," Carlo said. "There's nothing to be afraid of, really."

"I know," Sweet said, but his hands were shaking. "What did Polfax say?"

"He asked me what had gone wrong. I quote him. His very words."

"Well?"

"God knows. I don't."

"What did you tell Bentinck?"

"I mentioned Ritter, but you know what Bentinck's like. Inflexible. He'll never understand that we needed Manfred as a straw man. Why, David, what did you tell his lordship?"

Sweet exhaled yellow smoke. "Everything," he said. "I had to go behind your back, Carlo. Sorry."

"As long as it didn't get in your way," Carlo said.

"The thing was . . ." Sweet said, and hesitated. He was not a fluent man like Carlo. Not glib.

"Go on," Carlo said. "I'm listening."

"Well, treason is a matter of dates, Carlo. The thing was I couldn't understand why you continued to trust George after you knew that Ritter was in the clear. It's a funny thing, trust. You can distrust someone and still know that he's loyal, but it doesn't work the other way round. You can't trust someone whom you know to be disloyal, can you? It didn't make any sense at all to me until I realized what you and Owens were doing. I had to tell Bentinck about that.''

"Of course you did," said Carlo soothingly. "You took your time, though. Why?"

"I wanted to be sure that you were serious."

"And you were sure, weren't you?"

"Yes. All those memos. It would never have worked, Carlo. You *must* have known that."

"Not really," Carlo demurred. "Look at it from our point of view, Callwell's and mine. If George were Kim's successor, we had him controlled. He'd end up where he belonged anyway. If not, then we could still use him to find the successor."

"You hoped," Sweet said.

"No, we didn't. Everything was weighed in the balance. Nothing wanting."

"Really?" Sweet was sceptical.

"Yes, really." Carlo spoke as he would to a dog, chidingly, yet amused at the similarity between human and canine behaviour. "There was always the chance that the successor might find George," he said. "Or the recruiter or the controller—whoever and wherever they are. They would take remedial action, of course. Especially if they knew what had happened to George. And then their cover would be blown."

Sweet considered this statement, picking it over for flaws. There were times when he thought Carlo was either a very bright man or a very stupid one, and he did not know at this moment precisely which. So he grunted, as a dog often will when baffled by its master's expectations.

"Your reply speaks worlds," Carlo said.

"I was thinking," Sweet said deliberately.

"Ah."

"Safeguards, you must have had some safeguards."

"Oh, yes, plenty of those. What would the Russians think? That we'd trusted him for all those years? Unlikely, once they saw through the Ritter fabrication. And it was only a matter of time before they did. You knew that, David.'' Carlo studied Sweet, a mild, inquisitive gaze. ''That's why you opened negotiations for his release. Unofficially, of course. But the Russians weren't to know that, were they? They weren't to know that you forged Bentinck's signature.''

''Dorothy tell you that, did she?''

''It was a guess,'' Carlo said.

Sweet extinguished his cigarette, brushing the ash from his trousers. He smiled. His teeth were not good, but he had an aversion to dentists. ''It had to be done,'' he said, ''and you know why. They had him in the hospital.''

''I think you made a mistake,'' Carlo said. ''You prejudiced the security of a mission. You supposed that George was a traitor. You supposed, and you didn't have a shred of evidence.''

''He confessed, didn't he?''

''Under those circumstances who wouldn't have?''

''You're forgetting the network,'' Sweet said. ''Those men weren't exchanged, Carlo. I went to Berlin, remember? I saw what happened to them.''

''And it wasn't pretty? So a few agents get wracked up. It happens all the time. Really, David, you shouldn't let sentiment get in the way of your better judgement.''

''I'm not the one who's defending George,'' Sweet said.

Carlo laughed. ''You think I am?''

Sweet lit another cigarette. He had a subordinate's mind, and now it began to feel the strains of an idea. ''Bentinck,'' he said, ''Bentinck thought you ordered Stevens to betray Grove and Carmichael.''

''You smoke too much,'' Carlo said. ''Bentinck's not a Friend. What does he know about it?''

''I said you didn't. I denied it, Carlo.''

''That must have confirmed it, then.''

Sweet inhaled. ''You knew what George was doing,'' he said, aware that he was expressing himself badly. ''But you didn't give him an order—he could have questioned that. And you didn't frame him, not exactly. You let him frame himself.''

''All right, David.'' Carlo was feeling old and tired. *Copos*, that was the word: lassitude, weariness, sickness. ''Either-or thinking,'' he said. ''It used to be a fault of yours, David. Not anymore, eh? There are no totalities in our trade, you know. No man can afford to be totally false or totally loyal. But treason is more than a matter of dates, David, I must insist on that." And shall, Carlo thought.

He wondered how much he had succeeded in teaching Sweet, who had been opposed to the infiltration from the start. It must have irked poor David, playing second fiddle for so long. Sweet was slow but he was efficient; in his own way, quite artful. He was a forger by nature, an artist. Cheques—before the war. Hence D. He had also forged Johnson's papers. And he had been talking.

"Yes, I knew what George was doing." Carlo poured oil on troubled waters. "But neither that in itself nor the fact that he neglected to tell me is absolute proof of his malfeasance. He may have had any number of reasons, valid reasons, for going along with friend Dimitrov. Remember what Balthazar said about George never being twice the traitor he once was. And if he compromised himself in the process, so much the better from our point of view. It added to his credibility."

Sweet absorbed this in spongelike silence. Either Carlo was still unsure of George's loyalties and was afraid to admit as much or Carlo was *non compos*. There was another explanation, of course, but Sweet didn't want to think about that. Not yet. Instead he thought of something else.

"You were exposing George to risk, weren't you? Using him as a sleeper assassin."

"I didn't think that term existed in your vocabulary, David."

"No, but it does in yours."

"Those memos—you won't let me forget about them, will you?"

"I've just thought of something," Sweet said. "The cypher . . ."

"What about it?"

"It could have been a plant. Or else they read it. And if they read it, why would they let it go through?"

"An interesting question," Carlo said.

Sweet was incredulous. "And you sent Owens and Johnson to Moscow. Why, Carlo, *why?*"

"To preserve the appearances, of course."

"But they killed Soper. . . ." Carlo was over the hill, way over the hill, Sweet thought. "They killed him while he was trying to give Johnson the tape. Carlo, they've turned the whole thing round, and you're going with them!"

"Wheeling the flank," Carlo said. "The left flank."

"You're out of your mind," Sweet said, and immediately regretted it.

"Oh, no," Carlo said. "George is coming home now. He's found himself—your own words, David. You're right about one thing, though. Trust."

And then he asked if Sweet was carrying a gun.

Carlo had said that everything had been weighed in the balance, with nothing wanting. Someone must have been leaning on the scales, Sweet thought. Callwell was dead and Balthazar and Grove and Carmichael and at least fifty others, counting the nonnationals. Percival was dead as well, the Friends' former controller, presumably a suicide. But Philby was alive and *his* controller. The recruiter, too. Nemo and Niemand, respectively—names unknown. Were they the same? George Stevens was also alive, provisionally, and might have the answer to that question.

Carlo had a different story for everyone; the same facts, a different interpretation. There was nothing wrong with that in principle. People do change their minds. And their allegiances. Sweet, who hadn't liked the tone of Carlo's last question, began to search for a useful hypothesis. It was possible that Carlo could have recruited *and* run Philby, then spent the rest of his career looking for three imaginary people: the recruiter, the controller, the successor. Carlo had certainly done everything within his power to groom George in the role of heir apparent, Sweet thought. He also had one other qualification essential for the recruiter: age. But Sweet couldn't for the life of him understand why Carlo had gone to such lengths to set George up as the successor, then convert him into a programmed killer. His memos had used that term—conversion—almost in a religious sense. Of course, if Carlo had discovered that George was playing a double game, then his response was understandable. But no man would have covered as much as Carlo had for George if he really believed that the other was a traitor. Had there been a confusion of loyalties, perhaps, the interests of the service versus personal friendship? That was the easiest point of view, as it was also the safest—for the moment. The trouble was you eventually ran out of moments. Sweet didn't want to be around when that happened. Which was why he was carrying an Armalite Special, the automatic machine pistol with the collapsible stock and the illegal NATO 9-mm soft-core mercury bullets.

He stared at Carlo, who had fallen asleep and was snoring softly, a comical fat man. Carlo murmured something in his sleep—"tourney"—and Sweet suppressed the urge to laugh. The image of Carmichael's corpse came to him, and he imagined how it must have looked when they first found it, floating among the reeds at the edge of a German lake. That had been in the winter, and the whole of West Berlin had seemed like a mortuary, as cold as stainless steel under neon. Sweet had seen many corpses before but never one like Carmichael's. Whoever had stopped friend Patrick had taken a deal of pleasure in his work. Sweet had flown back with the cause of death and nightmares.

He cracked his knuckles to dispel the image and held out his hands, sensitive, fragile hands, unlike Carlo's bloated paws. Carlo had the hands of a blackmailer, which was what he was. Fat white hands, with larval fingers. Sweet lit another cigarette. He noticed that his hands had stopped shaking, a remission of symptoms. He wondered if he could kill Carlo. If his back were turned, yes. Or would he have to yell at him to turn around? Sweet had never killed anyone in person, nor, to his knowledge, had Carlo. Vicariously, yes, but that wasn't the same. Sweet, who possessed none of Carlo's saving abstractions, realized that he had no definite answer to his question. He would find out, he thought, when the time came, if the time came. And in some unformulated, wordless manner, he knew that this had always been the case.

The captain appeared, grinning, in the doorway, and Sweet asked how much time they had left.

"You mean flying time, don't you?" The captain was jocose.

Carlo awoke with a start. "Is there any other kind of time?" he asked, but no one understood.

"We'll be on the ground in twenty minutes," the captain said. "I've just been chatting with Lappeenranta tower, and it seems the Met people were wrong. There's a warm front moving in over Kymi, colliding with lots of nice Arctic air. That means snow and turbulence." On cue, the plane dropped through an air pocket, a sickening, stomach-churning lurch. "Oops. You'd better fasten the old seat belts. Well, here's to a controlled crash,'' the captain said, and departed cheerily.

"I've been thinking," Carlo said.

"What about?" Sweet felt dizzy. The plane sank again.

Carlo struggled with his seat belt. He clicked the ends together and the coupling sank into his abdomen so that it looked like a balloon with a twist in the middle. Carlo gasped.

"Those agents," he said, "the network. There was nothing I could do. Nothing at all."

"All right, Carlo," Sweet said.

But it was not all right, he thought. None of it.

22

On
the
Frontier

North of Vainikkala it was a frosty night, cold but clear, with a light cumulus covering the south, and Kilpinen had been watching the transport since it was a star among other stars. He had seen it before hearing it, way to the west, navigation lights blinking as it stole across the map of the heavens. That had been at 2330 hours, and Kilpinen assumed that Vyborg had already been monitoring the flight for some time. He hoped they were not trigger-happy tonight. Lappeenranta Airfield was just fifteen air kilometres from the frontier, and an unscheduled military transport that belonged to a NATO power could made a lot of people on the other side unhappy. Not that they had any right to be there. The Vyborg (Viipuri) sector of the Leningrad Military Oblast was Finnish territory, though the Russians would dispute this. And had disputed it, thought Kilpinen, whose father had fought in the Winter War.

Kilpinen decided that history could take care of itself for a while. He turned and walked into the hut, singling out the chief of the local *Poliisilatos*, a man called Melartin.

There were four men in the room, and one of them had just finished saying, "I've made a serious decision about myself and my life." Like hell, Kilpinen thought.

"They're coming in," he said.

"I'd better go and meet the plane," Melartin said.

The other three watched resentfully. They disliked Kilpinen for innumerable reasons: He was young, not yet thirty; he was a security man; he was from Helsinki; and he was an interruption.

"Somebody should," Kilpinen said.

He wasn't feeling particularly happy himself. His superiors had selected him for the job because he could speak English, on the assumption that their guests would not be able to speak Finnish or even Swedish. Somehow the thought rankled.

"You're not going out?" Melartin asked.

"No, thank you," Kilpinen said. "I'll stay here and watch."

Melartin left, slamming the door. Kilpinen heard his car engine and requisitioned a pair of night glasses from one of the men. He stood now in the long shadow of a row of huts, shielding his eyes against the glare of the landing lights, watching the Andover taxi to a halt. Kilpinen saw the landing truck crawl up to the aircraft, Melartin's patrol car following at a distance. In the darkness to his left, he heard the roar of the fuel bowser starting up. They were going to turn the aircraft round quickly in case the Russians hadn't noticed, which was unlikely. There had been some kind of security exercise going on all day, supposedly in connection with the fifty-seventh anniversary of the Revolution. Kilpinen knew better. He shivered, though not from the cold. It was the noise. There was far too much noise.

He raised his glasses and watched the two men disembark. The thin one, he knew, was David Sweet, current head of SIS-IX. Stevens, one of his forerunners, was supposed to be coming across in the morning at Vainikkala with a journalist called Johnson. But Heikki Kilpinen was much more interested in the first passenger off the plane, a man called Peat, for whom he had a message from a KGB colonel called Dimitrov.

"You will give this to Peat alone and in confidence," Heikki's boss had told him. "We do the English a favour and the Russians a favour. That way no one can complain."

Kilpinen was formal but correct with his guests, both of whom were armed. Kilpinen reminded them of Finnish neutrality. "I have a car waiting to take you to Vainikkala, gentlemen," he said. "You will find your accommodations simple but comfortable, and I am sure you must both be tired."

The man called Peat said, "The air is most refreshing."

"When the cement factory is not in operation, yes," said Kilpinen.

"What happens tomorrow morning?" asked the man called Sweet.

"In the car, gentlemen," said Kilpinen, who had no wish to discuss such matters before the locals. On the way out, he made a joke. "Only in the CIA do cement and security mix." The fat Englishman laughed; the thin one scratched his head.

Neither of them seemed inclined to conversation during the journey, which was a short one, and Kilpinen decided that if they would not talk, they could at least listen. "The train that is carrying Stevens and Johnson left Moscow at noon, their time, today. Barring any unforeseen accident, it should reach Vyborg at six a.m., also their time, tomorrow morning." Kilpinen looked at his watch. It was just a few minutes past midnight. "Or *this* morning, to be exact," he said in one of those moments when time is never more clearly a human invention. "May I remind you gentlemen that you have just lost an hour? It will be a short night for you.

"The Soviets will then clear the train for customs," he continued, "while the Finnish locomotive is being hooked up. At Vainikkala, the next stop, the train is boarded by our authorities. However, your people are leaving the train at Vyborg and—as you know—are being taken to the frontier by car. Because of the zonal time change, we shall meet them at some time between five-thirty and six a.m. our time. Certainly no later, because I have orders to curtail everything after that. The car will stop on their side of the frontier, and they will walk across. You will understand, of course, that in this latitude total darkness prevails at that hour. Despite the extremely short notice, I have secured extra lighting at the frontier post. The road will be floodlit, gentlemen, so there should be no problems with identification. At all times we shall remain on this side of the frontier. Do you understand the details?"

"Couldn't be clearer," said the man called Sweet.

"And your colleague?"

"Yes, I understand," said Carlo. "If all goes well, we should meet them on the Vainikkala road before they have left Vyborg."

"That is so," Kilpinen acknowledged, "an interesting thought. They will gain the hour you have lost. Let us hope that is not all they have to gain."

A murmur of assent came from the back of the car. "That is settled, then," Kilpinen declared. "However, one question remains. What do you think can be the reason for this extraordinary arrangement?"

Kilpinen, who was riding in the front passenger seat, noted in the driving mirror that the two Englishmen looked puzzled. "Perhaps I have phrased it incorrectly." He turned round. "What I meant to say was, why are the Russians not allowing your friends through on the train? Surely that would have been the simplest procedure."

"It is strange," Sweet said.

And Peat: "We've been trying to think of a reason."

"So have we," said Kilpinen. "Perhaps the Soviets anticipate an incident?"

"If that were the case," Peat said, "they would have flown them directly to London."

Encouraged, Heikki Kilpinen said, "That is what we thought — at first. It has not escaped our attention that there are also two of you." He paused meaningfully. "After Vainikkala the train continues to Helsinki." Almost as if it's a real train, he thought. "If, on the frontier, either one of you tries to walk in the other direction, I have orders that you are to be prevented. This is not an exchange, gentlemen. Do I make myself clear?"

When the Englishmen agreed that he made himself perfectly clear, Kilpinen relaxed. There was only the business of the note to dispose of now. "That is good," he said, and was silent until they reached Vainikkala.

It was a town that had no reason to exist. But not the Hotel Karelia, which still resembled what it once had been, a shooting lodge and summer retreat, though would-be hunters and tourists were asked, politely, to apply further on. The Hotel Karelia, with its smell of pine needles and floor polish, its deep corridors full

of glass-eyed trophies and surprising mirrors, had every reason to
exist—for those whose trade was best conducted under cover of
night.

"Your hotel, gentlemen," said Heikki Kilpinen as the car
bounced to a halt.

The entrance was unilluminated. A light glimmered farther down
the street, emphasizing the darkness.

"Grim-looking place," Sweet said humourlessly.

Peat tapped Kilpinen on the shoulder. "Aren't you coming in?"

"Why?"

"Well, it is your area HQ."

"In that case I'd better," Kilpinen said.

They were expected.

Kilpinen waited for half an hour, then climbed the main staircase
of the Hotel Karelia to the second floor. Two shiny black objects
outside Sweet's room caught his attention. The man had put his shoes
out. Evidently he had a sense of humour after all. Kilpinen smiled
and picked them up. They would be cleaned.

He paused before knocking at the door of the next room but
one. Light filtered through the doorjamb. Peat was still awake.

He did not seem surprised to see Kilpinen, though he looked
askance at the shoes.

"May I come in?" Kilpinen asked.

"Yes, of course."

"Didn't you know I'm just the shoe boy around here?"

"No, that I didn't know."

Kilpinen sat down in a wicker chair. "And the messenger,"
he said.

"You have something for me?"

"Yes."

Kilpinen gave him the message, which was unsigned: "Cancellation is the death of Poetry."

"This is from Dimitrov?"

Kilpinen nodded. "And now perhaps you will tell me what it
means."

Peat shrugged. "In confidence, it means that a number of people
have made a mistake."

"Have you?"

"Yes and no." Carlo sat down. "I have made a mistake but not the same one as—as these people."

"It has to do with Stevens, yes?"

"That's right."

"I see. Well, it is none of my business." Kilpinen sighed. "But what happens this morning is. We are a small country, Mr. Peat, but we know how to take care of ourselves and our friends."

"And your enemies?"

"Die with their shoes on." Kilpinen stood up, clutching Sweet's shoes. Peat was still wearing his, and the Finn gazed down at them bleakly. "Or off," he added. "On or off, according to the circumstances."

"You'll need some shoe polish," Peat said.

"Yes." Heikki Kilpinen smiled. "I was going to ask if you had some."

The Englishman shook his head. "A hotel without shoe polish," he began, "is—"

"Not so bad as a man without a country," Kilpinen said, cutting him off. "There's a phone in the lobby, by the way. In case you're wondering . . ."

"It's out of order?"

"Good night, Mr. Peat," Kilpinen said.

"Good night, Herra Kilpinen," Carlo said.

The car bounced over the brick-paved surface of the market square and turned southeast at the crossroads beyond. Darkness claimed the last of the human settlement, gigantic shadows leaping to the heavens and back, inviting, alluring, as if the car were preceded by a dance of demons through the forests of the night. "*Saata lunta*," the driver said. It had started to snow, a fine, drifting snow that swirled along the highway and accumulated on the windscreen with a hissing sound. The driver leant forward and peered into the vortex ahead. He dipped his lights and switched on the wipers. *One-two, one-two*. David Sweet listened to their metronomic beat, his mind preoccupied with demons of its own. It was like driving through a tunnel, he thought, and complained bitterly about the inadequacies of the Met people.

"It's nothing," Kilpinen said. "Just a squall from the gulf. It won't last."

"November is a depressing month," Carlo said. "All that waiting . . ."

"A fine day," Sweet grumbled. "That's what they forecast. A fine day. What happens if the train's late? Because of the weather, I mean."

"Then we'll see," Kilpinen said. "We have a saying in Finland."

"The evening is wiser than the morning," Carlo said.

Kilpinen turned round, surprised. "How do you know?"

"I spent some time here once," Carlo said. "Before the war, before you were born. They were building the Mannerheim Line then, and in the winter I used to go skiing. All across here and down to Viipuri. I know the country but not the language, not anymore. I've forgotten most of what I knew."

Kilpinen was surprised again when Sweet started to laugh, a low, racking noise that seemed to cause him pain, for he clutched at his side. "You!" He wheezed abrasively. "Skiing? Don't make me laugh, please don't make me laugh. What a sight you must have been!" And he coughed again, miserable in his mirth.

"I still think you smoke too much," Peat said, and then he saw the lights on the road.

"A checkpoint," Kilpinen explained. "This morning no one crosses from our side."

Sweet was still chortling in his cancerous way when the driver rolled down the window and a young soldier peered in. His face was red and laden with melting snow, an apparition that moved Sweet to further transports of laughter. The soldier shone a torch over the occupants of the car and waved them on uncomprehendingly. "The army," Sweet rasped as the car chewed its way uphill, "he's mobilized the army." Grinning, he turned to Carlo. "You're damned right I smoke too much," he said. There was a feverish glint in his eye as he cast around for another cigarette, abandoned the search, and jerked his thumb at the rear window. "You know what that was? I'll tell you, just let me get my breath. It was a—a *ski* troop!"

Sweet was abruptly quiet. "Forgive me, gentlemen," he said with admirable composure, "a touch of the sun."

The road was suddenly floodlit. Kilpinen had been as good as his word. Sweet made out the frontier post, a couple of trucks and a generator, and in the hazy, finite distance what seemed like an answering glare. Darkness returned. Mad dogs and Finnish men, Sweet thought. He blinked, and there were green spots before his eyes. In the darkness, with his eyes shut, he saw what he could not see in the light. There were four banks of reflectors, one on either side of the road and two in the centre, set back slightly. The retinal image faded.

"Impressive," Carlo said.

Kilpinen did not reply. He was listening to the sound of silence. He opened the window and sniffed the air. The weather was going to be worse, much worse, than anyone could reasonably have expected.

"We can wait here or inside," he said. "Inside they will have coffee."

Kilpinen heard Sweet say that he would like to stretch his legs. He listened carefully to that voice, which sounded quite ordinary now. Apparently the Englishman had found, in the subject of skiing, something that produced a condition akin to hysteria. Kilpinen made a note to remember this for future reference and also remembered that the phrase "to stretch one's legs" was a euphemism for one of two bodily functions. It was just ten minutes to five when Heikki Kilpinen announced that he, too, would like to stretch his legs.

An hour later Carlo was wondering if he would have declared anything to be impressive had he known how things were going to turn out. He sat at a wooden trestle table, his battered old portmanteau before him, and gazed into the dregs of his coffee, his mind moving between *kairos* and *khrónos*, between all time and time present. The future was like the horizon—the closer it seemed, the further away it was. This was not the first time he had waited for George to come through, though it would be the last, certainly the last.

It was extremely hot inside the frontier post, and Carlo dabbed at his forehead with a large white handkerchief. Sweet sat across the table, fidgeting. He kept looking at the clock on the wall, comparing its time with his wristwatch, which was still an hour slow. A denial of something, Carlo supposed. The two men had nothing to talk about. Only the soldiers maintained a kind of conversation among themselves, and every now and then one of them would walk in or out, admitting a blast of cold air. Carlo listened to the flat sounds of Finnish and the musical *yo-ho* of Swedish. They were happy, now that snow had arrived, and Carlo amused himself by trying to remember what little Finnish he had forgotten, especially the formula that required another to close the door. When even this modest exercise failed, he looked at Sweet, who was pondering the wall clock. It was five-forty-five, a quarter of an hour to the deadline. Carlo waved his handkerchief like a flag of surrender. Really, it was tiresome of George to be late. And Dimitrov.

"I wonder how they heat this place." Carlo broke the silence. "There's no stove, no fire or anything, yet it's boiling."

"Central heating," Sweet said. "Oil, most probably."

"Quite a show Kilpinen's laid on."

"Yes," Sweet said grudgingly. "I wonder where he's got to?"

"Looking for reindeer, I shouldn't wonder."

"Carlo?"

"Yes?"

"Did you really go skiing?"

"Yes, really."

The phone rang and was answered by a lieutenant who made odd gulping noises, which, Carlo remembered, was Finnish-Swedish for "yes."

"*Jö, Jö,*" he said—only it came out like *hoo* drawn on the inbreath—and delivered himself of one last inhalant *hoo* before abandoning the phone for the door, his distracted cries sounding from outside above the roar of the generator.

"*Puhelin! Puhelin!*"

"'Telephone,'" Carlo said. "'Speaking device.' Here's Kilpinen. . . ." The Finn picked up the phone and listened. "*Viipuriällä?*" he said, and his expression did not alter. He replaced the receiver and stared into the distance.

"It's off," he said.

"What's happened?" Sweet said.

"One of your children has gone to the woods," Kilpinen said. He spoke to the lieutenant, rapidly and in Finnish. "Gentlemen, I have orders to halt this operation forthwith," he said, and turned on his heels. Carlo followed with his bag in hand. Outside, the lights died.

"Listen," Carlo said.

"There is no point in protesting."

"I can hear something."

The soldiers ran back and forth like automatons, packing up their equipment in the snow.

"I can hear it, too," Sweet said, and he knew that Kilpinen could.

The sky to the south flared with the incandescent glow of Very lights. Starlight, burning bright, Carlo thought, watching the flares arc and fall.

The soldiers halted and stared heavenwards. There was a desultory crackle of automatic-weapons fire and a harsher, more strident note, the pulse of a helicopter engine, definitely audible now as the southern sky glittered under the brilliant canopies of falling parachute flares.

Sweet began unpacking the Armalite Special. "Turn on the lights," he said. "Turn them on again."

Kilpinen issued new orders, shouting above the racket. "There is going to be an incident," he said.

Sweet saw the lead helicopter. "Christ, it's a bloody submarine chaser!" Where were the submarines? He laughed. On skis, probably. Sweet laughed again. There was something wrong with that machine. It was making the most god-awful noise, and it was losing altitude rapidly, too rapidly.

There were four of them, Ka-26's, and the vicious *whip-whip* of their contrarotating blades was almost loud enough to drown out the whining howl of their turbines. "Air Sea Rescue!" Kilpinen yelled. "From Kronstadt . . ." He gazed in disbelief at the stupid *sotoväki* who were milling around in all directions, running and jumping and shouting and waving their hands at the oncoming machine, which blundered into Finnish airspace at a height of no more than a hundred metres, nose down, turbines wailing out of synch.

A convoy of cars had arrived, almost unnoticed, at the frontier. Kilpinen saw a Soviet officer standing with his hands on his hips at the barrier. Then he remembered his guests. "Into the hut, both of you!" he shouted, but neither of them moved.

Sweet was sighting the assembled Armalite, his lips drawn back over his teeth; and Carlo clung to his bag as though mesmerized. A cyclopean light shone from the belly of the first machine, and the others kept their distance, hovering on the Soviet side of the frontier like flying coffins. The soldiers had dropped to the ground, rifles aimed at the Ka-26, which seemed to hesitate, ponderously deliberating its next move, the light sweeping across the roof of the frontier post, probing and searching until it found what it wanted and the pilot began his descent.

"Run quickly!" Kilpinen's idiot advice was lost to the blizzard and the scream of turbine blades.

The helicopter flew in at an angle. Alone, illuminated in that awful radiance, Carlo registered everything photographically. He saw the bulbous black-glass nose and the pilot looking at him through some kind of contraption in the control pod; he saw the radome beneath, the naval-patrol markings on the belly, the undercarriage struts tilted out to the side, the radial treads on the landing wheels. Something tugged at his sleeve. Deafened, he took a few steps, then stumbled and fell headlong into the snow. The evil beast was directly above him now, the downwash of its rotors raising a maelstrom of snow and pinning him to the ground. Like a specimen to the board, he thought, crawling towards the portmanteau, which had fallen in front of him. The earth was swept clean around him, his coat flattened out like a cape, so that he resembled an overweight Bedouin in a sandstorm or an obese vampire desperately struggling to escape the rays of the dawning sun. It's going to be all right, he wanted to cry out, blindly clawing at the hasps of the bag and groping inside for the butt of the Webley. It's going to be all right, don't you see? He can't land on top of me. He can't! The undercarriage is too big! But Carlo didn't cry out. He knew, and then he saw what the pilot was trying to do.

Sweet began firing just as he expected to see Carlo clouted sideways to eternity. But the helicopter was out of range now, soaring around for a second pass, and Carlo was still there, kneeling like a man at prayer. "Get up, man!" Sweet cried, and steadied himself as the helicopter began another approach, laterally, like a huge and malevolent crab. The Finns, at last, had started shooting, wildly and erratically, but what the hell was Carlo doing?

He was still on his knees, the heavy revolver clutched in both hands, his forearms rubbing frantically at his face like a fly cleaning itself. Something black and hot and sticky had fallen on him, and his eyes were burning and he wanted to vomit and have done with it.

Mistily, through a red veil, he saw the machine sideslipping towards him for the kill. There was no use in standing up, no use at all.

He turned, and perhaps then he did cry out. Wearily, like a man bowed under the weight of the ages, he raised the gun and, taking aim, fired.

INTERMEZZO

From
the
Stevens
Papers

By late summer of 1973 I knew that my arrest could not be delayed much longer. Carlo was asking about the emergency procedures I had for contacting Volodny, and Macpherson had already moved in with a team of investigators. There was nothing I could do except count shadows.

The emergency contact system was very simple. For five years Vladimir Andreyevich and I had kept our *Treffen* among the bones of the long dead, in Huxley's fossil-hallowed halls, South Kensington. At the entrance to the Great Hall of the museum there is a postcard rack featuring, among other exhibits, portraits of our simian forefathers, those beetle-browed anthropoids whose cavernous orbits stare forth on modern man with pitiless recognition. Into this family group I was to insert another portrait—a picture postcard of a red-nosed potbellied Englishman in a blue and yellow striped bathing costume, his boozy-eyed gaze searching some plebeian strand. The caption read: "I can't find my little Willie," a statement that did not amuse Dimitrov, who was in some respects humourless. However, it amused Carlo, though his vanity was wounded when I told him that we had selected the card because the happy holidaymaker resembled himself.

This arrangement was, of course, dependent on my being able to reach the museum. Failing this, another such card, mailed to a KGB safe house in London, would alert my Soviet friends to the danger. Carlo was ignorant of the second detail, though he must have guessed that we had an alternative plan.

I had time on my hands that summer, and the first thing to go was the sense of time itself. My behaviour must have puzzled the Plods in Five. I would often catch myself staring into the lupine-clotted gardens of mews or into the infinite recesses of their courtyards. One night, on Waterloo Bridge, I gazed for an hour at the floodlit dome of St. Paul's, which dominated the city like the cowl and cope of a corpulent friar. I would count the river barges on the Thames or try to remember the constellations of freckles on my beloved Marjory's face. Should she read this, she might as well know that I failed. In Windsor one day I found myself walking in the grounds of my old school; in Euston station I bought a tomato slicer from a hawker. Slipping the fat man into the rack would have ended it, but time and treason had until September. On the first Saturday of that month, I gave Volodny the last of the ten agents, Eduard Chvalkovski, an official in the Czech Ministry of Commerce. I was now a spy without a security clearance and a traitor without a cause. The arrest itself came as a relief.

It was one of those spectral days in late September. The trees were turning, St. James's Park looked like an island of molten ore amid so much dross, and Broadway was full of flunkeys and cars with CD plates. I had just surfaced from the underground when my shadows, three of them, materialized. They were very civil.

"Mr. Stevens, Mr. George Michael Stevens?"

Do you know that voice, Dogberry's Sunday best? Humble and smug, ingratiating yet superior, leavened with a sprinkling of Wilsonite vowels, it is the voice that no Marxist-Leninist would ever understand. The arresting officer, a social revolutionary in ready-made mufti, held out the postcard as his warrant. It was stamped and postmarked, Carlo's idea of a joke. He must have gone to enormous trouble for Carlo, finding an identical card and then sending it to himself.

I was housed in the Scrubs for two months, twenty-five days, and twelve hours, deniable time for which I was allowed a lawyer,

Anthony Arlington Price, also known as the Catfish or the PF—the Prisoner's Friend. Marjory's as well. His legal training had left out the Official Secrets Act, though it had given him a word or two of Latin. *Habeas corpus ad subjiciendum.* You shall produce the body, preferably in court. As for Marjory, she was being ever so hugely loyal, totally committed to the idea of her husband's innocence. That was how the PF referred to me, in the third-person elusive. She was distressed, naturally, but she was coping. A brave and beautiful person. Perhaps that was how she summoned the courage to see me. Twice. The first time to model her new coat, the second to accuse me of selling state secrets. The two were not unconnected.

Macpherson was another, more frequent visitor. The Scrubs afflicted him with nostalgia. During the war it had housed the Plods' Central Registry until a German incendiary bomb fell through the roof looking for a fire. The enemy who drops bombs on you is worthier than the enemy within, just as it is worthier to kill a pagan than to burn a heretic. But Macpherson wouldn't let go of the war. Paris, January 1944, the rue des Saussaies. How did I get out? Everything he asked came round to that question. Finally, in a fit of exasperation, I told him, "The same way as I'm going to get out of here." He was a good interrogator.

Anthony Arlington Price showed up again a few days before Christmas. The deal for my exchange had been completed, and I think he was worried about the fee. Marjory was still being ever so hugely loyal, ignoring his strenuous exhortations on the facts of life without George. Reality was sometimes hard to face; it wasn't her fault that her husband was, well, a spy. Was the insurance paid up, and what about her pension rights? One had to be practical, after all. She had searched the place high and low, and still couldn't find a trace of the will.

"And I really do think, at this season, that one ought to bear such things in mind."

West Berlin was threaded with multicoloured baubles of light. There was serious carousing in Hallesches Tor, and the U-Bahn station was thronged with traumatized pilgrims bearing gift-wrapped packages to the East. It was Christmas Eve, and there was a heavy traffic at Checkpoint Charlie, which looked like a temporary isolation unit, clinical, white, and well patrolled. Spotlights played across the junction of Zimmerstrasse and Friedrichstrasse, and the sign outside the American hut: YOU ARE LEAVING THE AMERICAN SECTOR.

The Spirit of Christmas Present was tacked up on the wall of the American hut, a crease across her centrefold belly, her opulent flesh poured into a robe of fur-hemmed incarnadine. Underneath Sister Klaus sat an American major, discoursing quietly on the inanities of imperialism. He stared out of the window as he spoke, the spotlights from the wall probing his face, his voice accompanied by the distant strains of "O Tannenbaum." The barbed-wire stanchions were like musical staves on which the notes of the carol were played out: *"O Tannenbaum, O Tannenbaum, wir treu sind deine Blätter . . ."*

"A wall, that's why we're here, just because of a fuckin' wall? Naw, listen." No one was listening, but the major didn't seem to mind. "I'll tell ya something. There was a captain in Nam, a psychologist. Know what he did? Right in the middle of that village he made a huge big dollar sign and covered it with gold foil. He put it up in the village square and asked the VC to come in and do business with him. I tell ya, he had the only pacified hamlet in the entire Mekong Delta. Ya know what they did to him, the brass? Told him to get his ass right out of there before he was court-martialled, yessir! Goddamn red tape. That's what we're fighting — stupidity, not walls. Ya know what I'd do if I was running this crummy town? I'd ask them how much they wanted for that Jesus wall, that's what I'd do. . . ."

The bells of midnight interrupted the major's speech. He stood up and trained his binoculars on the Vopo hut. "Truck's coming," he said. "Right on time."

He licked his fingers and moved to the door. "They're getting out," he said, and with agonizing slowness began to count from one to ten. "Time for you fellas to go." He told us jokingly that he felt like the innkeeper at the Last Supper. On the table behind him lay the remains of a butterball turkey, all the way from Petaluma, California.

There are moments, in our weary striving for significance, to which we must return, as if we hope to surprise some meaning from life. I remember stepping out of the hut under the no-entry sign and feeling the shock of the cold night air. Volodny was behind me to one side, and I waited for him to catch up as we passed the sector notice. The barriers were raised on both sides of the zone now, and I knew that there were marksmen on both sides with precise images of us in their night scopes. We halted, as we had been told to do, at the tram tracks on Zimmerstrasse. There are three concrete blocks on the Eastern side, staggered to slow the traffic —a Roman touch. But what happened next was not Roman. It was like a scene from a Western movie, something the major would doubtless have appreciated. A man emerged from the defile and walked slowly towards the halfway mark. Another followed, then another and another until there were ten lined up on the other side of the tracks. Their clothing was motley and somewhat the worse for wear, but they were all clean-shaven and closely cropped, specially barbered for the occasion.

They had walked out in the order of their arrest, and I remember Volodny staring intently at the fourth man in the lineup, Anton Deriabin. Eighth in place was Manfred Ritter, with whom I had settled an old score. He gazed down at his feet. There was no real meeting, no confrontation. It was a shabby scene.

Volodny, who had gone earlier, raised his arm in the recognition signal and the line parted to let us through. It was only a few yards to the Friedrichstrasse control point, and I could see a man standing near the tailgate of the truck. He was about Carlo's age, and the duelling scar on his right cheek was visible in the light from the Vopo hut.

"Good evening, Mr. Stevens," he said. "It has been a long time."

It was Clemens.

Later, after we had climbed into the truck, Volodny remarked that the American major was right but did not know it. "Some people will sell anything," he said, "and not just for money." We were travelling down Friedrichstrasse and made a right turn onto the Unter den Linden. I had not been here since the end of the war, and the past, revisited, betrayed my expectations. From the back of the truck I glimpsed the shell-shocked ruin of Bismarck's chancellery, its great dome a baroque skeleton of tangled steel. Europe's collective nemesis was buried somewhere out there, his grave a no-man's-land of barbed wire and machine-gun posts. Judging from the sentries goose-stepping outside the Memorial Building, he could still have been around.

At the Polizei Praesedium, on Keibelstrasse, we exchanged the truck for a car and I heard Volodny give the address to the driver. It was Normannenstrasse 22, Berlin-Lichtenberg, the head-quarters of the Staatssicherheitsdienst, the East German State Security Service.

"It's nothing," he said. "They want you to look at some photos, that's all. You have a good memory. You must have, to recognize Clemens. You did recognize him, didn't you?"

"Yes."

"Well, then."

He was in that sort of mood. We had just crossed one of the canals of the Spree, which runs from the southeast to the northwest of the city, when he observed that some men were like rivers.

"You mean treacherous?"

"That, too." He grinned. "What I meant was that they ignore political boundaries." He was silent for a moment, and then he said, "There's an old saying."

"There always is."

"Yes, but this one applies to you, George. You can never go down to the same river twice. Did you know that?" And he repeated it, adding, as if there could be any doubt of his meaning, "The same man and the same river, but the man has changed and perhaps the river also."

Part Four STEVENS

I told him gently of our grievances,
Of his oath-breaking; which he mended thus,
By now forswearing that he is forsworn.
He calls us rebels, traitors; and will scourge
With haughty arms this hateful name in us.
—*King Henry the Fourth, Part I*

23

"My enemy's enemy . . ."

After his late-night session with Comrade Chairman Andropov, Vladimir Andreyevich returned to the apartment overlooking the Novo-Devichy Cemetery. But first he called in at his office, where there was a message waiting for him from Department 13, which handles the first chief directorate's communications: "Normannenstrasse 22, Berlin-Lichtenberg, 2400 hours. Clemens dead. Call Kron." Dimitrov had done just that. Clemens had been murdered, Kron told him, caught between two cars as he left the SSD building. The assassins, both East Germans, had been captured without a fight and had confessed that they were working for Carlo Peat. Unofficially, not that it made any difference to Clemens.

The sleep of reason brought forth monsters that night. Ivan the Terrible had celebrated the Revolution, leaving his frenzied challenge encrypted in blood and entrails: Catch me if you can! In Sverdlov Square the Greatest Teacher inveighed on silence, his granitic fist proclaiming victory to the proletariat. Icons were dusted off and refurbished, dialectic oiled like the gears of a tank. Limp banners draped the flanks of Exhibition Hall, and Vladimir Andreyevich caught the glow of a cigarette cupped in a sentry's hands—safe, however, at this hour. A missile transporter crawled down the *prospekt*, its carnivorous bulk cushioned on oversize tires. Tomorrow the army would unveil their latest toy. Vladimir Andreyevich did not think of its use.

"All this," he muttered to his driver, "and they still can't grow wheat."

He was in a bad mood and regretted his cleverness with the chairman, a superior cleverness for which there had been no need. He also felt personally threatened, though this had nothing to do with Stevens and the operation called Poetry. Clemens' death was an error of the first magnitude. A reflex action had killed the man, just as a reflex action had killed Soper, and Vladimir Andreyevich was responsible for both. He thought of an agent called Nemo slowly panicking, for panic had been slow in his case, until he could see no other course than to kill, had chosen the alternative of one.

Someone had desperately needed to make it look as though Carlo wanted Clemens dead. That man was Philby's controller and successor, the KGB's agent-in-place, Nemo.

"Drop me at the cemetery gates," he said to his driver. "I have a ghost to exorcise."

"A delta brain wave," Dimitrov said. "You must have been asleep, George—Carlo's sense of humour. We read the code. You know that, don't you? Or do you?"

Vladimir Andreyevich waited. As so often before when he tried to read the other man's expression, he was puzzled at what he saw there: a slightly aggrieved look, accusing rather than accused, yet passive at the same time, as if an abstract question had been posed, one that was unrelated to anything so material as life or death.

"Code? What code?" Stevens said. His pulse began to race. A lie detector. Infallible.

"We're rational human beings," Dimitrov said. "So let's be reasonable with each other. Let's talk."

"What about?"

"The truth."

"Treason to the teller."

"That depends on your point of view, George."

"Walls have ears, Volodny. I can hear them listening."

Dimitrov poured a large brandy and handed it to Stevens. "Have a drink,'' he said. "You'll need it for a change." He poured another for himself and began pacing the little room, which he seemed to fill. "It's too late for that now," he said. "My enemy's enemy is my friend. Do you know that, George? It's a good saying, up to a point. You and Carlo—we were friends during the war. So was Clemens. You know, in some ways he had a much more difficult job than any of us. He was everybody's enemy."

There was a kind of droll menace in this statement, and Vladimir Andreyevich used the moment to establish complete mastery over the room and its contents, so that even the furniture became his props. He set his glass down on top of the cabinet from which he had taken the brandy bottle, and Stevens noticed the sweaty print marks on the stem. George sniffed the brandy— Erevan, 114 proof—inhaling heady chains of esters. He, too, put his glass down, on a table at the end of the sofa. He wasn't going to drink it, not yet. There was something else, another odour in the room, rank as a mangy bitch in heat.

Dimitrov, who was still wearing his outer coat, unbuttoned it, crossed to the window, then turned round to face Stevens, rocking slightly on his heels. He said nothing but folded his hands behind his back. His eyes flashed with a dangerous, opalescent quality. Stevens had never seen him this way before. Be careful, he thought, be very careful. He was going to ask about Clemens, but Volodny held up his hand.

"You listen to me," he said, "and don't interrupt if the details are wrong. I'm not interested in the details anymore. There have been too many of those." Vladimir Andreyevich flopped into a low armchair, his voice a monotone. "You always claimed that Carlo trusted you. Transference, of course. It was you who trusted Carlo. That was your first mistake. Your second was giving us Grove and Carmichael. Years ago, many, many years ago—ten, twenty, but it doesn't matter—Carlo told you that Kim Philby's controller was still active among the Friends and that he was looking for a means to pressure him. This was the initial justification for Poetry, as it was represented to you. Setting you up as Philby's successor would force Nemo into an indiscretion, and at the same time Carlo gave you a blank cheque on how you went about ingratiating yourself with us. The slight matter of the ten agents, George, was for the sake of Callwell, who was then the Foreign Office adviser, or for anyone else who cared to look into the operation. When nothing happened, and when Carlo saw how literally you had interpreted his instructions, he came to you and said, 'Look, Nemo isn't biting. He doesn't think we're serious enough. . . .' Something like that. It was then that Carlo began to make a great deal of noise about posthypnotic amnesia and brainwashing. Two things, George. Have you ever asked yourself why Nemo didn't rise to the bait? In the first place, he would have told us that an infiltration attempt was under way, and that would have confirmed what you told me. And then he would have warned us about Owens. But he did neither of these things. Why?''

"He was waiting,'' Stevens said.

"So he was,'' Dimitrov said. "Think about it, George. The other thing is much more interesting as far as you're concerned. There wasn't supposed to be any brainwashing, but there was. You've been double-crossed, George. The target is a man called Chernukhin. Yuri Simonovich Chernukhin.''

Stevens' face was a blank. "I thought it was Andropov,'' he said. "That's what you told me. You said it was Andropov. Christ, Volodny, I've never heard of anyone called Chernukhin.''

"I know that you have, George.''

"It's the truth!''

"I don't disbelieve you.''

"But you don't believe me! How can I kill someone I've never heard of?''

"I'm trying to help you,'' Dimitrov said. He took off his coat and folded it neatly over the arm of the chair. "Carlo must have had a suspect,'' he said.

"What?''

"Just as he had Ritter set up, he must have had a suspect for Nemo.''

"Sweet,'' Stevens said.

"That's it, then,'' Dimitrov said. He reclaimed his drink and sat down again. "We were supposed to get rid of you, George. But we didn't. Tomorrow, when you play the tape and listen to that signal, you will understand. You will understand everything, George.'' Vladimir Andreyevich nodded. "Believe me, it will be a revelation to you. We've both read about artificially induced psychosis, but it doesn't *last*, George. Bear that in mind tomorrow. Carlo didn't have enough time, not nearly enough time. You're a free agent now, or you will be. We have no claims on you anymore. We're letting you go. Only, you have to play that tape, George. You must do that. . . ."

"Clemens," Stevens said, "what has this to do with Clemens?"

Vladimir Andreyevich swallowed his brandy. "*Proschai!*" he said. "Dead. Carlo killed him. About half an hour ago. A car accident. It was so unnecessary, George. But Carlo knew that you were coming home."

Stevens was silent. Among the permutations of the finitely possible there was one simple formula that equated Carlo with Nemo. It made sense, and yet it required faith to believe in a breach of faith.

"Why are you telling me this?" Stevens asked.

"I did a lot of reading when you were in hospital," Dimitrov said. "There was this one experiment in operant conditioning that fascinated me. There were three incurable madmen, each labouring under the grand delusion that he was the Messiah. The hospital authorities, believing that there is reason even in folly, put them together in a room. The youngest one said, 'I am the Son of God.' 'How can that be?' said the next madman. 'For I am the Son of God, and you are not my brother.' 'You two know nothing,' said the oldest. 'I am really the Son of God, and I'm old enough to be your father.' Tovarich, the result of this experiment was that the first madman was confirmed in his folly, the second was promoted to the rank of Holy Ghost, and the third was accepted by the others as the Heavenly Father. But, you see, they were only madmen, and Carlo is not a madman. He is the joker in the pack, the wild card. Don't you understand, George? It was Carlo who made sure that Clemens knew who you were during the war. Carlo is the traitor, George."

"Prove it," Stevens said.

"At Vyborg, George. I will have the documentation."

"You still haven't answered my question. Why are you doing this?"

"As the chairman said, Carlo's broken all the rules."

"What happens if something goes wrong?"

"Then I will see you on the frontier, George. You—or Sweet."

Vladimir Andreyevich stood up to refill his glass and noticed Stevens', untouched, on the table by the sofa. "Drink up, George," he said. "We have the arrangements to discuss."

24

Kalinin Oblast,
7 November,
1430 Hours

Weary clusters of people stared at the express as it pulled into the station. They stood like evacuees next to their bundles, then surged forward as though driven by contagion, the infectious hope, in Russia, that the next train is always the right train. Someone shouted in official tones and the crowd subsided as quickly as it had gathered, adrift among itself, disintegrating. In its wake Johnson saw an old woman flapping down the platform in pursuit of an escaped chicken. Her neighbours watched with heroic indifference as she fell on her quarry like an aged Fury, seizing the bird by its wings and forcing it into a cardboard box. She laughed and shook her finger at God, who allowed such things to happen.

"КАЛИНИН," the sign said in Cyrillic like mirror writing. Kalinin, all change to nowhere. Johnson saw another sign outside the waiting room, the now-familiar emblem of bottle and crutch.

He looked on from the corridor, isolated by a medium that seemed denser than air or glass. A child was playing a skipping game underneath the window. She smiled at Johnson, who returned the smile and thought of risking a wave. He decided against it. The gesture could be misinterpreted, everything could be.

For the last two hours he had listened to Stevens until he knew that history, objectively considered, was a delusion in which everyone agreed to believe and then set about rewriting, changing the plot to suit himself. Johnson could not rid himself of the awful look on Soper's face as they dragged his corpse into the hotel lobby. It was, he thought, the look of a man whose understanding had been finally perfected. Nor could he forget what Stevens had said after they left Moscow. Stevens could be mistaken, of course, but he had not been lying. According to Stevens, Carlo was the man (one of them? all of them?) whom Carlo was looking for. But Carlo had also told Stevens that he suspected Sweet of running Philby.

"Could he have?" Johnson had asked.

"Yes, and so could Carlo. So could I. Every spy like Philby has a nursemaid. Sweet was younger than Kim, but it made sense using a younger man because he could take over from his agent. The idea was that if I stepped into Kim's shoes, we'd soon flush out the controller. At the very least he'd have to contact me, sound me out—that was the idea. But it didn't work. So Carlo said, 'I want to try an experiment. We'll make Sweet think that you've been programmed to kill Dimitrov.' Volodny figured that out for himself. No one told him. Not Sweet, anyway. Funny, that—the controller was code-named Nemo. . . ."

"But you agreed?"

"Sweet seemed a likely candidate. He conducted the investigation into the death of Grove and Carmichael, and of course he drew a blank."

"Yes, but *you* gave them those agents. . . ."

"You think Sweet didn't know that? Carlo's reasoning was that David was biding his time, waiting to see if I was genuine or not. After all, it was a pretty big come-on. Then, of course, Carlo had me in a trap. So I had to go along with him. It was perfect, from Carlo's point of view. *He* gave those men to the Russians, or as good as, using me as a front. He didn't tell me to do it—he was too clever for that—but he knew that there would have to be some trading under the counter. He knew what I was doing. It wasn't until he brought in Owens that I began to suspect him."

"You let them brainwash you?"

"It was only supposed to look that way. But I couldn't remember— you must believe me—I couldn't remember a thing until Volodny started asking questions. Even then I couldn't remember the trigger stimulus or what I was meant to do or anything. The last memory I had was Carlo whipping me over the head with the gun, and I thought he'd done that to shut me up because Sweet was there. After that— nothing. I don't remember anything of those three weeks in May. I *still* don't remember. . . ."

Johnson had not disbelieved this, yet he could not accept it. His belief, or disbelief, was in a state of continuous suspension. Grove and Carmichael had been important agents. But there had been others before them, as Stevens freely admitted, and he talked about them as if they were so many counters. Calling another man traitor did not lessen the offence, Johnson thought. And so he had made some excuse about needing a breath of fresh air, had got up and left.

The train's hydraulics hissed and the station moved backwards as if jolted by an unseen hand. It was years since Johnson had travelled on a train, and the experience awoke memories of the irrecoverable region of childhood. He remembered summer weekends spent on the beach at Worthing in the years after the war. The beach was hard, too many pebbles, and he had not liked it. What a little bastard I must have been, he thought, and waved at the child on the platform.

The reporter amused Stevens, who could see why Carlo had chosen him. The man was a natural, too sincere for his own good. He must have made Volodny laugh like hell. That was the principle behind the whole thing, keeping everyone happy while he died. Suntse must have said something about that. One smile worth five spies. Great good fortune. And Machiavelli. Old Nick-olo.

He watched Johnson return from the corridor. The reporter closed the sliding door and slumped down in his seat.

"I've been thinking," he said.

"What about?"

"How long it was since I've been on a train."

"Me, too."

Last night's accommodations had evidently not agreed with Johnson. Bed and breakfast in the Lubyanka, it would make tomorrow's evening editions. The reporter was tired, and he was scared. Stevens could see that. Fear was understandable; a man could live off his fear. But not fatigue.

"You should get some sleep," Stevens said.

"Later. I was thinking about the cassette. Why don't you play it?"

"A hit tune, eh?" Stevens looked out of the window and saw his reflection in the corner. It was a pleasant enough face, middle-aged, a little pouchy under the eyes and slack about the jaws, where he had lost weight. Too much living, not all of it good, he thought. I'm tired, too. Christ, how I'm tired.

"Because I want to preserve my freedom of choice," he heard himself say. Now, that was absurd, really it was.

They were pulling out of the station now, a hundred miles gone. Vyshniy Volochek was the next station, and Bologoye after that. They would stop there at the junction. Plenty of time to think, maybe too much time. Some things were best done instinctively.

"No one has that anymore," Johnson said. "Freedom of choice —it's an illusion."

"Quite right, old man."

Stevens began to count flatcars. They were loaded with machinery from the engineering works. *Kalinin: an important communications centre situated on both banks of the Volga at the northern flank of the Mozhaisk Line. Its fall will* . . . Old history.

He stared down at the river and made a silent confession of his own fear.

"Look, I'm only trying to help," Johnson began. "I'm sorry . . . I don't see why you think it was Carlo, that's all."

"Is it?"

"Well, he doesn't strike me as the sort, somehow."

"And who does—strike you as the sort?"

"You do." Johnson smiled, then was serious again. "If Carlo was working for the Russians, why would he want you to kill Dimitrov?"

"Chernukhin," Stevens said, "his name is Chernukhin. A Jew. Maybe Carlo was afraid he was coming back to life again, the old *Yevrey*."

"I didn't know that." Johnson seemed shocked. "I mean, that Dimitrov is a Jew."

"Neither do I—neither does Volodny. It's a hunch, that's all. Yuri son of Simon—Chernukhin, it's a Jewish name. Carlo doesn't like Jews. Monotheists."

"It isn't logical," Johnson said.

"Oh, yes, it is. He doesn't like Christians either."

"I'm talking about motives, Carlo's motives. You know that."

"There's something you don't understand," Stevens said quietly. "Carlo doesn't have to make his reasons public. It's not a question of logic or rationalization or any of those things. If he has any 'motives'—as you call them—then you can be sure that they're not going to make sense to you, and I don't mean that personally. Anyway, I didn't say that Carlo was working for the Russians. I said he was running Philby."

"It's the same thing, isn't it?"

"Could be."

"Well, then," Johnson said. "You know or you *think* you know that Carlo was the controller—which means that you must have your reasons as well. You can't apply one law to yourself and another to the rest of humanity."

The man was insufferable, Stevens thought. Humanity? What did he know about humanity? He was like a puppy, assiduous, fawning, and very determined. Was this what England had whelped? This Fleet Street hack with his incessant prattle of values, concern, democracy, not—to be fair—that he had actually spoken of these things, but given half the chance he would, and *logic*, by God, for, yes, I am a reasonable man and so are we all reasonable men. . . .

The train clattered across a series of switches, and Stevens allowed himself to be lulled by its gentle swaying motion. Easy, easy, he thought, you are going to need this man's help. He gazed out on the endless muddy plain and saw his own image again, the reflection of a man on the inside looking out, a reversible image, as if the other were looking in. It was blurred like a double exposure, two images in one frame, the strobelike pattern of the rail ties falling aslant the window. Something there is about a train, he thought, something that annihilates time.

Advance units of Heeresgruppe Mitte broke into Kalinin on the fourteenth, outflanking the Mozhaisk Line from the north. . . .

"*Moscow won't fall, not while Uncle Joe's there.*"

"*How can you be so sure, Carlo?*"

"*They'll fight. For Mother Russia, Holy Russia, the Faith. You read his speech. They'll fight.*"

Past history, done with. Finished.

"Carlo isn't the rest of humanity," he said, but the reporter was unconvinced.

"You can't prove it was Carlo, can you?"

"No, too circumstantial."

"Dimitrov could have proved it," Johnson said. "If he really wanted to. He must have had documentation, things like that."

"I doubt it. He was doing me a favour," Stevens said. "He could have had me shot. He shot Soper personally."

Johnson looked up, surprised. The word "why" formed on his lips, and was silenced by the roar of an oncoming locomotive. He started. When the other train passed, he said, "I don't understand. Why would Dimitrov tell you about Carlo?"

"It's something to do with Clemens," Stevens said. "You know, I told Volodny everything about this operation. Everything I knew, that is, everything I could remember. Your line: I had no choice."

It was an appeal, Johnson thought. Stevens was looking for an excuse, a way out.

"Did you see Louisa in New York?"

Johnson was taken aback. "Yes . . . Why?"

"No reason. I just wondered how she was."

"Fine," Johnson said, "she was fine."

"And Marge?"

"Well, she was a bit under the weather. . . ." What a time to talk about his wives, Johnson thought. He suddenly remembered something. "How did you know I was in New York?"

"Dimitrov told me. Marge was under the weather, was she? Did she seem upset about, well, you know . . . ?"

Hell, Johnson thought.

"Sorry, old boy, I'm pissing on my grave. Not everyone has the chance to do that. Marge would never have stuck it out in Moscow. Too drab. She didn't, er, try to—"

"No, she didn't."

"That was a quick answer."

"Look, I resent—"

"Being interrogated? Gamesmanship? Life? There's a cure for that, you know. What *do* you resent? Don't talk to me about humanity, that's all. Leave humanity to look after itself. You and I will get along better then. Much better."

"I didn't ask to be sent out here."

"Come *on*. Nobody asks for anything. How in hell's name do you think I feel?"

"If I were you," Johnson said, "I'd find out what's on that tape."

"I know what's on it."

"Then I would play it."

"You would, eh? Then go ahead." Stevens threw the cassette deck across the compartment. "Catch!" he said.

It was just two-thirty p.m. when Johnson pressed the play key and the spools began turning.

George Stevens listened to the amplified sound of his own brain, the neural pulse of a sleeping man. *"Listen to the metronome, George,"* Owens said. *"We're going to knock out a few circuits, that's all,"* Carlo said. *"Strychnos toxifera—curare—you must have heard of it,"* Owens said. *"Nitrous oxide,"* Carlo said. *"The dental anaesthetic,"* Owens said. *"Laughing gas,"* Carlo said. *"Dimitrov is Chernukhin,"* Owens said. *"Yuri Simonovich Chernukhin is Vladimir Andreyevich Dimitrov is Chernukhin is Dimitrov Yuri Simonovich Dimitrov Vladimir Andreyevich Chernukhin . . ."*

So that was it. There was no blinding paroxysm of rage, no hatred, only the mesmeric rhythm of the telegraph wires dipping between posts and soaring up again—that and a dull, nerveless sensation for which there was no name.

Something else, too, Stevens noted. It had started to rain. Johnson saw him pitch forward, holding his head. Someone was yelling, *"K complex!"* Now, what the hell was that? And the tracks sang out, *Vainikkala kill Vainikkala kill Carlo Vainikkala kill.*

25

Bologoye–Leningrad,
7–8 November,
1700–0100 Hours

It was always the same dream. He was being taken from the rue des Saussaies to the Gestapo prison at Fresnes. During the course of that journey, his last, the back of the van became his cell. Carlo was there and said, "If you're caught, talk. That is the rule." Preparations for an execution were under way at the point of transfer. There was a guillotine in the courtyard, and when the curtains were drawn aside, he saw three executioners, who beckoned to him across the cobbled square, gravely comic in top hats and tails, white gloves. Someone called his name, but his legs wouldn't move. *"Marchez, m'sieur. Allons! Lassen Sie uns gehen! Schnell! Schnell!"* Suddenly he was in a small cubicle that was lined with black crepe paper. At last he understood, it was going to be a hanging, not a beheading, and they had the rope round his neck when Clemens appeared and said, "Your name is George Michael Stevens, and you were born in Kumasi on June the first, 1918. . . ."

And they were taking the rope down. " *'Raus! 'Raus! Kommen Sie heraus!"*

"I thought they were going to string me up," he told the reporter. "They didn't."

"It wasn't that way in your memoirs," Johnson said.

"No, a lot of things weren't. You got them back, did you, from Volodny?"

"Yes." Johnson smiled. That the things men do should live after them. Vanity.

The train had stopped again. Bologoye junction.

"Louisa said that I used to wake up screaming for help."

"What happened?"

"It was a long time ago."

"But it was important—it *is* important."

"Perhaps."

"I would like to know."

"Why?"

"Because . . ."

"They threw me back into a cell," Stevens said quickly, "a new cell. That can be a bit disquieting at first. You get used to a place, some sort of territorial imperative. *This* cell, the new one, was underneath the courtyard. No light and not much air. I could hear them hammering at the coffins outside. Now, this'll sound crazy, but there was something in the corner of that cell. I couldn't see what it was—it was too dark—but I knew it was there because they'd thrown it in after me, and I remembered the way it fell, with a sort of soft, wet sound. . . .

"For two days I sat there, with all kinds of foolish thoughts running through my head. Two days, it took that long before I summoned up the nerve to touch whatever it was in the corner of that cell, *my* cell. It was wet, all right, slimy and fibrous—like a lump of organic tissue—and it was beginning to stink. So there I sat, in the opposite corner, staring at that thing, which began to take shape in my mind, well, as if they'd thrown somebody's liver in there or something. That's what I thought, anyway. After a couple of days, when they must have thought I'd had enough, Clemens returned and the lights went on. I saw what it was then."

Johnson swallowed. "What was it?" he asked.

"A sponge," Stevens said. "It was a damned sponge." He laughed. "They'd thrown in the sponge for me."

"Clemens, what did he want?"

"Just a chat, you know."

"What about?"

"Peace."

"What?"

"The German Army wanted to give up. But only to the West. They wanted to go on fighting the Russians, who were the great menace to Christian civilization and all that. Maybe they were right. Anyway, you can see what a difficult position it put Clemens in. Canaris had ordered him to open a line to the Allies so all the nice Germans could leave France and go Red bashing. As proof of their devotion to the Allied cause, they were even preparing to bump off Adolf. But they had to have a separate peace, that's what Clemens said. Of course, I didn't know who he was then."

"Philby's recruiter?"

"That's right."

"What did Carlo say when you got back?"

"Well, he said that we ought to encourage Clemens, but not seriously. I think Carlo knew who Clemens was all the time. But that's hindsight."

"What happened to Clemens?"

"It's a long story but fairly typical in its way. After the July Plot he went into the cooler along with most of Canaris' people. Clemens was a true believer. But he wasn't directly involved in the conspiracy—none of the Soviet doubles were—so he didn't end up with a piano wire strung round his neck and dangling from a meat hook. He was lucky, though, that the Russians got to Berlin when they did. Another few days and there would have been no more Clemens. After the war they gave him a job with Komissariat Five, and when that organization was scrapped, he joined the SSD and worked his way up to a deputy state secretary. He oversaw the destruction of our network, and then he retired. But not soon enough. Last night Carlo killed him. That's what happened to Clemens."

"Why?" Johnson asked.

"I wouldn't be sitting here if I knew why. I'm sorry, but you'd have to ask Clemens and I don't think he'd grant you an interview now. Of course, you could try Carlo, but that might be rather difficult, too."

"What are you going to do?"

Stevens looked out of the window. The rain would turn to snow, he thought. It was getting darker, and he felt cold. Should eat, should drink, should sleep.

"I'm going to ask you a favour," he said. "When you get back to London, I want you to see a man called Bentinck at the Foreign Office. Understand?"

Johnson nodded.

"Tell him the recruiter was Clemens. Bentinck's pretty thick, so I want you to get this clear. FO Security keeps cumulative files on people like Clemens. I want you to tell Bentinck that someone pulled Clemens' file within the last week. Whoever it was must have signed for it, even if it was Macpherson himself. Tell Bentinck to get that signature."

"It's Nemo's?"

"Yes."

"How do you know this—about the file?"

"I don't. It's a hunch," Stevens said. He looked out of the window again and saw a helicopter moving in to buzz the train. "We've got company," he said.

They heard it again after Bologoye. There were four of them now, flying in a close diamond formation to the west. Johnson wanted to know what was happening, and Stevens told him that it must be some kind of security exercise. He looked at his watch: five o'clock. The sky to the east was a deep purple, burdened with heavy cloud; the land was black and full of long shadows.

Stevens asked if Johnson was feeling hungry. "We have to eat," he said.

"Where are we?"

"About halfway to Leningrad."

"I hadn't thought about food."

"Well, you should." Stevens stood up. "I'll go and see if I can find some. I won't be long, so you might as well stay here. Don't do anything I wouldn't."

Stevens made his way down the corridor, his hand going out to steady himself. At the next compartment he saw a pair of startled eyes regarding him through a half-open blind. And the next and the next: eyes in the dusk, watching. He heard a door slide open and knew that he was being followed.

The toilet was at the end of the car. Stevens opened the door, locked it, and urinated noisily into the bowl. He whistled as he washed his hands. The "Internationale." The sink was a little bigger than a man's head, and the taps were made of brass. COMPAGNIE DE WAGON-LIT, said the sign above the sink. Prewar rolling stock.

The man was waiting outside, thickset and heavy, staring down at his feet. He jumped when the door opened and peered into the vacated toilet. Edgy, Stevens thought. He gestured at the interior, stepped aside, and allowed the man to cross over. The movement of the train threw them together, and he felt the gun under the man's jacket. "So sorry," he said in English, and watched the other retreat into the toilet. Stevens knew that he could have jumped the Russian, but it was too early for that. The killing time was for later.

The fragment of a memory came to him: *"One thing known for sure about brainwashing is that its effects are temporary."* That was Balthazar's opinion, and Carlo had wanted to know how temporary. "Well, *temporarily* temporary. It all depends . . ." So it does, Stevens thought. Balthazar was all right for things vaguely psychic, but this wasn't the stage at the Variety.

Stevens continued down the corridor. *Vainikkala Vainikkala Vainikkala*, the tracks insisted, then he noticed a change in pitch, a syllabic shift: *kill Carlo kill Carlo kill Carlo* . . . The train was slowing, that was all.

He had reached the coupling to the next car. The floor plates cakewalked beneath him, and the accordion pleating compressed in the G force of the train's deceleration. Stevens hid behind the connecting door and watched Ivan emerge from the toilet. The Russian scoured the corridor, then slouched off to his own compartment, satisfied that Stevens had returned to his. Easy money, Stevens thought. The brakes locked and released, on-off, on-off, and the car bounced and swayed. Clenching and unclenching his hands, he listened to the rending cry of steel on steel. The sound jarred his nerves. And then he heard it: the unmistakable whine of a helicopter making its landing approach.

The train had come to a halt by the time he reached the dining car. He sat down, listening to the ticking noises all round him. Silence. He toyed with a silver teaspoon and gazed on row after row of tables, each covered with immaculately pressed linen, the places set for dinner. Someone was planning a banquet, a last fling for Iscariot. The bill for that had been rather costly, out of all proportion to the victuals consumed. But a banquet without guests?

He looked up. In the doorway: Kron.

The Russian was alone, and although they had not met before, Stevens recognized him at once. He knew him from innumerable files and from last night's conversation with Volodny.

"A man you can trust," he had said. That was unlike Vladimir Andreyevich.

The arrangements, Stevens thought.

They shook hands, Kron grinning broadly like a man who has just won a lottery. He was in uniform, GRU shoulder boards, insignia, medal ribbons, gun, and boots.

"Where is the reporter?" he asked.

"Back there," Stevens said.

A steward appeared and Kron sent him to find Johnson. He addressed Stevens. "Vladimir Andreyevich says he will see you on the frontier."

"I know that."

"Good! Very good!" Kron boomed. He lowered his voice. "Vladimir Andreyevich says he is sorry, but you dug your own grave."

"Is that so?"

"Yes, but then you know him. He is always apologizing for nothing." Kron grinned. "He says you threw away the spade, jumped in, covered yourself with dirt, and nailed up the coffin lid."

"That's quite a trick," Stevens said. "I had some help from the comrade in question, of course."

"*Da!*" Kron shook with laughter. "But that was only because he admires you. You shouldn't be so modest," he said, then was abruptly serious. "Vladimir Andreyevich also says that having done all this, you want to get out."

"It's the worms," Stevens said. "They bother me."

"*Worms!* Mr. Stevens, Comrade, you are a funny man. . . ." Kron subdued his mirth. "You understand the arrangements?"

"I think so."

Kron was unhappy. "Vladimir Andreyevich says that desperate diseases require desperate remedies."

"Yes, he would say that."

"We shall look after the journalist."

"How?"

"He will be taken by car from Vyborg to Vainikkala. After that it's up to your people. You realize that we are doing this from the kindness of our great Russian hearts. He is not worth a shit to us. Five minutes after Vyborg the train will stop again." Kron held up a massive hand, spreading the fingers. "There will be a Ka-26 waiting for you on the ground. Your compass bearings and flight path will be inside. We have even set up a DF beacon for you, and the machine is equipped with the latest topographical radar. It would be impossible to get lost and foolish to try. Is that clear?"

"Perfectly," Stevens said. "You're going to a lot of trouble. Why?"

"Carlo is expecting you to arrive by car. When he sees what has happened, he will think that you have escaped."

"That's supposed to make him feel better?"

"It might."

"The Ka-26, how does it handle? It's a long time since I've flown."

"They refreshed you in Plymouth. Two years ago. See, English," Kron said, wagging a finger, "I know. The machine is easy to handle. You should see our pilots. A blind man could fly it."

"What happens if the Finns start shooting?"

"Then there will be a war." Kron laughed. "Seriously, they will have been told that you are experiencing difficulties."

"What if there's a bomb on board?"

"Trust us," Kron said. "No bombs."

His eyes shot up, staring over Stevens' head. The steward had returned with Johnson, who loitered in the corridor like a truant child.

"Sit down," Stevens said, "join the party. . . ." Now, that was a crass remark, an incredibly stupid thing to say. But Johnson didn't seem to notice.

Kron inspected the reporter, a man of no consequence. The Russian turned his thoughts to other matters, grinding his molars and rubbing his hands together.

"Food," he declared as the steward reappeared with bowls of steaming borscht, beet-red and viscid, borne on a silver platter.

"You can't give up, can you? It must be like an addiction, that's what it is—some kind of drug. Why do you have to keep on dealing with them? They've got nothing on you. Or have they?" Stevens listened impassively to the reporter, who was behaving like an angry schoolboy. "You know what I think, what I really think? You can't prove a thing against Carlo, so you're going to kill him. Maybe you can claim diminished responsibility or something. Well, that's just fine, that is. But it's no good at all, not when you're afraid of what would happen if it came to a court of law. . . ."

The train was under way again, and Johnson felt slightly drunk. He shouldn't have had anything to drink, but the shock of seeing Stevens with that Russian had more than justified his indulgence. Christ, how he had needed a drink! His indignation was fired by a thousand petty treasons. He thought of Anna, the way she had tricked him, and of Carlo, who had lied about Stevens' death. The only person who had been telling the truth was Dorothy Winters, and he had been convinced that she was lying. Somewhere in all this Johnson sensed the makings of a scientific law. Absurdly he maintained that he mustn't lose sight of his objective, which he viewed as a kind of salvage operation. Mighty phrases rang in his head and evaporated. Last night in the Lubyanka he had dreamt of rats. He felt enormously tired, dead tired, like a man who could sleep forever.

"It's no excuse for murder, that's all," he said.

"Diminished responsibility or inadequate proof?"

"Both."

"Personal actions cease with the death of the plaintiff. It wasn't meant to come to a court of law." Stevens hoped that Johnson would see the fine point. He didn't.

"You're going to kill him! You really mean to kill him!"

"Are you speaking for the prosecution or the defence?"

"For Christ's sake, this isn't a *game*. He's an old man."

"So was Clemens. Anyway, Carlo's not so old. He's got sixty-five years of childhood behind him."

"That meeting, it was *arranged!*"

"You don't understand."

"I'm sick of people telling me that! Sick to the teeth . . ."

"You don't have to shout. You'll disturb our friends next door." Stevens wondered how much he could safely tell the reporter. Very little, he decided. "The meeting was arranged," he said, "because we're anticipating trouble. Kron's in charge of security for this sector. He doesn't want you to get hurt."

"Isn't that amazing! Everyone's so bloody well concerned for my safety. That really takes the piss out of the Easter bunny!"

"Yes, it does a bit. I'm sorry. You're an outsider," Stevens said, looking for the right words, "and you'd never understand, not in a million years. It's not your fault. There are principles involved, rules that go beyond national interest, even self-interest. It would be the best thing for everyone if you just got in that car tomorrow morning. No fuss, no problems. You just do as you're told, and nothing will go wrong. . . ." Stevens hesitated. "If it makes you feel any better, Carlo's an old friend and I love him like a brother. I've no intention of committing fratricide, tomorrow or any other day. I am not going to kill Carlo. Do you understand that?"

Johnson didn't reply. A queasy sensation invaded his guts. He remembered waiting for Soper, yesterday afternoon, at the Karl Marx statue. Now, why should he think of that? Johnson made a note to visit the Great Teacher's grave. It was in Highgate, where Hasketh lived—Terence Hasketh, Esq., who lived on the hill in a house with a view. Johnson remembered waiting for Soper at the Place of the Skull. He didn't want to think of Soper at all, so he thought of the British Museum instead. What was it the librarian had said about Lenin? "Lenin? Lenin? Oh, yes, I remember him. A nice quiet gentleman." Johnson thought of the tramp who had been reading Trotsky, the pub called the Half Moon, the Gissing girl. The train whistle screamed and everything came together: borscht and sour cream, Kron's cold regard, Dimitrov's mocking laughter in the graveyard of the Novo-Devichy Convent, the dead-fish eyes of Reginald Soper, the police smashing Gosling's camera, the tendrils of blood mixed with ice, and oh, God, that blood congealing just like the borscht.

He stood up. "It's the borscht," he said, and the word made him feel sicker.

Stevens watched him leave. Ten minutes later he returned, looking pale and ill.

"I was followed," he said. "The bastards watched me."

Laughter sounded from the adjacent compartment.

"You should get some sleep," Stevens said.

"It's snowing," Johnson said.

"Yes," Stevens said.

It was dark, and the snow swept across the window like static on a radar screen.

"Get some sleep now," he said. "You'll need it."

Johnson was snoring, and Stevens thought of Cavendish again, a man who could snore when he was awake. "Merely forgot to retract me adenoids." A sad, funny, clever man. Miles was talking about brainwashing, a subject that had preoccupied everyone in the days after the Korean War.

"No such thing. Just another name for bullying. More advanced, yes, more sophisticated, but bullying all the same. Hypnotism, now, that's different. The thing to do with these mesmerists and whatnot is to turn your mind off. Click-click, like a switch. It's all done by electricity. Turn off the lamp of your mind! It's easy, mind over matter and all that. Trouble is when it's someone else's mind and your matter . . ."

"A delta brain wave. You must have been asleep, George."

". . . no such thing as brainwashing, though. Yankee propaganda. Old wives' tales. You know why they confessed? *Kindness —* they were frightened by kindness. Owens will tell you. They went to school, see? There was an instructor who'd get up on the stage and say, 'Good morning, students.' Then everybody would chorus, 'Good morning, sir!' and the Chinese would think they were getting along famously. But if you were bloody-minded, the kindness stopped. Or it stopped anyway, just like that. Hot and cold. Pass the bottle, will you? Glug-glug, old fella . . . Where was I? Hot and cold, that's it, unpredictability, you know . . . The thing to remember is this. There's body without mind, commonly called a corpse, but no mind without body. Don't believe in ghosts, do you? Well, then, you can't get to a fella when he's dead. I mean you can't *influence* him. Same thing as when he's asleep, same thing *entirely*. Course, if he believes that you can put the 'fluence on him when he's asleep, then he'll believe all sorts of mumbo-jumbo. That's the weird thing about the mind. It has to be done consciously, understand? No rapport otherwise . . ."

Drunk again, Balthazar? No one can get to you now, and that's a fact.

There was a theory of mind, Stevens remembered, according to which the brain's function was to exclude stimuli, like a filter. What would happen if you were constantly aware of all sensations, slight changes in temperature or blood pressure, air currents, vibration, sound? Some people were driven crazy by their own body noises. Without special training it was impossible to regulate the autonomic central nervous system. Most people were not even aware of it; you don't have to think about digestion to digest a meal, though thinking itself could give you ulcers, could make the body digest itself. The same thing happened in death. Stevens wondered if it was possible for a man to think himself to death. Some kind of yoga, he supposed, might do the trick. "*A delta brain wave . . .*" There was a kind of anaesthetic fog in his mind, which he imagined would show up on an X ray of the brain like a shadow, except it was more palpable than that, something he could touch and taste and feel, velvet bile. And he was afraid, not so much of dying but of probing that shadow too deeply, as a surgeon would be afraid of cutting too deeply. It was an impersonal fear, and it was nothing new. In the Gestapo prison at Fresnes, after the second night, he had awoken not knowing who he was, had forgotten his name, age, identity, operational history, even his whereabouts, for perhaps just a microsecond, though in that millionth particle of time he had experienced enough terror for eternity. That was why he used to wake up screaming for help. *"Lassen Sie uns gehen! Schnell! Schnell!"* It wasn't a vision you could explain, to wife or stranger, friend or enemy, the thought that the man they knew or loved or hated, or towards whom they were merely indifferent, was nothing more than a husk, a confidence man who represented himself to the world as George Michael Stevens. This, he supposed, was how you felt after they had taken the brace and bit to you; it was like a prefrontal lobotomy without the surgical killing, the cutting and burning, of nervous tissue. Only one person had guessed at this state of affairs, and he, more than anyone else, was its cause—Carlo Peat. George Stevens understood only too well why Carlo had made no plans for his recovery. There was nothing to recover, but that was not something he could have told Vladimir Andreyevich.

Stevens closed his eyes. A revelation, saints and sinners know, is something you have to work on. He was in Owens' consulting room, off Brompton Road, and they had him strapped down to that table. The IV drip—what the hell was in the IV drip? Not a hallucinogenic. He remembered working on his pulse, trying to force it down to make the blood-brain barrier less permeable. Euphoria.

"Tell me about Philip Grove," Sweet said.

"Imperméable."

"What?"

"It's a French raincoat. Grove bought one, in Paris. It was blue."
Covered with plastic buckles and flaps and straps. Don't talk about
Grove, don't even think *about him. . . .*
"What was he doing in Paris?"
"Ask the Greeks." No aristeia, *that was his trouble, just a wife*
stealer. Lautrec, Henri Marie Raymond de Toulouse-Lautrec
Monfa, Le Promenoir. Baby Graebe, Julius. "He was a dwarf,
wasn't he? I don't know. What did they kill him for?" Baby warned.
Baby told Grove there was a Soviet double among the Friends. Did I
just say that? "He was minding the baby grebes, so they killed him
for the feathers."
"Who told you that, George?"
"No one."
So he had. Carlo. Grove had been Graebe's case officer, and
Graebe was the first agent to be blown. Grove couldn't be allowed
to walk around forever with Graebe's information in his head.
"Look at the necklace, George. You are tired, very tired. The
comrade colonel is going to ask you a few questions."
"Who are you going to kill, George?"
"No one!"
Druzula and Volodny—they hadn't been in Kensington Gardens.
Everything was mixed up.
"Listen to the metronome, Mr. Stevens. . . ."
Owens. He'd pronounced it like "metrognome." And he hadn't
been in the Kremlin Hospital. Crazy, crazy . . .
"Sergei, would you be so good as to fetch the comrade colonel's
tape recorder?"
Sergei, who in God's name was Sergei?
"Chernukhin Dimitrov Chernukhin Dimitrov . . ."
"Shelley-Jelly."
". . . spindling . . ."
"One hundred and forty volts. We can go twenty higher, forty
at the absolute maximum."
"One hundred and forty microvolts. Alpha wave."
Druzula hadn't always been there, in the hospital. There were
times when it was just Volodny and a technician whose name
was . . . Sergei!
"Chernukhin, Yuri Simonovich Chernukhin?"
"K complex, Comrade Colonel!"

Cheng: the Circus, twenty years ago. Burgess and Maclean—skipped. Philby—out of strategy. Denials all round and, later, the denials denied. Who made Kim run? Carlo made Kim run. How did Carlo make Kim run? He used yours truly, that's how, just as he would use him to take Baby out of the game.

Old friends, dead friends—the mind was like an attic: too many skeletons, too many faded photographs.

"Why are things always the wrong way round, mm?"

Balthazar had a saying, too: "If Mohammed will not go to the mountain, the mountain must come to Mohammed."

It had been the wrong side of the mountain for Kim. Carlo had known that: a dip slope and a scarp slope, the reversed image of Mount Ararat taken from the Soviet side of the frontier, peaks and valleys, *spindling*.

"Theoretically, there *is* a way of telling what's in someone's mind, even though he can't remember it himself. If you could measure the evoked potential of a signal, and if you had control, some basis of comparison, then the difference in amplitudes would be significant—but no more than that. It's what they call a psycho-galvanic response. Electricity again. You'd have to know what you were looking for, though. The ghost in the machine, old boy."

Stevens understood. The mountain had come to Mohammed. Owens had implanted the name Chernukhin and had then blasted out the conscious memory with electric-shock treatment, inducing so crude a state of amnesia that even the forgetting had been forgotten, seared over with a mental cicatrix. Only the deep memory trace had remained, buried under the rind of the cortex in the archaic convolutions of the midbrain, the lair of the great beast Id. Volodny and the comrade doctor had cornered the beast in his den, had mapped out the contours of the mind on a dream machine. They had done this because of the cypher, because he had been *clever*, because he had faked amnesia, as if his simulated derangement—that show of acoustical confusion that had fooled no one, least of all Dimitrov—somehow made up for and took the place of the en-gineered dysfunction. Hazard had ruled the *cheng* because of that code. Looking for one thing, they had found another. Yet behind this chance, this occult collusion, were years of planning and preparation, a degree of prevision that amounted to a psychic *diktat*. Carlo had chosen those code names. Could he have foreseen the cypher? It was not half so crazy, not half so paranoid as it would have sounded a week or a month ago.

Drunken laughter sounded from the next compartment; Johnson was still snoring. It was after one, and the train was pulling into Leningrad. They would stay here for another two hours at least, a dead time in a sealed train shunted into a dead siding. He could hear men talking outside in the snow. Someone swung a lantern by the tracks. The city lights twinkled along the Neva, and he could smell the salt sea air coming in from the Baltic. He did not want to sleep, a man afraid, perhaps, of dreams and shadows. Nor did he want to wake, afraid certainly of what the day would bring. It was not a breach of faith that troubled him now but the lack of faith; not a change of allegiance but the denial of allegiance. He owed nothing to any man, friend or comrade, he was through with them all. And so he allowed darkness to wash round him, adrift on that tide like a free man, freer than he had ever been, to wait, to rest, and not to feel, as if freedom and nothingness were the same, void of all feeling. He knew what had to be done, and how. *Aristeia*, the noble act even of a slave, freely to fight and freely to die. Yet—he did not know how much longer it would last—the conviction grew upon him that his freedom had never seemed more contingent, or anything more futile, more hopeless, than this lack, this denial, this zero.

26

Fellow Travellers,
Vyborg,
8 November,
0600 Hours

The man under the iron grey porch of Vyborg station wore his hat with the brim turned down and his coat with the collar turned up. Snow drifted along the tracks, flurrying, wraithlike, in the soft glow of the platform lights, and the man clapped his arms about him and stamped his feet on the station steps, his neat, shiny overshoes imprisoning the bitter cold within his feet. He heard the chatter of the telegraph inside the station and the muffled thud of a signal falling into place. The first of the helicopters droned overhead and the mournful wail of a train whistle was borne on the wind. Herr Keller from Essen counted four of the machines and consulted the oversized clock that projected from the faded yellow wood of the doorframe. Five to six, everything was on schedule.

The door opened and one of the green-hatted border police stood in the light.

"*Khaladna?*"

"*Nyet.*"

Keller lied about the cold. He thought of another such morning, the black morning after the German surrender at Schlüsselburg. With only an oil lamp for warmth he had endured that night in the company of the dead and the dying, watching the condensation trickle down the stone walls of the ruined fortress, counting the drops until eternity surely must come. Schlüsselburg was not so far away, the memory frozen into the marrow of his bones, a nightmare, a scar in the earth, defeat. But for Herr Keller, if not for his countrymen, it had been a victory.

The German watched the locomotive, a diesel, pull into the station. It reminded him of a Siemens generator on wheels, brute mechanical perfection, its steel grille crowned with a hammer and sickle. Snowflakes starred his vision. The driver and engineer swung down from the cab, and the rail crew attacked the coupling. Herr Keller from Essen looked forward to renewing his acquaintance with the English reporter Johnson, a meeting that promised to be interesting. It was just after six, Russian time, when he boarded the train and marched down the corridor, two of the border police following. Herr Keller tapped lightly on the glass pane of the compartment door, which was opened by the English spy George Stevens, for whom, at this moment, he had no time. A man of the past, George Stevens, obsolescent, but Johnson, *der junger Mensch*, was not too old to learn a lesson, and Keller had gone out of his way to teach him one.

"*Bumagi, pazhahlsta*—your papers, please." It was to Johnson that he spoke, keeping his hat pulled down and his collar turned up.

Herr Keller brushed the documents aside. He removed his hat and clutched it mournfully. "I hope you have enjoyed your stay," he said, "now that you have reached the point of expiry."

"Keller!" Johnson cried.

The reporter turned to Stevens. "He was on the plane coming out! He was on the bloody plane!"

"That is true," Keller said. "I was assigned to the transit."

"Where's Dimitrov?"

There was a coldness in Stevens' voice, a tone that Keller did not like. "Vladimir Andreyevich will see you at the frontier," he said. The train jolted as they hooked up the Finnish locomotive for Vainikkala.

"I thought he would be here," Stevens said. His face was a mask. Pharaonic. The Englishman had been too long in the tomb, Keller thought.

"On the frontier." He replaced his hat and shuffled his feet.

"Carlo arrived last night with David Sweet. The train will leave in a few minutes," he said to Johnson. "I'll be waiting outside, in the corridor." He retreated, leaving a puddle of melted snow behind him.

"They knew, then," Johnson said. "They knew all the time."

"It looks very much like it," Stevens agreed. "Your bag . . ."

"I can manage." Johnson reached for his case.

"How do you feel?"

"Tired."

There was a tacit understanding between the two men that Stevens would not be returning to London, and Johnson felt enormously depressed, weighed down by a sense of professional failure. Nothing had worked out, and the man who stood before him, awkwardly smiling, his hand extended, remained as much of an enigma as ever. A man with two sides to his head. It had never occurred to Johnson that George Stevens was basically an uncomplicated man.

Johnson shook his hand. "You made more sense before," he said.

"When I was dead?"

"Yes. Why did you have to let Carlo know?"

"Because he was expecting it," Stevens said. "Don't forget to see Bentinck."

"I won't." Johnson lingered in the doorway. "Well, good luck, then." He could think of nothing else to say.

"Thanks."

Stevens followed him out of the door and watched him walk down the corridor, shoulders bowed, carrying his case clumsily, as a man will when he is tired at the end of a long journey. The reporter did not look back, but Keller, Clemens' agent, did, tipping his hand to his hat in mock salute. Stevens wondered if Keller knew about his boss yet. He returned to the compartment and watched them disappear into darkness and snow. Stevens sat down and thought of his old SOE instructor, Pops—Popeye the Pole. Funny, but he had never known his real name.

COMPAGNIE DE WAGON-LIT, said the sign above the sink. *Vainikkala kill Vainikkala kill Vainikkala kill*, the tracks sang out. Stevens turned on the tap, the kind with a lever and spring that needs constant hand pressure to keep it running. He pressed on the brass lever until the porcelain handle sank into his palm. Well, that was practice, the pressure. He filled the sink and wondered about the goon outside, who looked as though he had a hangover. What was he thinking? It was not much of a job. Lonely. Most of the comrade goons had left the train at Vyborg. They were not expecting trouble now, a mistake. Water slopped on the floor and he let go of the lever. Time to go. He opened the door. Lurch, oopsa-daisy.

"So sorry . . ."

The man turned as he had before—the natural, unavoidable re-action in so confined a space—turned, flanking Stevens, who thrust his thumbs into the arteries at the soft junction of the neck and jaw, just above the hyoid bone, his fingers forcing the eyes back into their sockets against the optic nerves. The man blubbered as he fell and Stevens felt the carotid walls ballooning against the thyroid cartilage. He broke the fall with his knee, twisting the head back. A cervical vertebra cracked like a rifle shot. Galen, misapplied medicine: *karotikós*, *carus*, stupor, love, death. He kept the pressure on the arteries until the pulse ceased and he heard the man's sphincter ripple. The stench made him gag. He lugged the corpse into the toilet and wedged its head under the taps, facedown in the water. No bubbles. He felt the still-warm body, found the Russian's gun, and placed it outside in the corridor where it could be seen.

He retraced his steps and hammered on the door of the next compartment, shouting, "Hey, Ivan! Come on! Your comrade's been ill!"

The second Russian appeared with a drawn gun. He was in his shirt sleeves and half asleep, hence the cautious approach. Stevens backed off, raising his hands. There were no more goons in the compartment.

"How—ill?"

"Very."

"Show me."

Stevens wagged a finger towards the end of the car, but the Rus-sian signalled him to go first.

"Move, please. No trouble."

"I think he's had a heart attack or something."

"We shall see. Move now."

Tricky bastard, Stevens thought. His arms were aching, his shirt was blistered with sweat underneath his jacket, and he could feel his heart pounding against his rib cage. If I don't watch out,

I'll be the one who has a heart attack, he thought, and set off down the corridor with the Russian trailing cautiously behind. The train braked and shuddered, and Stevens gave another practised lurch, closing the distance between himself and the goon, who gasped when he saw the gun lying in the corridor.

He darted past Stevens, scooped the gun, stuck it in his belt, and spun round to face the Englishman like one who has spent a lifetime rehearsing just such a manoeuvre. "Feliks! Feliks!" he cried, kicking the cubicle door with his boot heel. Then he saw the liquid seeping under the door. "Back, back," he said, and put his shoulder to the door, forgetting that it opened outwards. The Russian swore and gave Stevens a rueful look, disconcerted by this conspiracy of objects. The Russian was young and nervous and he still held a gun on Stevens. Both men watched the door swing open on its hinges. The Russian licked his lips. He could see his comrade's legs kneeling by the sink, but no more. "Feliks?" he said again, less certainly. He backed into the cubicle. The floor was wet and slippery, and Feliks' head was in the sink—drowned? The Russian didn't panic, and Stevens had to admire this. It must have been a hell of a shock. With his free hand the Russian grabbed the corpse by the collar but its head was stuck fast under the taps. He folded his gun arm under one of Feliks', joined it with the other, and, clenching his gun in both hands at the back of the corpse's neck, tried a half nelson. It was then that he was distracted by Feliks' head, which was loose and floppy, and it was then that Stevens killed him, in the same way and just as dispassionately, though without apology this time.

He pocketed the clip from the first gun, which he threw out of the window, keeping the other. They were both the same make and calibre. It was quite messy and overcrowded in the cubicle, but before he cleaned up, he solved the spatial problem by inverting the second body, fortunately lighter than its predecessor, dunking it headfirst in the toilet bowl. DO NOT USE WHILE STANDING IN THE STATION, read the polyglot sign. Then he removed as much water as he could, absorbing it with a toilet tissue that was decidedly inferior in capacity to the three-ply stuff that people love to squeeze.

He closed the door and heard the clunk of feet falling and scraping on the inside. The train was almost at a standstill now. For God's sake, Kron, he thought, I hope you're not taken short.

27

Vainikkala
Kill

The Ka-26's power unit idled and whined, and the rotor blades flickered and drooped like the antennae of an enormous insect, a cicada, Stevens thought. The helicopter itself was blunt and functional, a coffin-shaped fuselage slung between a couple of tail booms and surmounted by two fat engine pods that looked like eyes from the front end. It seemed smaller on the ground than in the air, a paradoxical effect, and more fragile, almost delicate, now that it was out of its true medium.

Kron was standing under the cabin, aft of the Plexiglas nose. The pilot climbed out from the other side and walked round to the tail booms. He stared at the dull red glow of the engine exhausts, the snow hissing and melting on the hot metal. Stevens tried to think how he could get Kron on board without pulling the gun on him first.

"I'll want to do a cockpit check," he said.

"Of course." Kron called the pilot over. "We'll show you," he said complacently.

The train, marooned in the darkness, gave a blast on its whistle. Stevens wondered how long it would be before they found what he had left behind.

Kron gave him a hand up into the cabin. He left the door open and the pilot went through his drill, his face bathed in the grey-green nimbus from the instrument panel.

"The important thing is the DF beacon," Kron said. "But there's also a light intensifier for visual sighting." The pilot's hand swung up to disengage the device, which folded like a periscope. "Useful," Kron said, "for identifying and fixing a target."

Stevens crouched behind the observer's seat, massaging his hands.

"What about the beacon?" he asked.

"Operational at your cruising altitude."

"Which is?"

"Low. Eight hundred metres."

"How'd you get it that low?"

"The other machines will be relaying the beam. Two of them will be on station in front of you to the southwest and northeast port and starboard. The third will be flying directly in line behind you on the same vector. The beam is triangulated for a continuous signal over the Vainikkala frontier post. We weren't expecting this weather, so you may have to go down for a visual fix. There are parachute flares in the bay—the red toggle releases them. The searchlight is normally operated by the observer, but you should be able to manage it yourself. They will also have lights along the road at the frontier. You won't exactly be flying blind, Comrade."

"I'll get lonely up there, Kron."

"*Tovarich*, our thoughts will go with you."

"I know, but that's not the same. How about coming along for the ride?"

"This is the parting of our ways, Comrade."

"I don't think so."

Kron leant back, his head on one side. When he saw the gun, he knew that the Englishman had killed and would do so again if the need arose. He turned round, staring into the darkness ahead.

"What are you trying to do?" He sounded disinterested.

"You'll see."

Kron felt his own gun being eased from its holster. Those *svolochi* on the train! "We can't stay here," he said in the same bored voice. "The other machines will land."

The radio crackled and Stevens heard the Russian word *tualet* repeated several times. Someone must have found the meat. A pity the sign hadn't prohibited use while standing in the countryside. Tiny figures spilled out of the train and began milling about in the snow, their shadows long and frantic in the yellow light from the windows.

"Call them up," Stevens said. "This machine is out of bounds, understand?"

Kron did as he was told.

"You still haven't answered my question," he said. "What are you going to do?"

"Nothing for the moment. We just sit tight, nice and easy. Boyo here will do the flying. I told you, it's a long time since I've driven one of these things. But you wouldn't listen, would you?"

The figures were dancing and shouting now, waving their little hands in the air. One of the other Ka-26's clattered in and the figures scattered, throwing themselves to the ground. The radio spoke again.

"They want to know what the trouble is," Kron said bleakly.

The figures regrouped. They had found a leader, and Stevens heard shots.

"Those hooligans are shooting at the wrong machine," Kron said.

"You wouldn't want them to shoot at us, would you?" Stevens said.

"*Yob tuoyu mat!*" The radio barked incestuous obscenities, and the helicopter made another whining pass, nose down, searching. Recognition flares spluttered across the sky, Very lights falling like Roman candles in a display of multicoloured pyrotechnics. There was some confused chatter between the pilots of the airborne machines, then silence. Red and blue navigation lights made a Möbius strip, a figure eight vanishing to the east, and a momentary peace returned to the sky.

"All down, Kron. I want those machines on the deck." He felt enormously happy with the way things were turning out.

"Comrade Colonel"—the pilot spoke for the first time—"if they land, there will be no beacon."

Kron shifted uneasily. He was nervous because he couldn't see his enemy's face, and he tried to look at his watch but he couldn't see that either. There was too much light or not enough. Kron wasn't sure which.

"I can't order them down," he said. "I don't have the authority."

"You do now." Stevens tapped the gun barrel lightly on the back of the Russian's neck.

"As you wish," Kron said.

I wish, Stevens thought. He crossed over to the pilot's side of the cabin. "Be good," he said, "and I'll see you're taken care of."

The pilot nodded.

"Let's have some ignition, then."

The starter motor coughed and chugged, little puffs of white smoke drifting past the door. Shut the doors, Stevens was going to say, when he saw another of the buglike machines hovering no more than a couple of hundred yards away. Subliminally, almost before there was time to react, he saw the venomous points of flame stippling its side. *No! No! No!* The cry froze in his mind and the cabin rocked with the detonations, glass splintering like fractured ice, floating and slowly falling, the turbines shrieking as the pilot pushed the throttles to maximum revs, and the earth let them go.

"Close the doors," Stevens said, and asked if anyone was hurt.

There was no answer.

"Vainikkala now," he told the pilot.

"They will follow us," Kron said. "They will follow us on their radar."

"Then we'll go down, right down. Use the contour radar."

Stevens saw that the instrument panel was a shambles. The altimeter had been shot out; likewise the fuel gauges, flight-speed indicator, drift counter, and artificial horizon. There was an empty socket where the flight radar should have been and the electrical system reeked of ozone. Stevens could smell cordite and oil as well. The machine yawed in flight. Outside: nothing.

"Kron, you'd better tell your droogs to take up station."

The machine yawed again, and the pilot felt a shudder from the control column, which was slack and unresponsive. "We're losing oil pressure," he said. "There's a control problem somewhere. I'm not sure where. Yet."

Stevens thought, It can't go wrong, not now. "*Tovarich*, this set is dead," he heard Kron say.

"Keep trying. How are the controls?"

"Not good," the pilot said. "There's an oil line up to the pitching gear. I think it's been severed."

Stevens traced the line of fire across the cabin window up into the rotor transmission. A bullet, still warm, dislodged itself from the back of the pilot's seat frame and fell on his hand. Oil splashed from one of the holes like blood from a wound. He listened to the turbines. They seemed all right. Thank Christ there was no fire. The pilot will see us through. He's a lucky bastard, he *has* to be.

Stevens looked at the bullet, which had flattened out like a lump of putty. He remembered the flares and the searchlight in the bay.

"Circle left," he told the pilot. "Kron, let go the flares when I say so. Understood?"

"*Kharasho.*"

"Easy, easy . . . *Now!*"

Stevens saw the ground rocks, black on white, and the tree line illuminated in the phosphorescent glow. He guessed the altitude at around eight hundred metres, which was what it should be if they were going to pick up that beacon, not that there was any chance of that happening now.

"Switch on the bay light," he said, and Kron obliged. Flat country, heavily wooded. Lakes within islands within lakes, a canal, the railroad.

"The Saimaa Canal, and there's the Vainikkala road," Kron said.

The pilot saw the lights first, above the northeastern horizon, milkily diffused against the cloud base.

"Vainikkala," he said.

The machine didn't like flying to port, didn't like it at all, and the pilot was beginning to wonder why. He had needed all his strength and skill to pull out of the last turn, and his back and arms ached with the effort. The controls bucked in his hands, protesting as he brought the machine round in a lateral power glide towards the lights. Stevens heard a new note from the engines, an ostinato pulse, arhythmical and vibrant, like a weirdly syncopated funeral march. They were losing height and speed at quite a rate now, and he could make out the helicopter's shadow scudding along the road beneath them. When he looked up again, the lights had gone out.

The machine sagged, drifting to starboard. Stevens saw the pilot hunch over the controls, his back bowed like a weight lifter about to press a heavy load. The turbines were vamping now, but it didn't matter, nothing did anymore except this one thing. Shadows fractured the cabin and he was dazzled by the glare of beaded lights, strung out above them, which was impossible, or so he thought until he saw the ground hurtling up, angled at thirty degrees, and another of the machines drift by them, so close that he caught the pilot's startled gaze. He saw the customs post on the Vainikkala road, the trucks parked in the rear, the searchlights and generator by the road-side, the sky-gazers scattering, two separating amoebalike from the rest.

"The fat man!" he cried.

The pilot twisted the machine round in a slow passacaglia, a lumbering parody of the dance. Stevens saw Carlo turn, run, stumble, and fall, saw him taken up and blown aside in the down-wash from the rotor blades, his arms and legs splayed in the snow, moulding himself to the good earth like a great fat scarab, and he saw Sweet stagger from the eye of the storm—Sweet, the beetle's servant, clutching a skeletal machine pistol, shooting . . .

The horizon righted itself, tilted the other way, and steadied. They were hovering over the roof of the customs shed now, and he understood, with a kind of retrograde vision, that everything had been far too slow. "You can do better than that," he said, holding the gun behind the pilot's ear. "I *know* you can do better than that."

"Comrade Colonel," the pilot said, begging for instructions, "what shall I do?"

"Do as the crazy man says," Kron growled. "It makes no dif-ference to me." It was a lie. Kron wanted to live, more than he had five minutes ago, more than he had ever. The only trouble was Stevens. He turned round to look at the Englishman, who smiled at him. *"Tovarich . . ."* he began, and gave up.

The pilot reached out for the light-intensifier glasses, his arm mopping his brow. He was a good pilot and knew that the damage to his machine was more extensive than he cared to admit. He didn't give too much thought to this but concentrated on the task in hand. If the fat man was to be killed, it would have to be done this time. There would be no third chance unless he was very lucky, and the pilot wasn't feeling lucky.

He used the excess torque to advantage, giving the machine free rein and letting it fall into a sideslip until he judged that the fat man's head was in line with the landing gear. Then he shoved the control column hard over and down, coming in low and fast because the Finns were shooting at him and he made an easy target. But the fat man made an even better target, considering the size of the projectile, and the pilot couldn't understand why he held his ground in such a brave but foolish stance, like a man at prayer. Distantly the pilot heard a voice screaming at him to pull out. When he saw what the fat man was doing, his instinctive reaction caused him to do exactly that, forgetting even the gun behind his own head. Not, of course, that the crazy Englishman in the back would shoot (he was doing the screaming), unlike the fat man, who did, taking very careful aim just as the pilot felt something give in the controls and a terrible thud came from the landing gear, a bone-crushing jolt that sent a sickly tremor through the whole machine.

Carlo's first shot missed David Sweet, and that was unfortunate. His second shot also missed, which was doubly unfortunate. Carlo attributed his indifferent aim to the thunder of the great beast in the sky and the shock waves that convulsed the earth. Perhaps the rain of hot black pitch that fell, as though from a passing comet, also had something to do with it.

He was steadying himself for a third shot when Sweet, who had paid little attention to the report of Carlo's gun amid the discharge of so much ordnance, spun round, his face contorted with rage and hatred. He's going to kill me, Carlo thought, watching Sweet fiddle with the clip on the Armalite Special, which had apparently jammed. Carlo fired again, missed again. Instead of closing the range—it was about six feet, no more; how could anyone *miss* at that distance?—he took off with a strange hopping gait through the snow, pausing to look over his shoulder and shoot and miss, shoot and miss, until the Webley was empty and Carlo screamed. The underbelly of the great beast floated over him and the right landing wheel connected with Sweet's head, which dissolved in a livid red foam. Falling, Carlo screamed into the snow, clots of brain and gore splattering around him. And then he was up and running, still screaming, his arms flailing wildly as he sought to penetrate that crimson mist, to break out and escape.

He tore open the door of the customs post and rushed inside, collapsing at the table, sobbing. The great beast had followed him and the building quaked to its grotesque rhythm. Carlo looked up at the ceiling, not comprehending. Surely they must stop now and leave him alone, surely to God! But no, a bumping sound came from the roof: bump-bump, slither—a body. They were going to come in and kill him, and he couldn't defend himself because he had lost his gun, outside in the awful blood-soaked snow. Sweet, Sweet had a gun. He saw the headless corpse, squatting where it had fallen, or where it had tried to get up, perhaps, and *then* had fallen—it looked so unnatural, almost meditative—and he screamed again.

"George! Don't let them kill me!"

He covered his eyes with his hands and when he took them away saw that his palms were wet and sticky, messed with oil and blood, they were, and smelly, a deep, dark, carnal stench. "Help me! Oh, God, *please*, someone help me!" Bump-bump, slither. He heard it again, this time from the other side of the roof. Something bulky and vaguely human tumbled past the window, bullets rattled down the roof—ricochetting from the belly of the machine—and God, oh, God, help me—the thing was coming down through the ceiling.

Carlo was paralyzed. He sat at the table, wishing himself outside. Plaster trickled onto his neck and stuck there, the clock slid down the wall and broke into little pieces, the light swung in an ellipse that changed the shape of the room, and the green enamelled shade plummeted to the table, its fall masking the bulb, which exploded softly. Darkness. Carlo sprang to his feet and began a desperate search for the door, his hands clawing at the walls, the timbers splitting and cracking, bulging outwards. The pipes to the oil furnace broke and he saw a line of pretty green flames snake across the floor. He giggled hysterically. Among the many deaths he had imaginatively prefigured for himself, burning alive, next to being squashed alive, was the most horrible, and now it seemed only a question of which would come first. The roof beams groaned and sagged, and one of them fell, catching him on the right shoulder and snapping it like a wishbone. He collapsed into the flames, rolled over and over, and crawled to the table at the room's centre, using his good arm to lever himself to his feet as the pretty green flames licked greedily at the walls. He felt cold, so cold and tired and useless.

Reason must have fled him then, because he conceived of the headless Sweet knocking at the door and waiting outside. Carlo heard the susurrus of many voices. Weeping in pain and fear, he imagined that if only he could stop the noise, everything would be all right.

Yes, yes, that was it, but the difficulty, the *immense* difficulty, was that he couldn't cover both ears with only the one hand. He experimented by trying to raise his right hand with his left, but the grating in his shoulder forced him to give up. He hid under the table, lying in a foetal crouch, his left arm crossed awkwardly over his right ear, and in this position awaited the end.

The ghastly light from above compelled him to stick out his head. "George?" he moaned, shielding his eyes.

Carlo saw the black bloodstained wheel tear into the ceiling and retreat, taking half the roof away into the sky. There was a quality of mercy to this, for the downwash from the rotors doused the flames. Carlo moaned again and gazed into the jagged wound of night. He watched the great beast spiral aloft, a wounded killer bird abandoning its prey, its belly describing a majestic circle, once, twice, throughout the full three hundred and sixty degrees, its cry fading into oblivion, and he closed his eyes and saw that the heavens were full of light and warmth and peace.

Kron was shouting, "*Listen to me! There's something you should know!*"

The pilot knew it already. There was an incendiary device on board and it was meant to sabotage the machine, not its occupants. He dragged the door open and rolled out into the night, falling to the roof below.

The control column dipped forward, and Stevens scrambled over the back of the seat. Nothing like voting with your feet, he thought as he strapped himself in. Democratic. Somewhat anarchic, however. Nuggets of a white thermoplastic insulating material flew from the walls. The machine floundered a little. It didn't want to go anywhere except down and to the right. Stevens wedged his arms across the control column, holding it at an angle to his chest, the gun clenched in his hands exactly the way the second goon had held it.

"Just a little explosive charge, Comrade," Kron said. "The kind that causes a fire. It's not timed to go off yet, but with all this . . ."

"Get out, Kron!"

"Ordinarily I wouldn't, you understand—"

"*Out!*"

Stevens turned, but the Russian had disappeared. He saw him fall, hit the roof, bounce, and slide down to terra firma. Kron must have hurt his leg in the fall, because he skipped round to the other side of the customs post, where he began hauling at the pilot's arms, dragging him away to safety.

He saw this happen very clearly and was thinking that the machine should be easier to handle when it was shaken by a sustained burst of firing. Stevens took the first bullet in his foot, and he drew the leg up, rocking like a child. He felt a punch on his back, the second bullet, deflected from the seat frame, breaking his fourth rib, spinning off and nicking the subclavian artery. Until he saw the bright blood spurting from the exit wound, he was more concerned about his foot and the blood slopping around in his shoe. The intelligent thing to do now, the really intelligent thing, would be to follow Kron's example and get out, the only trouble being that Carlo was still in the shed.

Stevens saw the blood on his chest. A pity about Sweet, he thought, and fainted.

The shock of the helicopter settling on the roof brought him round. His foot was giving him hell—foot wounds were always so painful— but apart from that he was feeling quite all right, competent enough to assess the situation objectively. Vladimir Andreyevich Dimitrov wanted a distraction, and a distraction he was going to get.

Hell, Stevens thought. My foot hurts.

The control column jigged. Something was happening, something he did not understand. The machine rolled in a slow half turn, banking slightly as the nose came up. At the same time the landing gear tore away a section of the roof and the helicopter completed its turn, wallowing gently. I'm the automatic pilot, he thought, George the automatic pilot. The Ka-26 made another languid turn and the transmission started rapping like a poltergeist, vibrating with a metallic clangour that set the airframe juddering from stem to stern. He knew that it was time to get out, but he had no strength left and the machine was climbing now. It hesitated before the third turn, then the nose came up and round again, dipping in a threatened stall, down and round and up, so that he could see the ground rotating, lazily spinning, far, far beneath. The machine was climbing round its own axis, planing in a vertical cone. He knew that the lift was no longer coming from the rotors but from the airframe itself. The tail was wagging the dog, and that would have to be stopped. He tried focussing on one of the cabin spars, just to keep things on an even keel, but the torsive momentum increased with the fourth and fifth turns, and the G force was already stretching the skin over his skull, forcing more and more of that bright arterial blood out through the wound in his chest. He lost count after the sixth turn. He knew that the machine would stall and go into a spin at the apex of the cone and that he would have his chance then. With nothing to lift against, the rotors would freewheel until they spun out of the drive shaft. That, or the engines would blow. But you can't fool me, he thought, not old George the automatic pilot. If you're going to get out of here, you'll have to unharness. Later. Put the nose down, turn into the spin. A vertical spin—is that possible? How can you climb and spin at the same time?

Oh, no, no, Jesus, no!

Stevens saw the ground spiralling above him. The machine had flipped over. It was spinning upside down—diving, not climbing. His hand slipped from the throttle and the control column wrenched itself from his grasp. Even as he sought to establish final mastery over the machine, the turbines seized in a shrieking accelerando, short, sharp percussive blasts signalling the end of a main compressor. Slivers of titanium, each trailing a sonic wave, ripped through the engine pods and disintegrated against the rotor blades, which broke away cleanly and one by one fluttered to the earth. He felt almost ashamed in the presence of death, a man who had much to understand and much to forfeit—not that he was guilty of anything, the way he saw it, except, perhaps, an operational error. His hands drifted out to the controls and were drawn back by the centripetal force. It was an eloquent gesture, like that of a conductor laying down the last chord of a titanic symphony, and he felt no vertigo, only an iron heaviness as the blood sluiced from his brain. Why me? he thought. There was nothing he could do; everything seemed so distant and remote, and yet, dimly, he sensed that he had been through it all before. Like a rat, he thought, a rat in a treadmill that was being spun from the outside, faster than its little legs could run.

Johnson saw the helicopter plume flame like a gigantic catherine wheel. He watched it plunge to earth and heard the muffled roar of its impact. The three remaining machines climbed away to the south, and Johnson looked for Dimitrov and Keller, both of whom had slipped away in the darkness and confusion. He saw the Russians scramble into their cars and drive off at great speed. Dimitrov, who had been carrying a large document case on the drive from Vyborg, was not among them. Odd, Johnson thought, and began walking.

George Stevens had crossed his last frontier, Johnson thought, phrasemaking. Hasketh would like that; it had a picturesque finality to it and encapsulated things neatly. The reporter was too tired even to hate himself. He thought of Vikings and funeral pyres and Valkyrja, the winged goddess of the dead.

The Finns were housecleaning. Some of them had gathered round Sweet and were discussing, animatedly, what they should do with the body. The more intelligent ones battled the flames from the helicopter. Johnson collided with a Finn, who introduced himself as Heikki Kilpinen. "We must now go in search of Mr. Peat," he said, and they did.

They found him lying under the table in the frontier post. "Help me up," he said, and they did that, too.

Carlo's right arm hung loosely at his side; his clothing was scorched, and from his face, clotted with blood and oil, the whites of his eyes shone brightly forth. His tongue was pink and his teeth white, and he looked like Al Jolson after a slapstick routine with a human brain.

"I think I've broken my collarbone," he said.

Kilpinen looked at the shoulder and asked if it hurt. It hurt, Carlo said.

"I also think it is broken," Kilpinen said.

"Hello, Mr. Johnson," Carlo said. "I've broken my collarbone."

"Yes," Johnson said.

He was startled when the telephone rang. After the battering the post had taken, he was amazed that the instrument still worked.

Kilpinen answered the phone. It was the Hotel Karelia at Lappeenranta, reporting a UFO.

28

An
Omen
for
Nemo?

It was still dark but the Vainikkala frontier post stuck out like a rotten tooth from the jawbone of that flat land. The Finns had rigged up an emergency lighting system, using the generator and searchlights, and Carlo sat shivering across the table from Johnson, where only an hour ago he had waited for George Stevens with David Sweet. Johnson requested, and was denied, permission to call his London office. He tried explaining: His association with Peat was accidental, he was a journalist, not a spy, but Heikki Kilpinen's knowledge of the English language suddenly gave out on him at that point. Quite possibly it was a genuine failure. Besides, he had other things to do.

Carlo did not seem to notice when they brought in Sweet's headless body, but the reporter did, the reporter noticed everything. They had covered Sweet with his sheepskin coat. A little later one of the *sotoväki* added the Finnish flag, and there the body lay, a trunk of slaughtered mutton under a blue cross. "I'm cold, Mr. Johnson," Carlo said, "I'm cold." He was such a loathsome sight that Johnson ignored him. Instead he watched the Finnish soldiers bring in the garbage bags. It didn't dawn on him what they were at first, until he smelled burnt flesh overlaid with the sanitary reek of pine disinfectant. There were twenty-four of them, heavy-duty green garbage bags, each with a tie and tag, one for every hour of the day. Johnson closed his eyes. I'm not here, he thought, but he was. Mercifully there came an ambulance, for the mutton and Peat and the garbage bags, its Klaxon braying through the dark Baltic morning, hee-haw, hee-haw, all the way to Lappeenranta.

Johnson followed in an army staff car. The ride to Lappeenranta was just like the one from Vyborg to Vainikkala. Snow. Johnson recalled asking Dimitrov about the helicopters. What was going on? "You see," the Russian had replied, "I have to give George a chance." The reporter thought about that reply, as he had on the frontier, and it still didn't make any sense at all to him. A chance to do what? Kill Carlo, it seemed.

When the shooting started, Dimitrov had slipped away. Johnson thought about this, too. Carlo had set Stevens up to kill Dimitrov, and Dimitrov had set him up to kill Carlo. Both the principals were still alive; only the would-be assassin was dead. If Carlo was Nemo, Johnson couldn't see why he would want Dimitrov dead. And if Dimitrov was what he appeared to be, then there was no way he would want Nemo dead. It was as simple as that. Or as complex. If Carlo had been working for the KGB and Dimitrov for SIS, then Johnson could see why they might want each other dead. But that made even less sense to Johnson, who was feeling tired and sick and mortal. Dimitrov, a double agent? Everything was against that. So it was back to square one again. They had both tried to kill each other, using George Stevens as the go-between, and George had thoroughly loused up the job, Johnson thought.

He was reunited with Carlo at Lappeenranta Airfield, where a light aircraft was waiting to take them to Helsinki. There, Kilpinen explained, they would be met by a consular official and would board a regular commercial flight to London. No military transport this time. Consular official meant Special Branch officer.

The Finns had cleaned the mess of brains and oil off Carlo, sponging him down so that he looked like a newly polished old baby. His right arm was bound in a sling, and in the other he clutched, as well as his portmanteau, a brown-paper parcel tied up with string. The Finns had plenty of brown paper.

"It will have to go to the cleaners," Carlo said, and Johnson understood that he meant his raincoat, which was inside the parcel.

On the flight to Helsinki, Carlo sat with the parcel in his lap, picking at the string while he talked. It was good string, strong, hairy sisal such as he had not seen in a long time. The Finns had been very kind, he said, picking at that string like a man obsessed, a collector. Johnson watched, appalled, as Carlo unwrapped the gory relic of Sweet's death and stuffed it into his portmanteau along with the box of cartridges. The Webley revolver was deep under snow on the frontier.

Carlo went to the toilet then, trailing yards of string behind him. He was gone for some time, and when he came back there was no string. The meaning of this behaviour was lost on Johnson, who thought that Carlo must be slightly cracked. More than slightly, in fact.

"Nothing happens by chance, Mr. Johnson."

"No?"

"Indeed no. There's not much time left. I need your help."

Johnson edged away from the author of this appeal, thinking of others who had helped or hindered Carlo Peat. He wasn't afraid; it was just that he wanted to have a good look at Carlo.

Peat's face was bright and open, his eyes honest. He was a little pale, that was all; otherwise he radiated a kind of manic bonhomie. Some people never learn, Johnson thought. How can he talk like this? But talk Carlo did, gathering in those faint strands of the *cheng* that still remained within his grasp. It was an evanescent thing, this game, long periods of drudgery punctuated by occasional action. Though its physical manifestations were often crude and frightening (to the outsider), they were largely of a ceremonial character. Men like George Stevens, whom the reporter perhaps thought he had got to know, were easy to find. Ruthless, violent, criminal men, cunning to a degree—there was no premium on natures like that. Not to detract from George's undoubted talents. He was flexible, so much so that his loyalties had always been open to question. He had served two masters, and none. He had exceeded the mark in betraying Grove and Carmichael; he had been caught playing both ends off against the middle; most probably he had died as he had lived, believing in nothing. Yet, for want of a better, he had been a keeper of the secret. The game was quintessentially spiritual in nature.

Johnson couldn't stomach this. "Brainwashing," he blurted out, "is that spiritual?"

"Brainwashing, Mr. Johnson?"

"You brainwashed the man!"

"Good heavens, whatever gave you that idea?"

"The same thing that gave it to everyone else. You brainwashed him because you wanted him to kill Dimitrov!"

"Oh, no, Mr. Johnson. You've got it all wrong. . . ."

"You've got some explaining to do, you have."

"Yes," Carlo said. "I know."

Owens, hypnotherapy, the hocus-pocus with the laughing gas and the electroconvulsive treatment, the tape-recorded trigger stimulus, and the much-vaunted assassination plot—all that had been for Nemo's benefit. There had been no *actual* brainwashing, and if George couldn't remember what had happened to him, it was for the very good reason that nothing had happened to him, other than his being kept drugged and comatose for three weeks, during which time the brainwashing was *supposed* to have occurred.

"It was an entrapment, you see," Carlo said.

"An entrapment?" Johnson echoed.

"Yes. First Nemo learns that we're trying to infiltrate the KGB, then that an assassination attempt is under way. Sooner or later he had to crack. He was terrified that I was on the point of unearthing the wartime connection between himself and Clemens. You see what happened, don't you? Clemens told Philby that Canaris had ordered him to open a link with the British. Philby must have discussed this with Nemo, who said, 'George Stevens is going to Paris, let the Abwehr put him in the bag.' Anyway, Clemens talked to George, then let him go. Philby put a stop to the peace talk at our end. He must have been very pleased with himself that he'd helped his old recruiter serve two masters, Canaris and the Russians. The only thing he'd overlooked was that very few people knew where Stevens was going to be and when. Back in 1944 I added their names to Clemens' file. Only two of those people are still living," Carlo said, "and I'm one of them. The other, in case you're interested, is Donald Macpherson."

Johnson was interested. "Who else was on the list?"

"Sweet, Cavendish, Callwell. Five of us altogether."

"And one of you told Clemens about George's trip to Paris?"

"Yes. Or told Philby to tell him, which amounts to the same thing."

"But that's old history," Johnson said. "Why would Nemo be interested in the file now?"

"Not the file, the list. It's the only objective link with Clemens. The more dead people on the list, the more definitive it becomes. Nemo is the last man alive. At least, that's the way he wants it."

"And you think Macpherson pulled that file just to see if his name was on the list?" Johnson was going to say that it sounded like a pretty dumb thing to do, but something in Carlo's look silenced him.

"Not quite. He wanted to see if there *was* a list, first of all. You see, it was only three weeks ago that I told him about it, and then it was in connection with another matter. David Sweet had forged Bentinck's signature on a cable to Soper, and Macpherson was asking me about it. Did I know who'd done it? I said no and then I told him about that list. It was an accident, really, but he must have been brooding on it for the last three weeks. It would have seemed like I was putting pressure on him. It was a small thing, but coming on top of everything else, it must have loomed larger and larger, like an omen."

"Bentinck," Johnson said. "Stevens mentioned him."

"Yes, he would."

"The file as well."

"Really?"

"He said that whoever looked at the file would have to sign for it, even if it was Macpherson himself. But it was you that he suspected. He said that Dimitrov had told him you were Nemo and had killed Clemens because you were afraid of the connection being traced."

"Oh, no, Mr. Johnson!"

"He seemed pretty sure that you knew who Clemens was all the time. He wanted me to go to Bentinck and tell him to check up on that file."

"The access sheets, yes."

"But he said that it was a hunch. He couldn't be sure if Nemo had consulted the file."

"No? But I can, Mr. Johnson. You see, I didn't know about Clemens' death until just now. Nemo must have consulted the file and decided on the appropriate course of action." Carlo smiled. His eyes had never seemed merrier. "I don't have the authority to issue cancellations anymore, Mr. Johnson. That's something you can ask Bentinck about when you go to see him. Because you really have to go and see him now. Tell him to look at the access sheets. He'll find that Nemo consulted the 1944 volume within the last three weeks. He lives in Hertfordshire, in case you can't reach him at the office. Little Gaddesden. I'd do it myself, but I don't think they'll let me somehow."

"They?"

"Our friend Volodny." Carlo chuckled. "He's coming across, don't you see? Dimitrov is coming across and between them they're going to lay everything at my door. So it's a matter of some urgency to me, Mr. Johnson, that you contact his lordship as soon as you get back to London."

He was still chuckling when they landed at Helsinki, where they were met by the promised consular official, a man called Biggs, who had a warrant for Carlo's arrest. He cautioned Carlo ponderously, warning him that although he did not have to make a statement now, anything he did or said would be taken down in writing and could be used in evidence against him. "I've been framed," Carlo said, and Biggs transferred these words to the custody of his notebook. "I've been framed by Macpherson." Was there anything else? "Yes, but not for your ears," Carlo said, a statement that was allowed to remain at large.

Biggs, who was only doing his duty and said so, then handcuffed his right wrist to Carlo's left, and, thus siamesed, they boarded the plane together. The air hostess, checking their boarding passes, tried hard not to notice; and the passengers tried not to look as if they'd noticed, their heads buried in the sunny travel brochures found with the puke bags, diagrams of the nearest emergency exit, what to do when the oxygen mask pops down, and the remains of someone else's dinner in the pocket at the back of the seat in front.

The man from Special Branch unlocked Carlo once, allowing him to pick indifferently at a toy meal: a frog-sized portion of roast duckling swamped in orange sauce with lurid green broccoli and miniature carrots. The colour contrast was too much for Johnson, who felt like throwing up again. He did not even want to guess at the reason for Carlo's arrest, and when the hostess came round with coffee and asked how the meal was, he noticed that his hand was shaking ridiculously as the plastic cup passed between them. "The meal was fine," he said.

At Heathrow the air hostess said she hoped they had enjoyed the flight; and also at Heathrow—Macpherson.

29

Of a Modern
Major
General

Carlo went quietly enough, still handcuffed to Biggs, the pair of them flanked by a couple of Special Branch heavies. Donald Macpherson turned to greet his old antagonist of the press, in whom he was much more interested at that moment than Carlo Peat. "Now, then," he was saying when Johnson heard shots, six or seven irregularly spaced shots, followed by a child's scream and a hysterical Belfast woman yelling, "Yeu little swine! Yeu little swine!"

Men with drawn guns closed round Macpherson and the reporter. A jumping cracker—the kid had let off a jumping cracker left over from Bonfire Night! "I saved it!" he bawled, and the woman belted her child again and again, punishing him with violent apologies to the armed spectators, every one of them ready to kill, blow after blow raising livid welts on the child's face, his furious and bewildered cries sounding down that brightly lit corridor that led from nowhere into nothing.

Johnson looked at his watch. It was one-thirty on the afternoon of 8 November, and George Stevens had been dead for seven hours. Nine, if you didn't count the zonal time changes. Now, that was interesting, it really was. In whose time had he died? His own, Johnson supposed.

"Good to see you, Mr. Johnson," Macpherson said, and then, "May I offer you a lift home?"

Macpherson's Bentley was parked outside the terminal in the VIP area, past the row of double-decker airport busses and the taxi rank. The sky was brilliant and clear, and British Airways' new logo, a fractured Union Jack, was emblazoned everywhere. Johnson felt a little dizzy. He sank gratefully into the cowhide-upholstered seat and inhaled the smell of the Bentley: cigars and saddle soap, gin slings mixed with lime. Macpherson closed the partition that divided them from the chauffeur. His yellow eyes glistened, studying the reporter, who could not tell what was in that look. "I suppose you'll want to know why I had Carlo arrested," he said, and Johnson nodded. He could smell something else now. Peppermints.

The Bentley was under way before Macpherson spoke again. "A deception exercise, Mr. Johnson. Shall we agree to call it that?" Because, as he went on to say, the alternative was unthinkable, that Carlo had been a traitor for so many years, that he had set George Stevens up, expecting a primitive response from Dimitrov—this uttered coldly, with only the slightest hint of an accent: the Gorbals, slum tenements, the bailie man. "A deception exercise, Mr. Johnson. Theirs, not ours. For whatever else he may be, Carlo's no traitor." And he knew, oh, how he knew, had spent his life learning their little ways, the clubmen, the Friends, the jumped-up grouse-hunting squires. "Not that I'm looking through my fingers at murder, mind. Carlo's a fool, but not a traitor. . . ."

"Macpherson, what the hell are you talking about?" Johnson asked wearily. Something in Macpherson brought out the worst in him. That assured Knoxian tone; the way he wore his clothes (like a tailor's dummy in a Harris-tweed shop); his squinty rat face. Fuck you, he wanted to say. He said, "If Carlo's innocent, why did you arrest him?"

"Our Russian friend Dimitrov walked the same way as you did, Mr. Johnson. Across the frontier. He's asking for political asylum, in fact, and he has enough evidence on him to hang Carlo Peat several times over, if we still had capital punishment, which we do not." The major general sounded sorry. "Now do you understand?

I have to go along with them for the time being. I have to make it look as though I believe Dimitrov. You were there, man. Did you not see it?''

''I was distracted,'' Johnson said, ''by the fireworks display.''

''Aye, I cannot say I blame you for that.''

''So Dimitrov has defected. Is that what you're telling me?''

''No.'' Macpherson closed his eyes and opened them again. ''He's a plant. It began years ago, Mr. Johnson, Christmas 1960, with Sharpshooter. Goleniewski, remember him? What did George call him? The man who would be tsar. It was Goleniewski who betrayed George Blake to the Friends, one of their own agents, and Kim Philby, of course. But the Friends had known about Kim for nine years before that, ever since Burgess and Maclean skipped. Queers''—Macpherson's lips curled—''the Foreign Office is full of bloody queers.'' He recollected himself. ''For nine years, Mr. Johnson, Foreign Office Security had been feeding Kim Philby with false information that was then relayed to his Russian masters. It didn't make up for the previous damage, but it was a good thing, or so everyone thought until the Polish cavalry turned up.''

Macpherson frowned. ''By the way,'' he said, ''this is all off the record, you understand. You can see now why Kim was kept active for so long. He was a useful man to have around.''

''He must have known you were onto him,'' Johnson said.

Macpherson smiled and gave his foxy laugh. ''That's what Goleniewski told us. More than that. Kim was being controlled from this end by a Russian master spy whose code name was Nemo. Goleniewski had never heard his real name. Niemand, the recruiter, was handling the stuff at the other end, while Nemo made it his business to let Kim know which was fake and which was genuine material. You can imagine that this information had a salutary effect on Foreign Office Security, who gave themselves two new priorities in life. One was to end the spiel with Mr. Philby, the other was to find Nemo.

''Anyway, we now have Carlo, Mr. Johnson, his head full of wizards and demons, who decides that he'll be the one to catch Nemo, promoted, in his mind, after Philby's defection, to the status of successor. When another agent, Baby, whose name is Graebe, warns his case officer, whose name is Grove, that there's a Soviet deep-penetration agent in the Friends—well, there he is again, Nemo. But Graebe, and this is the amazing thing, Mr. Johnson, Graebe, if he was talking about anyone at all, was actually talking about George Stevens, whom Carlo was in the process of setting up to find Nemo, and when Carlo realized that, Graebe had to go. And so he was the first of the agents that George turned over to the Russians. But when Grove realized what was going on, Grove had to go as well, only with him there went Carmichael and the entire network, which was no part of Carlo's plans, or George's, or even a spy called Nemo, though he couldn't have done a better job of it had Kim Philby been back at his old desk. . . .

"Do you follow me, Mr. Johnson? Do you see the pattern? All hell is let loose; Friend Percival commits hara-kiri, Callwell, the FO adviser, dies, and a new one, Bentinck, who knows nothing of all this, is appointed. Carlo, whose mental apparatus is chock-a-block with cosmic riddles, I would say a sense of the weird, is now faced with the practically insoluble problem of maintaining the integrity of his own operation against prying eyes. It's three years since I interested myself in his business, but that's neither here nor there. All this, the loss of a station chief and the destruction of a network with the loss of God knows how many agents, could hardly be just Kim's legacy, and Carlo begins to wonder if he has selected the successor to find the successor. He can't admit that, of course, so he finds a stand-in, friend Ritter, and when Ritter's candidacy no longer bears too close a scrutiny, he goes the way of the others. Meanwhile, George, who from Carlo's point of view could well be Nemo himself, has made no secret of what's going on to the Russians, and that merely compounds Carlo's problem, because, you see, nothing is happening—no Nemo, nothing. That's when Carlo dreamed up his assassination plot, Mr. Johnson. Surely Nemo had to come out of the woodwork now, unless he really was George Stevens. . . ."

"But nothing happened," Johnson said.

"Nothing happened because there never was a spy called Nemo," Macpherson said smoothly. "Whoever invented him was very shrewd, you see, and understood the real meaning of treason. Nemo existed because the Friends wanted to believe in him. He was the lure, the mythical being they were set to catch, and they needed to believe in him because they could never understand that what Kim Philby did he did alone, unaided, without the help of any man."

Johnson thought about this. It was logical enough, as far as it went. The only trouble was, it didn't go very far.

"And you're going to kid Dimitrov along, are you?" Johnson said. "You're going to get a look at his proof and pretend that you believe it?"

"Aye, precisely."

"So what happens to Carlo?"

"We'll keep him for a while, until we've debriefed friend Volodny. And then he'll probably get a knighthood."

"Dimitrov or Carlo?"

"Peat, of course."

"Just like you."

"That's right, Mr. Johnson. Just like me."

You're going to have to hand your medals in, Johnson was tempted to say. "So who killed Clemens?" he asked instead.

"I thought we'd agreed, Mr. Johnson. No one killed Clemens."

"Are you trying to tell me that he's still alive or that he never existed either? Which is it?"

"Most probably the Russians killed him," Macpherson said.

"Is that why you looked at his file?"

"I don't quite follow," Macpherson said, and Johnson knew that he was lying.

"I think you do," he said.

"The Clemens file," Macpherson said, as if they'd been talking about something else. "Of course I looked at the Clemens file. What's so unusual about that?"

"Because you were looking for a forger," Johnson said, "and Carlo had already given you the names on the list. You knew damn well that you hadn't forged Bentinck's signature, and you knew that Carlo hadn't. So that left Sweet, and everybody knew that he was an artist. Because he was in D, Macpherson, and that meant documentation. You could have gone to him and asked if he'd forged Bentinck's signature, and for all I know, you did just that. You had absolutely no reason to pull that file unless you were looking for something else."

"And what was that, Mr. Johnson?"

"The context of that list. Five people, all of whom knew that George Stevens was going to Paris in January 1944 but only one of whom had told a German double agent whose name was Clemens about the Stevens mission. Now, wouldn't it be interesting, Macpherson, if the corresponding Abwehr file should turn up? Not to mention the KGB file. With your name—or Carlo's—as the informant. You had to look at that file, Macpherson, so that you could make sure there was a list. . . ." Johnson looked out the car window. Hammersmith. He understood why Carlo had sounded almost bored on the flight to Helsinki. It was so obvious. Dimitrov had been carrying the files in his document case, and Peat's name would run through them like a vein of gold through dross. Fool's gold.

"You had to make sure that Carlo's name was on the list,' Johnson said, "so that everything would match up." He looked at Macpherson, who had filled his cheeks with air, alternately filling and emptying them like little balloons. Johnson realized what it was that disturbed him about Macpherson. The major general was like a machine, with the real man hidden inside at the controls. He was afraid to come out of his shell in case he disturbed the mechanism or was caught up in it, the mincing machine. "And now Carlo's name will be on the Russian and German files," Johnson said, "and the thing is you can defend him, Macpherson, you can play the white man for as long as it suits you. You can be ever so loyal, Macpherson, and maybe even protect Carlo, because the guilty party would never do that, at least that's what everyone is going to think, and then, of course, the weight of the documentary evidence will finally overwhelm you. That's why you pulled the Clemens file, and I don't suppose there is anything particularly unusual about it. I imagine it happens to you all the time, Macpherson."

"That's just it—you imagine." Macpherson inflated his cheeks again. He deflated them, and the gasp of air was audible. "But it's an extremely good theory. I confess everything."

"Fuck you," Johnson said.

Macpherson seemed not to have heard the reporter. "I'm sorry all your trouble has been for nothing, Mr. Johnson," he said. "You're tired, you know, and a tired man makes errors of judgement. I mean, look what happened to George Stevens. Now, there was a tired man. You should go home and get some sleep. Stay indoors for a few days, take a holiday. We'll see that you're looked after. Would you like a cigar, Mr. Johnson?"

The major general took out a cigar case from the walnut cabinet beneath the glass partition. He opened it and thrust it at the reporter. "No? A pity," he said, toying with the gleaming silver cigar cutter, a delicate instrument, razor sharp.

It was nearly three before Johnson arrived back at his Crescent Towers apartment. He was always surprised that the place was still there. Everything was just as he'd left it; his books, mostly paperbacks, his desk and typewriter, a glass coffee table with a stainless-steel frame, the Sunday papers on top; nothing had been disturbed or was out of place, yet everything seemed wrong. The apartment was stale; returning to it was like revisiting a dream. He was strung out, of course. He had crossed too many frontiers and the day had too many hours. A good sleep and he would be all right.

Johnson looked at the phone. He remembered something Terry Hasketh had said after the IRA had blown the Half Moon to pieces and the Special Branch had towed his car away from the British Museum. "You've really pissed someone off, you have." That was true then, and it was even truer now. Johnson, who had enjoyed taunting Macpherson, decided that he would be a fool to use the phone. Then he remembered what Soper had said on the Moscow metro. The Baker Street underground—why not? Nothing so private as a public place. Johnson picked up the spare change that he kept in the upper left-hand drawer of his desk. Time to bell the cat, he thought, and he went out, slamming the door.

His first call was to Bentinck at the FO. Johnson spoke to his lordship's assistant, a man called Green. They were very keen to see him. Positively. Tomorrow morning at nine.

His second call was to Hasketh. "Macpherson is a Russian spy," Johnson began.

"You never did like him, did you?" Hasketh said.

"Listen, Terry. A KGB agent called Dimitrov is helping him frame Carlo Peat. The Special Branch took Carlo away at Heathrow about an hour and a half ago. Sometime in the last three weeks Macpherson pulled an FO Security file on a German double agent called Clemens, Johannes Heinz Clemens. He's dead, okay? It's a 1944 file and there's a list of five names in it: Callwell, Cavendish, Sweet, Macpherson, and Carlo. They all knew about that Stevens thing in Paris. One of them told Clemens. Oh, I forgot. Sweet's dead, too."

"Anyone else?"

"Stevens. This morning, both of them."

"He was alive, then?"

"Yes, but now he's not. About that list. Carlo wouldn't have made it if he was what he was supposed to be, and he certainly wouldn't have told Macpherson. If anything happens to Carlo . . ."

"You might care to write all this down," Hasketh said, "you know, as it happened. With an old-fashioned plot, Mr. Johnson."

"I'm serious, Terry."

"So am I," Hasketh said. "I'll call you later."

Johnson wondered if the office phone were bugged. He left the booth to a grey city type who was carrying a green-jacketed novel.

Back at his apartment, Johnson double-locked the door and sat down at his typewriter. He had a story to write, a story that began in New York with Monday's Moonies. "Father Sun Myung Moon wants you to know that the twentieth century is the landing site of Christ." Johnson remembered that and used it as a lead to his story. Moon's messiah had better hurry up, he thought, and imagined him as a South Korean militiaman with all the appurtenances of that calling: bonedome, night stick, tear-gas grenades, and sun discs for shoulder flashes.

He worked for five hours, drank two pots of coffee, smoked a pack and a half of Rothmans, and developed a sore spot in his mouth. I'm gonna die of cancer, he thought. He also made two carbon copies of the story, and in the morning he would post one to his father and another to Hasketh. Johnson trusted the mail.

When he had finished he treated the ulcer in his mouth to some plastic cheese that he found in the fridge. It was nearly nine before he lay down and, fully dressed, fell alseep for what seemed like the first time in a hundred years. The phone woke him around eleven. It was Hasketh, saying that Carlo Peat was dead.

"What? How?"

"Hanged himself. Apparently they took him down to the Scrubs for questioning, and . . ."

The string, Johnson thought. Then he remembered that Carlo had only one good arm. He must have been very determined, and Carlo didn't seem the suicidal type somehow.

"Terry, I've got to talk to you."

"Yes. Tomorrow morning. My place would be best. Eleven. How does that sound?"

"Okay."

"And, Bill . . ."

"Yes?"

"Take care."

Johnson cradled the receiver. He took off his necktie, coiling the ends around his hands until it tautened almost to the breaking point, then he threw it across the room and watched it slither along the glass-topped coffee table. Hasketh—how had he known that Carlo was dead? The reporter picked up a sheet of paper from his desk and screwed it up in his fist, for the longest time rolling it between his fingers, worrying at it with his nails. And then he went to bed, turning out the lights.

Lord Philip Bentinck studied the reporter, who had just told him that Major General Sir Donald Macpherson was a killer, which Bentinck did not for a moment doubt, but a Russian agent and Kim Philby's controller, a traitor of a goodly vintage then, and all this because he had consulted a file, an action that Macpherson did not even trouble to deny. Sir Donald had warned Lord Philip of this reporter, but the man himself exceeded all expectation. He was loud and abusive, and although it was only nine o'clock in the morning, he looked as if he had been drinking. Moreover, he smelled of vomit.

"I have a very full and competent report from Sir Donald, not that I don't appreciate your, ah, effort, Mr. Johnson," the adviser said, for he knew it was a mistake to alienate the press.

"Christ, are you in on it, too?"

"Now, there's no need to go upsetting yourself. If you go on like this, you'll be in no fit state to attend the press conference."

"Press conference . . . what press conference?"

"Mr. Dimitrov's, you know."

"*Mr.* Dimitrov?"

"In fact"—Bentinck looked at his watch—"it's due to start any time now, and I'd rather like to be there myself." He pressed an intercom button. "Green, would you show our visitor to the conference room? I have one or two calls to make here. . . ." The adviser stared hopefully at Johnson, who remembered the BBC television trucks he had seen in Whitehall.

"Press conference," he said. "Yes, yes, of course."

"Mr. Johnson, are you quite sure there's nothing wrong?"

"Not with me," said Johnson. "Do you know I was followed here? But it doesn't matter, Bentinck. You'll see."

"I'm not sure . . . "

"Oh, yes."

Johnson was so angry that he could hardly speak. It was a deep, cutting anger, and Johnson could have smashed his fist into Lord Bentinck's official smile. Trembling, he rose and followed the man called Green out of the room. The press conference was already under way, but that didn't matter, nothing did now.

Vladimir Andreyevich Dimitrov seemed shrunken under the klieg lights, a dark little man with bulging eyes and a neutral accent; he spoke softly, hesitantly, and was saying that his files, which dated back to the beginning of the last war, showed that a former senior British intelligence officer was a Soviet master spy code-named Nemo, for many years the controller of Harold Adrian Russell Philby. The Russian blinked as the press brayed for a name.

"Gentlemen"—Macpherson got up on his hind legs—"one at a time."

"Harland Caisho Peat," Dimitrov said.

"It's a lie!" Johnson yelled, and the flashbulbs went supernova. He grabbed the nearest microphone and clambered onto the stage, waiting for the cameras to pan round. "It's a frame-up. Don't listen to them, they're lying. *He's* the one, Macpherson. . . ." The press howled. "You can't touch me now, Macpherson. I dare you. . . ." The press roared, and Johnson saw the doorman and a police constable elbowing their way through the melee. A game of leapfrog started on the floor as a colleague knocked off the policeman's helmet. "Bloody good," someone said, and Johnson jumped down and was off and running through the corridor that opened in the press, out and away along the marble hallway, down a flight of stairs and into Charles Street, where he slowed his pace and remembered that he was seeing Hasketh at eleven.

30

Closing
the
File

The leaves were rotting in old Highgate Cemetery, where Johnson had gone to look at Karl Marx's tomb. It was more imposing than George Stevens', with a bust of the philosopher that made him look like a prophet of old, emphasizing his beard at the expense of his forehead. William Morris might have sculpted that beard. It was ornamental and it looked false, the Greatest of Teachers in his last disguise.

Marx was at home. Highgate Cemetery had all that ordered unruliness of an engraving from the Kelmscott Press: gnarled trees under a blustery sky, wrought-iron palings that looked like spears, bowers and seats for the despondent weary—a cultivated necropolis far different from the graveyard of the Novo-Devichy Convent. There were angels here, soot-stained guardians of a revolutionary's grave.

Marx was at home, but Hasketh had not been. Johnson hadn't liked that.

"You just missed him," said the young American who lived in the upstairs flat.

Hasketh had divided his house into flats as a precaution against

England's decline and fall. Every month he collected the American's rent, putting a little extra in the bank for his old age. His tenant was a research student in physics and enjoyed Prokofiev, Khachaturian, and Shostakovich. Hasketh tolerated the noise because of the money.

"He left about ten minutes ago," the American said to the accompaniment of *Spartacus*. It was eleven o'clock, and Johnson was on time, as he always was.

There was no message.

Johnson left without thanking the American, and on Highgate Hill he saw the man he had seen yesterday in the phone booth at Baker Street station. Johnson had seen him earlier that morning, too, outside the Charles Street entrance to the FO. After what had happened at the press conference he wasn't too worried, and he had decided to play games, trying some of Gosling's old dodges, jay-walking, staring in shop windows, doubling back up the hill past the school until there was no longer any sign of the man with the green-jacketed novel.

Johnson was thinking about this when he heard a rustling behind him.

"That Marx," a voice said.

He turned round. It was only a tramp.

"Make you jump, did I? Sorry."

He was about Johnson's age and the stubble on his chin was the colour and texture of cigarette tobacco. His eyes were large and green, his face gaunt, contrasting oddly with the roundness of his body, which was swaddled in a giant overcoat. He had on a pair of tennis shoes with floppy toe caps and his trousers were tucked into blue-and-white football socks.

"Haven't I seen you around somewhere before?" Johnson asked, though he knew where.

"Yeah, the British Museum. You get a good selection of papers in there," the tramp said. He was carrying a bundle of rolled-up newspapers, the morning edition of the *Times* on the outside. The tramp had a thing about newspapers. His coat was stuffed with them, and his trouser legs, too, and as he shuffled closer to Johnson he shed scraps of paper like some weird animal in moult.

"That Marx," the paper man said again, wiping his left hand across his nose and pointing at the tomb with his roll of papers.

"You'd better get a good look at him while you can, brother."

"Why?" Johnson's pulse raced.

"Because, Comrade, you won't be seeing him again, that's why."

"What the hell are you talking about?"

"Here, take it easy. You don't have to chew me head off. The council's closing this place down, mate. It's the tenants. They can't afford the rent."

"Oh." Johnson relaxed. "You mean the other place, the new cemetery. It's up for development."

"Is that what I mean? Capitalists. They've no respect for the dead. Me, I'm a Trotskyite, see?" The tramp lowered his voice. "I don't suppose you could see your way to lending me the price of a cup of coffee, could you?"

Johnson dipped into his pocket. As a rule, he didn't give money to bums, but now he made an exception.

"You know how it is," the tramp went on. "I didn't mean to make you jump. You must have been miles away. Daydreaming, you were." His hand went out to grasp the coin, an old florin, which he dropped among the leaves, fumbling with his newspapers. "Pick it up," he said.

"What?"

"My tip, my effing gratuity. Pick it up."

Johnson saw the gun, a wicked-looking automatic muzzled by a silencer.

Oh, no, God, no . . .

"Don't worry," the tramp said. "We're both in newspapers, aren't we? I mean, we're both gentlemen of the press."

"Yes," Johnson said.

"Well, then. Are you going to pick it up or aren't you?"

Johnson knelt. The coin had fallen heads up.

"I've got a message for you," the tramp said, lowering the gun.

Johnson looked up. He saw a face staring out from the upstairs window of a nearby house and watched it turn away as if answering a call. "Don't," he said, and heard the shot as if from a great distance. Two shots. He screamed. The side of the paper man's head burst like an overripe tomato and his body spun round, embracing Marx's head. He fell, grotesquely spread-eagled, on the bed of the grave, shredded newspaper settling like confetti on the ever-widening pool of blood. Johnson was looking directly at the little blue diamond label on the soles of the tramp's tennis shoes; VULCANIZED, it said.

The reporter stayed there, kneeling, for what seemed like a long time while old Highgate Cemetery filled with a flak-jacketed army of men with guns and dogs and sirens and flashing lights, until finally he stood up and said to the man called Hasketh, "I'm looking for my two-bob piece, Terry," and to the man called Peat, "You're dead. You can't come back to life again, it's against the rules."

"Oh, no, Mr. Johnson!"

"I'm sorry," Hasketh said.

"The string," Johnson said. "You couldn't possibly have known about the string."

"We had to make him go just that little bit extra, you see," Carlo said. "Poor Donald. We had to give him enough rope, so to speak. Well, Terry thought it would be a good idea if I were to die, pro tempore, for the time being, you know. I can't imagine why he chose hanging, but he said it would set you off—that was the expression he used, it would set you off. Poor Donald, you did rather provoke him, you know."

"The string," Johnson said.

"Come on," Hasketh said. "I'll buy you a drink."